Hypersexual

Copyright © 2016
Revised Edition 2017

All rights reserved, including the right to reproduce this book or portions thereof in any form whatsoever.

ISBN – 13: 978 - 1539143475
ISBN – 10: 1539143473

Hypersexual

by

Rory Aiken

Table of Contents

Foreword 8

Ch. 1 Dark Meat 10

Ch. 2 My Own Family – Part One 23

Ch. 3 Hypersexuals 25

Ch. 4 Seduction 32
  Cee Cee 32

Ch. 5 Pedophilia and Incest 51
  Hypersexual Prodigies 53
  Across the Line 54
  Protector 56
  The Voluntary Marking 57
  Educator 59
  Sexual Martyrdom 63

Ch. 6 The Worst Sound I Ever Heard 65
  My Own Mother 65

Ch. 7 Foster Care **69**
        Counselor 70
        Wynona & Carleton 73
        Secret Rooms 90

Ch. 8 Mentor—Déjà **92**
        Showering Love 92
        A little Pervert Returns 99
        Student 108
        Floating Blindly 113
        Promised 115
        The End of Time 121
        Arrival of The Goddess 126
        Eaten Alive 132
        Mission Information 141
        The Next Day 157
        Apprentice 162
        Historical Figure 182
        Picture Me 184

Ch. 9 Old Enough for Sex 192
      First Sexual Contact by Choice
      Abbey
           My first Attempt at Disclosure 205
           Legal Age Issues &
           Personalizing Sex Ed. 208

Ch. 10 Fucking Strangers 220
           Advanced Class – Abbey 224

Ch. 11 Rape 242

Ch. 12 Zoos 258
           Scruffy 258
           Zoophilia 262
           "They" are "Us" 263
           Donkey's, etc., etc. 266
           Consent 268
           Several Useful Understanding's 271

Ch. 13 Pimps & Prostitutes 274

Ch. 14 Necrophilia 293
      R.I.P &
      Unending Circle 299

Ch. 15 Inside Cee Cee 300

Ch. 16 Too Far 316

Ch. 17 Her Babies 346

Ch. 18 Help 350
        Chapter Epilogue 362

Ch. 19 My Own Family – Part Two 363
        The Earlier Years 365
        Moving Foreword 395
        Children's Education 396
        Golden Safety 425
        Returned to the Present 426

Ch. 20 Gravity 428
        Worlds Collide 430

Ch. 21 Defenseless 433

Ch. 22 Imprisonment 439

Ch. 23 The Illumined Visitor & Writing Wings 442

Ch. 23 Magnitude 448

        Epilogue 452
        The End 452
        Acknowledgements 453

Foreword

This is a fictional story that is overflowing with the truths of a great many people.

Still, any resemblance whatsoever to actual persons, places, or occurrences, is entirely coincidental and unintended.

Chapter One

<u>Dark Meat</u>

I took a bite of some dark sexual meat yesterday.

Perhaps the most aberrant girl treat I've ever eaten.

She was so lost, young, weak, pale white, intoxicated, and willing. Actually begging, as it turned out.

Taking my mail out to the street-side box, I met her at 11:45 a.m. on a Wednesday.

For work I manage a small commercial warehousing property that includes the home where I live with my family, and as I stepped out the lower level office door with my handful of letters, both business and personal, I saw her walking up the road toward me.

At first, she was too far away to distinguish much. But after I had walked the twenty or so steps to the mailbox, placed my mail in, and slipped the little red flag to the "up" position, I turned slowly around and back toward her—fully intent on taking a much closer look.

Being a hypersexual human, I would time my glance so that I could take a nice long gaze up the approaching female's body, certainly long enough for her to notice. And also long enough for her to consider how she might respond. And then, in an even more aggressive move, I'd also time it so that our eyes would meet just in time for me to say, "Hello."

I'm always very courteous, hopefully even charming, when my eyes first meet the females. But my long focused glances and seductive smile are purely and obviously sexual. I know that this behavior isn't "right." It is simply the best balance that I've been able to strike, so far.

And I can be trusted in saying that I stop short of going all the way over-the-line with my penetrating looks, because my every effort is positively against scaring a girl away. My constant secret goal is sex, not repulsion. At the very least I want to enjoy my long look, and the eye contact, and possibly the verbal contact, without any real negative penalty or noticeable ripple around me. My art is in being the friendly pervert.

Fortunately, I happen to be a nice looking man, which helps. I have strong broad shoulders, slim square hips, and athletic arms and legs, all neatly proportioned in a body size that is not at all threatening. I'm always clean shaven and freshly showered, I walk with smooth physical coordination and an air of confidence, and my clothing and shoes are nice and new enough. My medium-brown skin is vibrant, my expression is warm, and my aural colors are soothing and attractive. I'm professional, and casual, and lively, and inviting, and relaxed, and friendly—all at the same time. And my smile, which fully incorporates my almond shaped eyes, is so persuasive and camouflaging it is a truly dangerous thing.

However, regardless of my refined presentation and practiced boldness, the frequency with which I actually find the sex that I am constantly looking for is infinitesimal. Still, I do get a good thrill out of each and every girl or woman that sees the way that I am looking at her. I get an even bigger rush from the ones who spontaneously smile back, even though they too are quickly gone. And I'll even admit to achieving a disturbing kind of satisfaction from the women who know exactly what I'm about—and don't approve. Many mothers and grandmothers, for instance, have a knack for spotting me, so I don't push too hard around their types.

I have lived to develop a way of doing what I do in the midst of society, using what has always seemed to me like some kind of invisibility cloak that is created by the turning-away manners and muted responses of our culture, which neatly tuck behaviors like mine away, along with all the other unspoken things about sex.

On this wonderful occasion I had a lone female approaching me with absolutely no one else around, and I was going to get an exceptionally good look at her.

As a usual mid-December day for our mountain desert town, it was cold, and windy. And as I began to gaze up the form of the approaching girl the first things that I noticed were that she wore tiny worn-through tennis shoes, with no socks, and her legs were bare under a light skirt.

It was only 35 degrees outside, and blowing—what was wrong with this girl?

With my attention level decidedly raised, I slowed my step to elongate the moment.

When the passing "closeness" happens, it happens quickly. At twelve or so steps away my focus sharpened on her like a magnifying glass, and I began inching my stare up her body. I looked from her dirty shoes to her dirty white ankles to her skinny blue-white calves, and I saw that her skin was young, and shivering.

Not rushing, I looked up over her knobby knees and onto her lower thighs, where I marveled at the soft-looking and tight flesh. And my mind also began computing just how small she was.

At ten steps I saw that a yellow skirt or summer dress floated sensuously across her legs, tugged by the insistent winds. And just a few inches above the hem of the dress was a loosely wrapped and ragged white coat.

At seven steps away my eyes crawled farther up her body, and for a brief second I stared at her thin white hands clutching at the waist of the over-sized coat that covered her torso. Scanning quickly up over the blank and tattered covering, I then looked up to find her bare, slender, and beautiful neck, framed by the open collar of her dress and her fine red-blond hair. And finally, I allowed myself to look directly at her freckled little face.

This one was young, and she was so obviously poor, and so alone. And she was sucking on the last hit of her cigarette as if it would give her the warmth that she needed.

At five steps away I recognized that she was also weaving drunk—which, added to the other visual information I had absorbed, was more than enough—causing a terrible surge of unstoppable sexual energy to whip through my body, bringing the predator in me all the way to life.

If a soul can have claws, mine had just slipped out.

Focusing straight into her face, I locked my sight on the poor girl's eyes and held them for the next couple of steps, looking for *whatever else there was to see...*

Then, at only two steps apart, with no more time, wearing my sweetest smile I spoke to her.

"Hello there."

Surprising me, the girl took a last step forward and came to a dead stop barely two feet in front of me. And she was still looking right back at me. Most girls will glance only briefly into my eyes, and most girls will walk quickly by, even if they do reply or say "Hello."

Instead, this girl came to a halting stop, almost like she hadn't heard me clearly. And it also looked as if she was just tired of walking, and that she would much rather sit down somewhere.

Perhaps this girl was even drunker than I could have hoped for?

Still waiting for her to reply, I watched in growing curiosity as she continued to stand in-place staring at me with her unfocused eyes, looking at me as if she had a question, and then as if she had forgotten what it was.

She was so odd.

So, I just stood there and looked warmly into her gaunt and slack face, waiting. And still, she remained looking back at me as if she wasn't sure who was supposed to talk first.

After perhaps a full minute or so, and after taking a couple of deep and slow breaths, she suddenly attempted to stand up to her straightest and give me her prettiest smile. However, because of the unbalancing weight of her intoxication, her efforts came off as awkward. And her smile turned into an expression of, perhaps, dizziness? And try as she may, she still couldn't find her tongue.

I must admit that I was so surprised by the whole up-close vision of her, I wasn't quite sure what to say. She was so out-of-place...

But I did know exactly what I was thinking: *I want this one.*

And though I was astonished at the random appearance of it—I could feel that sex was close. I could feel it so strongly my ears were ringing.

I had to think of something to say. Looking at her simply drawn face, I began to concentrate.

And just then, without a word, the little girl let go of the grasp on her too large coat and let it fall open.

Looking down from her face, and down past her fragile neck, I saw her worn and faded cloth pullover dress lying closely over her pert young breasts. And below that I saw—in a moment I doubt I'll ever forget—that she was unmistakably and abundantly pregnant.

Looking quickly back up into her eyes, expecting something more from her, perhaps something verbal, all I saw was a wide-eyed and weary expression that said *"Look at me."*

Was she offering herself to me?

Looking deeper into her eyes, the only other thing I could see was the stillness of an impaired awareness.

Every day I wait so patiently, watching, searching for one who is ripe enough, and within my reach…

With what words should I snatch her…?

But, as I was deciding what to say, she spoke first, and with only the slightest bit of slurring.

"Hey.., do you haff a cigarette? Or anything else?"

Opportunity is the mother of all decadence; desire and appetite lie in wait; the prey begins the hunt.

She *was* offering herself to me.

We both knew what she was saying, once you've done the dance a few times you recognize the footwork. Just two short sentences, stuffed with all the other boldly evident visual and physical information about her, which she had done her fumbling best to present to me, now accompanied by that *certain kind* of eye-contact, told me that this little girl didn't give a fuck about anything; except having another cigarette, or anything "else" I had to offer her. And yes, her swollen little body might well be available for sex.

And finally hearing her voice, which sounded like dried-out honey, husky and empty, and smooth in a hard way, was like hearing the cough of a sick person.

Not even I had met a girl as palpably degenerate as this before, with such a plain and obvious disregard for all risks, both legal and physical, and maternal, and all at her too young age, and barely able to stand…

Every second that I spent with her felt like *falling*.

I know that such girls are out there, just like I'm out there. But I certainly hadn't expected to find one at the end of my driveway in the middle of this, or any other day.

And I've had all kinds of wickedly wild girls before, including countless who were seriously intoxicated in just about every way there is, including seasoned street hookers who were addicted to heroin. But this young girl seemed even more disconcertingly raw, and more openly dismal, in some way...

She was so...vacant.

I know what I know, and though it seemed early to make such a definitive read, standing next to this girl I could feel that she had come to me from some hellish life that was tormenting her, burning her down, and sending her out to me in smoking ashes. This girl was so burnt-out she couldn't even feel her own feet and legs freezing beneath her.

So, one way or another, I absolutely had to consume her. And I trembled in the power of my commitment. Mentally, I had gone past the crossroads and down the shadowy fork.

I would have her.

Breaking from her loose gaze for a moment I looked swiftly around, and up and down the street, and saw no one.

Looking back into her dull grey-blue eyes, my chest, stomach, cock and balls all began to ache in the most deliciously painful way. And I began salivating for the taste of her fresh, young, and fouled skin.

Yes indeed, I needed to eat down through all this girls openings, all the way to the place inside her that had left her ailing in this way.

Why? Because that is the feast that I was born to sit at, devouring the depths of a naked human through their sexual fruits.

Due to this girls woozy state of awareness, I had been able to let my mind absorb the details of this unexpected opportunity in what seemed like only a slightly extended amount of time. And now I was ready.

She had asked me if I had any cigarettes, or anything else.

Stepping a little closer, and smiling directly into her over-dilated pupils, I answered her still hanging question.

"Yes, you pretty little thing. I have smokes, and drinks, and a big hot heater turned on right inside my house."

"You...have a.., a house..?" She asked, with a confused and odd hopefulness, and perhaps a hint of envy.

"Yes, my house is right there, sweetie." I said, pointing behind her. "Do you want to come in? Come on in, it's cold out here."

Giving her the time she needed, I paused. Then, dropping my vocal tone toward a softer and more hypnotic pull, I continued.

"It's okay, baby. I really like the way you look. Come on in and let me be really nice to you for a little while."

Trying to be patient, I fought the urge to reach out for her. I could feel my relaxed and friendly voice working on her, but I had to let her make her own decisions.

Waiting for her answer, I couldn't tell if she was thinking or just resting. And trying to stand still was definitely revealing her inability to do so. And when she turned to look up at my two-story home, she weaved so hard I almost did reach out for her! And her slow stumbling return to "balance" was nearly comical!

Continuing to read her body language, it now looked to me as if she might be rolling past day two or three of a methamphetamine binge. Long hours of doing meth produces a different kind of mental fuzziness than alcohol, and it has a different kind of on-off effect on a person's movements and coordination. I still thought she'd been drinking, but there was definitely a heavier gravity to her impairment.

Of course, when I meet such a girl I am not interested in judging her legally, or morally, in her apparent lifestyle, or her personal choices, beliefs, or desires, any more than I am interested in questioning my own sexual identity or history.

In fact, those who are farther out on the edges of society have always held a special attraction for me. They make me feel less "different," for a while.

Perhaps most people are looking to accept only their own defined versions of "good" (or good-enough) in other people? Not me: The way in which total acceptance facilitates hypersexuality makes it way more important to me than considering what this specific girl had decided to do with her own body.

Obviously, this young mother was doing things that were health risks for herself and her fetus. Depending on exactly what drugs she was putting into her body, and how much of them, on top of the cigarettes she smoked, and perhaps her being out-and-about like this, I knew that she was very possibly creating some serious and irreversible damage. Which I grieved and accepted along with all her other fairly obvious life difficulties. (And we all know that pregnant women and mothers of all kinds, all over the world, do ingest, drink, smoke, and engage in all kinds of physically harmful actions.)

But I have nothing to do with what choices this girl might make in her own life, any more than I have power over the rain. And the way that I devour my sexual prey is focused only on who I have directly in front of me, and enjoying them as thoroughly as I can.

The truth I am trying to get at is this: No matter where they are coming from I don't judge the person I'm about to have sex with. I do quite the opposite—I start and finish by accepting them, totally.

And the part about my giving acceptance is much more crucial than it might at first appear. I don't just do it inactively, by saying little about nothing, or by carefully avoiding disagreements. I do it hyperactively, by following the tiniest leads, and starting with the smallest things. If the girl wants to talk about hating car traffic, we can start there. If she wants to get high, we will go straight there. If she wants to be quiet at first, I will be too. And I'll know where she wants to sit down by where her eyes fall when we walk into a room, and I will seat her right there. And if she stares at the stereo, I'll ask her what music she likes, and play it. And if she looks into the kitchen, I will offer her whatever food I have available. And in whatever ways, before she knows it the girl will tell me exactly what she loves, and hates, and wants the most in life. And I will love and hate those things with her, and I will dream about what she desires with her, reaching down inside her heart, climbing-in one lovely inch at a time.

Naked by then, I will continue inward as far as I can go, swimming down to stir-up her entire sexual being, including, most hopefully, whatever secret, hidden, odd, or even disgusting personal parts of herself she needs to have accepted, adored, and fucked openly.

Why? Why would I want to adore the disgusting and most secret and shameful parts of my sexual partners? Because when a naked person shows you the part of themselves that they have always hidden, that they can never admit to anyone, that they know *everyone else* in the world will find revolting and unforgivable, (and such depths can usually only be revealed after hours of spoiling personal connection and orgasm, and the descending layers of emotional and mental vulnerability that kind of attention can penetrate), sometimes—the sometimes that I live for—the last boundary is left behind and you can finally see all-the-way in: A spread-wide naked human being cumming and screaming and pulling and pissing and crying and begging to be fucked harder and harder and harder and finally exploding, *"FUCK ME!! OH MY GOD, FUCK ME!! OHHHH DON'T YOU STOP FUCKING ME!! FUCK ME UNTIL I PASS-OUT!! FUCK ME HOWEVER YOU WANT TO BECAUSE I HATE MY BORING AND NEARLY TOUCHLESS LIFE!! OH FUCK ME LIKE THE NEIGHBOR BOYS AND THEIR FRIENDS FUCKED ME IN THE GARAGE!! FUCK ME LIKE I WANT MY SISTER'S HUSBAND AND HIS FRIENDS TO FUCK ME!! OH DON'T YOU STOP FUCKING ME YOU GODDAMN HARD COCK FUCKING BASTARD GODDAAAMMNNNN IT!!!"*

My feast is the fully sexually opened person, guided out by the unbelievable acceptance and attention that I give them. And that screaming quote above is roughly word-for-word, from just one lonely housewife as she let go and fell over her edge.

Of course, the particular way in which those deeper sexual openings convey themselves, or come out of different people, can be amazingly varied and can involve any number of, or combination of, all the different possible physical or vocal ways of demonstrating ecstatic release. And they can contain all kinds of important personal information, too. Even a silent orgasm will usually be visible in the uncontrollably gripping and quaking body of the person releasing it, and perhaps in the tears flowing from it.

And, when the above mentioned housewife was done crying, and cumming, and crying some more, and playing with my un-hidden nakedness and fully available cock, and confessing, I was able to spend some exceptionally honest, understanding, and sexually progressive conversational time with her. Coming from where I do, there is always a part of my sexual self that I can show to people as a truly empathizing mirror of what they've shown me.

And sometimes the person I've been with will see themselves, or at least their sexual selves, more clearly, more fairly, and with a more helpful sexual recognition than they previously had.

Admittedly, the percentage of times that I am successful in this, even when I have a person naked and in my grip, is, again, fractional.

However, playing in my favor are the powerfully strong genetic roots, and physically and sensually pulling motives, and culturally learned imperatives in humans to seek, notice, and be pulled towards *the person who is passionately attracted to everything about them*, and who will not stop giving them that *special* attention.

I'm not trying to trick people, I truly do respect and adore them (sexually). But I do what I do out of a hunger that surpasses the search for love—I have love.

My pursuit is different. I am sexually created and compelled to uncover all that I can.

On this day, if I could get this odd, obviously uncared for, cold, street-wandering, pregnant, and dangerously wayward waif to enter that sexually releasing place with me—*if I could free her to reveal her whole self*—what would she show me?

I had made the decision. I was going to unleash my merciless hypersexual attention on this already heartbreaking one, until I had gone as far as I could.

I had a little over four hours to work with before my lovely wife and our college attending son and daughter would be returning home from their busy days in the city. I hoped four hours would be enough.

Of course, the ashen and only partly conscious street urchin was unaware of, and at this point in time completely unconcerned about, the power of sexual-will that I was about to assail her with.

When I spoke again, it was as if I had awakened her from a nap.

"Come on, sweetie. Come inside. Come let me fuck you."

"Yes…," she replied, as if that issue had been decided long ago.

And as I turned to lead the way, I heard her now softened voice reach out for me.

"Wait…, walk *with* me."

Chapter Two

My Own Family – Part One

As I mentioned, I have a wonderful family.

My beautiful wife Abbey, who I have known and loved since we were young teenagers, and to whom I have been married for thirty-five years, is the center of my life. And she will remain my dearest love even beyond our deaths, if such a thing is possible.

Now days, with our bright children Kye and Lula, both of whom are in their early twenties, both still living at home, and both studying in different areas of art at the nearby community college, we all enjoy a relatively amazingly good life.

Of course, no life is one-sided. And raising children and maintaining a tight-knit family is never anything less than a constant complex mixture of all of life's intricacies. But, with a concerted and steady effort, which has only grown stronger as the years have gone by, Abbey and I have managed to build and develop a decidedly safe and stable family life.

But it hasn't always been that way. Back before our children were born, and up into the first several years of their lives, Abbey and I had struggled through a great many difficulties, almost all of which had been generated by one edge or another of my persistent and widely varied sexual contact activities. However, due to something very special in Abbey's personality, my sexual roving and reputation was something that she'd striven to tolerate in me, rather than judge.

Eventually though, even Abbey's forbearance had found a limit.

So, as far as Abbey currently knew, I had left that "world" of hyperactive sexual contact behind, some seventeen years ago, when we'd moved half way across the Country to our current home to start anew and raise our children.

I suppose that my success with my secret hypersexual life is the one thing that I can claim has been perfect. In all those seventeen years, not one single second of my extra sexual contact pursuits have ever caused one single minute of negative impact on my wife or children. And, other than my being gone for the twenty-five hours or so a week that they believed I devoted to my bicycling, and the occasional weekend bike trip, my factual daily prowling and constant random sexual contacts have never detracted from any of my family members lives in any other way.

And, it is a record that I am extremely proud of. And the daily love and support that I, my wife, my son, and my daughter all feel for each other flourishes within that security.

All of which I would do anything in my power to protect—from anyone.

Chapter Three
Hypersexuals

I am one of the millions of whom I've already referred to as "hypersexuals," which is a word I came up with as a young teenager in the early 1970's to try to describe myself.

I can see, now, that I was simply trying to categorize myself in some understandable way. And I can also see now how imprecise categories and labels are. But what I saw back then is that there are some humans, like myself, who want/need/have sex, of some kind, almost every single day, every time we can, often multiple times with multiple different partners per day, every week, every month, and every year of our lives.

We also dream of sex, constantly.

There are, to be sure, far too many variations of hypersexuals to cover with any kind of blanket statement: there are so very many nasty nooks, niches, fetishes, fancies, compulsions and variant needs. And many hypersexuals willingly feed among a host of those deviant extensions.

I can say that in my experience there seems to be more male hypersexuals than female, though that number is definitely negatively influenced by the need for females in our American culture to hide their sexual drive even more effectively than males.

I will also say that the female hypersexuals that I have known seem to wield more power, and feed the most successfully.

My sexual mentor, my eight years older cousin Déjà, was a hypersexual Queen with power beyond measuring and an appetite for flesh that was as strong as a force of nature. And men and women bowed before her like reeds in the wind.

It is also true that some hypersexuals can occasionally go for a few days at a time without sex, or have an odd lull in their hunting for a number of weeks. Some even go into a depressed hibernation when the sexual conditions are cold enough—only to return in raving starvation.

But, for the most part we hunt daily, living from one quick sexual cohort to the next, occasionally going on a run of partners and letting that gratification last for as long as possible. Or, when necessary (sometimes as a way of self-protection), we exhaust ourselves temporarily through ruthless masturbation performed with nutrient-insufficient fantasies and pornography. Whichever the case, the hunger soon returns.

For us sex is not an addiction, it is a sustenance.

My people are born with, or at some point in their life develop, a human sexual drive that is in full dominance, just waiting to spring forward. Like a human who is born to be or becomes a charging sumo, or an earsplitting opera singer, or an unstoppable ultra-marathon runner; a hypersexual makes their way straight to the front of the sexual class with his or her over-developed strengths for carnal challenges—and never (willingly) quits the front.

Which means they will, if given any window of opportunity at all, have sex with and fuck the daylights out of anyone standing around them that fits anywhere within their extra-wide range of sexual desires.

Yes, some hypersexuals do have pretty specific sexual preferences. But many more of us have nearly none. In fact, *variety* is often the special spice of our favorite meal.

And everyone in society has met us: from birth we are a part of the population. In ways that many people have probably sensed, or strongly suspected, we *are* the ones who came hungrily towards their bodies in every different way. Often, as should be obvious, we are the awkwardly unstoppable flirtatious children, the too bold adolescents, the physically overly focused pre-teens, the effective seducers (even at very young ages), the suspicious seeming hiders, the smiling liars, the young bedroom teachers, the teen super-sluts, the unrelenting high school studs, the horny head cheerleaders, the secretive cheaters, the safe-feeling feelers, the beautifully desperate lovers, the sexually unsuccessful and suicidal loners, the silky smooth coaches, the ravishing educators, the wily bosses, the Cougars and the Casanovas, the relentless and too often unrefined hound-dogs, the swingers, the willing prostitutes, the pornography actors, the porn shop owners, the adult bookstore employees, the in-stall sex-givers, the public bathroom stalkers, and the next-door neighbors, friends, and family members you'd never suspect of doing any of those things.

And we come from every part and level of society, from the most illiterate and impoverished, through every level of the middle-class, to the filthiest rich.

And since hypersexuals are so often, out of necessity, adept at customizing their façades, gaining people's trust, and placing themselves in positions of powerful gatherings, too often we are also the out-of-control care givers, the dallying Doctors, the un-checked group leaders of too many kinds to count, the badly behaving celebrities, the hypocritical politicians, the unaccountable tycoons, and the prowling priests.

Nevertheless, for most of us our ways through life are made along much less affluent pathways, quietly and carefully eking out whatever invisible passages to whatever sexual contacts we can manage.

I, for instance, grew up in a very middle-class family and neighborhood, in a very conservative American City and State. My only "affluence" was my hypersexuality, itself.

Further, and making us even harder to clearly recognize or categorize, sometimes hypersexuals are only temporarily-active, or are an on-off type. But when their sexual light burns, it burns just as feverishly.

Sometimes people can see, or feel us approaching—but often we hide until we swoop.

And, if someone has met one of us intimately, they'll remember because we would have been the most sexually experienced person they were ever with—*by far*. And we would have been so much more comfortable, open, and easily insistent with our sexual contact, and our exploring desires, and our knowledge of the sexual body, and our familiarity with everything else about being naked and nasty. Plainly said, we are probably still an enigma to that person.

A sailfish doesn't brag by being the fastest swimmer in the oceans, it is simply an accurate description of the creature it is.

As I say, it's not that rare to know one of us, we do have to feed on all the different human sexual types. So a great percentage of people have, at the very least, been sexually stalked by one of us.

If, for instance, a person has had a run of more than fifteen or twenty different sex partners, perhaps during a spurt of sexual adventurousness, one of us who was near enough would have certainly followed-down their unfastened scent. Or, sometimes a hypersexual will be the one who sent a person off on their own sexual surge. Or, sometimes a hypersexual will be the one responsible for sexually unsettling a person, and turning them off and away from further sexual adventures.

Or, maybe some readers already know all of this—because they are one of us.

There are over sixteen million estimated sexual compulsives in America, which gives us a rough number of five percent of the population. My own estimate of actual hypersexuals is one-to-three in every one hundred humans. I could be off, we're a very difficult number to flesh out. And it could be different in different areas. I'm not entirely sure.

And, I should definitely remember to reveal the oddest thing (to me) about hypersexuals, which is that so many of them are so unaware of who and what they are—which works against them—and all too often, against those around them.

However, perhaps the most important thing that I should communicate here, is that among our number, whatever it may be, the majority of us are not aggressive or violent sex criminals at all. We are certainly sex criminals by many current legal definitions, no doubt, but not the kind that would ever have sex with someone against their will, or attack someone violently as a way of sexual release, or take a child, or abduct a person, or kill in a sexual venting.

Most hypersexuals, especially the more aware, do understand a lot more about the way such terrible urges and violent sexual acts can occur, largely because we are a lot more honest with ourselves about the power our sexual desires actually have, and often because many of us have been victims of sexual force or violence, in some cases having lived with a mixture of both those factors throughout our childhoods and adolescence.

But let me be perfectly clear: Wherever we may have come from, and whatever our experiences may be, the majority of hypersexuals are idealistically and very consciously as far away from sexual violence as they can possibly be. Sex is seen by us as a revered act of joining bared bodies and released lusts together—not acts that will cause horrible and permanent sexual fear and separation. Sexual contact is about intimate connection; hypersexualism is about pursuing the maximum possible depth and number of connections, and the supreme appreciation and gratification of those experiences.

We non-violent hypersexuals abhor the crimes of wrong and violent sex even more than the general public does—because those acts tread poisonously across our personal Holy Ground, and because we are way too close to the issues to ignore the realities of them—while others in society can pretend to have no part in it.

Most hypersexuals see violent sex crimes honestly: It is sex being taken, instead of shared.

The last thing I need to reveal about myself in this chapter, if my self-description is to be complete, (and it comes in two parts), is that in the midst of my rampant hypersexuality my only awareness of a primary sexual preference (which is frankly odd to me) is that I am unflinchingly aimed and primed for females—all females. And I mean *all females*—especially if they show *any* sign of sexual accessibility. The broadest possible variety of complete strangers and first time sexual contacts are my special favorites, girls who let me fuck them a second and third time, for whatever reasons, come next, and the women who continue to let me sexually maul them, even for years, come right behind them (sometimes one right after the other). And these sexual partners are unhesitatingly obtained from whatever sudden angle of availability they appear, of the widest range of ages, sizes, races, and of almost any relation, including family, co-workers, friends, friends sisters, friends mothers, other people's girlfriends or wives, sex workers, cross-dresser's, trans femmes, and *any* other female figure I come across, all of whom I see as equally sexually beautiful, all of whom I view as equally fair game, and all of whom I *will* have sex with no matter what specific things they will let me do, or what they may want me to do to them.

Still, for the whole of my life (and this is the second part), even with that wide of a range of potential, finding enough sexually obtainable females to feed a hunger as advanced as mine has been a very difficult and mostly impossible thing to achieve. However, because my prurient skills are born from a hypersexual genetic-line so ancient, so enormously intelligent, strong, and adaptive, my unrelenting sexual obsessions exposed, quite early on, a rather interesting facet in my sexual profile: If I can't find a nasty girl to sexually play with or fuck, I can embody one into my being, and offer "her" to other men. And for me, being treated as a nasty sexual plaything by an aroused man is, in the sexually embracing moment, just as fabulously releasing, and physically blissful, and personally important. And obtaining sex as that hyper-sexually-flexible person has been immensely helpful to me.

I realize that many people will have a hard time accepting my story, and that they may want to dismiss it. They might even believe that there is no such thing as a hypersexual human.

Long ago, I wrote one sentence that describes how it is for me in society at-large, and how it has been for me ever since the age that my hypersexual please-fuck-me persona came fully awake:

"People have always been more than happy to believe my lies, they cover things quite nicely; but when I try to tell the truth, when I pull back the covers, no one wants to see."

Chapter Four

Seduction
Cee Cee

As the weaving girl and I approached the door to my office, which also led to my home, I quickly began to arrange my strategy. This girl was cold (did I mention blue), pliable (deeply intoxicated), tired (pregnant and exhausted), dirty (un-cared for), and willing (desperate). And her only other obvious trait was that she was, at a currently reduced capacity, skittish (undoubtedly from a history of first-hand experience).

Fortunately, I had everything she needed.

As I opened the door and ushered her inside, it hit me again how clearly pregnant she was. Which, though I currently held no fetish for it, suddenly did give me a certain kind of primitive push.

After turning my office sign to "Closed Today," and then quickly putting my three dogs into an unfinished downstairs room, I led the girl out of my office and through the workshop area, then up the stairs into my fairly nice, large, and warm living room, which adjoins my open kitchen/dining area, creating a classic lower budget great-room. With a vaulted ceiling, and the lively yellow and green wall colors, and the sculptures and art work set around and hung on the walls, and the big L-shaped sectional leather couch, this room would serve as a pretty sweet sex-party location for the next few hours (though it was not my custom to use this room, or my house, for this function).

Like a hawk, I hovered around her.

"Do you…have a bed?" she said as soon as she came to a stop, dropping her ragged coat on the ground at her feet.

Hookers, or "sex-workers" as I would prefer they were called, are always in such a rush! The hardest part of the job ahead would probably be getting this girl to stay, to relax, and to forget time, so that I could have my slow and fully immersed way with her. I knew full well that a working girl keeps one eye on the clock, and the other on the door, out of strong habit. So I would have to earn my pleasure. Just managing to keep her in my house for more than thirty minutes, which is "flee-time" for most street girls, was going to take some clever maneuvering.

More intoxication would be a great start, if she wanted more.

"Where is the…ah…do you have some money?"

"Of course I do, sweetie. Sit down over here on my couch. Let me get some money for you. Do you like whiskey?"

"Oh…yeah. I like whiskey…yeah…I like it!" she said with a more chipper attitude, plopping herself into the corner of my long green-leather couch.

Clearly, and instantly, the fact that she was going to get some money (not having even specified an amount yet) was as soothing to her as a hit of heroin or prescription painkillers. I could see it in her body language as plainly as if I were watching her with subtitles. And I could also see that she had already decided she was going to like me.

As I left the room I looked over my shoulder and nearly swooned. She was so comfortable she wasn't even casing my house for something to steal. Instead, she had laid her head all the way back onto the high couch cushion and closed her tired eyes.

She would be all mine…

Less than two minutes later, when I came back from the other part of the house with the money, she seemed more than half way asleep.

In fact, she was so settled-in I couldn't tell if she had even heard me entering the room.

Quietly, I walked around to the back of the couch and positioned myself over her tilted back head. And still, no movement.

From this proximity I could smell her smoky breath, and sweet sweat, and cheap perfume, and her layered intoxication, all emanating up from her youthful and flushing white flesh. And I could feel that her cold little body was warming up, which released her scents to me even more.

Oh, how I loved taking that wonderfully deviant and degenerate breath into my body. And I knew at that moment that I would be able to recall the priceless erotic aroma of this girl for the rest of my life.

Poised above her, I looked down at her rough young face. Then I looked down across the worn-out and fading yellow dress hanging over her tiny and precipitous body. Seen from this close her stomach appeared quite awkwardly shaped, and almost the size of a basketball, but lopsided, and with nearly squared edges in a couple of places. And for the first time I wondered how different it was going to be to fuck such a body. I had certainly experienced sex with pregnant women before, perhaps dozens of times, but none had been so young, or small, or so late-term.

Looking back down to her square-featured and heavily freckled face, I decided to fall sexually in love with her. I fell in love with her that fast, even though she looked so hard, because her willingness made me assumed that she was soft on the inside.

Leaning slowly over, until my open mouth was just inches away from hers, I took one more long breath of her, and my deepest inner being shook.

Opening my jaw wide, with my tongue flexed outward, slowly, silently, and nearly dripping saliva, I lowered my tongue down in between her barely parted lips, and though she was slightly startled, she let me…

Lightly licking and kissing her smoky lips, I waited respectfully. And when she opened them, I kissed her deeply.

Reaching around and placing the palm and fingers of my left hand onto the front of her stretched out neck, and feeling the silk-thin skin beneath my fingers, I pulled her up towards me and filled my mouth with hers.

When I stopped the kiss, and pulled my face away from hers, she opened her eyes slowly. Focusing fully on my eye's, for the first time, she spoke as timidly as a mouse—and somehow, also totally unafraid.

"Are you gonna…fuck me now?"

As soon as she said it, I couldn't help but look straight down at her cunt. And before my eyes had finished moving she had opened her bare white legs in response. Because her protruding stomach was in the way I couldn't see much, but the movement had hiked her dress hem up onto her upper-most thighs, and I could almost see her triangular shaped treasure.

Smiling down at her, I took my hand off her throat. And then, reaching down over her rounded stomach, I smoothly stuffed that hand between her legs. Adjusting my view, I pulled the light flower print dress up until I could see her bunched-up white cotton panties (which were tattered and dirty, which thrilled me).

Letting go of the hem of her dress and leaning a little further, I pushed my open hand down over her entire crotch. Coming back with a firm but sensitive grip, I then gave her pussy a long, deep, fingering rub. Holding her soft fleshy vaginal mound like that, I looked back down into her now half closed eyes. In response, she let her eyelids fall all the way closed, and pushed her hips forward into my hand as hard as she could.

"Baby, I am gonna fuck you so sweetly! But not before we have a nice big whiskey drink, right?" I said, standing up and acting as if I hadn't just manhandled her pussy and pushed her hiding clit around for a minute.

"I'm gonna pour us some whiskey, and you're gonna tell me how much money I need to give you."

Though still slightly slow in her reactions, she fell in-step with my suddenly casual courtesies, acting as if I hadn't just finger-banged her through her panties and pushed her hiding clit firmly around for a minute.

Sitting up, she spoke in a fairly clear voice. "I wanted to get some cigarettes today…so…?"

"Sure Sweetie, how much do you need for that?"

"I can get a half carton for…around twenty dollars…?"

"Well then Baby, I would totally love to pay for a full carton."

Quickly snapping two twenties out of my pocket I showed them to her, and then walked over to her coat that was lying on the floor, and pushed them into the pocket as she watched.

Looking up at her with a smile, I saw that she was practically beaming.

"Thaaanks!" she purred.

"Now we can have that whiskey drink, girl! Do you like ice, or water, or anything else with it?"

"I like lots of ice!" She said, turning even more around to look at me.

"I like lots of ice, too!" I said playfully, and saw her giggle a bit as I turned to grab the bottle.

Picking small looking glasses I poured huge drinks, a generous quadruple shot at least, and then filled them with ice. I was hoping to send this girl out on another long loop of her already rocketing intoxication. I love fucking girls who love to be fucked while they are, shall we say, in an altered state. It shows an important level of trust, and release.

After grabbing a couple of cokes out of the fridge, and popping them open, I then transferred all the drinks to the low couch side table next to…?

Damn, I didn't know what to call this girl?

Almost all street-girls have favorite working-names that they'll give you. But, because their gut reaction to being asked their name is usually not a good one, I try to wait until they tell me on their own.

This quiet sweetheart seemed like she definitely wouldn't like being asked, and also as if she might not have a fake "name" ready at hand. But I was starting to get a little bored with utilizing all the common "cutie-pie" type nicknames. And honestly, I was starting to want to address her in a way that would bring us closer.

In that thought, I sat down next to her and picked up my drink. She had already grabbed hers, so I looked at her and said.

"Here's to meeting you…"

Hoping this salutation would lead to her telling me her name, fake or otherwise, I smiled and waited. I would definitely be giving her a fake name for myself, like Joe. Although, as I continued to stand there, she showed no signs of asking for one.

In fact, she didn't seem to have anything to say. So we took our first sip of the drinks, and she came away with a half empty glass.

Swirling my sip around in my mouth, an idea came to me: Sometimes come-and-go girls like it when you give them a fun nickname of your own making. And they'll like it as long as it sounds good, and you have some "hip enough" reason the nickname makes sense. For instance, you could say, "I'm going to call you Sadie the famous party-girl!" The word "famous" used with the celebratory designation "party girl" would make the nickname Sadie (or any other) work pretty well in most cases.

And giving a working girl a spontaneous nickname makes them feel as if you are really noticing them. It heightens their feelings of personal acceptance, which can accelerate a "coming closer".

It seemed obvious that this one wasn't going to give me her name, so...?

When I try to make up a nickname I like to pick something that will later remind me of the girl in a unique way, something descriptive of our illicit meeting. I never forget a girl that I've fucked, which is important to me. I'll especially remember her face, the way she smelled, her way of getting-off, and hopefully her name or whatever I called her.

"*Hmmm...,*" I thought to myself, she is giving herself to me for a carton of cigarettes, which could lead to the nickname C.C....

That's not bad? I thought, silently. Still enjoying the first sting of the whiskey drink. But as soon as I imagined saying it out loud, I saw the sounds in my mind's eye as being spelled-out "Cee Cee," which was more feminine, and better.

"Hey, Baby.., if you don't want to tell me your name can I call you "Cee Cee? You remind me of this super cute girl I knew a long time ago. God, I adored that girl! You look a lot like her. She spelled her name C-E-E C-E-E—Cee Cee—which I always thought was pretty cool. You're even more beautiful than she was, and way nastier I bet. I can tell..."

Talking slowly, I lured.
"Can I call you Cee Cee? It's such a pretty name, and you are such a pretty girl..."

Giving me a funny and somewhat confused look, she answered straightforwardly.

"Yes.., I like that name...*Cee Cee*..."

And now that she had spoken it out loud, she doubted it.

"Do you *really* want to call me Cee Cee...?" she asked.

Such moments are hard to equal, though most people don't see them the same way I do. What this girl had just asked me, in the language that I hear so clearly, was, *"Do you really want to be so nice to me? And adore me? And treat me like you did the beautiful girl you adored before?"*

Turning fully towards her, and smiling at her as if I were sharing a secret, I spoke with all the spilling adoration that I could muster, which was a great flooding wave—because now I was speaking from my position of power in this universe.

"Please let me call you Cee Cee."

She heard it inside her body as, *"Let me love you now."*

"Yes..., Cee Cee..." She replied, now hypnotized by her own dearest desires.

Every human being that I have ever met, from the lowest snakes to the highest whatevers, have wanted to be adored and listened to. There is no new knowledge in that fact. The discovery comes when you directly touch the unrestricted range of sexual things that people want to be appreciated for. Driving right past the good sense that keeps most people from committing themselves to so many passionate partners, so completely, so quickly, I habitually strip myself naked and dive directly in, swimming right over the usual personal questioning details and doubts, swiftly pulling myself and my lover all the way into the deep-end.

"Super!" I said, with charming enthusiasm. "I'm so stoked! A sweet new Cee Cee...for me!"

Raising my glass to my grinning mouth, I let our newly heightened relationship settle into the room.

Cee Cee, smiling widely, stared up at me like a trusting child.

"Hey Cee Cee, do you like to smoke good weed?"

"Yes! I want to smoke some weed!"

The party was on! And damn, it was going so wonderfully I felt like I was floating. And this little girl sure loved to stay high! And the more mentally-weightless quality of that kind of consciousness makes it so much easier for me to move a girl around. And it helps unwind the clock.

Smoking high-end weed these days is nearly the same as tripping on mellow psychedelic mushrooms, or some other lighter dose of psycho-active drugs. And, with pot, you have easy re-application just a few puffs away. If a person isn't used to the highest strength weed, and they smoke a bunch of it, mixed with other intoxicants, there's no telling how high, or semi-conscious, or crashed-out they may end-up. It won't really hurt anybody, but it can definitely zonk them out pretty hard. Of course this girl, though so young, already seemed to be sailing on even more strident chemicals, so I was confident that supplying her with a bit more "fun" would do no harm.

And I was right, and the ritual of smoking and drinking brought us even closer.

Sitting side-by-side at my long and low black coffee table, Cee Cee watched me work with my expensive looking glass pipe and my little bead-decorated leather stash pouch. I loaded hits, and she smoked them while I smiled at her. Then I let her load hits, and we smoked them together. Laughing next to each other, letting the buzz settle in, we made small talk about the skunky smell and the intense effectiveness of the buds, and the sweet burn of the icy whiskey drinks, and whatever other random observations came out of our loosened minds.

She liked the way I calmed her, and listened to her without interrupting, and laughed when she laughed. And I wondered how often she got to be the center-of-attention in her worn out world.

She talked and I goaded, and she talked a bit more. She told me very little about herself; and she told me so much. She was definitely from local Caucasian genetic stock: with her dry desert accent, her thin square face, her sun freckled skin, and her red-blond hair. She was also poor as hell, in every way: an unhappy foster child, a middle school dropout, no job, no money, no friends, no belongings that she was excited about or proud of, no plans for life, and no hope.

All she "had" was what she was experiencing at that very moment: she had an excellent buzz, a warm couch, some money in her coat pocket, and a shockingly affectionate and generous companion.

Suspended in that amazing way, for more than forty-five minutes we smoked and drank, and did "another round", until I was decidedly drunk and thoroughly stoned.

Looking at Cee Cee, I watched as the clouds of potent smoke drifted over her mind and the waves of whiskey washed across her swollen little body, mixing with whatever else was in there.

And now she was talking almost to herself as she drank, smiling sweetly even when she wasn't looking at me, and she was gliding off…

Seeing the opening portal, I seized the precious moment. Scooting closer to her on the couch, I looked over and asked her my all-time favorite question: quietly, clearly, and all at once.

"Cee Cee, when did you first have sex?"

"The first time I remember, I was nine or ten." She said without pause.

Not everyone answers that question. And when they do, it is hardly ever with that much unguarded spontaneity. And often, the longer the person hesitates the worse the story is. But that, also, did not necessarily apply in this case.

"Did you like it right off?" I asked plainly.

"Yes. I loved it."

Another instant answer, both given in a heartbeat. This girl was going to be full of surprises.

"I did, too." I echoed. "I loved it, and I still don't understand *how I knew* what to do?"

Purposefully, I let that hang for a second. And then I asked a third question.

"Did *you* know how, Cee Cee?"

"No. Not really. Well, yeah...a little."

She remembered...

"I knew that my youngest foster uncle was going to take my panties off and put his mouth on my pussy, even though he didn't say a word. That was weird... Why, what'd you know?"

"At barely seven years old I knew how to tell a girl that I wanted to take her panties off and put my mouth on her pussy—without saying a word."

Rolling her head sideways along the back of the couch, Cee Cee looked me straight in the eyes.

"You just made that shit up, right?

"No, not at all. It happened to me just like that." I told her, with all the honesty of truth.

Following Cee Cee's own frank tone, I just told her the story straight out.

"This is my very first memory of getting a girl to have sex me..."

Settling into the couch with her head comfortably facing me, Cee Cee listened intently.

"I saw her at recess one day, and our eyes met across the monkey bars, and I *knew* that I had to talk to her about sex—even though it was the first time I had ever had that thought or impulse. Inexplicably, I opened my mouth and told her that I was starting a 'nasty club,' and that she had a 'special invitation,' and that she could meet me after school to join the club. I had never said anything like that to anyone before. I didn't even know how I'd made it up. There was no thought. And she didn't think about it either. Instead, she asked me, just once, to repeat what I had said. And then she replied, 'Okay.'"

Looking at me with lively anticipation, Cee Cee held her eyebrows up and waited for me to go on.

So I continued, giving what I hoped I would get from her.

"We were in first grade, or she was a grade ahead of me, but I remember that we weren't in the same classroom, and that I didn't even know her. After school that day we met and instead of going home we walked about three city blocks to go behind a gas station that I knew about. We would have gone into the bathroom but the door was locked, so we slipped around a corner and into the concrete-block tire bin. Then we just looked at each other, and she did exactly what I wanted her to do, immediately lifting her dress up with one hand and slipping her panties down with her other. And then I dropped down on my knees and put my mouth all over her pussy—and she let me…"

"What else happened?" Cee Cee asked, clearly aroused.

"Before I was anywhere near done, or satisfied with kissing her wonderful smelling and tasting little pussy, she made me stop because she said it was 'her turn.'"

"She already knew how to do it?"

"She didn't tell me. She just pulled my tiny cock out from my underwear and sucked on it like she'd done it her whole life. And, even though I begged her to let me take another turn, she just kept going and sucked and slobbered on me until we heard someone coming!"

"Did you get caught?!"

"No, we almost did! But we quick grabbed hands, and ran out of the tire bin all the way out to the sidewalk, laughing so hard we couldn't even talk! Then I walked her home."

"That's good." Cee Cee breathed out, relieved.

"Yeah…, but we only hung out like that a couple more times, and we never did anything more than kiss on the lips a little, even though I begged her…"

"Were you nice to her?"

"Totally. Maybe too much, I think she got tired of me following her around the school yard all the time."

"Oh. That's cool that she already knew how to suck. I wasn't sure what to do, at first…"

"I'm going to get us another drink, Cee Cee."

Standing up, I walked around the couch and into the kitchen.

"What else happened with you and your youngest foster 'uncle'?"

Now, I should remember to say here that I absolutely cannot judge or hold back my open affection from someone who is telling me their truth about sex. Judging "badness" or "wrongness," especially in what is being shared with me about sex and sexual experiences, just isn't a part of the way that I collect my knowledge.

"We did just about everything that first time." Cee Cee began. "He already knew everything about sex, and we had all day. I'll bet we were naked for four straight hours!"

"I'm so jealous."

"Don't be stupid!" She said. "He was so nice to me…"

"What part of sex did he show you first, Cee Cee?" I asked from the kitchen.

She thought for a minute, and then started with a surprising sureness.

"I never knew what being touched so softly was like, and kissing the body. My old foster mother and father have never touched or kissed me with love—thank god! But when my uncle took his clothes off, without saying anything or acting weird, I just took mine off too."

From the kitchen I stared at the side of Cee Cee's head, smart enough not to say anything, even if she had paused.

"I was never scared of him, so I wasn't scared when he did that. And once he hugged his soft, and warm, and naked skin up against mine—I never wanted him to stop touching me!" Cee Cee giggled, and literally cuddled-up to herself as she told her story.

And again, I stayed silent, relishing in the wonderful moment.

"By the end of our first time he even got me liking cum inside my body, and having it dripping out of my body. Now I've been pregnant four times in my life, so far!"

Not knowing what else to say, I stammered, "Wow…"

Excitedly, she continued, "One thing that freaked me out a little bit was that I couldn't figure out why I was shaking so much. I didn't know, but I was cumming the whole time!"

"I saw beautiful lights…," I interjected, unconsciously.

And then quickly returning to her story, I asked another question.

"What else do you remember about that first time, Cee Cee?" I said, trying to envision this 'youngest uncle' character while putting ice in the newly filled glasses.

"The funniest thing I remember is how he moaned so much, and how he showed me his…face. You know…his *cumming-face!*" She laughed, clinching her shoulders up and pinching her face together in an imitation of him. "And at the same time, he was telling me in a kind of weird voice how beautiful he thought I was, and how much he adored me! That was the first time anyone ever said that to me! And it was the first time I ever fell in love."

"Cee Cee, that is so beautiful."

"Shut up, I'm not done telling you yet. At the end, when he was done cumming, I wanted more of it. Without asking him, I pulled myself down under him enough to get his cock into my mouth. Then I sucked on the head to get more cum. I don't know why I wanted his cock and cum in my mouth; *I just did!* And I kept sucking even though the sperm was so icky at first! And my uncle said that was the best thing he ever saw a girl do on her first time! That's *kind of like* what you said."

I so loved being together in that moment with Cee Cee.

"And you've been loving cock and cum ever since!" I joked, as I walked around to the front of the couch and handed Cee Cee another glass of whiskey.

"Yeah. *So?!*" She said, taking the glass almost roughly.

"*So?!*" I replied quickly. "So—today you are *my* cock and cum loving girl! That's what!" I said, as I sat down next to her and leaned in for a kiss.

Cee Cee, in response, stuck-out her tongue. Surprising her, I took her whole tongue into my mouth and pretended that I might bite it off, which made her laugh.

And so we shared the taste of the whiskey playfully. And the way that she kissed me back, told me just how much she was enjoying herself.

Even better, we had each shared a secret, safely, and each of us was equally aroused: We *were* alike.

And more than an hour had come and gone, and she wasn't even looking at the clock.

And I was still on my toes: keeping such a girl floating free can be like riding a banana peel; you have to keep sliding straight ahead.

I did want, terribly, to talk to her more about what she had said about being pregnant four times—by her age! *Holy shit!* But she had gone quickly past it for her own reasons. So instead, I followed where the current was flowing.

"Cees," I said, affectionately shortening her new nickname. "How old was that sweet 'uncle' of yours when that happened?"

"Thirty-four, then, I think…he's about twenty-five years younger than my old-ass foster dad. Their weird old mom, whose dead now, had like ten kids all spread out." She stated, without a shred of hesitation or guardedness.

What…? Hearing the uncle's age stopped me, but I shouldn't have let it. I guess it was because I'd imagined and expected that he was just a few years older than her, or a teenager at most. In an uncommon unconscious-of-my-words moment, I spoke too quickly.

"You said you were nine or ten…, *right?*" I asked, turning to look directly at her.

In answer, Cee Cee's quickly changing facial expression said it all. She had thought that my last question was a judgment, and I could feel the reactive locking-mechanisms tumbling and falling through her heart and mind. And her face tilted heavily toward her lap.

"Cee Cee! *No!* I didn't mean *that*! Look at me! I already told you who I am! I've been nasty since way before you! But I didn't tell you about my oldest cousin and me; I'm just like you! I loved her! I love her still! *I don't care about shit like that!*"

Desperately unwilling to let this rare treasure go, I reached in with my burglar-like emotional reflexes and took hold of Cee Cee's full attention.

"Cee Cee! Listen to me! I think my oldest cousin had sex with me when I was just an infant! My parents always said weird stuff about her and me, and then my other cousin, who I learned sex from since I was only six or seven years old, told me once that she thought our oldest cousin had probably done way more sexual stuff to me than I could ever know! She also told me that she believed our family had generations of what she called 'extra-sexual' members going back as far as she could imagine—just like us, and your uncle!"

Pausing, I gave her time. Even the smallest part of a communication like this holds great meaning. And it can take an entire combination of meanings, all falling into place, to re-open a locked heart. After a short silence, she looked back up at me.

"You were..? I mean...your cousin told you that?"

Slowly, Cee Cee came back to me.

"My cousin Déjà' told me that, and many other things, Cee Cee. And when I was barely thirteen she showed me so much more about what people really do with sex, it makes you and me look like a couple of dorks! Believe me Cee Cee, we don't have anything to feel weird about! Déjà said she had fucked more than four hundred men by the time she was twenty, and from what she showed me when we were together, I totally believe her."

"I fucked at least thirty, already!" Cee Cee blurted out, as if a score were being kept.

With great relief, I could feel her resistance and doubt letting go. That's another virtue of deep and steady intoxication, it can often help thoughts and emotions slip along a bit easier.

"Cee Cee, I love how you loved your uncle, alright? In your own heart you can love anyone you want to. And no one can take that away from you. You were just a kid!"

I wanted to set that specific point straight.

"He *was* sweet." Cee Cee replied. "But after we got caught we're not supposed to see each other anymore." She finished, with a tone of unrequited confusion.

Prompting my absolute most genuine reply.

"My parents said that too much physical affection could ruin a child for life. Fuck that! I ain't ruined!"

Yes, I know that I protest too much, and about something we all know is wrong. But I was, at that moment, alive only to be Cee Cee's clear and loving reflection. And I shudder to think of what it might take to make me release such an unusually amoral quarry. To me, successfully hooking into this girl felt like a matter of hypersexual survival.

"What did your oldest cousin really do to you…?" Cee Cee asked, trusting me again.

And so I told her. "I only know some, and some is a guess. But I do know that when I was an infant my oldest cousin Maria, who was actually adopted, and who was still a teenager at the time, was my main babysitter for over a year. One time, when my parents returned home from a vacation trip to Canada with my three older brothers, who were just toddlers themselves, Maria locked herself in her room with me and tearfully refused to hand me over. When my dad broke through the flimsy door, I guess she was holding my naked little body wrapped in hers, and in the very center of our nakedness…I think she was pretend-breastfeeding me, or something."

"I've pretended that with a baby too." Cee Cee responded, seeming thoughtful. "I did it really quick, once."

"But later," I continued, "when I was still years younger than you are Cee Cee, my other cousin, Déjà, whose actually my second-cousin, told me that she knew of some 'extra-sexual' people who did way more to the children they touched. I'd always wanted to know exactly what happened to me, but my cousin Déjà was crazy, and it seemed like she only wanted to tell me some of the stuff she knew."

"Why?" Cee Cee questioned.

"I'm not sure. She would tell me the wildest sexual things about herself, and about other people, and about me, and then she would just stop and refuse to talk about it anymore. One time she started talking about one of our relatives who got rich somehow, and then went 'sexually insane', and then she wouldn't tell me what that meant, or even their name. But I'd never heard anything like that from my dad about anyone in his family. Anyway, Déjà imagined that Maria taught me how to 'sexually feed' and suck on her whole body when I was a baby, and that she kissed and sucked on my whole body too."

"Oh."

"Maybe that's how I knew what to do the first time I was with a girl?" I wondered aloud.

"Maybe." Cee Cee replied.

Fully regaining my momentum, I brought us all the way back together.

"Cee Cee, I'm going to cum so hard inside your body!"

"You better," she threatened teasingly, shaking her finger at me with a wanton smile.

And then, almost to herself, she added, "I wish I could get pregnant from you . . ."

Chapter Five

Pedophilia and Incest

Cee Cee and I are both born from this: Children of hypersexuality gone wrong, the progeny of other hypersexuals who reached in the wrong direction, creating the too young and too often touched.

In my case, pedophilia and incest are so intertwined into my sexual origins the braid of them feels like my own spinal column.

Beginning in my infancy, by the end of my fourteenth year I had experienced both deviations in perhaps a hundred or more sexual incidences with older, and much older partners, both related to me and not.

In truth, I have no conscious memories before my desire for more-sex.

When I was a kid and anyone older than me included me in their sex, of whatever type, I looked up to them as my secret heroes. My oldest cousin, my eight years older second-cousin, my oldest brother and his friends, and the adult and elderly men who began to find me in all kinds of places, were all my idols.

Similarly, beginning at age nine or ten, Cee Cee had her new foster uncle, who was both an unhindered pedophile and the only person and only adult that had ever been closely attentive to her. And she adored him.

I realize how confused that might seem to most people. But it is also true that confusion, especially when worked on so persistently, can sometimes lead to an unexpected depth of understanding. I have always believed it would.

Perhaps even more confusing and difficult to make sense of, during my eleventh and twelfth years of age, in addition to my other sexual activities, I was also physically forced and anally raped by strangers, twice, and violently abducted into a vehicle by my throat once, all while seeking sex in public park bathrooms. And, Cee Cee had been abducted and raped by her uncle's sneaking and threatening work friend, repeatedly, and was eventually impregnated by him (her second pregnancy) when she was barely twelve. And still, neither Cee Cee nor I had ever thought of sex—itself—as anything but wonderful. And neither of us had ever been turned-away by those bad experiences from actively seeking a continuous string of partners, and nearly daily sexual contact.

But, what does our American society call a child who experienced incest or pedophilia, especially repeatedly? *"Crushed."*

Unless they are like Cee Cee and me—in which case we should consider it more carefully and say, *"Created."*

I've always supposed that it was my in-born hypersexuality that protected me from the worst consequences of my abuse and attacks, and I suspect the same is true of Cee Cee. And I also realize that this form of protection isn't the reality for most victims.

So, because I am their risen raped twin, it is my dream to help heal as many of the crushed as I can, and to bring back the sexually mislaid and lost. In my hypersexually ambitious vision, my denial-shattering honesty contains the power to change the world. We have to try something.

One way or another, I believe we all need to know how to better rise above our sexual ordeals, and challenging histories, however difficult to accept, for our own, as well as society's self-preservation.

For myself, like Cee Cee, I feel fortunate to know that I am exactly as I was meant to be. And we both know exactly *why* we are like this, which is to give what should not have to be wrongly taken.

Hypersexual Prodigies

Though everyone instantly relates to the children who are hurt by sexual abuse and/or a sexual attack, no one that I've ever come across wants to talk about the "other children." The children who instantly adored sexual contact no matter what form(s) it presented itself in, and the children who exalted ecstatically in their too young experiences, with their naked rapture unencumbered by mature awareness, or "normal" boundaries, or legally defined limits, no matter the age, or relation, or specific behaviors of their older partner(s).

I will talk about it.

What does society call those sexually awakened, invisibly branched-off, and constantly aroused children of too-young sex? We call them "sick." But I didn't feel sick as a child, I felt wildly enlivened.

Those children, however they came into being, should be acknowledged as "hypersexual prodigies"; attracted to, and excelling in sexual congress, released into the oceans of human sexual-contact ahead of others, set free with hunting skills that have been passed directly from body-to-body and mind-to-mind, with an unrestricted hunger, and destined to become gargantuan among sexual-feeders.

When I was touched as a child, it was I who sighed the deepest. I remember it as clearly as I remember my own face. I was always the one who opened my mouth the widest, first, begging to be sexually filled.

Cee Cee, as well, was literally swollen with her desire to be sexually touched.

In our humming little hearts we believed that when those older than us found themselves touching us, it was they who had been seduced, and that we were born to be this way.

As a child I believed that *something* had sexually touched me even before I was born.

An "abomination," I know, my mother told me. And I'm sure many people would agree.

But, as an adult, and a now fully matured hypersexual, I also know that my mother, and all of that kind of fearful sexual judgment—against me and other hypersexuals—is just plain wrong.

Hypersexuals *are* special, in their own ways. For one thing, they intimately know innumerable helpful sexual details, and thoroughly useful specific information, and they can communicate those things directly.

For instance, I can begin by telling you these three important things: Without my early confusions I would not have had to begin understanding what sexual respect is—and isn't—so face-to-face at such a young age; and due to the power of that understanding I have never sexually reached for a child; and I can show other hypersexuals and hypersexual prodigies, as well as any other potential pedophiles, *exactly why and how* they can achieve this same kind of sexual respect.

Across the Line

Some hypersexuals and hypersexual-prodigies do reach across that line, I know. As do a whole range of other sexually searching people whose personal beginnings have nothing to do with pedophilia or incest.

The heinous bottom line though—and a hated curse of my kind—is that the most common sexual abuser of children is the one who was, himself or herself, a child who experienced sexual abused.

This is especially hard for me to accept.

To be truthful, because of my history, I suppose I can imagine how a crushed and too-confused victim might reach for a child to try to take what was taken from them, or to break the rule that was broken on them, or are for some driving reason exploring what was done to them, or have let themselves become sexual bullies because they are finally big enough to be in control, or are perhaps reacting in some delayed kind of ultimately tragic self-hating and self-damning act.

But the fact that they have acted against a vulnerable child—just as they were—is beyond my tolerance.

And frankly, I can also envision how, when a child's sexual confusion has been shamefully hidden and locked away since their too-early experiences, and their pain and halting uncertainties have been left unheard and unprocessed or educated, they might become so terribly and mysteriously starved for a return to that "left-unfinished sexual circumstance" they would seek it out, and even hunt it down.

But I can't forgive it.

And I will be even more honest.

A hypersexual prodigy, like myself, might consider engaging a child because they remember how wonderful their own first sexual encounters felt and seemed. It is important that these things be spoken out loud, so that the reality can be acknowledged. For us such sex is not a dirty fantasy, or a fetish, or a perversion, or a painfully forced incident—it is simply an example of ecstatic sex that we have already experienced.

This, and similarly shocking truths from our hypersexual worlds, is what scares the sex-fearing public the most about us. It scares them so much they can't even bear hearing the start of a conversation like this. They can't even allow the beginning of a thought like this, let alone the potentially valuable completion of the open contemplation of it.

But again, what those frightened people fail to appreciate, or even consider, is that many hypersexuals, perhaps especially those who had been hypersexual prodigies, contain whole storehouses of strenuously built and crucially important sexual understandings. And further, for those hypersexuals who, for whatever reasons, have become positively empowered like myself, the very best ways to help children, and the simplest ways to prevent the sex crimes in the first place, are what we see the most clearly—and can offer to society.

<u>Protector</u>

What if our children could know the powerfully protective parts of what I, and others know?

I believe they can. And, I'm not too shy to try.

I think we should straightforwardly explain at least the basic reasons of how and why some people, both from within a family group and outside it, might sometimes seek inappropriate sexual contact with too-young partners. To do that all we need to admit is the truth about the multi-layered positive side of sexual contact, for people of appropriate ages, and how the attempted satisfaction of that completely natural human desire is sometimes aimed in wrong directions. Why are such simple things so beyond discussing in our culture?

As a barely five or six year old child living in the American mountain-west I was taught how to spot a dog that might be a danger to me—perhaps even a mortal danger—from quite a ways away. I knew that when a dog focused all its attention on me, and its head dropped, and its ears laid-back, and its body movements became more deliberately aimed, and it began to slowly creep toward me—I knew that I absolutely had to be afraid, and that I had to move to safety.

And this part is also true: Within no more than a year or two of that same age, by seven or eight years old, when an adult was looking at me with sexual intentions—*I knew*. Cee Cee knew, too. And I know that I am unquestionably correct in that awareness and claim because I always moved successfully toward it. And once I knew it—*I owned it*.

Some truths are discovered in the oddest of ways, which certainly doesn't negate their validity. And I'm positive that children would trust this kind of honesty and helpful sharing. Kids are way more intelligent, and even intuitive, than they get credit for. But they still need the important framework of information to work with, and way more depth of open details and conversation than we currently give them.

If I could, I would make sexual predators as easy for a child to distinguish and evade as an approaching bus.

Of course, even with a better kind of education, we still wouldn't protect every child or victim. But we would surely be making a genuine and meaningful difference.

What we'd still need to accomplish is a much more effective way to stop the offenders before they even reach for the children.

The Voluntary Marking

Perhaps because sexually seeking individuals have been so easy for me to "see" from such a young age, when I was twelve or thirteen years old I started having a terrible reoccurring dream about how society could take away the invisibility power of predatory sexual criminals. And when I was awake, even though I knew that this kind of system could never be used, and I was absolutely terrified of its implications about my own life, for years I pretended that this idea could be, and perhaps should be used. And, for a number of years, I practiced a personalized version of it on myself in mostly small ways, like bruising myself with a hammer, scarring, burning, and a few other relatively harmless ways. I called it "The Voluntary Marking."

In my nightmarish dreams the idea went like this: Those who commit sexual crimes ranging all the way from being the willing child partner of pedophilic sex, to panty stealing, to public acts of masturbation, homosexuality, and prostitution, all the way up to the adult acts of abuse against children, as well as rapists of all kinds—if allowed to wander free in society—would have to agree to wear fearsome and warning face tattoos and even brands—like a grim new version of the old puritanical red-letter "A" for adulterers.

If they were a violent offender, or had ever forced someone in any way, they would also lose their most dexterous limb, and be castrated. And they'd still be treated as dangerous in society, but they'd be ninety percent less so, and impossible not to spot.

And these difficult dreams, in which I was always being chased-down with my heart-pounding until I awoke, continued for at least ten years. And they evolved and morphed in several weird and upsetting ways. And for most of that time I felt that they were trying to tell me something important about myself.

But, as a more matured hypersexual I came to understand that no new-age version of branding or marking sexual perverts and deviants and criminals is ever going to be the answer. And I knew that no mark or brand or label could ever describe me.

Markings, or even the most modern versions of categorizing or labeling perverts and deviants and alternative sexualities are imprecise to start with, and an immature and ineffectual idea no matter how sincerely intentioned. The hammer I used as a preteen, and the bruises it left, didn't help in the least. And the nearly exact realities of our current criminal classification system is what made my old dreams and nightmares seem worth describing at this time, because we all have to put away our ineffective ideas and come up with something that *will* work. Something that acknowledges everyone, from A to Z.

Educator

Here is an especially significant and commanding piece of knowledge about trying to categorize sexual criminals and behaviors, and it has a million-times the power of any marking: The most recent progressive clinical studies on pedophilia and pedophilic incest reveal that *perhaps all so-called "pedophiles" are actually not-at-all exclusively sexually attracted to children.*

This clinical confirmation is huge, and it directly parallels my own hypersexual experiences and investigations. Sexually driven and hypersexual people who are attracted to the idea of sex with children and youth, and/or rape—are also attracted to sex with all kinds of other partners. In plain honesty, this also parallels most human experience: most people are admittedly attracted to a variety of possible sexual situations and potential partners, even if only in their fantasies; but the sexual contact they actually have is restricted within only a small or singular range of their desires, usually defined by what is socially appropriate.

In other words: Most humans consider a wide range of sexual possibilities, but their actual range of sexual contact and available experiences is limited. Obviously, in our society, those options are severely limited by religion, cultural mores, and law.

Hypersexuals expand their sexual contact options by walking right through and beyond as many of those social and legal limitations as they can, in as many ways as they can—rather than steering solely toward one unalterable, perhaps criminal goal. For sexually driven persons, and plenty of others, attaining a *variety* of sexual contact is a much more prevailing and influential reality than strict adherence to any one sexual fixation.

This reality about sexual deviance could be the breakthrough society has been waiting for, because it means that we can offer sex criminals of all kinds, including pedophiles, something they want—which is sex, of *some variety*—so that they can stop committing crimes in order to obtain their sexual contact!

Ultimately important to this discussion is the fact that, as an adult, I have been that *variant* partner for deviants who admitted pedophilic attractions or desires a great number of times. And I have had many informative conversations with them, along with the deeply encouraging experiences of living this (above explained) essential reality of sexual contact with my own flesh.

In fact, on several occasions throughout my life I have successfully talked hypersexuals and other deviants out of their misdirected sexual intentions toward children, usually by unhesitatingly sharing certain parts of my own life's experiences and understandings, supported by the relevant stories of other people that I've heard and collected throughout my life. And I've had these kinds of conversations.

so spontaneously, so many times, I never really thought of it much—until now.

In one case, I managed to turn a confused mother away from sexually approaching her own adolescent son as a way of attempting to complete her own unfulfilled sexual desires with her pedophilic father. She'd even built-up an idea that experiencing the (imaginarily life-continuing and positive) sexual contact with her own son would somehow also solve her remaining issues with her own mother's failure to protect her. It can be so complex.

Still, by repeatedly showing that woman that there was a much more direct route to the sexual gratification that she felt such a dire need for, through fucking the begeezus out of her in every other way she desired, which sadly no other man in her adult life had been able to supply, definitely helped return her attention to where it belonged—which was on her own body and sexual being, not her sons. And she did understand that.

Sharing some of my additional knowledge with that mother, and empowering her through openly discussing her whole hoary host of personal sexual confusions and life-long difficulties—not unlike my own—all without a shred of hesitation, or fear, or disgust, or judgment—and also vividly discussing some of the worst possible outcomes of enacting the sexual scenario that she had suggested—with genuine empathy and powerful personal details—also greatly helped her understand why both she and her son must never come to that kind of sexual harm.

In another situation, I respectfully moved a man away from his pre-teen nephew, who he had surreptitiously observed masturbating in his bedroom. Interestingly, and revealingly, in this man's history there was absolutely no pedophilia or incest experience. Instead he had begun his sexual encounters with other young men in his early twenties, in what he experienced as a painfully unguided and awkward path, which he had always felt was a far-less-than what it could-have-been introduction to his sexual pleasures. Now picturing himself as a suitable guide for a sexually earnest young man, he'd let his mind go too far in the direction of his nephew.

However, candidly talking with that man about many of the general realities of being a pre-teen, like the overall emotional, mental, and social unpreparedness of a boy that age for handling such a serious and deviant relationship. And the extremely unlikely possibility of having the pedophilic relationship he had described without also having all the social and legal consequences eventually catch up with both of them, which would lead to possibly even worse consequences for his nephew than it would for him. And even reminding him about the common inability of a boy that age to actually keep such a big secret—and the reasons why such big secrets can be unhealthy at that young age, like the habits of deceit and walling off oneself. All of which was communicated to the man without condemning his fantastically imagined, and positively intentioned, sexual designs—before bending our conversation back toward my fully-naked and fully-available sexual invitation.

And then I held still and let that man fondle me, anyway he wanted to, without interruption, until he came on my stomach and genitals.

My being a model of unhindered sexual availability, not to mention matured skills, had left no room in that man for doubt. And in this way, the unrealistic and less-than truly respectful illusions of his finding sexual satisfaction through any kind of advantage-taking or levered-control over a youth were dispelled.

And, over the course of the next several months that man had both thanked me for helping him in this way, and also mentioned that his nephew had moved with his family to a different place (which that man was, quietly, acknowledging as a "safer" place).

Unfortunately, for that man and all the other people in our culture who are caught wondering which of their limited sexual options they should pursue, the exacerbating issue of our society's nearly total lack of easily available sexual contact options remains.

All of which brings me to the final part of my vision.

Sexual Martyrdom

To all those who would sexually gratify themselves with our children, or commit rape of any kind on any person of any age—I give zero mercy.

Instead I will give them myself, and Cee Cee, and any other willing sexual meat behind us.

Let the sexually ravenous of the world gorge themselves on our nakedly offered flesh in unrestricted orgiastic celebration and fully released salacious feasting.

Just let them do it before they abuse another child, or anyone else!

I always wanted to grow up to be a sexual martyr.

If my oldest cousin Maria, who may have been a hypersexual prodigy herself, really had fully engaged my infant body orally, wetly showering my infinitely sensitive flesh with what my second-cousin Déjà called "the pleasure of a thousand kisses," and had then placed my suckling infant mouth all over her own gushing sexual body, it certainly could have produced a rather insidious push to my sexual consciousness.

However, it is also a well-known scientific fact that human fetus', of both sexes, have been observed masturbating-to-orgasm while still in the womb. As human beings we are born with an awareness of sex; we came swimming out of sex, which makes us sexually sensitive.

I wasn't created by a violent attack—I was lovingly embraced, though wrongly. Maria and Déjà could not have known what individual being they were sexually engaging.

But I would never want to mark their faces, or amputate their hands and tongues.

After a lifetime of ardent hypersexuality, I believe this: If Maria and Déjà could have somehow utilized their sexual energies in their local communities in an open, legal, and fully-exercising way, they wouldn't have had the pent up sexual energy or gnawing hunger to push the idea of putting me into their mouths.

And I know this: If Cee Cee and I could have grown up with the opportunity to apply our deviant desires and our over abundant sexual energies in socially acceptable and readily available ways, we too could have avoided our dreadful danger and mistakes.

The answer isn't for society to mark, or categorize, or label, or continue to try to corral hypersexuals and sexual contact seeking criminals: The answer is for society to *use* us.

Children, and everyone else, should be sexually safe.

I'm defensive about the way in which I was created, and Cee Cee, because I believe that sometimes nature creates a kind of genius out of madness, sometimes in an attempt toward balance, and sometimes to save itself.

Chapter Six

The Worst Sound I Ever Heard

One day, when I was eight or nine years old, as I was sucking-off my oldest brother Burt in our downstairs and darkened laundry room, our mother unexpectedly came in and turned the light on.

My brother, who was nearly five years my senior, was laid back on the top of the washing machine with his legs sprawled to the side and his pants hanging down around his ankles.

When my mother saw me pull my wet little face up-and-away from my brother's lap, revealing his quivering cock, she made a sound that no child should ever hear.

She spoke only two words, *"Ohhh, Roooory..."*

But the sound of her words was so filled with stomach wrenching disgust, so gutturally vomited up, and enunciated with such shaking revulsion, ending in groaning sobs that I can only describe as mourning—it made me feel as if someone were dying.

And then, with her arms flung up to protect herself, and in trembling horror, she fled the room as if from the presence of Satan himself.

She had choked-out only *my* name...?

Why'd she do that? My brother Burt was the one responsible for teaching me to suck him and his friends' cocks when I was just eight. Why did she say only my name?

Why did she blame and condemn only me? And for something she obviously found so unbearable and inexcusable? *Why only me?*

And my mother's flight was so complete, and her back turned so finally from me, all I could think to do was move my head back toward my brother's lap to finish what had been started (and was then quite surprised when he kicked me off.)

I cry now, but I didn't then. I didn't for a very long time.

Equally devastating in the coming days, was my father's silence. I had expected hell-to-pay when my father got home that evening; but not a word was ever spoken. Was he, too, *that* revolted by me? Or, was my mother so sickened she couldn't even tell my father?

If my father did know what happened, as a caring physician who dealt with young patients every day, how could he not help me?

If he didn't know—how could he ever help me?

Even with his medical credentials, my mother may have feared that my father would beat me too badly. This is perhaps odd sounding, considering her emotional treatment of me, but physical discipline was different back then, and a cultural norm, and like many women my mother was the only thing that stood between her children and their father.

It's a tough call. If my father had thought that I was "ruining" his family in any way he very well may have beaten me. Burt, on the other hand, was evidently beyond blame. I say this because he, also, was never talked to or disciplined in any way (and he soon returned to me).

Or, the final truth was that my mother's vehement sexual judgment and the fully encasing silence it demanded ruled our home.

I never knew—so I decided that it was all of those things.

All these years later, as a proactive parent I am vigilantly aware of how careful we need to be if we catch our children in an act of sexual contact, regardless of what kind of sexual act it is, or how surprising the discovery may be.

Preferably, sex education in the home would start as young as possible, which would certainly avert a great many difficulties. But we all know that in our culture—even still—most often that education doesn't happen early enough, if ever.

If we are talking about beginning a conversation with a pre- or adolescent child, as I was, before all else I would make sure that they know how much I love and respect them, and that I have no overwhelming aversion to the sexual contact they are involved in.

Smiling warmly at that child, and making them feel calm, I would then explain that sexual contact is a natural human behavior and occurrence. And that parents, too, engage in sexual contact. Sharing the fact that very nearly all mature human beings have engaged in sex, of some kind, including the kind the child themselves was engaged in, is a straightforward, honest, and unifying place to start.

Then I would tell the child, in a welcoming way, that we would talk more later, and that there is no trouble, or reason to worry.

And explaining all this to a child is just as simple, and easy, and direct as the five sentences I just wrote, though it does require genuine follow-up.

Later, as soon as I saw my child again, I would open my arms and affectionately hug them to me. And while talking with them—being careful to listen as much as I spoke—I would make sure to wear a tranquil smile, and to make the loving eye-contact that holds a child secure and tells them that "All is truly well."

That way, I wouldn't rip my own child's heart into dying shreds inside their own little chest, and they wouldn't become deaf to me, and emotionally lost from me.

I also know that for the older child or teen involved in an abuse of this kind, who initiates sexual contact with a younger partner, having a parent or adult who reacts with indirect revulsion, followed by repulsed inaction, followed by silence, is one of the worst and most dangerous eventualities possible—for that older child and everyone else.

An open and ongoing exchange of truthful and real-world information about sexual contact, including the positive and powerful importance of understanding complete sexual respect in all its many parameters, is the only thing that can save them, and their potential future victims.

I had younger siblings, of both sexes. They should have been better protected.

From the perspective of my experiences as a boy, as a young man, and now as a parent, I strongly believe that keeping too-early sexual contact an un-discussed, uneducated, and blindly turned-away-from reality is a sex-crime not yet identified.

And I will never forget the soul-rending sound of my own mother's voice.

Chapter Seven

Foster Care

When I was young I only knew a few foster children, and something about them pulled at me. There were very few of them in our town, which made them stand out even more. And trying to be friends with a couple of them gave me a glimpse into how differently they could be treated. And without a doubt the kids at school, and the teachers, and everyone else around town also seemed fully aware of their singled-out status, which was odd and irritating to me.

One of the first sexually active pre-teens I ever met was a foster kid. And Cee Cee is a foster kid.

Of course, being a foster child or juvenile ward of the state isn't always a separating and sad experience, no category or position in life is that homogenized, and I'm not trying to make it sound that way. I'm sure the full range of experiences exists. I know it does.

Most people agree that being adopted is a big step forward, but barely fifteen percent of the hundreds of thousands of children left in the state welfare systems will ever be adopted. And the rest, won't. (Adoption outside the welfare systems, and all kinds of other private adoption options, have their own numbers and rates of success.)

In the State welfare systems, by the time a child is approaching their later adolescence and pre-teens the chance of ever being fully adopted into a family is cut to nearly nothing. So, categorically temporary stays in the homes of random foster parents and/or host families is all they can even hope for. And being decidedly more disconnected or severely less-connected to the parent figures and the "real" family is a simple reality of life.

And the less connected a young human is to fully invested and committed adults, or caring parental figures, the less safe they are in every way.

From my side, I know what just several serious degrees of separation from my parents resulted in. So I'm sure that is a part of my sympathetic connection to all such children.

Statistically, foster children suffer substantially more sexual abuse and rape, and a much lower rate of reporting the crimes, which means there is definitively a less genuine kind of familial protection going on—on a massive social scale—which enrages me.

If we could save even one of those ill-treated children we might save the ten who come after. If we save ten, we will also save all those who would have become victims of some of the original victims who have become wounded attackers. I'm not great at math, but I know an exponentially expanding problem when I see it.

Just one foster or adoptive parenting sex offender can do massive and lasting harm to a long and constantly rooting-off line of victims, and we are dealing with thousands and thousands of them.

As for those readers feeling shocked by my assertions, or led astray, I can assure them that there are pedophilia-farmers working the child welfare systems. I've tasted their work, and kissed away the bitter tears.

Counselor

Please consider this idea: Send a hypersexual counselor out to visit with every foster and newly adopted child, especially between the ages of six or seven all the way up to seventeen—and what is hidden will be revealed.

We can't send a less-than hypersexual person, the sexually abused (or activated, or over active) sense the non-understanding and trapping judgment of the sexually close-minded, fearful, and denial ridden people—and they hide from it by iron-clad habit. We have to send a counselor in who can see through the hiding veils, one who is already on the other side of the veils.

Come to think of it, every child could benefit from a session with a counselor like that at least once or twice a year throughout their childhood and puberty. Why don't we have something like that—anything?

The point being that as a child Cee Cee could have been saved from a great deal of her suffering with the help of hypersexually adept foster care counselors. I could have uncovered what was happening to her the moment I saw her after she had been through her first sexual experience—negative, positive, or neither—because I would have simply asked her about sexual contact in a purely honest, authentically open, and receptive way.

If any would doubt that claim, which is totally understandable, let me remind them that I'm the hyperactive opposite of shy. And for my whole life I've been an especially trusted person with children. In fact, I'm so easy and natural with kids I would even say that people feel I am the "most trusted" kind of person. And not only is it easy for me to make friends with almost any child, of any age, it is just as easy for me to ask them—in a completely easy, simple, and smiling way—if anyone, or any friend, or any family member, or anyone else has ever touched their bodies in certain ways. And my questions themselves would be a friendly sharing and educational kind of thing, like the best of today's pediatricians and child psychologists (with the addition of my hypersexual understanding). And once the child is communicating, a properly skilled hypersexual counselor could quickly sort out the important information.

I did that with my own children when they were starting day care. And I've done it for a couple of close family friends who felt much less comfortable with the necessary questions and conversations their children needed to hear and have. And, because I care so deeply about this issue, I could do it all day. And I'm certain that many hypersexuals, especially former prodigies, feel the same way.

If Cee Cee had been genuinely connected to, understood, helped, and educated about her sexual experiences by a hypersexual counselor, or in any other way, there would have been no need for me to get so involved with her dilemma, and I would not have had to supply the compassionate care no one else had.

Of course, sexual abuse is only one of the many forms of abuse children in the welfare care system suffer at a higher rate than other kids: lack of authentic affection, forced religious involvement, nutritional privation, physical bullying, poorer education, state enforced indentured work (for the host family), and/or living conditions in which they have no legal ownership of their belongings, and less legal control over their lives than "normal" children, is too often their actual lot. And all of these issues are equally awful failures, and they are also equally correctable. Why do we, as a society, fall so short on so many of them? Admittedly, I am only focusing on one of them.

We need more people who know how to look straight into the face of sex abuse without blinking. We need the strongest, and most aware, and most empowered sexual survivors.

Long before Cee Cee, I met another little foster girl who I will never forget. In a way, her rather short and tightly contained story is one of the most mind-bending and heartrending memories I carry. And my total inability (inactivity) to help her, in her moment of need, remains one of my greatest shames.

Wynona & Carleton

This encounter happened during the time that I was working as the manager/caretaker of a small suites-style hotel that served visitors and tourists that came to our small city for a wide variety of reasons. Because I was also the on-site after-hours manager, my family and I lived in a separate building on the same property. All of which made my relationship with that job quite a bit more intimate.

Each of the identical suites had a large sized kitchenette, and a dining and living room area, which sat forward of the two separate, extra-large sized bedrooms, each with two queen sized beds and a full on-suite bathroom; all together equaling one-thousand square feet of spacious, quiet, multi-person accommodations. Families, of course, were often attracted to the layout.

One afternoon, a stiffly dressed elderly man and woman showed up at my check-in counter.

At first glance, as I looked up from the paperwork I was doing, I saw that they looked like staunchly conservative elderly white folk, with almost comically flat expressions, and plenty of obvious concern for appearing as prim-and-proper as possible.

Being more-or-less a hippie-at-heart (though well disguised in my Manager's attire) they almost made me laugh. But I'm sure I smiled, anyway. And when I looked up more completely, and my field of vision widened, I also noticed two little black children hiding behind the legs of the grandmotherly woman. With one quick look, I saw that the children looked to be an approximately seven or eight year old boy, and a smallish twelve or thirteen year old girl.

"Hello, welcome to the Creekside Suites." I said in my friendliest tone. "How can I help you folks?"

Speaking with a practiced and professional tone, and wearing my unreserved "Hotel Clerk" smile, I gave them my full attention.

The man, probably in his early to late seventies, stepped forward and asked about weekly rates in a very dry and business-like way. And I answered all his questions, selling my property and its amenities to him, and his purposely plain wife, in as pleasant a way as possible.

While we spoke, the black-as-night children stayed tucked silently behind the woman, and more or less motionless.

I like well-behaved kids, and I admire the people who raise them (even though I had to guess that these were the "grandparents" of the obviously adopted kids, or something like that). But, it was already seeming to me that these kids might be too-well-behaved.

Having children of my own, it was easy to see that these children were reserved to the point of being distant.

Taking the lead of the conversation again, with another of my welcoming pitches, I spoke half-way in the children's direction. "I can also tell you folks where all the parks are, and the other places that the kids will like to go while you're in town."

Smiling directly at the children for the first time, and unabashedly trying to get their attention, I shared the information as a way to try to connect with them. But the old woman stayed stiff, and actually moved sideways a little in order to block them from my view. And the man, seeming to catch my deeper drift, replied with a rigid smile.

"These children are on medications for behavioral problems. We rarely encourage excitement, and so forth. They are very good readers, and we have books on video that they enjoy a great deal. We also go to church each day. I used to be a preacher, but I gave it up to foster children full-time. I assume each room has a full-sized television with a DVD player? The children have some good Christian shows and lessons they like to watch."

God damn it, I just freaking hate non-activity for children. Children with behavior problems can especially benefit from daily mental and physical exercise—I know.

"I see…," I said, lying. "How about a nice walk around a nature park? Or our local zoo? Most kids really enjoy those attractions. And there's a very nice creek-side walking trail that comes right up to our property line, right at the end of our sidewalk."

Cutting me off, the old man replied with an obvious lack of enthusiasm. "Perhaps, but that is not our usual routine."

Pausing, he looked directly into my eyes. And for a just a moment, I saw what seemed like anger, and pride, and a forceful demand for respect come across his face. Curious, I waited for him to continue.

"My wife and I are proud to have accepted many racially-mixed and non-white foster children into our home. We've had these two children since they were barely old enough to start educating. Sometimes, if they learn to behave well enough, we keep them all the way until they can become adult wards of the state. These children are numbers thirteen and fourteen."

Saying the last part without even twitching his head in their direction, (which pissed me off so bad I could hardly stand still), he held my eyes. And I held his.

Son-of-a-bitch..., you don't call children by a number! What an asshole! (I thought to myself).

And then, as if noticing the way my stare had changed, and sensing my awkwardly frozen response, the old man reluctantly spoke their names.

"Wynona and Carleton."

"Pleased to meet them." I responded in smooth acknowledgment. And moving my head to the side so that I could see them a little bit, I smiled toward the kids. But neither of them looked back at me.

Seeing their stillness, and approving, the old man continued.

"We've been fostering for over thirty-four years now, and we've found that every single one of these children needs to be medicated with Ritalin, or other similar drugs, in order to help with all the behavior problems they got from being conceived in sinfulness, and then neglected in every way by their godless birth-parents. That's why getting these children wound-up is never a good idea."

Turning to his white-haired wife, they shared a knowing nod. And looking back to me with an expression full of confidence, the old man continued.

Too shocked to process what he had just-now said, I listened in growing horror.

"We had our own blessed children long ago, before we started fostering, and they were normal, so we know the difference. And we never adopt."

Finishing with a firm shake of his head, which the woman echoed, the absolute un-self-questioning certainty of the old couple was bone-chilling.

Inside my own head, I was reeling (as much as you can "reel" behind a hotel cash register). I simply couldn't believe what the man had just said. I just couldn't believe it...

My first grade school teacher had bitchily requested that my parents put me on Ritalin. Fortunately, my educated father had refused. I am absolutely sure that those drugs would have had me psychotically depressed, and who knows what I would have done with that kind of foul fuel. So, my whole life I have angrily wondered at what originally drove parents and adults to medicate children, instead of giving them the vital and specific attention, and extra activities, and special educations they needed and deserved.

These old Christian control freaks had permanently pushed down fourteen children, one after the other, with forced Ritalin! It was psychopathic!

I looked at the kids again, and they were as still as lamp posts, and being talked about as if they weren't even there.

I've tripped on a lot of LSD in my lifetime, and I'm glad, because when a freak-show moment like that comes along I can somehow manage to absorb it.

I was standing in a room with two fully licensed serial mind-fucking foster child abusers, and two of their current victims!

My head started to ache. And when the old man spoke again, I think I actually flinched.

"My dear wife and I have even been honored with the 'Foster Parents of the Year' award in our home state, for our lifetime commitment to fostering."

Saying this last sentence the old man beamed with satisfied authority, as if the award itself proved that he was, beyond question, a magnificent man.

Because I was in a situation that was making me extremely uncomfortable, out of my own peculiar habit, I pushed forward and directly into it. Resuming my Hotel Clerk voice, and practiced performance, I also tried to resume control of the conversation.

"Well, then. Let's see if we can't find the perfect suite for you all. I have a two-room suite at the scenic end of the row that should work great."

Getting closer to weird shit has never scared me, I'd experienced so much of it before in my life. With darkest humor, I immediately considered poisoning the elder foster freaks, and setting the zombied children free.

As a first move, I quickly rented the foster family a suite for a four-day stay and promptly finished the check-in process, and then walked them down to the suite. And though I continued to take every opportunity to try to make eye contact with the children, and the older one did glance at me once, they both obediently held themselves to the no-contact training they'd so obviously received.

As we walked to the suite, down the lovely outdoor stone walkway, which wound along under the swaying green willow and elm trees, I pointed out the wonderful shaded creek area that lay below us, and the emerald vine-covered hillside that sloped away to the bottom. And even when I told them that the trail down to the creek actually started right by their doorway, I still got no response from the kids.

That evening I told my wife, Abbey, all about it when she got home from her office. But she was understandably tired, and much less interested in my "hotel clerk horror stories" than she was in how our own son and daughter's day had gone.

In those days, it was so nice that I got to be home waiting when our kids, Kye and Lula, came back from school, and then when Abbey got home from her office. The dogs and I greeted both kids at 3:25 p.m. every weekday, unless I had a customer just then, in which case the dogs mauled the kids by themselves. And we all greeted Abbey, in a happy pack of five, when she got home at around 5:30 p.m.

Abbey did understand my concern and anger for the medically-deadened foster children, (though she usually doubts how much I read into things). But I just couldn't let go of the sadness of it.

Later that night, after dinner, the old man rang me up and asked for some local driving directions, so I went up to meet him at the office.

Smiling politely, I gave him directions to the area of town that he had asked about, and to the best grocery nearby, and a few fast-food places. Using my most charming manners and my very warmest behavior, I answered his every question.

I was also wearing my less formal shorts and cotton t-shirt, so acting more like an attentive butler made the after-hours transaction seem as professional as it could be.

Alone, the old man stood more relaxed, and engaged me in a more conversational way. And somehow, perhaps because of his less formal attire, he actually looked many years younger. Listening to him from my seat behind the counter, and staying calm (as I have looked at many demons before), out of my always over-active curiosity I genially submitted to his bantering.

And that old vulture sensed my submissive vibration one second after I turned it on.

Feeling it like a spark, his head came up brighter and he looked down at me with his yellowing smile. Coming closer to the desk, with a warming expression, he looked slowly down at my whole body. And with his voice dropping in tone and cadence, he spoke with an affected tenor that reminded me of old velour.

"You're a very nice and professional young man." He began. "And you're so healthy looking, and so young for a property manager of such a nice business." He continued.

If I should attempt to explain this in terms of seeing human auras, I would say that even though this one was a black-hearted man, his physical/sexual colors expanded at that moment, and flowed out into a wrapping dark orange-yellow glow. He was thinking of something extremely beautiful to him, and he wanted to surround me with it.

If I had unbuckled and unzipped my pants, and taken my cock out in that late evening locked office, sexual contact to the un-corked pouring-end would have begun within milliseconds.

Instead, I hesitated and sat there stunned at the surprisingly bizarre sexual moment, which is, as you know, something I have a very hard time turning away from.

Even with what I knew about this man, (and actually because of it), I spontaneously wanted to give him the sex that he craved from me. Because of who and what I am, I *almost needed* to know where he would go sexually, and where he would ask me to go with him, and what he would reveal to me about his evil soul. And, I had an un-rented and empty suite less than fifty steps away…

I've been having sex with older men, even of his age, nearly my whole sexually active life, and plenty of them had come from all kinds of staunch backgrounds, and strictly held religious beliefs, and otherwise sexually stifled lives. And the truth be told, I have also always appreciated how most elderly sexual partners have matured to become extra soft and unhurried in their sexual movements, and their quaking sexual touches. And I've always like how their skin is so delicate, and feathery, and papery. But I digress.

Plainly said, if Abbey and our children hadn't been waiting to have dessert with me, already expecting me back, I would have had sex with that old man right then and there.

Was he just an insanely sexually repressed Christian man who had no idea how terrible his drug-induced foster parenting methods were? If that were the case, perhaps I could get through to him through his own personal openings?

However, there did seem to be something aggressively creepy, and perhaps consciously disrespectful and domineering about this man. And I just didn't have the time.

As a devoted husband and father, I had learned to make my extra sexual contact decisions fast and with one priority in mind: Keeping my sexual life hidden from my family.

When I dimmed my shine towards the old man, by simply having the thought *"I can't"*, he pulled back and away from the desk as if it were I who had been speaking out of place.

With an almost palpable air of offense, the momentary connection snapped apart. And with one last condescending glare in my direction, he was out the door.

I'll admit, I'm disgusted by that whole scene too. And I'm quite used to dealing with myself after moments like that; I move on to the next set of minutes, and do the best I can to forget the former set of minutes.

I did wonder if sex between us would come up again during the week. And I wondered what I would do. And I still had those kids on my mind.

For the next couple of days, around his old wife and foster children, the old man never even looked at me. In fact, they spent most of their time away from the room. And in the first three days I only ran into them on a few more occasions.

When I did see them, the children were always walking in perfect one-step behind the old lady, never laughing or even talking! It made me so sad. And I never once had a chance to talk with them, or introduce them to my kids.

Then, in the afternoon of the third day, after the maids had gone home, I watched as the whole foster group shuffled glumly from their room toward my office and the parking lot area. And I was surprised when the old man poked his head in the office door and quickly asked me to check the toilet in the children's bathroom while they were gone, which would be approximately forty-five minutes, depending, he said, on how long the family "was in prayer".

Nodding, I replied, "I'll get right to it."

I was also busy with five other things just then, so one more chore on the list, especially a toilet-mystery, was about as welcome as a kick in the shins.

Fifteen or twenty minutes later, as I approached the room, I remembered that the creepy old foster freaks had asked that our maids only deliver new towels to the door each day, rather than clean the rooms. They even put their own trash out on the sidewalk so no one had to enter the suite. That wasn't really unusual, especially for just a handful of days. But it was always more interesting to go into those kind of guests rooms, because you never knew what you'd find.

Plunger in hand, I entered the front door of the suite with my master key.

The ungodly mess that I beheld as the door swung open and the daylight flooded in was beyond anything that I could have expected.

Three days of half-eaten food, open take-out boxes, old pancakes in Styrofoam, partially full paper-plates, filthy napkins, and half empty drink cups were stacked and congealing and spilt on top of each other on every flat surface of the large open kitchen and living room areas, some spilling onto the floor. Their drab clothing was also thrown around in piles here and there, on chair backs, on the couch, and on the floor. Religious kid's books, coloring books, video boxes, assorted candy wrappers, tissue-paper, and kid's discarded clothes also littered the floors.

I stood in the doorway shocked, and repulsed.

I'd seen worse, barely, from college kids. But this was totally unexpected. These people seemed so stiff, staunch, tucked-in, buttoned-up, and spotless in public?

But this room said "deep mental chaos" to me. Fucking disturbing! And now I had a whole new reason to feel sad for the kids!

But I didn't have time to ponder my sadness, I was too damn busy, with ten things left to do at the front desk before the end of the day. And I dreaded even more, now, finding out what was in the toilet. High-stepping and wading through the disgusting detritus to the suites hallway, bracing myself for a gross discovery, I was preparing to enter the bathroom when…something stopped me in my tracks.

Right there on the floor: *Panties.., sexy, lacey, high-fashioned, nut-hardening panties…*

Holy Grail! Chalice of…,

"WAIT A SECOND?! WHO'S FUCKING PANTIES ARE THESE?!" My mind shouted to itself.

Reaching down I snapped the expensive panties up into my right hand. And I knew, instantly, that there was no way these panties belonged to the old woman (which would have been so weird, too), they were way too small—and they were way too fashioned for sex appeal. My neck and the back of my head began to crawl.

Having a daughter of your own should cure you of going too far down the Lolita fantasy-lane with something like this (if it doesn't, consider getting yourself some meaningful help). Still, for *me*, finding myself trying to un-overlap the raw sexiness of a ripe pair of dirty lace panties from the reality of them belonging to this eleven or twelve year-old permanently drugged foster girl was extremely uncomfortable for me.

Moments like that make me feel emotionally cross-eyed, even knowing all that I know.

And my stomach hurt. Something was terribly off...

How could these slut-cut panties belong to the silent little foster girl of those crazy old creepers?! These were super high-end lingerie panties (with the familiar label hanging out as clear as day). And they were made of tan flesh-colored satin, with lacey leg and waist hems, with a heart-shaped lace window over the entire pubic area, a nearly thong cut rear end, kept slim along the entire crotch length, and with the tiny inside cotton piece stained by overuse.

What kind of weird old people dress their little pre-teen girl like this? And the old woman knew..., she had to, the panties were just lying on the floor...

Was I tripping out? I'm well aware of how sexually over-focused and borderline-crazy I am. Don't think for a minute that I don't question myself on a daily basis. But holding the panties up in front of my face, and looking at them again, I began to regain my own footing. These were definitely expensive professional-grade fuck-me panties, and that was all there was to it.

I couldn't help it, I was in the midst of something sexual—*I could feel it.*

Spontaneously standing stock still, and closing my eyes, I pictured Wynona wearing them—only them—and tried to *"see"* with my hypersexual vision.

Instantly, two other powerful pieces of information jumped into the front of my raging brain: the Ritalin abuse, and the old man's obvious, bold, and even anger-tinged extra-sexual behavior with me on that first night.

Like being struck through with lightning, *I could see...*

I was standing right in the middle of the ongoing heinous and hellish crime of drug controlled pedophilic foster care.

I felt sick.

I felt twelve years old again, and afraid.

And I felt full-grown, and angry.

And I felt hyper-mentally-activated: *I was going to dig through this whole disgusting suite!* I had to see what else I would find!

What I expected to find first, and I always remember this as clearly as if I had actually found it, was a small dildo. And, almost as surely, I expected to find a cache of something even more sinister hidden among the foster parents' belongings. Perhaps even a stash of pictures or videotaped evidence.

How insane was this going to get?

Completely forgetting the world outside the suite, and one-hundred percent caught up in the immediate and burning issue, I looked toward the children's room, and then at the parents' side, deciding where to start my search—and then suddenly all the sand fell out of the hourglass.

Someone was coming...

And those are all the facts that I ever had a chance to gather, and deal with, which is probably why this incident sticks with me so clearly. Being suddenly deprived of any resolution in the middle of something so intensely personally connected and mentally pulling can leave a permanent impression.

Since I am a living and heaving hypersexual-adept, you can guess how badly I would have wanted to know more. Even though, of course, I knew that their reality would have horrified me to my core.

Why would I want to know *even that*? I just do, desperately: the continual search for, and gathering of any widening sexual facts, as well as artifacts, so to speak, makes me feel less distant from the world around me.

Plus, there was a chance I could have helped those children.

If I'd found pictures or something like that, of course I would have taken them to the proper authorities. But even then, to step into a legal accusation like that, with your professional position and the owner(s) of the business possibly liable for the consequences of that accusation, you better have all your ducks neatly lined-up, and your long-term legal team ready.

Should I have risked my job, our home, and my own family's financial safety? At the time I couldn't, not on a suspicion and an "if", with nothing else heavy enough behind it. And not when I knew damn well that those old people might have their asses covered six ways from Sunday. Maybe those panties were the only slip they'd ever made.

In this always wanting to turn-away from anything sexually difficult-to-face society you have to be able to come forward with irrefutable evidence, or risk the serious legal consequences. In a culture where you *could* question such things without becoming an instant target yourself, and possibly being sued out of existence, I certainly would have pursued those foster monsters to the end.

I also had the problem of having to explain my reasons for believing what I believed, which was centered around my deep personal hypersexual observations of the pair of panties that I had found, combined with the momentary details of my flirting and sexually revealing encounter with the old man, and what would certainly sound like my insane accusations against the elderly couples serial chemical torture through forced Ritalin.

In a world where I *could* explain my story to someone who would really understand it, like a hypersexual officer or a hypersexual foster care counselor, instead of endangering myself in the instant suspicions of our current brand of enforcers, of course I would have given it my best try.

Instead, in this case; the maddening experience was suddenly in front of me, and then I was caught in the middle of it, and then it was over. I had only been in the trash-strewn suite for about four or five minutes when the fiendish foster parents, with their pharmaceutically deadened children in tow, suddenly returned.

In fact, I barely heard them coming two-steps-before they arrived in front of the wide-open door of their suite.

The panties were still in my hand—and then they were in my front pants pocket. Had I even tried to drop them, it could have been seen.

When I turned around to greet the old man, he spoke first.

"Is the toilet fixed?"

"No sir, I just now got the chance to come over to take a look at it. If you'll give me a minute here, I bet I can have you all set."

"Leave it. We can all use the toilet in the other room. We'll be leaving in the morning."

"I don't mind, sir. I wield a heck of a plunger..."

"Leave it."

"Okay."

As I walked past the old couple, and the children hiding behind them, my eyes dropped down to a respectful level. And then, at the very last moment, I let my head swivel quickly left and my eyes darted directly towards Wynona's—only to catch a glimpse of the side of her head as she shoved her face into the back of the starched and tightly tucked-in blouse of the old woman.

I'd wished then, and in a way ever since, that I could have left those panties. If I'd have gotten into that bathroom by myself I would have ditched them, they were burning a bulging satin hole right through my pocket. But there was no choice, they went with me.

I've also wondered why that old man sent me in there, and then returned so quickly.

I just hoped that the mess those freaks lived in would make the loss of those panties disappear, or at least make it less-possible for them to pinpoint with any certainty.

I'd also quickly realized, that from the second that I'd walked out of that suite I was criminally guilty of the theft of a very legally sensitive item, which among other things, would completely disqualified me as a witness worthy of voicing any kind of suspicion against anyone. In anyone other than another hypersexual's view, what I had taken would surely be seen as evidence—against me.

My world has never been easy in that way. I have existed in this state of "sexually questionable being" ever since I can remember. I know what I know, but finding ways to share and communicate my knowledge helpfully, coming from my too intimate angle, has been incredibly difficult.

And, though the shadowy and infinitely saddening foster family was out of their suite and gone down the road the next morning before I even opened the office, because *I knew*, I continued to agonize over Wynona, eventually for all these years afterwards.

At the time I thought obsessively about how I might be able to construct some kind of anonymous letter or report on what I had seen and observed, or make some kind of effective phone call, but it just wasn't possible to do with any anonymity or protection for me or my family. And the longer I waited the more idiotic my story and observational evidence seemed, even to me. And every day that went by buried the chance of my ever doing anything even deeper.

But I never stopped thinking about Wynona, and the quiet horror of letting what I had seen go without a single word.

It is a scar on my heart that will never fade away.

And, I still have those panties, tucked safely away with all my other super-personal artifacts and sexual relics in the kind of place that every hypersexual should have: A fully hidden (and thereby safe and protected) masturbation room—a "masturbatorium".

When I see Wynona's panties hanging in my masturbatorium, I remember being twelve. And I remember that I wasn't sexually safe, either.

And I grieve for her, in a deepest-reaches of human tragedy kind of way, because of how her adult tormentors had also put a permanently childhood stealing chemical leash around her body and mind.

And my being cringes to imagine what other kinds of psychologically devastating, emotionally chaotic, educationally twisted, and religiously bent madness those old fostering phantoms assailed those kids with.

Worse than the worst: It all exists.

Secret Rooms

      As I have also just revealed, it turns out that all kinds of people really do build secret sex rooms, trick closets, unknown basements, and concealed attics, etc., all hidden-off right behind the façades of the normal world.

      Some of the things that are done in these hidden places are beyond belief, and are absolutely beyond ignoring. Wynona and Carleton were trapped behind one of the most multi-leveled, hideous, invisible, and mobile examples I've ever seen.

      However, some of these secret spaces and rooms are safe-havens of sexual privacy, designed as places where those persons can be more nakedly honest with themselves, and where, in lieu of direct human sexual contact, they can care for themselves.

      Mine is a purposely kept darkened space where I hold nothing back from myself: Where every existent aspect of my sexuality, sexual experience, and prurient history is laid out in the open, consisting of collections of every kind of pornography, and all my personal photos, and video clips, and letters, and scores of other panties, and bras, and necklaces, and bracelets, and other remnants and memorabilia, like the small wooden sexual sculpture/choker-necklace that my oldest brother carved all those years ago. Added to all that, are all the other memento's I have like hotel keys, and blindfolds, and hand-ties, and dildo's, all of which are hung and plastered on the walls, and draped from the ceilings, and stacked on all the dresser tops, and lain on the bed, and set on the chair seats, and even strewn on the floor. And the dresser-drawers are full of lists of names and numbers from over the decades, accompanied by more stacks of private pictures, and rarer magazines, and all kinds of rubbery accessories. A stack of towels and bottles of water for washing-off occupy one wall shelf, while shaving razors and hair-cutting scissors have their own small drawer, and beer and liquor are kept inside the little economy fridge, with a glass jar of weed and pipes on top. And, of course, lubricants, cock-rings, and other wearable gear are strewn generously around the entire room, where the final decorating touch is the multiple mirrors, both large and small, set in several places around the dim menagerie of sex-reeking furniture, giving the fully enclosed rectangular space a reflecting and rabbit-holing effect.

When I am in there, fully stripped of all the guarded pretenses of the outer world, freely feeling my real-self—when my sexual pulse rises high enough and even my mind becomes untied—I feel as if I am standing in a hallowed hall of my always sexually aroused ancestors, happily masturbating amongst all the warmly smiling, hotly inviting, and sex-smeared generations of my hypersexual race.

Of course, all this deviant rambling must seem as if it has nothing to do with this chapter's chosen subject of foster-care: Unless you are me, with a story whose details deserve to be told honestly. The piece of Wynona that I kept, belongs with me.

In the darkness I dance on the wicked edge of the wide-wide river of sex, peering directly into its curling currents with my sparkling eyes so that I can see everything—*including the monsters swimming ashore near me.*

"Foster Parents of the Year"—*I saw you.*
Goodbye Wynona and Carleton.
There is so much danger.

Chapter Eight

<u>Mentor</u>
<u>Showering Love</u>

It is time for me to tell you the more complete story of how I was first led to the edge of that wide-wide river of sex, and then washed out into the rolling oceans of my own hypersexuality.

It is time for me to properly introduce you to my ancestors.

My mentor was my second-cousin Déjà. She is eight years older than I, and she is an empathic hypersexual with power beyond measure.

During a period of seven years, from the age of seven to the age of fourteen, my sexual experiences with Déjà and her influence over me was such a pervasive and relentlessly drowning wave I can barely imagine gasping out a description of it.

It is also something that I have been waiting to tell, for my entire adult life.

I'll begin:

The first time I met my cousin Déjà was on the first day of my first trip to Southern Florida, the birth-place of my father and the home of his family. With roots that traced themselves back to Venezuela, and through Cuba to Southern Florida, all the way back in the 1800's, my father's family ties to the most colorful and verdant part of the great peninsula were deep. And though his siblings and their growing families were by then spread out, and not especially close with each other's families, my father's brothers and sisters were still more-than-happy to welcome their prodigal family member, who'd left the peninsula to pursue his dream to be a physician, along with his children and Caucasian wife (the only Caucasian among the entire family), into their homes for a long looked-forward-to family reunion.

With six siblings in my father's family, all with their own large families, the total number of relatives was a whopping forty something. Which was filled-out by brown skinned children and teenagers of every age. And smack in the middle of that throng, was Déjà.

I was seven and a half years old, Déjà was fifteen, and I had a full-blown crush on her before she even finished her first welcoming kisses on my young cheeks.

In mine and everyone else's eyes Déjà was a natural born "Star", both beautiful and brilliantly sharp. She was so gorgeous, and lively, she was easily the center of attention in any room—if she wanted to be. And she was so pretty, and so aware of it, she could tune the level of her attraction to whatever effect she wanted to produce. In fact, she was so naturally stunning she could act as if it didn't even matter.

And others made way for her, happily, whether they were conscious of it or not.

Even then, I wanted to be like her. I wanted to be looked at the way she was, and listened to the way she was. And I wanted people to like me and laugh with me the way they did with her. She was so good with people.

In the afternoon of the second day, after coming back to my Uncle's Quintus' house from the nearby ocean beach, with my little head swimming in all the wild new realities of the amazingly lush tropical world, several of us similarly aged younger boy cousins were herded into the large outdoor showering area behind the immense historical house. As I remember it, as the youngest and wildest boys we were the first group of cousins to be wrangled together for the rinsing-off.

The impressive house was a stone-built mansion located not more than a few hundred yards from the massive undulating Atlantic Ocean and the bright sandy beach that edged up to it. My Uncle, who was married to one of my father's older sisters, had been successful enough in local real estate, and then specifically in resort-style condominium properties, he had earned himself enough of a living he could afford a truly premium chunk of property. With the breaking ocean covering the entire front view, and a thick green, deep, noisy jungle growing right up to the back, it was an almost overwhelming paradise. I also remember how the towering trees stood like shady columns spread out across the huge and rough mown lawn.

I'd never seen an outdoor shower before, but I thought that it was totally cool! Size wise, it was an approximately ten-by-ten foot open area located just to the northwest side of the mansion, and just below the old-style wooden-paneled rain-gathering tank, which was built out over the edge of the foliage-covered roof. A fifteen-foot long steel pipe, with a huge showerhead at the end, led out of the water-tank at a droopy angle to hang directly over our heads. Above, the wide open blue-white sky and overhanging dark tree limbs created the only roof; and beneath our bare feet was a rough circular cement pad with a big central drain. Wrapped around us was a tall, fully encircling shower-curtain that had been custom-made with thick white linen sheets hanging down, which enclosed the showering area from the view of any who might pass by on their way down to the beach front.

Though I'd expected to do the group showering with our swimsuits on, I immediately notice that my Floridian cousins had stripped theirs off and were rinsing them out with soap.

Now we were naked outdoors. I liked it, of course, but I was far from comfortable. And when Déjà suddenly walked into the showering enclosure I felt like I had been kicked in the stomach. *What was she doing here?* She was so beautiful, and I was so naked.

Interestingly, when she walked into the showering area my cousins hardly seemed to notice, and I was the only one covering myself, and the only one even looking at her.

Wearing her tiny bikini, barefoot, and moving with the clear authority of an experienced babysitter, Déjà told the rest of the boys that she needed to show me how to wash-up the right way. And, holding out her hand for the soap bar, they just nodded obediently, put their swimsuits back on, and left.

When Déjà turned her eyes on me, I felt that I had never been so aware of my nakedness, and the aching nervous feeling that sat edgewise against it.

And I can tell you now, and this is important—*I felt her coming.*

Walking over to me without hesitation, Déjà lathered-up her hands and, kneeling down in front of me, reached out for my body. Intently, her eyes lay squarely, and only, on my exposed genitals.

"The most important thing, Rory, is to wash all over this area," she said, as she put both her hands to work.

Unseen by the rest of the world, I held perfectly still. Her concentration was so focused.

Just outside the shower I could hear all five of my father's siblings and their families, with all their many kids, meandering around in the front yard laughing, and going in-and-out of the nearby house, all eating snacks, and telling stories.

And as Déjà held onto my naked little body, behind my willingly closed eyes I could "see" my relatives all around us, with all the grown women in the wildly colorful loose dresses, and all the uncles in their wide shorts, wearing sandals, and sporting short-sleeved tropical style shirts, and all the kids wrapped in big towels or running wild in their swimsuits. I can even remember listening for a few seconds to the odd mixture of the wild bird-songs from the trees above us, and the clanging sounds of pots and pans in the big kitchen of the house, as the early preparations for dinner began.

But all I could feel was the cascading rainbows of penetrating pleasure that kept arcing up through my body as Déjà, now on one knee in front of me, rubbed and slickly stroked my entire genital area at the same time, all the way from my tummy and tiny cock-head, across my little anus, and all the way through my bottom crack.

I have never been exactly sure if my eyes were open or still closed, but I know that this was the first time that I saw aural-light—shimmering off everything around me, and all around Déjà and the whole shower area. And if the shower curtain had been thrown open—I believe I would have seen the blazing aura of the whole wide world!

And I remember that my head was pounding and my ears were ringing.

The only thing I can remember Déjà saying was the word, "Good."

And when my shivering little brain-collapsing orgasm had faded, she said, "Okay."

Then she stood up and, looking right into my eyes, she smiled and left me there.

What more can I say about it, when nothing more was said to me?

What more could I have thought when, obviously, there was nothing more to be thought over?

Slipping my wrung-out swimsuit back on, as my cousins had done, I left the shower.

Walking around to the front of the house I returned to the active, and loud, and totally oblivious world around me. I could still feel the sexual touching inside my stomach, but the dimmer-colors, of everything, had returned.

About a half-hour later, still wandering around by myself, when I knew that Déjà was in that outdoor shower with some of the other older girl cousins, I unhesitatingly snuck into an upstairs bedroom that overlooked the area. And, leaning out the window as far as I could, I saw her!

Completely forgetting myself, caught in my unmindful desire, someone in the yard noticed me nearly falling out of the window, and sounded the alarm.

When you're a kid and suddenly everyone in the whole party is staring up at you and laughing—you never forget it. I felt frozen in time, and in such a weird way, because while I should have been burning-red in embarrassment—I was still filled only with my desire to look at Déjà. I didn't really care about anything but her.

I've also always remembered that my punishment for being caught was as odd and surprising to me as all the rest of that day had been, because all the punishment consisted of was mass laughter among the Floridian family, and my cousins unrelenting teasing.

(Back in my family's mountain-west hometown, near where my mother was born and raised, I would have been spanked black-and-blue for that same behavior. And, there would have been no laughter. If nothing else, my parents were drill sergeants when it came to their kids having good manners, especially in public, and none of this would have passed.)

"Rory loves Déjà! Rory loves Déjà!" was the chant that my younger relatives adopted. And they were right. And I have always wondered why they instantly knew that it was Déjà I was spellbound by. The outdoor shower had at least four or five girl cousins crowded into it at the time. And, continuing to baffle me, after only a few short minutes the Floridian grown-ups seemed completely uninterested! And then, my parents let it go too!

  As for Déjà, though she was nice to me in the same way that she was to all the other kids, for the rest of our ten day stay in the outskirts of southern Miami, she never again seemed to have the slightest intimate thought in my direction. I tried everything to get her fleeting fifteen year-old attention, and literally followed her around whenever I could—but it was as if she had forgotten that she had ever touched me.

  Also missing, and something I only became aware of during the final days of our visit, was the adopted oldest cousin, Maria, who had been my caretaker as an infant. I never heard why, and so her absence was the only thing added to the one other thing I knew about her.

  And then we were on an airplane back home.

  As for Déjà's touches, I never forgot about them. In fact, from those days until now I have never forgotten anything sexually important that has happened to me. Somehow, Déjà set off something in my head.

  Some people's minds remember numbers without fault, or names, or complex formulas: I can mentally re-live my significant sexual occurrences down to the tiniest fraction of a sensual second, with full visual, tactile, and even aromatic memories blooming in my mind. To me, it has always seemed like I basically started "thinking" when Déjà touched me.

  Also, I never stopped masturbating daily after that, often times with both my hands lathered with lotion or soaped-up as she had done. And, maybe a month or so after getting back from that vacation, sometime around my eighth birthday, my oldest brother Burt began to have me suck his cock, and soon after I was also sucking off several of his friends.

And my first sexual experience with a total stranger, a white haired elderly man in a Y.M.C.A. locker room shower, happened later that year. And I also seduced my first girl, a second grader, within the following school year.

Regardless of all that, from the time that I met Déjà I thought non-stop about much older girls and women—wanting every one of them to be exactly like Déjà—and often imagining that they were.

At that time, I was an eight year-old non-stop touch-me boy; and three years crawled slowly by. My desire to be touched and cuddled and kissed by females was manic, and my attempts to obtain that attention were barely tolerated. With few exceptions, the sex that I got to have during those years was the (ever expanding) cock-sucking, and the constant masturbating that I did.

A Little Pervert Returns

When I saw Déjà again, during my family's next trip to Florida, I was eleven and a half years old; Déjà was nineteen—and gorgeous beyond words.

When I saw her in the group of relatives waiting for us at the airport, she was so beautiful I felt sick. Holding a welcoming present and wearing a smile so big I wanted to climb into it, she walked straight up to me and placed her welcoming present in my hands. Staring directly into my eyes, and smiling warmly, she then kissed me slowly and moistly on both sides of my neck, which made me feel so much sexual-love it was overwhelming.

And now that my feet were on the ground, I could finally feast in the fact that we were going to spend more than two whole months on the tropical peninsula this time! And I was beyond myself with anticipation.

Walking through the airport parking lot I noticed the amazing and unique texture of the air. Because it is surrounded by the always close and churning ocean, the air at the southern end of Florida is so clean and moist it feels like it is stroking your skin. And the tropical aromas and bright colors of everything natural around you are so varied and clear they are completely immersing. Even the sky looks different, a warmer blue. And your senses are filled by it all, as if by a meal you didn't even realize you hungered for.

But for me there was only Déjà; sharp as a razor in my focus, smelling like a delicious female fruit just out of reach, causing me to writhe.

On the drive to my Auntie Silvia's house (Déjà's house) my erection became so stiff it was painful. If I'd been alone in the backseat of that station wagon I would have masturbated (which was something that I had started doing around that time in the back of cars, buses, classrooms, etc.). Instead, as we headed out of Miami I stared at the back of Déjà's head, seeing her luscious face and big red mouth in my mind's eye.

I remember becoming aware during that drive of how much I had changed since the last time I had visited. I thought about how, during the years since then, I had become quite the proud little pervert. For one thing, it had been almost three years since my mother had caught me sucking off my oldest brother in the laundry room, and damned me, and I had dealt with that meanness by sucking even more cock. And it had been more than a year since I started going to public park bathrooms (which I learned about from one of my oldest brother's older friends). And, by that time I had also managed several seductions (of varying degrees) of girls my age, though the sex never progressed beyond awkwardly fought petting, kissing, and some attempted oral adorations.

Riding from the airport that day, still remembering every detail of what Déjà had done to me in the outdoor shower during my first trip to Florida, I realized that she must be "different" too. Understanding this, I was then determined beyond care of consequence to do something sexual with Déjà again, as soon as possible.

I would even say that I somehow felt *certain* that we would. But how, or what I might be able to do to make that happen, was totally beyond me.

And I was completely innocent of the fact that Déjà had already marked me as a target of her own hypersexual agenda, which I would find out soon enough.

As soon as we arrived at the house and began to unload my family's luggage, Déjà announced that she was going to take me with her to the store so that I could carry some needed groceries for her.

Leading me quickly across the dirt and grass driveway, with her bare feet and chocolate brown legs filling my field of vision, I followed closely behind her.

In the busy mix of all that was happening, the only person that even noticed us leaving was my oldest brother Burt, and he gave me a look so strange I can still picture it. At first I thought it was one of his familiar "I'm going to beat the shit out of you" looks, but there was something else added-in that changed the glare to one I wasn't afraid of. I can describe it now as submission; and in that instant, I began to guess that Déjà had been sexual with him too.

With barely a push of her chin she directed me to run around the side of the small yellow pickup truck that was sitting in the taller grasses next to the station-wagon that was being unloaded.

"Climb in," Déjà chirped at me.

To have an idea of what Déjà looked like you would begin by picturing a slightly short, athletic, always scantily clad, unusually focused, super feminine eighteen year-old Venezuelan beauty queen. Then you should envision all her exposed chocolate skin a few shades on the creamier side, making sure that her barely covered breasts and nipples are poke-you-in-the-eye pert, with nearly black colored nipples and areolas that showed through all her shirts. Finally, you would add a faintly extra rounded-face, with pouting fat dark red lips, lovely wide cheekbones, and brilliant hazel colored eyes shaped like big shining almonds that held the power of soul-swallowing.

Now open her irresistible wet mouth, and picture her bright red tongue snaking out towards you.

To have a working description of me, at that time, you could start by picturing a healthy and vital looking pre-teen boy with wonderful light brown skin. With a Caucasian-blooded mother I was a shade lighter than Déjà, but still quite brown-skinned. I also had long jet black-hair that framed my friendly and moderated ethnic facial features. And with hyper-activity and a hyper-athletic father as the forces behind my physique, I was a lithe and fast athlete, and handsome in my own boyish way. But I was also a little bit smallish, with regular brown colored eyes, not so many friends, and I was from a place not nearly so beautiful.

What Déjà and I looked like was a couple of south-peninsula kids; what we really were, was somehow invisible.

When I opened the door and jumped into the truck, Déjà looked at me with a smile that melted my brain and filled my nutsack with electricity.

"You and me are going to be *special* cousins, Rory. You're going to be my 'little helper,' yeah?"

I had no idea what she meant, specifically, and didn't care. I would have done anything she told me to. And pulling out of the hedge-lined driveway, away from my family, I felt more freed and sexually exhilarated than I ever had before!

As Déjà concentrated on driving through the muddy ditch and out onto the country highway, I stared at the side of her glistening face, and I worked up the courage to speak.

"So, where are we going?"

"We're going to the grocery, like I said." She replied with a friendly firmness. "And…I think we're going to make one other stop." she added, with a widening smile.

"Okay." Was all I could think of in reply.

At the small roadside grocery Déjà was loud and cheerful and behaving in a clearly local-style, quickly introducing me to everyone as her very favorite little cousin from afar. As always, her way of being amidst people was flawless. Her manners were bright and welcoming and people noticed. And again, I realized how much I wanted to be just like her. Keeping up, I followed her closely, shook hands, and hugged and kissed people, and said "thank you" a hundred times, and carried everything that Déjà handed to me.

As we left the store she leaned closer to me and whispered.

"Hurry up, already."

I did as I was told, and we were off and moving before I'd closed the pick-up door.

Déjà drove back in the same direction, as if heading for her house. Then, surprising me, she quickly turned off onto a winding and rutted dirt road, and sped along it as if we were driving some kind of baja-buggy!

"Where are we going now, Déjà?!" I shouted over the noise of the rattling speed.

"We're going to go to a special place!" She replied, as she made another fast turn onto an even smaller and more tightly jungle-surrounded road.

I remember being so impressed with her driving skills. Even though I was just eleven, I was already a very good motorcycle rider, especially in the dirt, and I could even drive a stick shift car or truck. But I had never seen anyone drive a family car quite like that before! As indiscriminate foliage and flowers whipped by the sides of the truck, slapping the windshield, and tearing apart around us, Déjà steered aggressively over the furrowed and twisting terrain. I looked over my shoulder at the groceries, and although they were bouncing around they were still secure in the netting-pocket where I had put them.

Suddenly, very suddenly, she braked hard and turned the truck into a side nook that I wouldn't have even seen. Coming to a stop, and switching off the engine, the moist cloud of dirt settled around us, and almost all sound ceased.

By now Déjà was breathing heavily from the driving effort, and tiny beading sweat wetted the sides of her face, neck, and her bare shoulders. And before she even turned to look at me, or said a single word—*I felt her coming, again.*

Looking across my left shoulder at her, I sat waiting, with my heart beating like a panicking humming bird—and I was absolutely willing…

When she turned to look at me, she must have seen exactly what she wanted.

"Take off your shorts and underpants, Rory."

I did, instantly, but I was oddly nervous. It was so different than when I was with my brother and the other older guys. And I knew exactly why: with the guys I *knew* that I was going to please them. With Déjà I wasn't feeling any of that confidence—and I wanted to please her so badly it was making my throat and chest hurt. And, because she was staring directly into my naked lap, I immediately became aware of how small and shrunken my young cock was.

Déjà actually laughed at it.

"Oh my God, it's so tiny!" She giggled.

I felt like vomiting. Maybe she saw my emotion on my face, maybe she didn't.

"It's alright, Rory. It's alright!" she said soothingly, still staring down intently.

And then she leaned her hot sweating body over mine, and she pushed her face down into my lap, using her left hand to first spread my legs a little, and then to feed my entire tiny cock *and* ball-sack all the way into her surprisingly hot lips and mouth.

And then there was: *A kind of singing peace, sweet, and safe, and slickened, and terrifyingly wonderful, filled with hot hungry liquid flesh, and bathed in beautiful and bad abandon. And a rainbow opened up over us...*

After less than a minute, Déjà lifted her wet face slowly up and, while holding my stiff cock out with one of her hands, she spoke affectionately.

"See...now it's not so small, Rory-boy!"

And then she put her pumping head back down and continued.

After being pinned beneath perhaps five more minutes of the beyond-delicious sensation, with my head throbbing, and my body writhing in submission, Déjà lifted her magnificent mouth out of my lap, kissed my cheek, and then moaned clearly into my ear.

"Tell me when you are going go cum, okay? And no matter how sensitive it feels, make sure *not* to take it out of my mouth."

And just hearing her say that, before she sunk her purring hot mouth back down over my straining cock and surging little balls, made me go over the edge! And I hardly had time to tell her before I began my bucking orgasm, stomping my feet against the metal floor, and pushing my back up against the squeaking seat, with my body and brain consumed in the lightning flashes that were bouncing off the inside of the pickup truck, over and over, while Déjà held me down with both her arms and her hungrily swallowing face pressed down across my lap.

Finally, when she had sucked up the very last drop of my young squirting sperm, she lifted her wild and smeared face all the way up to mine and, grabbing me by the back of the head, she French-kissed me like I had never been kissed before. And it was not just the surprising depth of her hard reaching and fat-tongued kiss, or the taste of my own cum that she was sharing: it was the absolute unleashing of her pent-up sexual emotion, directly into me, that was so overwhelming!

Déjà rose up and broke over me like a ravenous force. Her mouth was pushed so far into mine it was almost too much for my lower-jaw, and her tongue filled the back of my throat in a way that threatened to gag me, and she was holding my head with both her hands so roughly I almost wanted to pull away! Even her face was pushing against mine so hard my nose and outer lips hurt. And her aggressive kiss went on for so long, maybe ten minutes or more, I eventually felt that I was going to suffocate—but I could also feel that Déjà *needed* this forceful release, so I made myself relax against the trucks seat and continued to let her.

Even if I had started to choke, I would have held still for her until my brain shut off.

I already knew that I would never say "no" to Déjà. That was something I knew before I was born.

And I was stunned at how strong she was, and how powerfully she came-out in her sex. During that kiss her body was literally shaking from all the power and tension, and all the internal build-up and release, and all the obvious searing lust that she had boiling through her body.

I know now that Déjà kissed me like that, with the demented strength of her over-built body of sexual knowledge, for a very specific reason: She was claiming me as her own.

I found out a couple years later that when Déjà was a young teen she had accidentally come to know about my oldest cousins "problems" with my family when I was an infant, and why she was sent away. And for Déjà, in her too young and too often touched mind, that secret knowledge translated itself into the irrefutable idea that she had all-rights to my naked little body, and a no-holds-barred freedom to pursue sexual explorations of any kind with me.

At the time of her overwhelming kiss, because she had her body wrapped so tightly around mine, and her face pressed so intently into mine, I simply understood on a physical level that Déjà was claiming me, and my sexual-soul for her own.

While driving back to the house, when she slowed down, Déjà told me what to do next.

"You won't tell anyone about us, Rory-boy. We have to protect our 'sweet secret' from everybody. When we get to the house don't stare at me, or try to talk to me all the time. You know what I mean. You keep *helping me*, yeah…? When we get to the house you just take the groceries in, and go about the day as if nothing happened, okay?"

It wasn't a question; and I didn't need to answer her. And it was thrilling on a whole new level to be in a one-on-one sexual connection with such a beautiful and powerful person.

And then, when she climbed out of the pick-up truck, her attention left me, completely. When I got out, I could still taste, and smell, and feel Déjà and the sex that we'd just had. And my body and brain were still sizzling, and I was still seeing the aura of the world.

As we walked toward the house there were instantly thirty some relatives and friends moving around us, many of them greeting us loudly, (though they seemed somehow muted), some taking things out of my hands, the rest milling around in the larger ripples of the crowd, all of them seeming to me to be very distantly related beings, and all of them engulfed in a quiet glittering yellow vibrating light dance, which was part sunset magic and part aural display.

Then, when one of my immediate family members grabbed my arm and pulled me in some important direction, the sensually separate-reality bubble popped and left me stranded back in the other world.

A world that I now knew had a closer-than-expected escape route to a perfectly heavenly body.

Student

Trying not to stare at Déjà, or talk to her, was so mentally and physically difficult for me I thought the constant battle with myself was going to make me ill after only a few days. And Déjà could tell.

On the sixth or seventh morning, after a crowded and busy family brunch, and after most of the relatives and my family had headed into the city, I wandered out alone onto the large wooden-deck of my Auntie

Silvia's house, looking, as always, for Déjà. I'd noticed that she wasn't going with the others, so I had made some excuse to stay back. Gazing out over a bright green bamboo forest that fell away towards the distant ocean, and marveling at the soft and cool breeze, Déjà suddenly appeared from behind me.

Motioning to me with a pointed chin, she sent me out toward the uncut jungle.

"Go over there and wait for me." She said, with a hushed tone.

Delaying long enough to observe if anyone else had notice my departure, she soon followed and caught up to me. Walking several more strides into the thick stand, we were soon well out-of-sight. And as Déjà approached me, I demurred in the erotic expectation of an over-sexualized eleven year old, reaching with both hands towards my belt buckle.

"Don't do that!" Déjà said firmly, as she came through the curtain of bamboo stalks toward me.

Shocked, and confused, I dropped my hands to my sides and held still.

"Damn it, Rory!" She continued angrily, "You have to stop making yourself so damn obvious! I told you! Don't stare at me all the time! And don't ever follow me around! Like *just now,* you were looking for me, weren't you! And my mother is right inside the house! What's wrong with your head, eh?! Do you want me to *never* talk to you again?!"

With a face full of whipping fury, each of her words and sentences lashed at me. And my head fell to my chest, and I began to cry. This wasn't fair… Turning away from Déjà, and trying to sniff back my tears, I looked deeper into the shadowy grove for escape. Unable to face her, or think, I gathered myself to run.

"*Don't you do that!*" Déjà ordered, as she saw me start to take a step. "*You stay right there, Rory!*"

Frozen in my tracks, (even with all the searing reasons I had to flee), I put my tear-stained face back down towards the ground.

Stomping towards me, Déjà increased her vocal focus and strength. And grabbing me by one upper arm, she forced me to look up.

"You crazy little fucker..." she started with a growl, "Do you have *any idea* what would happen if we got caught, Rory?! Or if someone figures out why you're always following me around?! What if someone asks you why you're crying, right now?! *Why the fuck can't you do like I told you?!"* She continued, "And don't you *ever* run from me!"

Sharpening her next words, she cut me all the way through.

"If you ever tell anyone about us Rory, I'm going to say that you tried to rape me." She hissed. *"Maybe I never should've trusted you."*

Hearing her horrible threat, and choking on her vicious rebuke, I finally broke and began bawling-out and begging her. "I would never tell anyone anything, Déjà!!! I would never do that! They could cut my tongue out before I would ever say a word to anyone about how I love you!" I wailed with tears literally pouring down my cheeks.

"You don't even have to say a word, Rory!" She spit. "Are you stupid in the head or something?! Everyone can *see* how you stare at me!"

And suddenly understanding exactly what she feared—which was losing her power of invisibility—I stopped myself from crying and looked directly into her eyes.

"I can do way better, Déjà! I promise! I know what to do! At home I'm the best liar of everyone! I'm *the best liar* of anyone I know! And no one knows anything about what I do! Ask my brothers, Déjà! I am! I can do it!" I pled, but with a building note of confidence.

Calming myself down, I tried to show her. "I can act like I don't even know you're standing next to me. Let me show you, Déjà. I can."

Turning my face sideways to her, I instantly adopted a totally nonchalant and "oblivious of her" expression and attitude, showing her my acting abilities. Behaving as if she wasn't even there, and as if I were all alone in the forest, I turned and walked away.

"Get back here." Déjà commanded, but in a softer voice.

Turning slowly around as if I was in some other place-and-time, and as if I was surprised to find someone so near to me, I continued my exhibition of cold-deceit by facing her with a fully relaxed expression that said, "I don't even recognize you."

And Déjà *saw it*; and I believe that she saw a piece of her own reflection.

And after a very still moment, she spoke slowly, "That's better, Rory…maybe you can…"

"I can." I promised.

Lifting her hands up in front of her, and making an exasperated sound, and pinching her expression a little, she scolded me one more time.

"I'm still too mad at you to feel-good right now. You better keep your promise, Rory-boy," she said with a serious edge. "If you do, maybe I'll reward you."

Then, in her more usual manner of control, she gave me my orders. "Go hike out over there, and then walk back up the dirt road to the house. If anyone asks, just tell them you went for a walk. And from now on, you act like you don't even see me. Okay?"

"Okay, Déjà."

And for the next week or so I showed Déjà what I could do when I was really trying. And she noticed. And when she followed me into the downstairs bathroom one afternoon and locked the door behind her, I knew that I had done well.

Quickly stripping off her tiny shorts and panties, and then sitting on the toilet with her legs spread open, she led me.

"Pee on my pussy, Rory-boy. And make sure you don't spray all over! Just pee right on this spot…" she purred, as she opened her bright red pussy and started to rub it.

Luckily, even though I wasn't expecting this particular turn of events, I had played with pee during sex already, including allowing my brothers and their friends to pee in my mouth and on my face, so I didn't hesitate in the least. And neither did Déjà; before I could begin my own stream of pee, she had already begun to squirt her own piss out and over her masturbating hand, which sent my own rushing stream of pee out and onto her moving hand and her dripping wet pussy. And I was so turned-on by her being so tuned-on my little cock hardened, which slowed the stream of pee, which made Déjà lean her head forward far enough to take my drizzling cock into her mouth, which made me cum.

And Déjà took my little cock and everything coming out of it into her mouth as deeply as she could, and sucked on it like an erect drinking straw full of her favorite delicacy, until I was shaking in helpless ecstasy and was totally emptied—which made her cum.

And the whole time it seemed like the light bulbs in the room were exploding.

Slipping my spent cock out of her mouth with a push of her tongue, and quickly reaching for a giant handful of toilet paper, Déjà began to unceremoniously dry off her legs and abdomen. Looking up from her seated position, she groaned at me.

"Good boy, Rory. That was so NASTY! A lot of boys and men get so nervous when I tell them to pee on my pussy, but not you. Good boy, Rory."

"Jesus fucking Christ Déjà, you are so fucking NASTY I can't believe it!" I gushed.

"Don't say 'Jesus Christ' like that Rory-boy. It's not right. Just tell me how much you love to cum in my mouth. You do love to cum in my mouth, don't you Rory-boy."

"Oh My God, Déjà!" I exclaimed.

"Shhhh! And don't say 'Oh my God', Rory." Déjà interjected out of obvious habit. "Next time, I want to pee on your face…"

"I want you to pee on my cock, too…" I replied, in anticipation.

"Yes, that too…" Déjà imagined. And then, coming back to the present, she returned to instructing me. "Go out first, Rory. I'll come out in a few minutes."

After that day, it was terribly hard for me to take a piss without having to masturbate. And on some days I would masturbate four or five times, until I absolutely could not get a response from my cock. It was exhausting, which is exactly what I needed.

Floating Blindly

I'm not sure, but I think that Déjà had sex with my oldest brother during that long vacation, too. But I wasn't positive. It wouldn't have mattered, or had any effect on the way I felt towards either of them. I just wanted to know.

Otherwise, I spent my time concentrating on constantly proving to Déjà that I wasn't staring at her, or following her around.

In truth though, with her busy beauty-queen social schedule, and a boyfriend often in tow (a big sports jock), I was lucky to see her for more than a few minutes each day.

Déjà actually was a Floridian Beauty Queen that year, which had been her senior year of high school. And since she had started school a year later than most kids, her one year of extra physical maturity had long played in her favor.

And though my mind was relentlessly filled with the loud clanging thoughts of sexual desire for her, I could see that Déjà could make her mind go silent and blank to that inner call. Or, at least she could make herself go blank towards me.

And even when I knew that she would be gone all day from the main house, it was still frustrating to me that I was constantly being forced to go out on planned adventures all around the coastline.

What I wanted to do, (all I wanted to do), was make myself available to Déjà. I spent nine weeks that summer running wild all over southern-most Florida with my cousins and five siblings, with all the local privileges possible, including access to private beaches, and even areas in restricted Indian Reservations, with boats to roam the everglades and swamps, and small sail boats and catamarans to play with on the ocean— and almost all I can remember is wanting to look at, and be with, Déjà.

(Although I could admit that all the bikini clad women running around everywhere were somewhat of a relief to me—but none of them ever looked at me the way Déjà did when it was *time again*—so they did not hold my attention.)

Big family-meal parties, which seemed to happen about every three or four days for the entire time we were there, were the most reliable moments that I knew I would get to be near her. But I learned very quickly that I was invisible to her during those events, too.

It seems impossible (now) to me that I never even once tried to talk to her about my side of what was going on, or straight out begged her for sex. Instead, I obeyed Déjà's sharp instructions better than I had anyone else in my life (including my parents), and I kept my eyes off her and stayed quiet.

And I knew that Déjà *knew* when I was skillfully keeping her within my peripheral vision. In fact, something in her subtle body and face language told me that not only did she know it, she adored it. And she was proud of my skill. And she relished that she could ignore me so completely. In time, I came to feel as if Déjà was playing herself like a movie in front of me, a silent and always seducing movie.

Promised

I also knew that Déjà could step right out of her illusive movie-like life anytime she wanted. I already knew firsthand that she had the power to stop the whole world around her, and take her sex whenever and wherever she wanted it.

Eleven year old humans aren't stupid. They can't distinguish the complexities of long term consequences so well, yet, but they can be impressively focused on the information they do have, and persistent in waiting for their next opportunity at something they are focused on. I tolerated all the daily vacation duties as best as I could, moderated a little bit by the family-wide acceptance that I was the "solitary kid" of the family, which gave me bits of time to myself, mixed-in with the hustle and bustle.

It took at least two weeks for Déjà to stop the world again, and come for me.

In the middle of one late-late night, with my four brothers and sister scattered to different cousins' homes, and with our parents crashed-out after a long night on the town drinking and eating, Déjà woke me up out of a sound sleep and whispered to me to follow her.

"It's time again, Rory-boy." She said softly, lifting my sheet off and taking my hand.

Just touching her hand told me that her body was humming and hot...again. And as she led me down the hallway she pulled me quickly along.

It may seem like an exaggeration, but Déjà's hypersexuality was so severe it would light an almost frightening level of fever in her body. It made her muscles hard and tight, too. And the peculiar way her body trembled, which I could feel through her pulling hand and arm, made me want to tremble too.

And the tingling soft light began to surround me, making the dark house glow.

Quietly, she led us all the way into the smaller secondary living room in the far end of the basement of the house, and to the couch in the farthest corner of the room. Luckily, everyone who was staying at the house that night was asleep in upstairs rooms. Plus, in the dark we would be hidden from sight there because the couch, which faced a backyard patio, had its back toward anyone entering the room.

And more, Déjà's obvious confidence and assuredness with the location created an air of security.

Still holding my hand, Déjà directed me to follow her in a low and commanding voice.

"Come over here, to the front of the couch."

Standing in front of the couch, she made both our bodies completely naked. And when the heated tremulous skin of her stomach and breasts pressed up against the front of my body, and her burning arms wrapped around me—my being immediately caught fire, and I began to shake in the sexual flames too.

Lifting my arms up to reach around her, I whispered, "*Déjà...*"

Lifting her hands up to stop me, she guided, "No-no... Don't grab me, Rory. Slow down. I'll show you..."

Standing face-to-face in the gleaming darkness, and controlling our igniting bliss with a masterful patience, Déjà then spent the next thirty to forty-five minutes teaching me how to touch bare skin in an extraordinarily soft-and-slow-way: moving our hands, and lips, and bodies against each other in almost slow-motion and so sensitively we could actually feel the individual ridges of each other's fingerprints dragging over the other's skin, and nipples, and faces, and lips, each touch lingering lightly, so that each exquisite sensation could sink-in as deeply as possible. And the quietness, and the darkness, and the extra slowness of the sexual touching lit my mind up like never before. And everywhere that our steaming and beaded skin touched, liquid tactile light-ripples were stirred-up and sent flowing out over us.

Then, laying us both down on the couch, still face-to-face, Déjà took that slow flowing touch and applied it to my lower tummy, pubic area, and around my entire tingling and pulsating cock and balls, staying far away from the kinds of repetitive motions that would make me quickly orgasm.

After lying beside me and spoiling me with her warm and feathery hands and lips for what seemed like another half an hour, Déjà skillfully slid her hips a little to the side and turned her body to lie on her back next to me. Lifting her knees up and spreading her legs out like wings, she took both my hands and led me into lessons of female masturbation, moving my fingers however and where ever she wanted, sometimes holding my fingertips to some quivering part of her wet and wide-open vagina, sometimes sinking several of my fingers inward, sometimes running my hands all the way down and back up the full length of her dripping girl crack—staying just short of making herself fully orgasm—all the while staring right into my inches-away face and openly telling me how good each particular touch felt to her.

And her sopping-wet, sparkling cunt, beamed open before me, visibly swollen and aflame with nerve-ending luminosity—pulling me into itself with the gravity of a sexual sun.

Then, putting her now slickened hands back onto my cock, we performed mutual masturbatory touching while she initiated me into long-long mouth kissing: consuming me with twenty-minute and perhaps even thirty-minute long kisses, which were especially drenched, soft, licking, and slow sucking kisses, filled with heated breath, and laced with words of unfettered adoration.

And how can I possibly describe the ecstasy of looking into Déjà's face so closely? A faultless face of pure unhindered pleasure haloed in tiny pinpoints of exploding sensual radiance: For me, it is still the image of "Goddess."

Like an echoing reflection I did everything to her that she did to me, trying at the same time to do anything else that I thought might feel good to her.

Then, moving both our bodies around, she put me on my back and placed herself in her favorite version of the sixty-nine oral sex position. With her body all the way on top of mine, she sat down on my mouth and told me to both kiss and touch her pussy, using both my mouth and my hands in the ways she had just shown me. All of which I wanted to do more than anything I have ever wanted in my life.

As a reward for my instantaneous passion for deep, long pussy kissing, and sucking, and stroking, and steady clitoral worship, I was given the unmatchable honor of swallowing multiple gushes of female ejaculation, as Déjà finally let herself begin to orgasm.

And the musky-sweet-slippery taste of oozing girl cum was an elixir to me more perfect than any other on earth, similar in texture and taste to pre-sperm, but richer and much more gratifying—and forever-after my favorite fluid and flavor in the universe.

And it was fascinating to me how, because I was so focused on my own oral adulations of Déjà, she had sucked on my cock the whole time I was sucking on her—without it causing me to cum. Instead, the sweet sexual bliss of all the different cascading physical sensations lengthened themselves out with the new, unhurried experience.

Sometime later, with us down on the floor in front of the couch, and with Déjà laying on her back again, with her legs spread even higher and wider, I was then given my first experience of cock-in-cunt fucking, made absolutely perfect by her allowing me to cum inside her blazing hot vagina (as she was on the pill).

And, because of the lack of size of my eleven and-a-half year old penis, Déjà had shown me how to put it all the way in, at the best possible angle, and to then mash my whole abdomen up and down and as hard as I could against her pussy.

Not hurrying, but definitely pushing with all my strength. Using every muscle in my body I'd tried my hardest to thrust and rub myself against her with the power of a full grown man. And when Déjà let out her first grunting exclamations, I knew that I was pleasing her.

And while I fucked Déjà her whole body shone with an ethereal glow, which seemed to come both from her super fine heated flesh as well as the dancing electricity in the air around her.

And then I came, with Déjà's legs wrapped and locked around my waist, holding me inside her. Keeping me inside her, while my torrid orgasm ran out of my body and into hers.

Huffing and puffing to catch my own breath, likely hyperventilating, and still buckling in the lingering aftershocks of my drowning-inside-her orgasm, Déjà had held still until I had become still myself.

Then, guiding me slowly up from the floor, she laid us back onto the couch, again facing each other on our sides, with our bodies touching from our tummies down to our toes.

Lifting my sweaty hair off my face and neck, she cuddled and cooed at me.

"Yesss…that was so nice Rory-boy…I was feeling so twitchy all day…and I was so busy all day long…but you took care of it, Rory…Ohhh…, you took care of me so good tonight Rory-boy! You really 'get it', Rory. You sweet, sweet boy…"

When she sent me back to my room, it was with a promise.

"I am gonna need you again soon, Rory. Oh my sweet boy, I'm gonna need you again soon!"

That night we spent at least three full hours together: totally removed from the world; and so close to each other we were as one.

And I've always remembered how much I loved the remarkably relaxed and elongated flavor of that meeting. And I've especially held dear to my mind the way that Déjà spoke so softly into my mouth while kissing me, and touching me, and fucking me, filling my being with her breath, filling my mind by telling me exactly how to please her, and filling my heart by telling me how much she loved my touches.

The End of Time

    Because the most recent experience had been so ground-breaking, it actually lasted me an unexpectedly long time. Happily following my family around without even a thought of complaint, because I was still inside the memory of being inside Déjà, a couple more weeks of our summer vacation passed by in a blur.

    But, when I realized that we had only one week left, and I also realized how insanely bad I needed to be with Déjà, at least once more, time slowed to the speed of an old slug dragging itself across cold shattered glass.

    Painfully, and in a mood of dread caused by the fear that Déjà would ignore me until it was too late, I waited. And it was hard—so hard—but I never once had even the slightest trace of a negative thought or feeling toward Déjà. I worshipped her, and prayed that she would need me naked and alone again.

    I waited dotingly (almost staying too close to Déjà); and I waited in silent burning desire; and I waited dying in my soul, already sure that she would never come for me.

    Which, unbearably, she didn't.

    Until the very last day, at the very last minute.

    While a final meal was being prepared, and the final packing of my families luggage, and gifts, and other last minute things were being done in a frenzy. And the full mass of our relatives were standing around both inside and outside my Auntie Silvia's house. And with everyone expressing their final familial emotions all over us, Déjà finally caught my eye and led me straight through the crowded house and back into her mother's sewing and laundry room.

Alone and hidden inside the large walk-in closet, with hardly a word said between us, standing ankle deep in the dirty laundry, I received Déjà's grace once again.

Lifted into rapture, Déjà suddenly adored me above all others. Barely pushing her hands down on my shoulders, she sent me to my knees in front of her. And before I had even settled into my kneeling position she had stripped her tiny shorts and panties down around her feet, and had kicked one leg free and wide.

"Put your mouth on me," was her short instruction. "We won't have much time, Rory. So go ahead and jack yourself off, okay?"

Hurriedly pushing my face into her quivering cunt, and quickly centering my sucking mouth and hard lapping tongue on her overly developed, poking-out, and tightly quivering clitoris, Déjà set me to devouring her.

Too soon, losing her control at the first chance, pulling on my hair and bucking against my face, Déjà let herself go into the fury of her terrible need.

Like splashes from a welder's torch, the lights behind my closed eyes exploded as Déjà pounded her cunt against my gaping open mouth.

Clinching her arms and legs around my head as she railed through the coursing bursts of her sexual bliss, Déjà's powerful and rather long-lasting orgasm eventually shook itself out.

And when she began to force me to stop, while trying to regain her own composure, I tucked my head tightly in-between her thighs by locking my left arm around the back of her legs, hurrying to finish jacking-off onto the pile of clothing between her feet—holding onto Déjà to the last quivering micro-second that she would allow...

Benevolently, she let me act as if I had a measure of control, and gave me the hurried moment I needed for my own quaking release.

And I squirted cum on her feet.

Picking me up out of my devotional position, she talked fast and with a note of compassion.

"I'm sorry I haven't spent more time with you, Rory-boy. But you are the youngest."

"The youngest of who?" I remember thinking.

But that was just another question, among all the others, that would remain un-answered.

Stepping her loose foot back into her panties and shorts, and yanking them up, Déjà then ushered me out of the closet.

"Come on already, Rory-boy." She whispered firmly.

And then, suddenly stopping in her tracks just as she was preparing to open the bedroom door, Déjà swore out loud, "Oh sweet Jesus, I almost forgot!"

Turning to face me, Déjà let out her furtive news.

"I'm starting college next month, Rory. After one year here, if I do good my parents said that I can travel wherever I can afford for my second year, so I think I'm going to come over to your city and see you then."

"That would be incredible!" I blubbered.

"I know…" she said, with a kind of distant tone.

"Wow, Déjà! That would be great!" I agreed again, enthusiastically.

"Don't tell anyone. Just be good and wait, okay? When I get over there, I'm going to tell you lots of real sex stuff I know. I love you, Rory-boy!"

"I love you, Déjà." I moaned.

And then, with a squeeze of my hand and a quick nod, she was out the door and gone down the hallway.

Abruptly teleported from Déjà's enclosing vortex into a hallway noisy with the competing voices of the crowd of relatives in the great-room at the other end of it, I already felt as far away from her as I would be the next day, when I would be nearly two thousand miles north-west across the American Continent.

When I got home from that extra-long, mind blowing, heart opening, virginity losing, and physically torturous vacation, I loved Déjà beyond words and without question, and I desired her in a destiny-rooted way. And, I had absolutely no real idea of when I would ever be seeing her again (even though she had indicated it might be no more than a year or so).

I remember asking my father one night, not long after we had returned home, when we would be able to go on a family vacation to Florida again. Of course, trying to hide any hint of my real reasons for asking.

And, I remember his blunt response.

"Go to bed."

Returning with a re-doubled intensity to my efforts of seduction with the usual neighborhood and school girls in our hometown, I crept forward with little success (sixth grade not being a very conducive environment for sexual contact—for obvious reasons that were not at all obvious to me at the time).

Instead, for the most part, I made due with the sexual contact and cum that I intermittently sucked out of my oldest brother and his friends.

And then, after learning about it from one of those older guys, I expanded my cock sucking to the local city public park bathrooms whenever I could, where I experienced the delight of knowing that I might obtain sex with a different adult perhaps every time I went.

Soon after, I also experienced my first physically forced sexual contact in those parks (as previously described).

I also began stealing and hoarding porn, and even porn-like pictures, from any possible source. And I also started having several different kinds of reoccurring sexual nightmares: those where I was doing sexual things I really wouldn't do, those where I was caught and gruesomely punished, and those where I was doing all the sexual things I wanted to do—and would wake up in the real panic of knowing that it was just a dream.

I even considered our family dog "Scruffy" as a possible sex partner during that year.

At that time, when I was turning twelve, to save money our family had moved to one of the outskirt areas of our city. Buying a house in a suburban neighborhood that was surrounded by small rural ranches, our family finances were substantially relieved. And because I was able to convince my parents that it would help burn off some of my excess physical energy, they agreed to let my start youth boxing. And at the beginning of the next year I began wrestling at my junior high school. And I ran track. And during that year I did have some very limited and short lived success with girlfriends my own age. But to be honest, I was not a suitable partner for those girls, and I scared all of them off within a few make-out sessions.

All the while, in the aching front of my brain, and in the squirming pit of my gut, and with a never ceasing need in my groin, I lived with Déjà always in my mind.

Then, the vast and unpredictable universe answered my constantly pounding prayer.

Arrival of The Goddess

Just before my thirteenth birthday, ostensibly so that she could attend our State College, Déjà left her home in Southern Florida and moved to our city, and into our house.

The pertinent realities of my family's home life at that time were fairly simple. And I suppose that the fact that both my parents worked more than full-time, and were gone from the household for as much as eleven hours a day, would be one of the most important of those facts.

My mother, an often physically and emotionally stoic woman, did not like me (as you know), so I was good at avoiding her notice. My father, a family physician, had reached the point in his demanding career where all his energies were used-up before he returned home each night. And with so many kids, it was always the most stand-out pieces of news that got focused on. And, since well-behaved children lined-up and ready to sit down at the dinner table was what they both expected to see when they got home, for the most part that's what they always saw.

A fervent believer in achieving the best education possible, my father was strictly determined to see all of his children attain a higher education. In line with that my three older brothers, who were five years, four years, and three years older than me, had all graduated from high school with honors. And all of them were off at their own universities.

Two of them were out of state, and my oldest brother Burt would be in his second year at the State College that was located in our city, (which was the same college that Déjà would be attending), but he lived more than twenty miles away in an apartment with several other college guys, and because of his less than good relationship with my parents, I didn't expect to see much of him.

Because of Déjà's arrival, I couldn't have been happier with the timing of the last of my older brother's departures from our home.

As for my younger siblings, my one year younger sister was very nice, and popular, and smart, and busy with her own school and social life. She was even a part of the Jr. High School student government. And my youngest brother, who was three school grades below me, was young enough that he had all his own aged friends, and no interest at all in anything that I did. Which meant that neither of them would be any hindrance to me.

Being the middle-child, and the lesser-achiever among my siblings, I had long considered myself to be the lucky-one who "faded from sight". To myself, in all the important ways, I felt that I basically lived by my own directions and more or less controlled a fairly big part of my own existence, and a great deal of my own time.

So, when Déjà walked through the front door of my house—into my world—I could hardly believe my eyes. Standing in my living room, shining with unbounded beauty, now twenty years-old, if anything she looked somehow more petite. And her facial lines were more definite, and finer, which I quickly realized was because she'd finally lost the last of her baby-face—and she was even more gorgeous than ever!

Walking across the room to greet her, as she shuffled her suitcases in and set them down, I stood up to my tallest, (though trying not to be noticed by anyone but her). And not being too obvious or gushy, I spread my arms wide for a welcoming hug. I had grown, too. But as I wrapped my arms around her, and felt her face against mine, I felt our age difference perhaps more than ever.

"Déjà! Welcome, cousin! Welcome, welcome!" I said, being happy and loving; but not being *too* happy or loving.

Speaking in an appropriately tired after a long day of travel kind-of voice, Déjà responded, "Hello, Rory! Oh, I'm so tired! I took three connecting flights to get here!"

And then with my mother and my younger siblings giving and getting their hugs, I backed up and prepared myself for the necessary acting job I had ahead of me. Terribly wanting to offer to carry Déjà's suitcases downstairs—instead, I didn't. Staying back and seemingly unconcerned about anything in particular, I paid peripheral attention.

Fortunately, my father gave the order for me and my little brother to carry her things downstairs, to the room she would be staying in. And the whole thing began to feel real.

I had, of course, been informed that Déjà would be moving in with our family, about a month previous, which, of course, had pushed me beyond my happiest imaginations. But I could only live each of those days by blocking that information out, and deciding that I wasn't going to believe she was really coming until I saw her with my own eyes. But, even when I saw that Déjà was actually standing right in front of me—as stunning and outrageously sexy as any penthouse pet that was ever born—I still couldn't fully believe it!

I wasn't going to be able to believe it until I could touch her, and feel her, and taste her!

On her third night, sneaking through her new surroundings, Déjà came for me.

In our basement there were three bedrooms. Mine was the big one that the last of my older brothers had just moved out of, which was positioned right below my parents' upstairs room. My younger brother was still in the room we had shared, which was adjacent to mine and directly below my little sister's upstairs room. Déjà was using the third basement room, a spare room that had been my mom's sewing and laundry room, which sat on the far side of the basement separated off by the main washing and utility room that was located at the base of the stairs. The kitchen sat above that central basement area, and only the far corner of the upstairs living room was above Déjà. As best as my mother could organize, Déjà was purposely meant to have her privacy.

When she came into my room on that third night, I was sound asleep.

Awakened by her warm breath and the touch of her lips on mine, I opened my eyes to see, again, the most beautiful thing I'd ever seen in my life—Déjà's sparkling and sex-hungry face hovering over mine.

"Rory...," she whispered.

And so began the furious and by far the most extensive chapter of my sexual/experiential/training period with my hypersexually insane mentor.

The first meeting in my house was really just a friendly warm-up, though personally memorable for me, with a few notable high points: foremost among them, how Déjà knew exactly when and how to back her sucking mouth off my peaking cock just enough to keep me from spilling my sperm-load—not once or twice—but time-after-time for what eventually began to seem like a kind of tortuous game.

Once, in response to her hot and wet vacuumous cock-sucking, as my bottom muscles tensed-up so hard the small of my back lifted off the mattress, she actually pinched me with her fingernails at the neck of the underside of my scrotum! She didn't pinch me that hard, and I didn't cry out; but it most definitely did distract my body and brain away from the cresting orgasm.

Also during that meeting, Déjà licked and sucked and kissed my nipples, which was a big sexual "first" for me, both because I had never been touched there like that and also because it was something I was so unaware of as a sexual point(s) for a male! And when she sucked on my hardening little nipples the exact same way I sucked on hers, and touched them with her saliva slickened finger-tips as if coaxing them to grow, I felt shock, deep arousal, orgasmic eroticism, and then confusion (of a kind I can only relate to feeling when I later, immaturely, feared that I was "gay").

And I had two orgasms right in a row that night, barely thirty or forty-five seconds apart, caused by Déjà's incomparable sucking mouth and pulling hands.

In contrast to the mostly one-sided cock sucking I usually engaged in, including the illicit sex I had at the parks, and my daily fantasy filled masturbations, Déjà's sex was a shining and floating galaxy far above and beyond the smallness of everything else I'd known.

At the end of it, after kissing me for a while and quietly looking at my face, while showing me an extra warm expression of unguarded happiness, which held a calmer maturity than I remembered seeing on her face before, she leaned down and whispered three instructions into my right ear.

"Don't tell anyone here about us, not even your best friends. And don't masturbate all the time—wait for me. And from now on, when you go to bed take off your underwear and hide them under your pillow, so you can be naked for me. Goodnight, my sweet Rory."

"What about what you promised to tell me, Déjà?" I asked, as if that distant promise had been made just minutes before.

"Yes.., Rory." She acknowledged, "Tomorrow night I will begin telling you. Go to sleep, now."

"Alright Déjà, I love you."

"I love you," she responded, as she tip-toed out.

Hearing Déjà say, "I love you" sent me falling all the way. And more than anytime that I could remember before, I fell blissfully to sleep looking forward to the next day, certain for the first time in my life that the world held everything that I had ever dreamed for, because the next day held *Déjà*.

But the next day didn't really hold Déjà, which totally bummed me out because it was the end of summer and I had all day to do whatever I wanted. But she had been busy all day signing up for her fall semester classes, learning the layout of the college campus, and riding the public buses all the way across the city and back, right up until just before dinner time when she finally arrived back to our house.

After dinner, if I could have moved the earth and sun forward by any power, I would have. Honestly speaking, at that juvenile time, I would have stolen time from all the world and creation to have been with Déjà more quickly. Instead, I stayed in my room and kept my concentration centered on the raging anticipation (and my cock, and my newly found nipples).

Waiting for her that night, with both my hands trembling in the effort not to masturbate too quickly (and cause an orgasm), I do remember one other interesting line of thought that I processed: I thought of my eighth grade school friends and what they would have been doing that same night, which was watching Monty Python, or Dr. Who, or Mutual of Omaha's Wild Kingdom, and eating ice-cream, or popcorn; and in my hidden differences I felt like a somehow secret-nomad-wanderer leaving them behind.

Slipping my underwear off and hiding them under my pillow, I lay brightly bared, trying to get used to the amazingly increased level of tactile sensation that came from lying in bed naked.

Eaten Alive

It took *forever* for Déjà to come, but I was still awake when the rest of the house fell still enough, for long enough, and Déjà finally crept into my room.

I remember being surprised to see that it was after midnight when she led me into her new guest-room, still crowded with her half unpacked suitcases, and then told me to lay my unclothed body on her bed.

Of course, I could not know that this second sexual meeting between us in my house, our sixth sexual encounter so far in our lives, was going to be such a defining moment, going completely beyond anything that I had ever heard of, or read, or fantasized about. The overwhelming impact and influence of the occasion simply cannot be overstated.

This time Déjà would reveal to me how much more I was than just a "little pervert."

This time Déjà would touch me even more fully—and give me Power.

The stage was set in part by the way that Déjà's bedroom was tucked off to the far side of the basement. As far as my parents were concerned, she was expected to be given privacy. And her door was expected to be locked. It was so well tucked away we could even talk to each other, at a reasonable whisper, and move around without worrying, no matter the time of night. From the beginning, we felt extremely comfortable and hidden.

Déjà, who seemed to have a curiously concentrated focus that night, told me to lie in the middle of her bed, on my back. Lifting her nightgown over her head and slipping her panties down and off, Déjà stood naked and perfect in front of me, and paused. Looking up, I could see the gathering attentiveness on her face.

"Lie still Rory, I'm going to love your whole body now. You can watch me, but don't move unless I tell you. And stay quiet..."

As she approached my eyes flew up and down her body.

But it was her face that I had to stare at—to stop and see the *special way* she was looking at me, and my naked body—before or since, nothing has ever surpassed that look: I felt like a beautiful gift or a sparkling jewel set before her.

And when Déjà crawled up over my body, and surrounded me in the tremendous heat of her sexual being, I laid still and gave myself unconditionally.

"The Pleasure of a Thousand Kisses" is what Déjà called the sexual event that she was about to begin. What we name it is of little importance; but what it actually was, to Déjà, is a procedure of intimacy that is of such penetrating brilliance and sexual power I am still astonished by it.

What I couldn't have known ahead of time, was that the *way* in which I responded to her penetrating sexual procedures, and absorbed it, and understood it—or didn't—would determine if I was worthy of Déjà's continued special attentions.

The "Thousand Kisses", as Déjà enacts it, is an extremely rare sexual experience at its lowest level; a thoroughly baring sexual test in its middle; and a diabolical way for her to take permanent and pervasive control of a person at its hypersexual apex.

Unfortunately, it would be literally impossible for me to completely describe to you the outrageously delicious and lengthy experience of the entire thousand kisses. For one thing, there were way more than a thousand kisses, and touches, and penetrations, and fluid exchanges, etc., which all flowed together in the complex patterns of sexual concentration. Plus, it would take me nearly five hours to describe the entire event, because that is how long it lasted.

Yes, Déjà really did kiss and suck and rub herself on literally every single inch of my body: using her big lips, and her hot wet mouth, and her unbelievable tongue, and her breasts, and her cunt, and her bottom, and her hands, and her face, and nearly every part of her body. Progressing exceedingly slowly, sometimes with her hands or fingers touching lightly down beside the tip of her tongue, sometimes rubbing her swollen nipples slowly back-and-forth across the spot receiving attention, sometimes even squatting her open cunt and amazingly over-swollen clit down to touch or rub herself onto the spot-of-the-moment, before kissing and spreading her own slippery juices around with her tongue and her sex-hungry mouth.

And yes, she did turn me around and around and positioned me like a teen boy-sized doll in every position she could think of: flat on my back with my hands under my head and my legs folded Indian-style, on my knees with my head covered in pillows, flat on my stomach with my arms spread out, and even rolled up on my shoulders with my knees behind my head and my skinny ass in the air. At one point she sat me upright against the headboard, placing my legs apart with the knees up, and then while kissing my hands, she squatted in front of me and humped each of my shins and knees to orgasm.

Déjà also sat on my face, several times, in many different positions, slowly humping my head and often intentionally smothering me a little bit.

She also rubbed her sizzling-mound on the small of my back, the back of my head, my chin, my hands, my hands closed into fists, my forearms, my chest, and on many other places.

And yes, it all felt just as outrageously wonderful and sexually expanding and overwhelmingly satisfying as you'd think it would. But it was also somewhat torturous at times. And frankly, there were even parts of it that weren't really sexually enjoyable to me at all. I did not like it when her mouth was on the bottoms of my feet, and I thought it was a waste of time when she stayed at my ankles and the backs of my calves (though the rear of the knee is a surprisingly erotic point), and I disliked it when she wetly explored my nose and ears (though her kisses on my eyes were very nice), and it was hard for me to kiss her back in some of those places too, but she was insistent.

And Déjà took her time at every point regardless, treating each electrified area as sensitively as a mindful acupuncturist would. Every wide-open mouth-sized area of my body, one after the next, and overlapping, was given her spoiling saliva slickened and sexual organ rubbed treatment: my elbows, armpits, back of the ribcage, between the shoulder blades, back of the ears, wrists, eyeball-sockets, where tears come out, center of the chest, center of the spine, each vertebra descending down past my tail-bone to my anus, inside the belly-button, the front base of the throat, the third-eye, and behind the ball-sack astride the lowest stem-root of the cock shaft, and the anus again (and again).

And there were some completely unexpected areas that she touched hotly down on that made me shake like a leaf, feel actual shocks, moan in different tones, breathe in different tempos, hyperventilate, stop breathing altogether—and one very central spot that she sucked on and then penetrated that made me cry tears of happiness like a freed fool.

And yes, she also sucked-off and masturbated my cock as a stop in-between other areas of oral focus, sometimes teasingly and sometimes more torturously. And she did the same thing with placing my cock into her cunt-hole and her anus, keeping it brief because it made the pleasure feel infinite.

She also rubbed and finger-banged her own pussy and anus, and then pushed those fingers into my openings, and would then use those same fingers to play with her own lips and mine.

And throughout the timeless tingling stretch of ecstatic eternity there were rolling orgasms of different lengths and intensity, for both of us, rising and falling, some with just a momentary quake and leaking, some with sheet shaking and spraying spasms beyond tempering.

At one point Déjà made me cum, again, by simply blowing her boiling hot breath up against the bottom of my balls and twitching cock-head. At another, she made me orgasm by squatting absolutely still over my face and holding her deep red hanging open cunt and arching up clit-nub just an inch above my mouth's reach.

Whatever she did touch down into my mouth, I was allowed to kiss and suck on; but she controlled those moments strictly and kept them mostly brief, except for one especially notable set of minutes when she took that squatting position and then dropped her pouting red pussy and pink anus into my waiting mouth for a longer and deeper ride. In that position she let me French-kiss and suck on both her sexual holes for quite a while, just as she had done to my one.

At every moment, at every point of my body, she was so tuned-in and feeling what I was feeling I could no longer sense any boundary between us.

Was it just her burning mouth and body that was being penetrated by me? Because I was dead certain that I was also inside Déjà's heaving heart and deliriously storming sexual mind. Beyond separating sanity, I felt the inside and outside of both of us. Completely immersed, I floated with the tidal sensations of our two sexual beings.

All of which is exactly why Déjà was exerting such a painstaking attention on my body: She was reading my flesh and fully opened sexual self like a blind genius reads whatever he or she touches. But, because she was bred in a hypersexual tribe, Déjà used her snaking tongue, swollen lips, reaching mouth, and female sexual organs to achieve and gather the very most perceptive contact, results, and soul exposing sexual information possible.

I absolutely believe that Déjà has sexual abilities beyond scientific measurement or understanding (unless she had a naked scientist in her grip). Like humans able to heal internal organs with just a touch, or those who can see into one's great past, or even those who can calculate impossible mathematical problems in a blink, Déjà has real powers.

She can lift out the full-spectral sexual spirit of a person—and then swallow it into herself.

Déjà is an empathic-hypersexual of the highest order; in her embrace I felt like I had been cumming ever since I was born.

The idea of ever being anything but naked, or anywhere but deeply wrapped in the bare nakedness of Déjà, or another human body, became distasteful to me to the point of angry sadness.

And I did not want to remember or acknowledge the world as it had been before. How had I lived without Déjà?

At the time, I slowly realized that I was thinking these broader kinds of thoughts because Déjà had stopped touching me. And I realized that my eyes were closed. Finally backing off from her exhaustive hyper-investigation of me, Déjà had lain quietly down on the bed beside me.

After ten or fifteen minutes of still-spinning around inside the exquisite sexual after-quakes of our bodies, with our heart rates calming down, our breathing patterns slowing, and our barreling brainwave activity gradually subsiding, I opened my eyes and sat up a little.

Looking over, I *saw* Déjà with radiant diamond-white refractions of light dancing brightly above her perfect caramel skin, hanging like an aural mist, and softly framing her resting face on her pillow. On her closed eyelids, I saw tiny exploding stars: *My Goddess*...

After another silent group of minutes, as I watched Déjà, she finally took a long breath and then gave out a longer and stronger sigh. To me it sounded like a deeply satisfied, "*Yesss.*"

Sitting up and scooting back to lean against the headboard next to me, Déjà spoke in a language so direct even a thirteen year old boy could understand it. When Déjà decided to tell me something there were no subtleties or shyness. When she really wanted to tell me something she spoke straightforwardly, openly, and alarmingly bullshit-free.

"Only one man before you was able to last that long, Rory. And you let me go everywhere...I'm so proud of you!"

Scooting up to the headboard I sat back, listening to her. But her pride in my ability to let her have her way with me did not seem that important or surprising, to me.

"Oh, you! You don't even know!" She exclaimed. "I've had men last less than five minutes under my mouth and tongue!"

Noticing the way that Déjà was looking at me, so wide-eyed and unswervingly, I sat up even more.

"Rory, what you've just let me do is absolutely amazing! I've had men slap me after teasing them with my mouth for just a few minutes!"

She continued hurriedly. "Most men are so impatient and pre-set in their sexual ways, you wouldn't believe it! And sometimes they are just plain stupid about the weirdest things when it comes to sex!" She paused shortly, "And most of them can't be submissive..."

"Weird about what kind of things, Déjà? And why can't they be submissive" I asked, using a word I had just then learned (and instantly understood).

Answering quickly, Déjà continued. "Like when a man gets in a big hurry, and then tells me he wants to have some kind of sex that he already had with some other girl before, and then he starts telling me exactly how to do it!" She snorted with distain. "And it's worse when they get pushy about something stupid. I want to yell at those men 'You never had Déjà before!!' I want to yell at them to 'Shut up and see what happens if I take over!' I can't stand stupid and boring sex! Like grunting frozen-stiff already-over sex!" She exclaimed with a tone of disgust and disbelief, and then paused for a moment again. "And then they act all 'Oh, I have to run out of here as fast as I can!' That kind of sex makes me want to kick somebody right-in-the-balls!" She finished with a growl, like an animal happy to be in a fight!

I'd never seen Déjà with such a loudly offended attitude. And the stronger her words got, the more her deeper personality came out. And even though I wanted to ask her questions, I didn't interrupt her.

"Rory-boy, I've even been beat-up and thrown out of the room for just trying to go near some of the places on a man's body that you let me go tonight! So you don't know how much it means to me! I had my whole thumb up to my wrist inside your bottom-hole, all the way up Rory-boy, and my fingers too, several times! And you just let me! You never even flinched!"

Using slower sentences, she got even more serious.

"Really Rory, it's rare for anyone, man or woman, to be able to let another person go sexually free like that, for that long, and go everywhere in their body. And the way your body so obviously begged for every second of it has great meaning, because if you can be kissed and sucked on and sexually entered anywhere; and if you can kiss and suck and put your tongue and body inside someone else, anywhere, and everywhere; and you can go for more-and-more sex with anyone—then you are one of the extra-sexual people—just like me!!!" Déjà's gushed, and her spilling delight finally hit me.

"I…I…" I stammered at first, "Do you really think that *I* can be like *you*, Déjà?! The way you can have sex whenever you want to?! The way that you make sex whatever you want it to be?! Is that what you mean, Déjà?!" I asked in a sudden fantastic panic.

"You silly boy!" She sang back, "You already are like me! You'll see! Wait until you see what I can do! What *we* can do! We are going to have some very crazy sexual fun, Rory-boy! We can make some money, too. If you want to…?"

What she had said before was true: I would let anyone do anything sexual to me. But I hadn't ever realized that being that way was such a special thing. I certainly hadn't ever thought of Déjà in that way. I saw her as the one who had control over everything, not the one who had to give it up. I hoped that difference was something Déjà would explain to me soon.

"Déjà, you have to tell me more! How can I start to really be like you? Do you fuck my older brothers? How many men have you had sex with? Who else in the family do you have sex with? *Do you know what Maria did to me…?*"

"Rory, Rory, quiet down! I'm way too tired to tell you all that stuff right now. I have to sleep for at least a couple of hours. I'll tell you lots more tomorrow night. Just fuck me a little more now, Rory. I'm going to close my eyes. Fuck me a little bit while I fall asleep…, then go to bed."

"Okay." I replied, resigned—and also so fulfilled I didn't care if I had to wait to hear more!

And so, as the Goddess lay back I pushed my way up between her legs. Lifting her knees gently up and back, and then rubbing and shoving my hard-again little cock into her still wet and burning hot vagina, I performed my adoring worship.

Then, kissing her sticky-pungent cum soaked and sweet glowing pussy goodnight, I retreated respectfully.

I should have had a million questions raging through my mind as I slipped back into my own bed; instead, I had a body full of answers and a promised date for the next night. Emotionally, I snuggled with the most treasured nugget of personal knowledge and power I had ever been given—*I was like Déjà.*

Mission Information

The next night, our third night in a row, again floating through the after-midnight hours, Déjà equaled the comprehensively penetrating lessons of the night before by telling me almost all the information I would ever come to know about whom we really were, where we came from, and why she had come for me.

At the end of that night she even gave me my own dark recognition, and a sexual title.

To prepare for the conversation Déjà played with my body for a while, returning to some of her favorite touch-sites from the night before.

Then she gave herself some pounding release by having me fuck her while she was practically standing on her head (to increase the penetrating depth of my rather small cock).

Then, still naked, Déjà sat me down on the edge of the bed facing her.

I thought I was ready. She started fast.

"Rory, your oldest brother Burt told me what you used to do for him and his friends: Do you know why?"

"Do I know 'why' what?"

"Why you sucked their cocks."

I didn't know what to say; and I didn't know what she was trying to say. The usually overpowering sexual-light that surrounded Déjà face and eyes was somehow dialed down to a more tightly defined beam, which made me feel different.

"Do you remember your first trip to Florida, Rory-boy?"

"Yes."

"When I touched you in the outdoor shower?"

"Yes."

"You were a good boy."

"Yes…"

"Your oldest brother Burt taught you how to suck his cock right after that trip, didn't he?"

"No." I said quickly, mostly because I couldn't exactly remember right then, but also because she sounded oddly accusatory. So it was a reaction.

"*Yes he did*, Rory. I know exactly when it happened, and I'll tell you why. When I was fifteen and your family came to visit Miami that first time, I thought that Burt might be a super-sex boy for sure. He was so handsome and big for his age, so I damn near sucked his little cock off during that one visit! He was just a little younger than you are now. Of course, you were so young then, but I already knew that you had been touched, so I touched you too. And you liked it so much! I remember you told me that you could see 'blinking lights in your head' and that 'you loved me', which I thought was so cute! Anyway, at the end of that visit I told Burt to tell you to suck his cock—and I bet him that you would!"

"You told Burt to make me suck him..?" I said with obvious doubt. *"Why?"*

And it was weird that I didn't believe her. I wasn't offended, so much as surprised and confused, I guess. I'd never tried to connect the two things together before. And Déjà's facial expressions and vocal tone were different and odd to me (I suppose because they weren't, as usual, restricted to only those tenors that are flagrantly sexual).

Even with what she had said the night before, about our being sexually alike, in that moment I felt like I was being caught-out at something. Or that I was already caught, in a trick of some bizarre kind.

And the fact that this awkwardness was happening with Déjà, at this important moment, was making me feel especially uncomfortable.

I spoke without thinking. "You're lying Déjà, Burt would have told me!"

With white fire shooting out of her eyes, and leaning quickly forward, Déjà exploded back at me in response.

"Don't you ever call me a liar!"

Then calming back, and seeming to enjoy the drama, she finished with a forceful hiss.

"Burt didn't tell you because I told him not to! Just like you will never tell anyone about us!!!"

Her conviction was complete and fully confident. And with her voice returning to the tone and volume of a controlled and conspiratorial confessor, she continued on as if she had not just coiled-up at me.

"Anyway.., I was right, Rory! You did want to suck him, and more than just him! I sure found out the second time you came to visit. I think I could tell the minute you got off the plane. You are definitely the super-sex boy in your family. Your mouth was so good...especially for being so young!"

Pausing, Déjà considered her next words a little more carefully.

"I told Burt to teach you how to suck his cock for his pleasure, and to see where he would take it. But, even though you were so young, it turned out to be for *your* pleasure, and that *you* are the one that took the sex over! Burt told me how you are! He said you sucked and swallowed five guys one after the other! He said you will even let them pee in your mouth! And he said you never say 'no'. That's amazing! That's just how I was!"

Pausing, again, she seemed to finish her final internal considerations.

"Ever since I heard about our oldest cousin Maria touching you as a baby, I thought you might be..."

My oldest cousin, Maria...?! So Déjà *did* know something about that?! I had always believed that was my own family's secret, buried all those years ago!

With the impact of an emotional and mental concussion, the long unspoken secret and most guarded mystery of my lifetime stepped out of Déjà's chest and into the middle of the room.

My parents had avoided this subject so strictly, and so strangely for my whole life it was definitely the secret-est secret in our entire household.

And there was nothing I wanted to know about more.

Jumping on the moment, I raised my voice.

"What do you know about Maria touching me Déjà? You have to tell me!"

Perched tensely on the edge of the bed, all the short hairs all over my naked body were standing on end. Leaning toward me again, Déjà smiled and let go:

"Rory-boy, you are so cute! And you want to know everything so badly! I love that about you. And I know that you've been waiting for so long. So listen to me, now. Where should I start…?"

"Start with Maria!"

"Did you know she's adopted?"

"Yes. I've always known that."

"She's adopted, but she's still from family."

"Whatever, I don't care about that part. Tell me about when she took care of me."

"No Rory, let me start before that…"

With my brain on fire, I kept my body motionless and listened.

"Okay Rory…, in Florida, especially Miami, I know lots of people just like us who are super-sex people, like you wouldn't believe! And I have been this way ever since I was eleven years old, Rory. That's when my 'teacher' saw how much I liked to be touched, and he took me for his secret student. Since then I have met and had sex with hundreds of extra-sexual people and tourists, from all over the world."

My eye-popping amazement went without saying, and Déjà was rolling into her story at full-speed.

"Rory-boy, there have always been super-sex people like us. I think maybe ever since before history. That's what my teacher told me. And I bet some families have more of us in them than others. In my family I am one; in your family you're the one. Maria is one, too."

"Do other people know?" I couldn't help asking.

"Yes, sometimes people know. But the people who aren't extra-sexual almost never talk about stuff like that. You know how that is, already. So our world is 'secret', yeah; but it is also not-secret, yeah?"

Something so important shouldn't be so ridiculous, or make such perfect sense when explained in this way. But what she said made more sense than any other explanation I could have heard—because it was true.

"But what matters the most Rory, and what I have been waiting to tell you, is that for us sex is 'no-shame' and 'no-shy'—it is our 'special place' in society. For us sex is just as natural and unstoppable as the oceans touching all over the Earth! And all the different ways of having sex are beautiful to us! And each of us is different, like the fish in the sea; and we're all the same too, because we all adore being naked and nasty with all kinds of people! And that is a big part of what makes us special too—we really do have a deep and real love for all the different kinds of sex-people. For instance, we have a cousin you've never met in Key West who is now completely a girl in his mind! And so many people and rich tourists love him! And he makes so much money it's crazy! Oh Rory-boy, he would love to meet you!"

At that time in my life, in the year 1973, I had barely even heard of gay sex. And when I had, it was never in a positive way (but rather in an openly hateful and violent way).

What Déjà was saying was so eye-opening and mentally releasing it was making the skin on my neck and the top of my head feel tight and tingly. Of course I had seen pictures of Hippies in communes, and heard (totally un-detailed) stories of events called "love-ins", and I had my own little collection of traditional porn magazines, and I had even seen street hookers in my life—but none of that reality spoke about anything but fairly straight forward hetero-sexual activity.

And my own oral sex with my brother and other male partners, including those in the public parks, which had always been me performing the service ninety-percent of the time, was such a hidden and absolutely never discussed thing, and something that I had been doing since such a young age, I had somehow (in young denial?) never begun to consider my behaviors in this more openly stated kind of way. For one thing, I'd *never* thought that I or any of my male partners were anything other than heterosexual. I thought I was "different", but different and still heterosexual.

What Déjà was talking about—just like what she had done to me—was sex of a whole different elevation.

At this point I also remember that Déjà started showing her sharp pride, actually lifting her posture and her chin as one who stands "above" others.

"I can make a man leave his wife with my eyes, Rory! And I have! I bet I could make a woman leave her husband, too! Some women adore me as much as the men do. No lie, Rory! Because of what I am, and what I can do, I have been one of the highest paid 'working girls' in Miami ever since my teacher first started letting me work! And I've worked at all the best hotels in southern Florida, and the Key's! I even got flown to Honolulu Hawaii by one big customer, for a whole week! And he offered me a job in one of the best hotels there! But I said 'No' because I'm a Florida girl."

Literally beaming, Déjà seemed to be enjoying this release of concealed information almost as much as I was.

"And even at the very first, my teacher said that no 'girl' in all of Florida—or maybe the whole world—was more-sexual than me, and he was right!" She squealed! And then suddenly changing her tone to one of confused wonder, she let out her next surprising fact. "I can't believe it

Rory, but half of the 'working girls' I know don't even like the sex! Some of the girls even hate the sex! They must be crazy or something... I don't understand them..."

Of course, I was marveling at everything she was saying, and I struggled to keep up. Her uniquely brazen pride and happiness in her sexual-self was something that I had always noticed about Déjà, and knew I had never felt about myself. She spoke about herself like a world champion does when they celebrate their victories. I wanted to hear more, and I wanted to be able to talk about myself the way she did.

"And Rory, you wouldn't believe who some of those people I fuck are! Sometimes I meet really famous men, and super rich men, and even Royalty from other Countries! And I am fearless, and I'm always ready for any kind of sexual excitement! I even have sex with people who don't speak a word of English, all the time, and it doesn't matter to me in the least! My teacher thinks I'm one of the most daring super-sexual working girls he's ever seen in his life!"

I knew that it must be true. Everything both sane and insane about what she told me made me believe that I was in the presence of a girl so fiercely sexually turned-on no other could outmatch her. How could they?

"We are like this, Rory" she continued with unfettered enthusiasm, "...because we are *meant* to be exactly like this! My teacher showed me that we really are 'special'; *I could feel it in his hands the first time he put them on my body*. Now I am here to show you how to be the most-special too, Rory—just like last night."

I did want to be "special" like that.

"You know exactly what I'm talking about, and what you are, don't you Rory? You're a terrible little pervert boy and you can't help yourself, right? You want sex every day, all day, even if you already had some, don't you?"

"Yes." I did know that about myself, of course, but no one had ever spoken about it out loud before.

"That's because you're a *real* extra-sexual person, Rory."

"Who else is like us, Déjà? Who was your teacher? Is there anyone else in our family? Tell me everything! And what about Maria?!" I begged.

"Too much to tell about everything…," Déjà shrugged. "Besides, when it comes to other people's sexual business my teacher always said, 'If you weren't there, maybe you shouldn't be talking about it. Otherwise, it's better to respect the privacy and keep the secret.' That's why you can't tell anyone else about us, Rory-boy. No one, *ever*."

Stopping, she emphasized the point with lifted eyebrows, and by waiting for my acknowledgment. When I nodded in agreement, she continued.

"But I will tell you about some stuff that happened to me, and what I think Maria did with you when you were a baby, those stories belong to you."

And this is when Déjà sat back and told me with devious delight all the bare and transforming details of what she had always imagined happened to me when I was an infant, as well as what had happened to her when she was eight or nine, and then again at eleven years old, along with an almost countless list of other incredible, nearly unbelievable, and unstoppably orgiastic sexual accounts that she had personally been a part of, including her unchecked prostitution up to the time she left Miami to be with me.

And the more she told me the farther I sailed away from my immediate family, my school friends, and all the other people who lived in the world that I had lived in before.

Up until the day I heard these stories from Déjà, I'd made up all kinds of possible explanations about the mystery of my violated childhood: But none of my imaginings were anywhere near as explicit, outrageous, clearly defined, or as formative as what Déjà was describing.

In the throes of an obviously long treasured arousal, Déjà told me how she had always envisioned that what my then nineteen year-old cousin Maria had done to me, specifically, was nothing less than an infant-aimed version of what Déjà had done to me with her mouth and body the night before. For Déjà, no picture could ever be more perfect than my being originally sexually birthed in that same kind of extraordinary sexual immersion.

She was actually envious.

And now that I knew I really had been touched sexually as a child, which was something I wouldn't have thought would make me feel so calm, I realized that I rather needed to be "special."

With everything else that Déjà was telling me, and showing me, and doing to me, she was my absolute authority. Who in this universe could know more than her? Who could possibly be more special?

Continuing her wrapping account, Déjà told me how when she was fifteen, just before my first visit to Florida, she had accidentally overheard her own parents discussing the hushed story of how Maria had been caught with me, and was then sent back to Miami by my parents.

(All of which was something that her teacher, as far as she knew, was totally unaware of.)

When Déjà had hypersexually reasoned-out the untold details of the story to her own satisfaction, she had then begun to build an idea of how she might someday have me as her own sexual "apprentice."

For Déjà, the opportunity to take control of such an "already touched" sexual apprentice was beyond resisting. Even the nearly two thousand miles between us, and the stark cultural differences of our upbringings, and even the bone-chilling differences in our geographical locations, had meant nothing to her limitless way of seeing and seeking sex. And so, Déjà had touched me the first chance she had gotten, and mixed herself into my destiny.

Four years later she had tested me, and initiated me as her own.

Now six years in the making, her time as Mentor had finally come.

Layering her story, she began to tell me more about her own mentor.

In Déjà's view, her teacher's most laudable sexual achievements centered mostly around his constant daily sex with teen and twenty something year old girls, both local and tourists, both amateurs and professionals; and the way that he had patiently prepared Déjà for her work as a self-empowered professional seductress of the highest order, and of the highest-paid kind—all of which he achieved in conjunction with his trusted job as a top-shelf Hotel Concierge.

Déjà also noted that he had never once, in all his years, had a serious sexual incident or scandal break on him. And she claimed that he had also taught her that "magical skill."

He had also prepared Déjà so well that, as a private high school student living in Hollywood, Florida (a separate city from her parents), she was quickly working the top-client lists of the very best hotels, escort services, as well as directly from her own list of clients in the greater Miami area, making as much as several thousand dollars a day any time she was in the mood.

And Déjà's sexual mood was a constantly rising matter.

She also told me with disturbing amusement that even her best paying repeat customers often languished for torturous months or even years, leaving unanswered messages one after the next, because they were too-boring to ever get an invitation or return call from her. And she talked about how her scheduled new clients (meaning strangers, a favorite of hers) and her waiting-list were so full she could usually be as choosey as she wanted.

As far as long term sexual partners, or other apprentices, it seemed to surprise Déjà (just as much as it did me) how hard it actually was for her to find sexual partners with a real actionable potential for the kind of energetic sexual expansion she saw as necessary.

In my mind, I thought that any young man would have followed Déjà to their eager death. But in reality, she told me how she could capture almost any boy, or man, or woman—who could be seduced—but that she would inevitably sexually tire of them, or overwhelm them, and/or just plain scare them away.

Déjà also told me that babies and little children had never made her feel very sexually aroused because they had nothing interesting to offer her—unlike me. And she explained that, though little boys old enough to have a crush on her and a hard-on had been "in-bounds" when she was a young-teen, very soon after that point in time it was the older, mature, and more successful men of the world who became her undisputable attraction and forte, which I understood completely.

And then she asked me if babies or really little kids had ever been sexually arousing to me, which, even at that time, seemed like an insane question! And I vehemently denied ever having had any such thoughts. And I told her how, instead, my sexual attention had always been directed toward older girls and women, like her.

Staring at me as if she had other questions in mind, Déjà instead moved-on to telling me about several other specific kinds of sexual acts, most of which I had never heard of before.

Because she had gathered her clients from one of the most concentrated and affluent tourist pools on Earth, with year-around domestic and international traffic, for at least five years so far, she was especially proud to have experienced and absorbed an enormous list of sexual experience, acts, and skills. During those years wealthy Asians, Germans, Eastern Europeans, French, Italian, Eastern Indian, African, Middle Easterners, North and South Americans, distant Islanders, and well-to-do persons from nearly every other Country and part of the globe had enacted whatever wild varieties of sexual behaviors they desired, or could imagine, across Déjà's outrageously willing body.

And she described them to me one after the next. And I saw that her hyperactive fascination and physical sexual enjoyment was boundless, and it made me feel so high I was dizzy. And after completing each of her short stories or elaborated descriptions, which were graphically and unhesitatingly communicated, she would ask me in total open candor:

"Have you ever done that?"

To which I would reply, "No." (Except in a couple of cases.)

"And I can't wait to see what kind of sexual partners I can find in this city, and at the college! What do you think, Rory?!"

"Geez Déjà, I don't know…" I struggled to respond, "I don't think we have anything like the big hotels and tourist places you had in Miami…"

"I'm not here to do that, Rory! I just want to have sex with a whole bunch of people from a city I don't know anything about! I want to do something different for a while. This is a big city, Rory. And I know that I can find what I'm looking for. I bet the college professors will be fun. And I might see what being in a sorority is like, but I'm not so sure about that…I just want to see-and-do something different! Who knows how long I'll stay…."

Pausing, I thought she might be done talking. But I had nothing to say or interject.

"Rory, tell me a story about what you do!"

"Déjà…, I don't do anything…"

"Yes you do! Don't lie, Rory! Tell me the most exciting way you have sex—or try to have it."

"I have sex with men I've never met before in public park bathrooms…"

"I've heard about that! And I've never done it!! See Rory-boy, you already did one thing I never did! You really are my perfect apprentice!"

And so, she enthusiastically got me to tell her exactly what public bathroom sex was like, as well as anything and everything else sexual from my life that she could get me to think of or remember. And she asked about my friends (which were few) and their levels of sexual experience (which was none). And sometimes, in the middle of what I was saying, she would spin off and run in some surprising direction with a sudden additional sexual memory, or thought, or idea of her own.

And the longer Déjà talked the softer and closer and more profound and totally trusting her connection to me developed. And as she began to slow down, with her eyes looking up and back into her own mind, she seemed to be reaching into her memories for anything else that needed to be exposed at this time.

Until, seemingly satisfied that she had completed what she had set out to do that night, her divulging declarations came to an end with this:

"I never told you yet, but my teacher was our neighbor from down the street. He had no wife or children of his own, but he is very nice and everyone likes him. Everyone in our town also looked up to him because he had an important job at one of the best hotels. And when I was eleven, because I was so smart, he told my parents that he had a little helper/assistants type job for me at that hotel. And that was that. As far as anyone knows I've been his good employee ever since, now eight years, until I came here. And no one else in the family has ever known anything more. And I only tell you this, because I'm *your* teacher."

Finally ready to stop, Déjà became quiet. I had emerged as her dearest little brother and sexual-student, with both of us tucked away together in the pre-dawn darkness for all the same reasons.

Even knowing all that I have come to know since, over the entire vast arc of my own experiences, I still cannot say whether it was what Déjà told me that night or what she had done to me the night before that shaped me the most.

Or, is it our adopted oldest cousin Maria that I should be bearing in mind?

Or, did my creation begin when my parents first used the word "ruined?"

Or, was I hypersexual even before I was born?

It is impossible to argue out: But it is definitely Déjà that I have always sensed in my hard beating heart, and seen in my mind's eye, and smelled inside my head, and needed inside my stomach.

During Déjà's heavy strokes of information I also became aware that an inordinate amount of my mental and emotional rush was coming from the fact that so much of this sex and the information it communicated was, by the cultural standards I was aware of, so terribly and obviously forbidden, wrong, sinful, illegal, and damned in every possible way. And the more outrageous, irregular, or even hideous the information was the more it meant to me in some struggling and unsettling way.

I became distinctly conscious that night that a part of me actually disliked and distrusted all people who didn't have abnormal sexual experiences and appetites. And the feeling of proudly having such unacceptable sexual beginnings, with no remnant of respect for the obviously irrelevant social control and judgment mechanisms in-place around me, suddenly made me feel strong, instead of weak.

Up until that moment in time I had been but a lowly beggar of sex: Now I was fully a part of a secret sub-culture of extremely active sexual abnormals and I LOVED IT! And I couldn't wait to know more! Maybe I wanted that even more than I wanted physical sex at that moment!

That night I became two people: my fake self, which was a shallow image held in place by my family, Jr. high school teachers, and my closest society's obvious expectations of me; and my *other* absolutely uncontrollably sexually driven and determined self.

From that night on, if I were to greet you honestly I would have to say it in two different ways.

"Hello."

~ and ~

"Hello, I am the one who will fuck you now..."

Admittedly, being two people at once is disconcerting, especially at first, no matter how excited you are about it. Sure, the liberty is unbearably enticing; but the vertigo of having a second soul that is falling so far and so fast is also a gut wrenching and unbalancing edge to step over.

If you have ever lied really, really big—and just barely gotten away with it; or broken a core family rule completely beyond tolerance—that wasn't even noticed; or if you almost died in something sudden like a bus hitting you while you were out doing something horribly sneaky and wrong—feeling partly dead inside and shockingly alive at the same time—then you would have an inkling into the flooding emotions that I was overfilled with that night.

Somewhere along the way, at around five o'clock in the morning, I could absorb no more.

"Déjà, I'm so tired…"

"No.., you're not too tired Rory-boy. You're my sweet *'Son of Midnight.'* Come lie down with me for a while."

An hour or so later, as dawn lightened the room, I awoke surprised to be in Déjà's glazed embrace. Feeling in-danger of discovery by my family, without a word I quickly slipped out of her bed, out of her room, and into my own new world.

The Next Day

Because it was still summer vacation, I crawled into my own bed and slept until late in the morning. When I got up, of course my first thought was for sex.

Breakfast, or brushing my teeth, or something along those lines would have been more normal, but I don't think I even ate breakfast that morning.

I knew that Déjà was going to be gone all day. And though she had already told me that she would be busy over the next several days, I couldn't help but hope that she would at least take me into her arms during the now unbearably alluring wee hours.

And though I also remembered that she had told me not to masturbate all the time, and to wait for her, on that day you better believe I was going to have sex of some kind, with somebody!

Out of habit I thought of my oldest brother and his friends first, but most of them were gone. And even when I tried to think of any who might still be living near, I remembered that I had never been the initiator of those kinds of meetings. And it was interesting to remember then that even though they knew how much I liked sucking their cocks—and they knew how much *they* liked it—all but one of them had "grown out" of having me do that a couple of years ago.

I then thought of all the girls in the neighborhood, including all my old so-called "girlfriends", and all of my older brothers' former girlfriends, all of whom I'd constantly hounded for kisses and tried to feel-up whenever I saw them. It was possible that I might be able to find one of them still around and bored enough to make-out with me.

My "sort-of girlfriend" at that time, (basically a girl at my school who'd let me act like we were going-together), wouldn't even let me kiss her on most days. I still adored her, emotionally, because she let me, but it was a one-way love affair. Plus, she'd been gone for most of the summer and just got back, and I hadn't talked to her yet, so I didn't even know if she still "liked" me at all. Regardless, I thought about her because she was so pretty to me. Just staring at her creamy-white face, with her lightly freckled cheeks, all framed by her thick curly brunette hair, felt sexual to me. (I'd also tried to hug-up on her older sister, who got mad, which almost got me into serious trouble with their mother.)

I then thought of my retarded neighbor who often wandered around behind his garage, for hours, unsupervised.

And I thought of doing a panty raid somewhere, maybe on one of my friend's moms or sisters (actually stealing the panties out of the homes, and masturbating while smelling them, as soon as I possibly could, always gave me a serious rush).

I also thought of my friend up the street who had a really nice fifteen year old sister, Ruth, who had several unfortunate and serious birth defects. Forced to live severely crippled and in a wheelchair, she was also a real sweetheart of girl who was deeply lonely for any kind of normalcy. And I knew that she dreamed of having a boyfriend. And it was painful to watch her when occasions like school dances came around, or even just on weekends when everyone else was going somewhere with their friends.

In my head I *knew* that Ruth and I were going to be together someday, for sure, and that I was going to make her feel beautiful, and that she would (even if only for a few minutes) forget her separation and seclusion; but that would require the perfect opportunity because she was watched very carefully by her parents.

And I thought of the public parks, even though finding sex at one of them at this early time of day would be highly unlikely. And, those parks were far away.

Pacing back and forth in my bedroom, not even dressed yet, already feeling sexually pressed, and knowing that jacking-off would not stop the desire, I logically decided that I had to try for the easiest and closest possible contact first: which would also mean having a kind of sex that was insanely against the social grain—which felt just right to me.

My next door neighbor Dwayne was almost my age but, because of his severe retardation, he acted like a kid half our age. Over the course of the time that I had lived next to his family he had learned to perceive me as a person who smiled at him, and who said "hello" to him in a kind and simple way. I might have even been the nicest kid on the block toward Dwayne, and he always tried to wave "hello" back at me.

His old-as-hell parents were also impressed enough by my kindness, and they often waved and smiled at me. And no one ever knew why those old folks had just one mentally handicapped kid, because no one ever talked to them. All I knew was that the old lady would let him (or maybe made him) stand around by himself in their backyard for hours at a time, almost every day.

Because I was horny enough that day, my mind went straight to the first place that I thought I might find a niche of leverage for my sexual knowledge.

Since he was a thirteen year old boy, I surmised that if I could get Dwayne to let me touch his cock, even from outside his pants, and then to suck on it, he might go right along with it; and maybe he would spontaneously repeat what he had seen and felt me do.

Whenever Dwayne tried to talk to me or say "hello", which he could not do, I could always tell which sounds were the more positive and happier ones. And I had always behaved toward him as if that was all I needed to know. And on that day, I still believed it was all I needed to know.

Climbing up onto the roof of our garage, I looked over into Dwayne's yard to see if he was out there. Making a careful visual sweep, I didn't see him anywhere. Sometimes he would be inside the garage, but only if the old man or woman was out there with him.

Tucking myself up beside a raised section of the garage roof, and hidden by the overhanging trees and the shadow of the deep shade, I unzipped my pants and decided to play with myself while I waited to see if Dwayne would show up. And of course, I fantasized about what I was hunting and hoping for...

When Dwayne finally appeared, because I was already so close to my orgasm, I just finished while I watched him walking around in his semi-conscious state of constant mild wonder. Because his head was usually twisted over and staring downward, I hoped that he at least found the grass, and the ground, and the cement of his driveway interesting and perhaps even beautiful.

And I was glad that I had cum from just thinking about having sex with him, because I knew that I could no more take Dwayne for a sexual partner than I could my own unwilling sister. What I sought was sexual connection, and adoration, and bliss, perhaps sometimes with a dash of seductive coercion, sure—but not with the taste of outright trickery, or potential fear, or personal disregard.

I wanted to be sexually *wanted*, so I climbed down off the garage and rode my bike to one of the big enough public parks some five miles away. And after spending a couple of unfruitful hours there (as it was still too early), I rode my bicycle to get some lunch and then continued to the next closest park, which was about another five miles away. After spending another several lonesome (and manually stimulated) hours there, I rode approximately three more miles to the nearest highway truck-stop bathroom where I finally serviced a big quiet fella who took less than five minutes of my time, and spoke only two words to me, which were, "Thank you."

Realizing that it was nearly dinner time, which I was obviously going to miss, I raced myself back towards my side of town and made it to my evening boxing workouts barely on time. And after spending the next two hours practicing footwork, and punching, and sweating, I was finally mentally free enough to realize how terribly hungry I was. I had only eaten one hamburger since I'd woken up.

And by the time I got home that day I had ridden my bicycle approximately twenty miles, and I had jacked-off to orgasm at least four times, and sucked one cock, which was disappointing but sufficient because it was actual sexual contact, and finally late evening had arrived and the sky was fully darkened. After a quick hello to my television watching parents, I devoured two big sandwiches, a big bowl of potato chips, and two big glasses of milk before descending into my basement bedroom.

Waiting for Déjà and the absolute sexual power that she wielded, I wished for midnight so badly you'd have thought I was a vampire child.

A sad vampire child: because Déjà did not come for me that night, or the next, or the next, for the next twenty or so days after that.

And during that time, not only had Déjà begun to have almost all her daily meals, including dinner, at the university—or wherever she really was—when she did arrive home for the night, other than the briefest of smiles and nods, she politely but completely ignored and avoided me.

Which, I guess I should have seen coming.

And all my heated follow-up questions about everything that she had told me about went cold. And I began to wonder if Déjà had moved on to other sexual adventures with more interesting people, in bigger and brighter places than my basement.

And for three wretched weeks I waited, and wilted.

Apprentice

Regardless of how long I waited, no amount of time would ever influence how much adoration I felt for Déjà, or how ready I was to take sexual flight with her again—in that sense, I was her faultless and faithful student. And in my mind, because of what she had already given me, I considered her my perfect mentor.

However, as far as the world at large is concerned I have to admit that Déjà did not seem sufficiently aware of, or considerate enough of the way she left all sexual and relationship boundaries shattered and wrenched open. Déjà was concerned with Déjà—which seemed right to me—she was the Goddess.

Obviously, I was born for the hypersexual life. So I found ways to endure. But, what Déjà had told me about my oldest cousin and others like her, while arousing to me for all the wrong reasons, was also frightening to me for all the right reasons.

As I mentioned, I had become "of two minds." And the saner one simply could not reconcile the actual kinds of sex that Déjà had described with the social world that I lived in. In my early nineteen-seventies religiously dominated mountain city society everything about anything other than marital sex was fully repressed. What I had grown up doing in my stolen moments of sexual desperation was already so far out of bounds I had basically taught myself to immediately forget what I had done, and put it behind me. But Déjà had introduced a whole new level of sexual experience, knowledge, and vision that I couldn't and didn't want to forget. But all rhetoric aside, the hard fact that so much of Déjà's sexually unhinged and pedophilic story was actually my own—made me afraid of myself.

At barely thirteen years old I stopped worrying only about "getting" sex—and a growing part of me started worrying about "what kinds" of sex I might create.

For instance, a couple of years before Déjà came to live with us I'd tried to get my youngest brother to have sex with me the way I did with our oldest brother, but because my little brother had not wanted to do it I had immediately stopped my advance, and never approached him again. But after Déjà came I began to fear that I might start ignoring that kind of signal altogether. I already did that more than I should with the neighborhood girls. And I'd had so many crazy sexual thoughts all my life: If I had to worry about actually *doing* those things, I was in some very deep trouble.

Quick sucking sex, like the truck stop, suddenly seemed relatively harmless, because all persons involved knew what sex to expect and could easily express a mutual agreement: Déjà's kind of sex seemed almost as if it did not require a mutual agreement.

I never saw her ask.

Déjà did steer me away from my one-year younger sister, who had also already refused me. And she rebuked my request that she teach my aforementioned younger brother (whom I had suggested out of what I now realize was an immature and misguided attempt at brotherly kindness). But neither of those decisions of Déjà's had anything to do with a moral or considerate boundary-mark that she recognized; she simply saw the much-much dimmer sexual lights in their too young eyes, as well as their lesser willingness to be so deceitful, and she was right.

As far as sexual intuition, seduction strategies, and carnal ability, Déjà was always undeniably right on the bulls-eye. However, as far as the after-effects that her sexual actions had on others, she had zero inhibitions and no definition of wrong.

For Déjà, the fact that the universe allowed her to do what she did was the only proof she needed of its rightness.

As her student, following her path, I left all the existing limitations and boundaries that I was aware of behind, including any hope of having any kind of control or say in my relationship with Déjà.

I also quickly gave up any hope and lingering illusions of ever getting any answers to all my questions. The very first time that I asked Déjà to tell me more about her teacher, and anything else that she knew more about, she'd looked at me with a weird mixture of annoyance and what appeared to be pity, and she answered me with a flat tone of finality.

"I told you that, already."

Déjà's sexual way was always forward. Everything I would learn from Déjà from there on out would come from my own observations, or from any random conversations that Déjà started, which were almost always about what we were doing at that very moment.

Describing it now makes it look disturbingly harsh and one sided. But the relationship definitely made a quick study out of me. And I knew not to waste any of Déjà's time.

Still, along with whatever other sexual explorations she was getting herself into, I did have something Déjà wanted—and wanted to continue stretching open.

In the beginning, as described, when she came to me it was always late at night and we would steal away into her room. But, as soon as that bored her it never happened again. And the rest of our sexual adventures took place outside my house, and far outside our suburban/rural neighborhood, which seemed uninteresting to Déjà.

The approximately thirty-five or forty additional sexual experiences that I had with Déjà over the course of the time that she lived in my family's house averages out to just one starved-for-feast every eleven days or so. Sometimes our sexual contact was more often, a couple times it was a couple days in a row, and sometimes I waited for weeks.

Thirty-five or forty sexual experiences with Déjà also equaled such a mind-blowing ladder of descent, in reality I hardly had time to absorb one new depth before the next one dropped me further. And sometimes what we had done would fulfill me so much, or blow my mind so much, it would last for days and days, perhaps even a week or two.

As a quickly growing teenager I was getting a little more muscular, and I was just tall enough, and smart enough, and confident enough to pass for being a few years older than I was. All of which helped me to move with even more freedom through all the loose curtains of my multi-layered world, which was the only way I could hope to keep up with Déjà.

When Déjà did let me run with her, not only did she plow me with whatever kind of sex she had in mind, whenever and wherever she wanted, she also took me out into her fully unfastened world to witness her powers. Usually, it would start with a phone call.

"Rory-boy, meet me at the Seventh Avenue bus station at five o'clock."

As if it were nothing more than a trip to the movies, in the beginning of the third month Déjà started our city outings with what she was most familiar with. Having rented a hotel room in the downtown area (with money from her own secret bank account from Florida), she had then taken me out into the evening for a nice dinner and to watch her pick up a man for "paid sex."

Standing on a dark corner or walking the streets in the shadowy part of the city was not at all Déjà's style for hooking a man: She could read men so well, she was the one fishing. In lieu of the super high-end hotels and resorts of Southern Florida, Déjà gravitated towards the high-end shopping district and our most upscale and brightly lit malls.

"All the men here have time on their hands, right Rory?" She explained. "And they have money, right? And, they think they can buy whatever they want…" She giggled. "Watch me from over there, Rory."

Observing her as carefully as I could, I sat on a bench and kept my eyes peeled. And it took her less than thirty minutes to spot and capture her prey.

Riding the bus home by myself, all I could think about was the way that she had simply walked around as a pretend shopper, moving her body in a slightly slower and more sensuous way, and placing herself in convenient pools of light, until she saw a man watching her *in that way*.

Immediately catching the man's full attention with a direct smile, she had then boldly walked straight up to him and begun talking in a very relaxed and inviting way. And once she was that close to him, it seemed as if the seductive artfulness of her physical mannerisms, and the smoothness of her conversation, had the effect of an inescapable magnet. In fact, I sat there and watched that man slowly close the last twelve inches between their bodies, first with a tentative hand, and then with a brushing leg, and then with a wrapping arm, and finally with a hug and a kiss on the cheek. After which, they left.

On my way home, and while I lay in bed trying to fall asleep, I repeatedly marveled at all these specific points, and at the overall deep rippling confidence that Déjà had displayed. And I eventually realized that these things were exactly what Déjà wanted me to be thinking about.

A few weeks later, when she had found the right man/john, she took me to watch them fuck, which was so uncomfortable for the man (even though Déjà had gotten him to agree) he almost couldn't perform (which Déjà quickly cured). And watching her like that was both erotic as hell, as well as a study in the psychology of sexual maneuvering. And I was absolutely fascinated by how differently she had spoken to this man. The tone of voice she was using was one I had never heard her use before. And in the conversation that we had sitting in the farthest backseat of the city bus following that event, Déjà tested me.

"Rory, why do you think that man agreed to fuck me in front of you?"

"Because…, he would do anything you told him to?"

"No. No, he wouldn't. He almost didn't go along with it tonight, because that whole situation was definitely beyond his limits. I know because when I met him and brought the idea up, he laughed at me. But I convinced him by challenging his manhood, in a sexy way of course. He went along with it, Rory-boy, because he thought that he was in-control, and that he was showing *me* how sexually strong he was, so he could continue to think he is the boss of me. He has no understanding that he was being submissive to my desires. And he could never think of himself as being anything but dominant, which is so stupid!" She laughed. "He's the opposite of real-extra-sexual—he's less-sexual."

Putting her explanations together with what I had seen, brought the whole scene into focus.

"That's why you were talking so differently to him."

"I felt like I was whispering, so I wouldn't scare him away—or make him mad! See how stupid! Lucky for him I thought of a fun enough reason to let him fuck me one more time. But that idiot will never see me again."

"He had a pretty good looking cock…"

"Ha, ha, ha, Rory-boy, you really are crazy! Now unzip your pants already, so I can suck on *your* good-looking cock, before the bus gets all the way to our stop."

In one of our next outings, when she had seen the right look from the right man, she pointed him out to me and calmly told me exactly what to say, and how to say it, and how much to charge him when he agreed to take me home with him. And that man, my first try ever, fell right into the heart-thumping open-aired perversion of it, and he took me right to his house and fucked me in his wife's bed.

As Déjà had instructed me (while standing there looking at the man), I'd told him that I was sixteen (a lie), that I was very-very attracted to him (a straightforward seduction), that I had noticed him looking at me (an admission of flattery), and that I was a little short of money (a position of evident "submission"). Standing right there in the middle of that mall, in less than five minutes, she had also showed me how to better move my body around, and how to barely touch myself while I talked openly to him about the sex we could be having. And she showed me how to make small sex-noises in my throat while I talked, and how to use them for punctuation. And she showed me how to use unflinching eyes and my smile, alternately staring at the man's eyes and then directly and longingly at his crotch, which she said would lock it all down.

And I realized that I already knew some of this from the public park bathroom's, (although many of those meetings required absolutely no conversation), and that Déjà's abilities were advanced extensions of a language that I *did* understand.

And I was so excited to have "worked" my first john at the age of thirteen and a half! And Déjà was just as proud as she could be! And the fifty dollars I made (in less than fifteen minutes of actual sexual contact) bought us the best dinner we could find!

And for a few weeks Déjà dressed me up a little and took me out more regularly. And she showed me a rainbow of angles and approaches to opening a sexual dialogue with people in all kinds of public places, like clothing stores, and other retail shops, restaurants, hotel lobbies, art galleries, banks, and even parking lots. And because Déjà usually used the weekend nights when I could say that I was sleeping over at one of my school friend's houses, I could stay out all night with her.

Within a few months though, catching johns with me was already becoming a bore to Déjà. So, after taking another lengthy break from me, she returned and commanded me to show her what public park bathroom sex was about.

Of course, Déjà blew the doors off every park bathroom that she entered: attracting men in like bees to honey, absolutely unafraid, sometimes surrounded by three and four men at a time—and always with me no farther away than a naked arm's-reach.

And it blew my mind how her self-possessed attitude and different way of behaving changed the sexual scene inside those bathrooms so significantly. Compared to the usually in-all-ways muted demeanor of such places, what Déjà was able to do inside a public bathroom seemed like a magical transformation. For instance, because she was smart enough and brazen enough, she always made sure (through confident and unhesitating verbal commands) that someone was on the look-out (even if it had to be me) so that everyone else would have the earliest possible warning if a patrol car entered the park, which created an actual "environment of safety", which in turn created an almost unimaginable difference in the energy and vibration of the sexual contact and events that she spontaneously engineered.

I had seen occasions where men did the same kind of "look-out" thing, but that was a rarity because it required at least three men, and a more complex non-sexual conversation, rather than the ruling experience of two men meeting and having sex as quickly as possible, and with as few words as possible.

I was also surprised that during the trips we made to the park bathrooms I never saw a single man turn away from Déjà—even though the sex that went on in those places, day in and day out, was strictly man-on-man. And for those men, the differing reasons for deciding on a potential partner had always seemed to me to be a strictly hit-and-miss kind of thing. And many, many men had turned away from me. But as soon as each man that I observed saw Déjà, they were at first surprised (even shocked), and then they headed straight for her.

Interestingly, because of my ultra-obvious and special connection to Déjà (which she made sure was clear), I never had a single one of those men physically challenge me, or ask me why I had to be there (which I worried about). Many of them did look at me with a rather burning curiosity, and sometimes an admiring jealousy, and I think that some of them assumed we were brother and sister, but ultimately they were too busy obeying Déjà to ever question exactly how or why we did these things together. And if she ever wanted to move a man's attention away from me, she would simply say something like:

"HEY YOU, come over here and show me your cock already!"

Eventually, during our fourth or fifth trip to the biggest park in the city, in an interesting turn of events for everyone involved, Déjà began taking her greatest delight in having the men we met do anything and everything sexual she could imagine, or fancied at the moment, to me.

(And yes, you may imagine—and I can guarantee that it happened).

Sometimes she liked to make the men do the exact same sexual act to one of us, and then the other. Or, sometimes her sexual mind might go in the other direction, and she would make the men watch us do sexual things to each other. And I saw many men cum helplessly onto their hands and the floor before they could even get a turn with either of us, because just the sight of us doing what we did was too much for them.

I also saw Déjà, naked and half covered in cum, respond to an older man who had become too aggressive with her by grabbing him by the naked-balls and dropping him to his knees—screaming into his face that she would rip them off his body if he ever touched her again! And even though everybody else in the room had more or less frozen in-place, Déjà had then looked straight at the biggest other man in the bathroom and commanded him to throw the injured older man out, which he did instantly. And which, sent Déjà straight back into her whipping sexual feast, setting-in on the big guy who had served as the bouncer first. And even though I think she had been scared of the older man—she was something *else* even more (hypersexual, and a fighter instead of a runner).

I also remember that during our next trip into the city, while we were again riding in the back of a city bus, she had nonchalantly handed me a single-blade fold-out pocket-knife, and had then told me that if anyone ever grabbed onto her to "stab them until they let go."

And when I seemed surprised, and inadvertently showed some fear or hesitation, she had looked down at me and said derisively, "My teacher gave me my first knife when I was your age. I thought you were a fighter?!"

Stung, and smart enough not to talk back to Déjà, I had sat quietly for a handful of minutes. And as I worked the knife open and closed, and felt it in my grip, imagining how that blade would augment my boxing skills of striking fast with either of my hands, I became certain that I *could* stab someone if they ever tried to hurt *my* Déjà.

Another lesson came from how I saw Déjà instantly veer away from certain men, on several occasions, even when they had seemed to be looking at her. And what I finally noticed they shared in common was an obvious air of physical and self-confidence mixed with aggression. It's a hard thing to describe, but for whatever group of reasons in the arena of sexual contact humans usually, somehow, clearly reveal how submissive, or dominant, or aggressive they will be. (Note the word "usually" because those who purposely hide their intentions in moments of human contact like this can be extremely clever and dangerous.) But, as for all the other men, it seemed to me then that they were all too surprised and sexually happy to see us to even think of causing trouble over being too aggressive. I also think that the fact that Déjà and I were together—meaning more than one lone-person—also made a big difference. And trouble is just something that most sneaking perverts avoid out of practiced habit, if they can. Trouble isn't what they're looking for.

I also saw, only once, how she dealt with a man who decided to take public offense at her sexual advances. When he had stepped backwards from Déjà, too surprised at what she'd said, and then his face changed into that judgmental-and-shocked look, and he lifted his hand up to point at her *in that judgmental way*, and he opened his mouth to admonish her—she lit up like a siren and started yelling, "HELP!!! STOP THAT YOU PERVERT!!! SOMEONE HELP ME!!! SOMEONE HELP ME!!! PERVERT!!! PERVERT!!!"

Occupying the "stage" like a professional actress, Déjà had held her arms up and waved them around like a struggling victim, and screamed at the top of her lungs—all the while looking that man in the eyes with a dead-calm stare that was gut-freezing—which made him turn in terror and hurriedly stumble in the opposite direction.

I would say that most of Déjà's flashing anger had come from that man's judgmental accusation against her, which she rejected wholeheartedly, and the smaller portion from her own failure to seduce him. But she had never really considered herself in danger of him, or perhaps any sexualized situation that I saw, which I now, these many years later, know was her own form of denial.

More importantly, observing first-hand how Déjà really affected people with her searing temper, her explosive power, her quick action, her razor-sharp mind, and her insanely confident behavior was an education in itself: visceral and valuable, and immediately empowering.

Somewhere past the mid-year, when Déjà seemed to hit another wall of boredom, this time with her college life, on four occasions she asked me to take her to a porn theater, of which there were only a half-dozen in my city. I knew them all, and I had gone into every one of them to steal magazines. But, because of my age I was usually kicked-out of them before long. With a hat and sunglasses on I could pass for a short eighteen year old for a while, but not much longer. And I didn't care in the least when I did get caught and kicked-out, because I usually already had a magazine tucked into my pants or jacket. I had also hung out a few times in the alleys looking for sex by the rear exits behind each of those theaters, but the police cruised those alleyways too often, and it felt too exposed and risky compared to the parks (and most often, I think the men coming out of the theaters had just had an orgasm, which severely decreases their immediate desire for sex.)

However, Déjà's differently informed attitude was that she could walk into any sexual situation and totally own it. And, she had been in some theaters in Florida with clients (which she said had been exciting but also disappointing, making me think that the men had been in-charge).

And, as I expected, Déjà did things in those theaters that I have never seen equaled or topped in any of the perhaps one thousand porn theaters and shops that I've visited since. Simply said, in a public setting of this kind I've never personally observed an individual who was born with the kind of sexual wings that Déjà could spread open.

Similar to her incautiously released behavior in the public bathrooms, in the porn theaters Déjà had no interest in being careful, or sly, or secretive, or choosey, or slow about creating her own sexual realities.

On one occasion she walked in the front door and straight up to the man behind the counter, and as she unbuttoned her thin shirt and hiked her short skirt up over her naked hips she said, "You get to be first; lock the front door."

Grabbing a "Will Return At:____" sign, the man ran to the front door and back. And this started a spontaneous gang-bang in the front magazine and video room that lasted for over an hour and blew every man's mind who was already inside the store and wanted to join in, many of whom had wandered in from the theater room and couldn't believe their eyes or their luck!

On another occasion Déjà walked into the main theater room and did the most humorously released strip-show I've ever seen, right in front of the movie screen, giggling and laughing so hard she sounded like she was singing, whipping her few clothes off and placing them on a seat right in the middle of the front row. And another ten or so shocked men got mega-fucked that day like lascivious lottery-winning idiots.

And like royalty of some odd kind Déjà and I never paid to go into those theaters, and none of the store workers or managers ever asked how old I was when we walked through their doors holding hands and sporting smiles that bespoke of our higher sexual station and power. Not one porn shop worker ever even questioned us, accept one female worker (whose presence behind the counter, circa 1974, surprised the hell out of me) but she was immediately told to "shut-up" by her senior manager, who immediately invited Déjà into his office. I, of course, gave the female worker the "inviting eye", but she wasn't into it (I think because she was too busy being pissed-off about how beautiful Déjà was).

And almost always, whether I had been included already or not, Déjà finished our porn theatre visits by having some man, or men, fuck me silly in some way that appealed to her on that day.

I thought then, and think still, that in many of those sexual events she was—watching me, being her—in a boy's body. I know this because of the way she would talk to me during those moments, holding my head in both her hands while some random man fucked me or played with my cock: She was actually talking to herself.

And I was honored to have heard her self-aimed dialogue.

"Ohhh, that's good Rory... That's it... Let them all fuck you... Let them all do whatever they want to you... Yes..., you can make those sounds even louder... Tell them how much you love it... Tell them not to stop..."

By that point in time Déjà was staying in inexpensive hotels that she used for days and perhaps weeks at a time. I didn't know for sure, because she didn't tell me what happened between the times I got to see her. And her cover story to my parents for why she was sleeping away from our house so often was that she had made friends with some dorm girls and some other girls with apartments in the city. I did know that she had plenty of spending money, most of which her parents had no idea of. I also knew, by then, that she had dropped out of most of her college classes.

Of course, whenever I got to go to one of her hotel rooms I wanted to stay with her and never leave. And a few times when I concocted a weekend long sleep-over excuse with my friends as cover, and was able to convince her, Déjà did let me stay for one or two nights and days with her, which are my very favorite memories. During those times I would imagine that we would live together forever. And when we went out in public she would dress me up and hold my hand and pretend that I was her boyfriend, but she would still do all the talking at the hotel desks, and the restaurants, etc. However, eventually I would be dismissed from our beautiful escape with a curt "You better go home, Rory-boy."

Imagining all of what Déjà did with all the time she spent away from me was like envisioning the life of an actual super-human being. I still bow in wonder.

In the ninth and tenth month, in another change of venue, we started spending the afternoons and evenings that we were together wandering around the more affluent college area of the city. Walking hand in hand along the streets that had all the shops and restaurants, or around the student housing neighborhoods and condos, going to the coffee shops and pizza houses where the students and professors gathered, looking for odd sexual adventures and interesting pick-up opportunities for each other, or both of us. And our conversation was all our own, and no matter where we were we talked about things ranging from cock size, to vaginal dryness, to emotionally controlling a random sex partner, to clothing fashion, to skin lotion, to favorite TV characters. It didn't matter what we talked about, it only mattered that I was talking to Déjà.

During that period I got to have sex with a couple random college girls, with Déjà's giggling help and match-making. And I blew those older girl's minds, and fucked their pussies, and sucked their mouths, and bodies, and cunts so good they couldn't believe it.

I also got to watch Déjà pull in a bunch of random lucky fellows, both younger and older, who attracted her unpredictable attention. It was fun, and a proud victory of our peculiar friendship for us to watch each other walk away to have sex with a new person.

And, though we often agreed to wait for each other in a pre-designated place, as a reassuring re-connecting point, we didn't always meet back up. And at those times, it felt extremely invigorating to me to be alone and free like that.

Déjà told me then that as far as the college guys went she definitely preferred professors rather than partners her own age. Though, for all I knew, she had fucked the whole football, basketball, and wrestling team, as well as my oldest brother and all his friends on her own time. But I did believe her, and understood why she would be even more attracted to older men.

And I remember wondering a few times what all this was like compared to the amazing sexual life and power that Déjà had described enjoying on her home ground in Miami. And I worried that it might be disappointing to her.

And so our intermittently manic and unbalanced sexual explorations continued to progress for dizzyingly deviant month after outrageously salacious month, until the next summer had arrived.

Amazingly, that was also one of my best years at school, even though I missed more days than anyone would believe (exactly one day less than half, which was the minimum requirement in those days for being graded). Because of those missed days I did have to quit the wrestling team part way through that year, which made me a "loser" and an even more pronounced pariah in my family. Fortunately, my after school boxing training could continue at a more patient rate, and with a lot less pressure on a weekly or monthly basis. Boxing competitions were spread out to only a handful per year, and each boxer usually ended-up doing only two or three at most. And, because the boxing gym's main trainer was an unapologetically contrary man with differently angled points of view from most conservative people on almost everything, my parents also left that part of my life alone, which was a great gift. When I did show up at the gym he worked me as hard as I could stand; and when I didn't show up he never asked or seemed to care where I had been.

But, as far as school work went that year, when I wasn't with Déjà I was doing whatever I had to, or could do, to be ready to take off with her whenever she beckoned me. Because of my need I was always as far ahead on my homework as possible in case Déjà told me to miss the next day. And I made sure that my grades were good enough (3.8) that neither of my parents would have a second thought about me (school grades being the only part of my life they actually did keep track of).

And not only did I keep Déjà completely secret, of course nobody from my neighborhood or family ever saw or heard anything about my public park, or porno shop, or truck-stop sex, or my slowly growing penchant for daytime mall prostitution, or my developing sperm-bulimia (which I had started doing when I swallowed sperm as my own idiotic brand of protection against sexual diseases, though I, like Déjà, took absolutely no other precautions).

And even though my family had noticed that I was missing dinner much more often, and that I was usually gone somewhere until as late as possible, and that I almost always seemed to have money of my own—the stupidest string of excuses worked on them like a charm bracelet.

One of the best "cover stories" I invented toward the end of that school year was my "landscaping helpers" job, which I told my parents was run by exactly the kind of grease-stained and rough manual laborer they would never want to meet, which gave me both an excuse for the money I had, as well as a good deal of the time I spent away.

For me, the hardest thing of that time was dealing with all the hours and days that Déjà and I weren't together. And in all those months we had *never once* talked about anything having to do with ordinary relationships, or anything like that, especially something as boring and common as clinging attachment.

Déjà lived and breathed according to her own mercurial intuition to the exclusion of all other modes of consideration. And questions or hesitations about anything were just stupid-doubts to Déjà; so I never questioned her. But when I just followed her, flowing along with her like water, she was one-with-me as intently as if the world might end in the middle of our immediate sexual journey.

At those times Déjà always shined and shimmered and seemed to somehow dance in-place even when she was holding still. With her body's aura lit by the raging sexual-synaptic-storm that was almost constantly going on inside her brain, there was no hiding her presence.

And men could sense her bristling sexual energies the second they laid eyes on her.

Eventually, about a month after the end of Déjà's spring semester, in the first part of July, she told me that she wanted me to accompany her to the house of a professor who had given one of her sociology classes a lecture on "The Non-Majority Religious Nature of American Social Sexual Morality" or something like that.

She also told me, with a snort, that he had flaunted his pair of Ph.D.'s and issued a challenge to the students to "Explore the freedom of finding your own sexual moralities and philosophies."

Déjà, it seemed, was planning some kind of extra-credit summer project as an answer to his challenge. And before I'd even met him, or heard a single word of his lecturing, even though I was still a month shy of fourteen years old, I knew that this professor had talked-down to the wrong "student."

As it turned out, and was explained to me at the last possible moment, as we approached the upscale downtown high-rise apartment building, Déjà had already begun her personal project with this professor. And now, she had decided that it was time for the nearly sixty year old man, Aaron, to break some of his own long held boundaries and accept his heretofore unacknowledged homosexual side, which is why she had brought me along.

I remember thinking, "Cool, I love sucking cock in front of Déjà."

However, according to her nature, Déjà took it a lot farther than that. And she started with a simple command.

"Professor Aaron, I'm only going to tell you this important instruction once: You're not to speak—not one word. If you speak, I'll leave angry. Today is the day that *you* get to listen, and learn."

And it seemed to me that Déjà had brilliantly taken away this man's most powerful personal ability, and mental-shield—his power of verbal dominance.

In order to compel Professor Aaron through a full regimen of flamingly gay and bisexual acts—much of which she forced him to look-at and watch in his massive bedroom mirror—Déjà exercised and vented an extraordinary amount of physical spirit and mental marksmanship. And in the process Professor Aaron experienced an array of mind-melting sex with me in so many ways, mixed in with sex with Déjà in so many ways, he could hardly keep his own personal footing. And at one point, when I was sitting on top of him astride his penetrating cock, and Déjà was sitting on his face smothering him with her flowing wetness (she may even have been pissing a little), I'm sure I heard him cry-out, but the sound was instantly cut-off by Déjà's repositioned and fully muffling ass-crack and pussy.

By the end of it, the Professor was irrevocably and erotically gay, and inescapably bi-sexual, and I believe he had been implanted with a whole new level of sexual hunger.

I'd felt it. And even if he wasn't sure what it meant, yet—he'd felt it. He'd also had sex with a young teenage boy, and lost himself in it, and I had a good sense that this fact was going to cause some lasting conflict for him.

For one reason, Déjà had initially told him that I was sixteen (which was legal age at that time, in that state), but then at the end she revealed that I was still a few months short of fourteen years-old. And then, astounding me, she also suddenly told the Professor a shortened but challengingly detailed version of how she believed I was sexually created by our oldest cousin, all as a pointed response to his theoretically supporting a "personal sexual moral-model." All of which was so inundating to Professor Aaron, who was still forbidden from talking, all he could do was make a facial expression of helplessness.

When we left, the look on Professor Aaron's face was that of a man seriously perplexed by his recent momentous sexual experience. And I felt some empathy for him. I also felt a shamelessly mounting power over an unsuspecting world.

As we walked away from the high-rise building, Déjà spoke one sentence to me.

"I'd like to see him philosophize about that."

As we rolled back toward the city center that night, staring out the big public bus windows at all the passing lights, I told Déjà that I would bet my life that she could have sex with the President of the United States—if she wanted to. And when she didn't laugh at that, but instead smiled, I knew just how confident she was.

Historical Figure

A few weeks later, when I hadn't seen Déjà around for maybe ten days or more, one evening at dinner my father told the family members at the table that Déjà had gone back to Florida.

No additional explanation was given, just a decidedly strained silence.

I didn't even get to say goodbye to her.

I would have thrown up right then and there, but my father violently hated when anything untoward disrupted the dinner table. And, to be totally honest, there was also something all-too-familiar about this sudden and total lack of such important details, and all the wandering emotions that kind of void will leave.

Part of me just hit an emotional flat-line, and coldly viewed the emptying moment as perfectly fitting. Part of me was so broken I lost all feeling in my body.

And the special place in my mind that had "seen" all those exploding lights, and raining colors, and aural glowing around Déjà's naked body and the sex it exuded, was also lost.

I still "see" a certain shimmering at the edge of my vision during sex and orgasm, occasionally, more with some partners than others, and my pleasures are certainly nonetheless. But the beautiful cascading and nearly blinding mental lights that had surrounded Déjà were gone with her.

Déjà had lived with my family for exactly eleven months and ten days. And I had to believe that it had been a sexual incident that forced her out—what else could it have been? I was never told, as usual. And not one additional word was ever spoken about it.

I always thought that she must have sexually approached my father. Why would I think that? Because I knew what was irresistible to Déjà, and that her habitual attraction began right where things became forbidden or would normally be considered sexually impossible.

Or, it could have been something that happened on the university campus. Or, she could have been arrested at a shopping mall—how could I even hazard a guess?

Regardless, for months I held out a hope that Déjà would return (while progressively picking up from my parents that such a thing would never happen).

So I began building a dream of going to Florida when I had graduated from high school and was old enough to travel wherever I wished, which was about five years away.

Then, sometime during the next year, the one additional piece of news about Déjà that did make it all the way to my ears was that she was now planning to attend university somewhere in Pennsylvania or New York. And my dream of finding Déjà and being with her slipped even farther away.

The truth was, I knew damn well that I'd never dare to mention such an idea to Déjà because she would have laughed in my face. Attachment or common relationship behaviors were the antithesis of her always expanding sexual movement.

And how could I have ever sustained a relationship with her anyway, anywhere? We were cousins (second cousins, but same thing in American culture). Before six months had past, my most honest intuition, however personally obliterating, was that Déjà, as I had known her, was gone forever.

Imagining all the myriad possibilities of what sexual calamity had taken Déjà away was, as usual, my only way of filling in the blanks; and I'm also pretty sure that this method is a less than healthy way to have to process life's most important matters.

At the age of fourteen I realized that I was on my own. On occasion, to ease the pain, I would smell and wear the one pair of lacey panties that I had dared to steal from Déjà, touching myself more slowly and more thoroughly as a way of being with her again.

Picture Me

During the following year I was living every day on an even sharper razor's edge of sexual danger than I ever had before. If a day neared its end and I had not yet achieved some kind of deviant gratification—I was out my basement window and into the night until I had.

Wandering around in the darkness, sometimes stripping myself completely naked, sometimes lurking around homes, sometimes masturbating in a backyard while I watched the family inside, or in the back of a city bus while I looked at the people on board, making my way from public bathroom to public bathroom, the porno theatres and alleys, and the one truck stop I knew of, traveling across the lonely nightscape, burning with sexual needs that could be so torturous sometimes I wished my breath could stop.

And though it was potentially even more dangerous than all the rest, because I had to go into their homes or to a hotel room with them, I did continue to find mellow-looking johns (as Déjà had taught me) and made a little money while I sought my full range of sexual rushes.

However, even though I had learned to move instantly away from any men in those public arenas that I felt a certain kind of aggressiveness from, and I was definitely becoming much more physically confident, I was caught off-guard in a bathroom by a much bigger man and I was raped again (though not very violently, because I quickly and very obviously submitted).

Even more confusing, sometimes I couldn't quite tell or clearly remember later why I had chosen to submit to certain things that happened. And in some cases I thought that perhaps I was just getting too sensitive to being told what to do. And though I loved to be touched, I started to notice when a "touch" became a forcefully guiding "push" or a differently "insistent pull."

At the end of that year, in the mid 1970's, as I began my sophomore year at High School, I had also started smoking and selling weed, and then dosing and selling LSD, which I got from Burt, who was in his third year at the local State College.

(He had only asked me once what it was like having Déjà living in our house. And when I had given him an evasive answer, he just took it with an oddly accepting shrug. And when I later asked him if she had ever come to see him, and he blew me off with another shrug, that conversation was ended.)

I was also drinking any kind of alcohol that I could, which I did on the weekends with the kids that I sold weed and LSD to. And my school work turned to shit, skating all the way down to the first "D" grades of my life.

But my training at the boxing gym had stayed steady and even increased. Sometimes working out at the gym, as early as I could (often when skipping the second half of school), was the only thing that kept me sane. And even when I did workout, as soon as it was over I was getting intoxicated in at least one way or the other (which became a pattern I've eventually lived with for decades). But no matter when I showed up, the main trainer, Mel, would always greet me with a surprised, if-gruff sounding enthusiasm, sending me right to work with whoever was moving around on the floor that evening. And that was also the year that I started taking the new self-defense classes, and situational awareness courses. They even had a three week knife-fighting course that first summer.

As an unexpected development, along with being the new drug dealer in the high school I also, all-of-a-sudden became somewhat of a sexual figure (for lack of a better term) to the teenagers of the freshman class, and then the sophomore, and then the junior class girls! Even my old reputation as a "groper" suddenly turned in my favor!

And again, it was the mid 1970's, so Déjà's layer of reality was an intricate overlap to the still alive-and-struggling peace-love movement that had begun in the late 60's.

At fifteen years old, it seemed that the sexual interests of the rest of my age group were finally catching up (a bit), and many of the girls who already knew me also started seeing and feeling something different about me. And what they started letting me do to them delighted me, though it far too often stopped short of what I really wanted to do, even when they let me touch or kiss their pussies, or finger fuck them a little.

And I began to see an unexpected side to what Déjà had left me with: Along with the incredible drive that she had accelerated in me, she had also given me the power to easily and reliably carry other people to the destinations and the limits of their own sexual curiosities and desires.

As long as I didn't go too far, too fast, or tried to go somewhere unwelcomed too many times, the sexually transporting effect I could have on people was starting to be productive

During that school year I was even asked by several slightly younger girls to teach them how to French-kiss. So, for a couple of hours I held instructional court at one girl's home: taking each girl into a bedroom for five or ten minutes at a time (while the rest of them waited and giggled in the kitchen and living room), teaching each girl very carefully, requiring at least three or four rounds—for good practice—with fully open and relaxed question-and-answer breaks in between. I even got to stop for a milk and cookie break that the girls had very considerately thought of. And I remember feeling good about my ability to help even those girls who wore braces (two of them) to be much more relaxed and confident in their kissing. And it was extraordinary to me how much, and in such a different way, I was excited by that so innocent sexual incident.

In fact, being willingly accepted at any normal social level had a certain taste that I was finding more attractive than I would have expected. Now that the girls were more receptive, just kissing and making out with them seemed somehow on more of an equal sexual level with sucking cock or letting a man fuck me than I could easily explain.

Still, no kind of sexual contact that I was able to find was as powerfully flowing, fully confident, totally encompassing—or just plain pushed-past-reasonable—as the sex that Déjà had created.

At the time, I really didn't know if the more usual and acceptable types of sexual interactions were just another new flavor of my sexual exploration, or if they were now a meal that I would need as part of my continuous sexual diet. Either way, it was a strange and ominous feeling because I was thoroughly aware that I could never be part of any truly customary relationship.

In that same year, I would be arrested twice. The first arrest was for loitering near a park bathroom, which I was able to explain away to my parents much too easily, with some lame lie or another.

(I had actually been fully engaged in masturbating outside the bathroom when the cop suddenly appeared from around the back of the building barely six or so yards away from me. Fortunately, because I had [barely] managed to tuck my cock and balls back through my zipper while making about twenty running steps, before the cop got hold of my arm, all he could conclusively say in his report was that I had been "loitering". I guess because I was a minor they didn't charge me for running or resisting.)

The other arrest happened when a city bus driver smelled pot on me, and two cops got on the bus and found a pipe and a bag of high-end weed tucked into the seat crevice right next to where I had been sitting.

And again, because I was a minor, legally speaking I walked away with little more than a slap on the wrist.

However, that arrest basically finished off my relationship with my father, because to him "the law was the law", and he was especially disgusted by illegal drugs. And, though I was sorry toward him in a certain way, I couldn't help but be glad because it meant that I was fully free from both my parents.

So, not unlike many other teenagers, I lived without even the slightest shred of adult supervision, or real connection, or trust.

Interestingly, those two arrests made zero difference in my sexual hyperactivity. Having only two bad legal incidents occur among all the hundreds of illegal and creeping sexual things that I had done during those years of my life was, if anything, quite encouraging.

Also encouraging to me, was the fact that I had gotten into several fights with bullies at school, and one really crazy fight with two guys I didn't even know at a city bus stop—and I had won them all! I'd even pulled my knife out once when I was threatened by an older drunk one evening while I was walking the downtown strip! And I liked the way it felt to know that in a street-fight I would never be so afraid that I would freeze-up or fail to make my own moves—no matter who was fucking with me.

Even if I had to temporarily sexually submit against-my-will again sometime, I had become determined to at least escape my next sexual attacker, the reality of whom I had come to expect.

What was really bothering me was the fact that it was (nearly, or actually) impossible to create anything that held the same amount of sexual charge that Déjà had brought into our experiences. I could get close, especially by doing some of the things that we had done together, or by getting together with a brand new girl I'd met somewhere, but even then it was still missing "Déjà."

By then, now more than a full year since Déjà had gone, I was also having as many as five or more orgasms every day, and hopefully at least one or two of those orgasms was experienced in the midst of a person-to-person interaction.

Too often, though, I would find myself somewhere alone late at night, prowling around in my never ending search for sex. And in those quieted times, when I would find my mind suddenly outside my hypersexual body for a moment—what I would see was so shocking it alarmed me.

I'll describe it in a kind of snapshot.

Place the scene at roughly 11:00 p.m. to 2:00 a.m. on any random night of the week:

...a fairly intelligent and otherwise physically healthy teenage boy finds himself laying his completely stripped naked body and sensitive skin onto the dim glowing tile floor of a public park bathroom (or porn theatre, YMCA locker room, truck-stop shower, college library bathroom, etc.), closing his eyes and deeply breathing the sharply tinged air into his lungs, he openly masturbates his aching red cock and wet pulsing anal sex-hole as slowly as he can possibly stand, going on for thirty or forty or ninety minutes, straining back at the very edge of orgasm again and again, desperately waiting to share it, with a thousand inescapably perverse visions exploding in his brain, and all fears and concerns black-holing away in the insanely dangerous exhibitionism and erotic delirium, until, against his every will to make the internally burning bliss last forever, his own star glistening sperm explodes out into his cupping hands or, through gymnastic positioning against some cold wall, he drains his life-singing-load directly down into his own gaping mouth—still hoping

fervently that some sexually demented stranger will walk in and do something even more depraved to him…

"Click." Picture me.

She is Déjà, the Dark Sexual Goddess: I am her Roaring Son of Midnight.

Chapter Nine

Old Enough for Sex
First Sexual Contact by Choice

About a year and a half after Déjà left me, I met a girl at school who was so completely from the other side of the sexual range of experience she stopped me in my tracks.

Not expecting it, this virgin girl would expose me to something sexual I had never seen or known before, or even imagined: Having first sexual contact through fully aware personal choice, and at an appropriate age.

I am the wide witness Rory, and it is my honor to introduce you to Abbey.

Abbey

When Abbey was a perfect little devout Catholic girl in elementary parochial school she started to touch and rub and play with her pussy on a very regular basis, especially in bed as she fell asleep.

After progressing into a more rushing type of masturbation, which was aided by the water faucet of the family bathtub, and which made her very happy for another several years, she then began to explore deeper.

Without much extra thought or hesitation, when the desire arose, Abbey then started her inner vaginal worship with a very small, smooth, and thin handled comb, which she intuitively knew would be perfect for the delicious penetrating pleasure that she suddenly craved to the point of undeniable need.

At that time Abbey was no more than a skinny little eleven or twelve year-old girl, with ivory-white skin, and long legs, and long curly brunette hair, and hazel-brown eyes, and breasts that hadn't even sprouted yet—the nasty little thing.

But she was most certainly *not* ready for sex with another person, by many years yet. And if any person had tried to have sexual contact with Abbey at that age it would have terrorized her.

Fortunately, inside the guarded quiet of the locked bathroom in her family's home, Abbey's sexual pleasures and explorations were granted undiscovered and uninterrupted bliss for year after lovely year.

Which is what makes Abbey's own descriptions and revelations about a person's private early sexual life so vital and important to me: I believe that Abbey may have had the most un-complicated, unpolluted, un-swayed, un-pressured, unhurried, and un-worried early sexual life of any that I have heard of (or at least the equal to any other.)

The only so-called traumatic or shocking type of sexual occurrence in Abbey's young life was that she had once found a folded-up pornographic picture in the weeds near her home that depicted sex in the doggie-style position, which had actually been a huge turn-on for her rather than any kind of negative experience.

The only challenging sexual "issue" that Abbey had been forced to struggle with was that—when seen through the eyes of her religion and strictly religious family—her daily masturbation sessions and fantasizing about sex was an unholy and detestable sin. But Abbey didn't see her own personal pleasures through anyone's eyes but her own. Perhaps because, as a sweet preteen Abbey had already *known* that she wasn't "bad", so neither was her sexual enjoyment.

I also think that it is exceedingly important and instructive, and even enlightening, to acknowledge that Abbey's sexual story also started around the same age as Cee Cee's, and Déjà's, and myself. But I don't want to digress.

For whatever reasons or fortunate happenstance, Abbey's early life sexual experience seemed to me (I suppose especially to someone like me) to have been so much more healthy than so many of the other stories I knew, and came to know, and her privacy was somehow more respected by her surroundings, and her desired physical expansions were guided solely by her own personal choices.

In line with all that, Abbey's slowly maturing desires for actual sexual contact with others came to her only after she had, over the course of several years, worked her way through the whole comb and brush handle selection in her family's bathroom, and she was feeling ready for something bigger, and something even more exciting.

As she told it to me, by the time she was contemplating something distinctly larger, like the small end of her un-plugged curling-iron, at the age of about thirteen and-a-half, she was definitely beginning to desire and fantasize about sitting on a hard cock. And by the age of fourteen, she suddenly could not stop thinking about sitting her naked body into the hot and hairy lap of an older boy or man, and then getting on the floor on her hands and knees.

When I came into the picture Abbey had still never met or known a boy or older boy she felt anywhere near close enough to, or safe enough with socially, to even talk about sex with let alone have actual sexual contact with. But she dreamed of it nearly every night. Abbey knew that she wanted to be fucked, and she knew how she wanted to be fucked. And she also knew that what she wanted would require a certain kind of male partner: certainly one with experience, and his own means and abilities, who was also completely separate from her family's church or other social circles.

When we found ourselves sitting next to each other in a high school geometry class, she being one of the freshman in the class and me one of the sophomores, she was soon confident that she had finally met the older boy she'd been waiting for.

As a girl who'd always been cautious and tried to do everything well and "right", from straight A grades to going to church every week, to never speaking ill of others, etc., etc., Abbey was well aware of my reputation as a sexual mauler, a young drug dealer, a sports drop-out, and an outsider, which is why it was so surprising to me when we began to flirt with each other, and then continued to flirt with each other until we agreed to meet at an upcoming school dance.

I knew damn well that Abbey was way too "good" to be trying to hang around with me. She was so pure, and fresh, and beautiful, in what seemed such an untouchable way, I felt out of place with her. Even my two closest friends were worried about what I might do to upset, or scare, or disrespect, or even damage her.

What we didn't know was that the basis for Abbey's powerful attraction to me, and the reason for her odd and unwarranted trust in me, was that she was *certain* that, because I was such a "bad-boy", I wouldn't think what *she wanted* was so bad.

After the dance, where we more or less made-out on the dance floor, we made-out again on a darkened sidewalk by the parking lot of the school. As we kissed, I rubbed my knee and thigh up into her tight jeans covered crotch, and then followed with my skillfully exploring hands and rubbing fingers. Unexpectedly, I discovered that Abbey had gotten so wet I could feel it on the outside of her pants—and so, I knew exactly what she wanted—and I didn't think it was bad at all.

Pushing my hand and fingers even deeper into her crotch, and pushing my tongue even deeper into her mouth, while my other hand held her tightly by the ass, I did my best to assure her that I understood.

By our fourth date, Abbey was ready. Taking her into a quiet room at a friend's house whose parents were out of town, I then slowly slid my body between her long, slender, porcelain white legs and carefully and caringly gave her everything she wanted, just the way she wanted it, eventually "taking her from behind" just as she'd always dreamed about.

I also gave her an unhesitating and totally open verbal sexual conversation, which had begun with my first kisses on her lips and had never stopped. In fact, Abbey quickly became quite the chatter box during sex, and almost immediately enjoyed assuming a verbally leading role, as in:

"Rory, let's smoke a little more pot and then you can lick my pussy again while we listen to some more of that music you brought. Then you can fuck me again. Okay? Please? Smoke me up and then make me cum again, Rory."

After that date, we became damn near inseparable. And we were so openly loving and sexual with each other—all the time—an older friend of ours called us "The Siamese-Twins: joined at the hips-and-lips." And because Abbey trusted me so completely, I tried my hardest to never fail that trust, especially during sex, which became an incredible lesson for me.

Of course, at that time Abbey had no idea of my compulsively deviant sexual habits and my other sex life. She only knew that I was the answer to all her bodily desires and all her expanding sexual questions. Because my willingness to satisfy her desires had shown up precisely when she had made up her own mind, and because I was so skilled in following her body's desirous requests, and because I never rushed her or pushed past her own depth (out of some kind of newly found patience and respect)—I felt like I was in the right-place at the right-time in a way I'd never been before.

I'd certainly never used the word "right" when thinking about my own sexual behaviors before, even though I'd envisioned many other positive descriptions like "powerful," "skillful," and "confident," my way of being with Abbey was a new sexual experience for me.

Further amazing to me, Abbey's transition into sexual contact was so well-timed, and so wonderful for her, she couldn't help but spread her happiness by telling her friends that "first sexual experiences" weren't anywhere near as scary or as difficult as they had all thought it was—*if* they could get the right kind of guy, who knew what he was doing, and who wouldn't be pushy or impatient, etc., etc., etc.

From locker room talk, and sleep over gossip, and whispered conversations during competitive sports trips with her school girl friends, as well as the girls that she studied ballet with, Abbey knew only too well how scary the thought of first sexual contact was for most of them. And it was a much more complicated mixture of worrying points than I had been aware of.

Creating a two-way sexual openness with other people can have so many important benefits. For instance, you can learn at least twice as much about anything sexual you approach that way.

My sexual mentor, Déjà, had taught me how to do so many sexual things, and how to perform so many specific sexual acts, and how to be exceedingly physically sensitive, and how to be unfailingly bold, and how to drive the sex forward—but she had never taught me to be a patient "listener", or bothered with any considerations about how or *why* the other person's pre-, early, and especially current sexual contact concerns could be important to respect, or how an experienced person could make those first sexual contact experiences so much better by acknowledging the inexperienced partner in that much more genuine and sexually courteous kind of way.

Abbey taught me that.

In colorful fourteen year old detail, Abbey explained to me that for her and her girlfriends there were so many considerations and fears about first sexual intercourse the actual event seemed too complicated and threatening for most of them to ever actually do!

Speaking matter-of-factly, which was so cute, Abbey ran down the list of their worries: First, there was the physical pain part, and the anxiety of having a "first man" who wouldn't be at all aware of how to deal with those feminine difficulties, which Abbey made sure all the girls knew I had helped her with, as she'd had just a bit of remaining tightness, which I was very patient with before putting my cock all the way in.

There was also a complex distress they had that their first wouldn't be an overall "good enough" experience, which was a vague romantic kind of worry based on the man being a combination of handsome enough, a good enough kisser, have a tender enough touch, have a good cock and knowledge of how to use it well enough, etc., etc. All of which was dually important for the obvious in-the-moment reasons, as well as the less obvious reasons of the girls not wanting to have an eternal memory of dissatisfaction or even disillusionment over their first sexual intercourse experience.

They all, I found out to my bursting amusement, were specifically terrified of running into an ugly, or surprisingly weird looking, or a funny shaped cock! And most of them were worried that if they did, they might not be able to continue!

They were also afraid that their first wouldn't have a good enough personality for the extremely close moments of sex, even if he was good-enough as a regular boyfriend. They'd all seen famous men in Hollywood movies that had the right mix of charm, and dash, and focused sexual attentiveness, but they rightfully doubted finding that kind of guy in their own neighborhoods (or inside their own boyfriends).

I remember thinking to myself then, "How *could* a girl expect to find almost any of those qualities or abilities in a boy or older boy anywhere near their age?" And when Abbey kept telling me that she and her friends would fantasize about their first sexual experiences as being with an older man, I was confused (because everyone knew that wasn't allowed). But it should have made more sense, right off.

When the idea of the bad-boy image was discussed, I learned that it is all about the combination of the outer appearance of "badness", which facilitates the girls' excuse of being seduced. But once they are naked those same girls want a man who knows how and when to be sweet, and slow, and sensitive, and soft enough, if also powerfully so.

Before that, as a kid, I had actually thought that women really did have some kind of weird attraction to ignorant-acting, inconsiderate, socially mean, disrespectful, and even totally disinterested-in-them men. But that isn't true!

The "loner" part of that classic character, on the other hand, which represents someone with enough emotional depth to stand on one's own, turns out to be a truer and more meaningful turn-on.

Abbey and the other girls also had the very valid concern that the man or boy might ruin everything afterward by handling the delicate information wrongly in society.

Of course, they also suffered from the fear of pregnancy, which they mutually agreed was something the guy would have to be completely responsible for—because they were all religious girls.

They also felt the serious pressures of losing a relationship if they refused to have sex at a moment when they weren't prepared, or whenever the boyfriend suddenly demanded it.

And the specific anxiety of being terribly hurried, with a quickie, through a moment they so sincerely felt should be a wonderfully elongated one, was another possibility of a bad memory, and its intuited potential for lasting and life altering negative effects.

And, of course, there was the fear of God: but in the end, as usual, He wasn't going to stop these girls from getting laid.

However, the fear that surprised me the most, the dread that was so important it was the one that could hold them frozen from sex even when a significant number of the other desired aspects seemed aligned— was their panic at the thought of sexually-stumbling, in any way, in their own sexual performance: the anxiety of "sexual awkwardness." And the consequences of a stumble could be disastrous, including private and public shaming, and perhaps worse—a permanent reputation. And since few of them, if any, had ever had any kind of meaningful technical sexual knowledge handed down to, or shared with them, I definitely understood their distress. Awkwardness goes hand-in-hand with ignorance.

That's an awful lot for a teenage girl to work out, or to expect to go well on a wing-and-a-prayer, especially in our culture. So I could definitely see their problems, and relate.

Still, it was definitely the final piece of information from this extended conversation that became especially instructive, and especially important when considering their debilitating concerns of sexual awkwardness. Because it became Abbey's fervent belief that my extraordinarily easy way with sex, my thoroughly relaxed attitude, and my comfortably informative, easy-paced, interactive, fully attentive, always friendly, and unfailingly enthusiastic way of handling every part of our constantly expanding sexual encounters (a behavior that Abbey, herself, had evolved in me), was *exactly* what all her friends needed in order to go through their first sexual intercourse experiences—without all their fears, on both sides of the equation!

Abbey had already seen the velvety-smooth and deliciously penetrating answers to all those challenges happen right between her own trembling legs—and she just couldn't help but share that truth.

And, because Abbey had always been completely without guile or false intentions, as outlandish as it should have seemed (in our small, conservative, and religiously dominated community), her friends immediately believed that they too would experience the passionate and safe first-sex-magic that Abbey claimed lay inside my hands, and my mouth, and my pants. And in this way, Abbey "gave" me as a sincere gift to five different virgin friends over the course of the first two years of our relationship.

Her thinking was that no conversation or description alone could equal the actual experience of them being with me. She had felt like she had been both fulfilled and released without worry to all her current and future sexual desires during the very first time we were naked together.

And so, Abbey's friends did trust me. And I did respectfully follow each of their personal streams of sexual choice all the way to their running sources, holding each one as tightly or loosely as I could sense she wanted, kissing each one where they wanted to be kissed, talking softly when needed, and quietly taking control when it was time for that.

And some of the most wonderful "connecting" that I did with those girls happened in the conversations we had about sex, which seemed as out-of-this-world to them as the sex that I covered their bodies with.

For instance, I made sure that each of those girls also lost their phobia of weird shaped cocks by simply being super open with them about all the different stages of my own cock's appearance, showing them just how different a single cock and balls can look at each different moment of arousal and/or lessening-arousal. Talking without any awkwardness whatsoever about other kinds of cocks, like bent ones, and uncircumcised ones, and pointy ones, and lumpy ones, etc., etc., which made them giggle a lot, I allowed them to realize that every cock is going to be different *and interesting*. And, I was also able to set each of them at ease about the way their vaginas looked, bringing the conversation about cocks in as a literally perfect parallel (which I thought was pretty ingenious at the time).

(It may have also helped that I was dearly fondling and kissing their pussies in open-worship while I told each girl how beautiful they were.)

I also explained some of the differences between female and male orgasms, the most important of which being how they could let-go to their orgasms as many times as they wanted to, while most males will build up to one mighty orgasm. I was also able to make sure that I didn't cum inside them because of my incredible sperm control built-up over tens of thousands of orgasms (mostly masturbation, which I considered a training tool that they should definitely tell their boyfriends about). And I also made sure to show that skill to them when I pulled my cock out of their quivering bodies and then neatly finished my orgasm outside of their fertile little pussies, so they wouldn't worry later.

In addition, I explained to those girls how I didn't believe that good sex technique or the kinds of knowledge that I was sharing with them was some kind of secret science. In fact, I made sure they knew that I thought the opposite. Even basic sensual and sexual understandings would suffice as a solid starting place for people, I explained, *if* those kinds of understandings were at all shared in our culture.

Abbey's fawning descriptions of our sexual play, as well as those girls' precious memories of my sexual skills, did have plenty to do with where they were starting from relative to where I was at. But there should be no question that their initial sexual experience(s) were filled with genuine attentiveness, satisfaction, and safety.

It was also significant how helpful it was that each of those girls knew ahead of time that I was coming to them for a very specific purpose. Completely unlike the common surprise-push by a boyfriend, they had all the time they needed to consider and give their fullest consent. Clarity is always helpful in relationships, and in this case even more so.

Also, the fact that the girls were not alone in their experiences, but were instead sharing and processing these sexual events with each other, also created an uncommonly relaxed air among them. Other than Abbey, none of those others girls would have been brave enough to invite me in to their bedrooms, or lives, at that time, without the support of close friendship.

To be clear, I'm not talking about peer pressure or some kind of group initiation; I'm talking about the value of open sexual sharing by-choice.

As for what I was given: Among other things, I was allowed to see that Abbey and her friends' most specific and treasured erotic dream is to find a seriously horny man—whom they can trust, in a multi-layered way.

I found that singular fact the most important and fascinating of all—that *trust* and a feeling of complete safeness with sex, including physically, emotionally, mentally, and socially, is the most erotic setting a girl (or boy) could experience—because it allows them to let themselves go to all the rest of what floods through them during sex, including all the parts that feel less-than-safe, rushing, and even out-of-control.

I had been introduced to sex in a way that was attached mainly to the aggressively lusting and boundary-breaking urgency of blinding sexual-feasting. And by the time I met Abbey and her friends, I had already created a number of inelegantly over-pushed sexual encounters, and I had immaturely prodded at too many border lines and limits.

What Abbey showed me, and taught me then, was that respect and trust could open sexual doors in a much more deeply welcoming way than pushing and pounding against another person's sexual boundaries.

In terms of adding something meaningful to help balance my unevenly developed sexual personality, what Abbey gave to me was probably life, or at least sanity saving.

And, it would be no exaggeration to say that whenever I was with Abbey, whatever we may be doing, I was as careful as I could be, and I consciously kept us as far from harm as possible, in every way I could—so that part of my sexual life was actually protective to me, which was new.

And though I would like to say that my sexual growth and understanding was securely completed by the knowledge, and my wonderful relationship with Abbey, the truth is that my never ending search for more-and-more sexual contact was in full effect whenever I wasn't with Abbey.

So, in reality, I just put that new knowledge to work for myself, and I worked it as hard as I could in my neighborhood and whatever other options came up. For instance, during the summers of those years my older brothers got jobs at the high school swimming complex in the school district next to ours, which opened up a whole new population of similarly aged girls to me.

The beautiful girls Nikki, Chris, Ada, Lisa, Laurie, Tracie, Teri, Joni, Jill, Cathy, Ann, Jillian, and Joy to name the ones I can recall just now, all came from my daily efforts during those two summers.

As far as quick sex with men, which I continued to engage in when I could, this new knowledge made less of an impact. (Though random male partners in fully public sex arenas do expect, and seek, their own levels of safety and respect, and they do have to give trust).

However you look at it, what Abbey gave me then and would continue to give, should be acknowledged in the highest regard. In the end, her love does rescue me.

My First Attempt at Full Disclosure

When Abbey and I had been together for about two years, her love for me had grown so strong, and her honesty with me had been so complete and humbling, I decided to tell her about my early life sexual experiences with my family members, and about my current compulsive and most-often homosexual activities.

Because of the incredible way that Abbey loved me, I felt assured enough to take such a risk. Or, maybe it was the bravest act of love I ever tried to show Abbey. Maybe I was trying to warn her.

Either way, I learned an important lesson in the attempt of that honesty, though I cannot say that it was an easy lesson to understand.

Having waited for the right kind of moment, when I saw it I jumped on it.

Laying together after making-out for a couple of hours, I simply thought of the first words I needed to say, and started.

"Abbey, I want to tell you about some of my first sexual experiences."

With a beaming face framed by her shining brunette hair, she replied without hesitation.

"Alright, my love."

"I was only seven years old when my oldest brother Burt taught me how to suck his cock."

"Oh."

"I've also been having sex with one of my older girl cousins ever since that age, too."

"Is that Déjà?"

"Yes! *How did you know?*"

"I guessed. You've mentioned her name a few times."

"Yes, it was Déjà. And she told me and showed me all kinds of wild sexual things about…"

"But you haven't seen her for more than three years now, right?"

"Right…"

"How long did you have sex with your brother?"

"Well, right after I started sucking him I started to do it to several of his friends."

"Oh Rory…, for how long?"

"They had me do it, whenever they felt like it, for quite a few years."

"You poor thing…"

"It's always bothered me that I could never tell anyone about it."

"You don't have to say another word! I understand my love! None of what happened to you is your fault. You have me now. Just lay quietly with me."

"But I wanted to tell you about how I…"

"No. Don't say another word! You don't have to tell me anything more. Nothing you can tell me could make me love you any differently—I will love you forever."

"But there is so much more, I…"

"Rory! I'm not like other people! I know exactly who you are in my heart. You don't have to explain yourself to me—ever."

"Abbey, sometimes I feel so sexually driven it's hard for me…"

"You have me now! And if you ever did have sex with some other girl, sometime, you already know that I wouldn't care! We don't even have to talk about it, Rory. I will love you like no one else ever could! Please stop worrying about this, Rory. You're making me sad…"

"Abbey, I have even had sex with…"

"Rory, please! I don't need to know! It is all alright. Please just let me love you."

"Abbey, I'm worried that I'm not *normal!*"

"Oh my god Rory, you're NOT normal! You're so much better than normal! The way you hold me and kiss me makes me melt inside and I never want to be without you! You're better than any boyfriend I could have imagined! Don't you see it?!"

"*I am…?*"

"You are to me, my love! Now don't talk about all that stuff anymore. Come kiss my mouth, Rory, and tell me that you love me…"

"I do love you, Abbey. Open your mouth…and close your eyes."

At the time, it felt like a valid victory. At seventeen years old I had finally told someone about my early family sex and homosexual hyperactivity—and I had been instantly accepted, and forgiven, and loved.

Intuitively, it also felt like a failure.

In any case, whatever we successfully shared in that moment it was honest, and deeply joining enough, that it was, and is, a big part of why we have been together ever since. And on Abbey's eighteenth birthday, we were married.

Yes, we have certainly been challenged to the breaking-point in every way by my hypersexuality and its struggling evolution, and by the difficulties of partial truths—and we're still together.

However, the story of this book is much bigger than me, or Abbey, or Wynona, or Déjà, or even Cee Cee. So let's keep the wider telling going. In this case, there will be no one to hush me.

Legal Age Issues & Personalizing Sexual Education

Sexual freedom of contact at fifteen years old by consent, with no age-of-partner limits, would be very reasonable and helpful.

The age of consent in most of Mexico is fourteen, with legalized prostitution. And the age in Canada is sixteen, with legal prostitution in limited provinces. And in both these Countries, our nearest neighbors, legislated age-bracketing designed to limit the contact between age groups is not used.

In the State I now live in the legal age of consent for sex is eighteen. Everyone under that age, and anyone older having sex with someone under that age—even with consent—is committing the crime of rape.

To reveal more of the insanity: If a teen is nineteen or under and they have sex with a teen that is only two years younger, in brackets going down to the age of fifteen, the within-two-year boundary can (potentially) be used as a legal defense—even though the act is still deemed illegal sexual contact. But, that teen may just as well face very serious charges (resulting in a lifetime designation as a sex-criminal). But there's no way to know what will happen. Which is threatening and confusing.

I personally believe that the youth suffer worse from this maddening complexity than the adults do. Plainly, way too much of our American youths' first and earliest sexual contact experiences have been proclaimed illegal, which we should also remember equals "immoral," "psychologically sick," and "perverted" in our religious, medical and cultural definitions. What does that teach our youths? How is it helpful?

American teens aren't supposed to have sex with each other, and they can't learn about it from an older person. Sex is legally defined as a crime, and immoral, and sick—and then all of the sudden it okay, as long as it is with someone your own age (who, by definition, will also be sexually ignorant). I can hardly think of a more idiotic system.

Incredibly, our American society also severely stigmatizes people who have sex later or never in life; openly calling such persons old-maids, or derisively looking down on them as elderly-virgins, a stigmatizing judgment that is passed on them even by their own families, or groups of supposed friends, or work office colleagues, or gossiping neighbors.

If we were half-honest with ourselves we would remember that for almost the entire span of known world history, cultures from all over the planet have had a place for the traditions of having older more experienced adults educate the younger ready-to-learn adults—including instruction in the realm of sexual contact.

Doesn't every other kind of human knowledge and skill follow that instructional pathway to the greatest benefit?

One of the high social functions that prostitution used to handle in many cultures, including early parts of our American society (for those affluent enough), was the much less awkward and potentially much more instructive introduction to sex, for anyone, of any age, including those who became ready later in life.

If we were even more honest with ourselves we would also see and admit how valuable younger prostitutes could be to some of our current criminal concerns. Imagine how many fewer rapes and kidnappings of young girls there would be if you had available and affordable fifteen year-old professionals everywhere. Even if the law required a one-year training period, smallish sixteen year-old professionals who enjoy acting as if they are much younger during sex could clear the streets of a substantial percentage of the takers of too young sex partners, who (in an anonymous system) could then become happily paying customers, or perhaps even medically sanctioned and insured clients. Socially speaking, I'll support the development of that insurance.

At full honesty, I would tell you that fifteen year-olds and teenagers like myself, Cee Cee, Déjà, even Abbey, and so many others that I have met in my life, would have made wonderful professional sexual partners and healers who were more than happy to play-nasty with older partners, especially in a fully protected and cash paying forum.

Many, many teenagers are up-to and ready-for sex of all kinds, with a wider variety of partners, and more often, than most people in our society might believe, because our culture is erroneously being taught that teenagers aren't even ready for sex! What bullshit! That is exactly what a great many teenagers are the *most* ready for!

It is a simple social and sexual truth: older people like to have sex with younger people, and vice-versa, with every mix of age and gender combination you can think of coming into play.

Some older people want to have sex with younger people so badly they take it in the worst of ways. And we have to try to fix that.

To do that in the most effective way, along with correcting the legal age restrictions, we would need to have a much more proper, broad, open, honest, and even more personalized sexual education for our adolescents and pre-teens who are approaching the age-of-choice.

Abstinence "education", and all of the other currently legally allowed sexual education programs are so ridiculously tongue-tied and ineffectual it is downright irresponsible. And the confusing absurdities that kids often share with each other, as a way of "alternative" learning, is in far too many cases plain stupidity.

How have we gone so far in the wrong direction?

Maybe the anti-freer-sex sector of society is scared because they correctly sense how sexually inept they are?

Most people can hardly talk about sex in anything other than a humorous or somehow well-removed way. And if you can't even talk about sexual contact, how are you ever going to understand, or educate, or evolve sexual knowledge, sexuality, sensualism, personal choices, skilled partnering, fetishism, or any of the other actual fields of comprehension that come into play within the consideration of the greater sexual subject?

When kids can converse, and question, and share any and all serious sexual contact topics with adults—we'll be there.

When a pre-teen or teenager can speak to the adults around them in a comfortable and confident atmosphere of respect, and positive understanding, and sincere helpfulness about specific issues like masturbation thoughts, or fantasies that they don't understand, or anal arousal, or desiring the taste of sperm, or the painfully intense and emotionally sizzling brain activity they are experiencing toward physical contact—we'll be there.

Unfortunately, our culture is anchored to the idea that these sexual issues and specifics are too difficult to discuss, especially with our youth. But they aren't.

Here is an example of a single conversation that I had many years ago with a fifteen year old male:

Because of knowing me for several years through the gymnasium where we both worked out, and because the young man had learned of (some of) my sexual reputation from some of the other men who knew me (and whose own experiences at the edge of my sexual world were difficult for them not to brag about), I consequentially seemed to him to be a very logical choice for sexual information. So, one day after workouts, in a "casual dude-to-dude way", he told me that he had been enjoying some porn magazines recently, which I smiled and nodded knowingly at (staying quiet so as to let him maintain his lead role in the conversation). Continuing shyly at first, he started by hesitantly describing to me how beautiful the girls that posed in the magazines were to him, which I also agreed with. Gaining momentum, he began to less-hesitantly celebrate his favorite types of girls in those magazines, and their fully revealed body parts, and best picture angles, and his personal fantasy wish-list while he stared at them. All of which I quietly replied to with knowing smiles, and well-timed nods of my head.

Then, after ten or fifteen minutes, the young man became suddenly serious. Turning to face me, he bravely asked why vaginas (which he'd studied in his magazines) are *so complex*, and why they look so differently from each other, openly showing his confusion with a series of knotted-up facial expressions. Looking up at me, and seeing the totally secure understanding in my eyes, he then wondered quickly and out loud if I could tell him what all the different parts were..., and stuff..., and how to do stuff...?

At the end of his stuttering inquiry I told him, "Yes, I can tell you about plenty of stuff."

In quick reply he said, "I'll go get some of my mags."

So, after quickly riding his bike the few blocks to his home to grab one of his porn magazines, he returned to the now deserted locker room and excitedly sat down next to me. After finding a really good set of pussy pictures, some with the outer lips pushed tightly together and hiding everything, and some with the labia spread wide and wet with the clitoris swollen and prominent, and some with the labia so swollen it was hard to tell what was what, we then spent a while exploring the very specific details of what, and where, and why, and how to best touch a pussy with your hands for the sake of pleasuring it—and I actually touched and stroked the pictures in visually instructional ways.

Then we talked in unhurried detail about cunt kissing, licking, and sucking (all with vivid descriptions), followed by a frank discussion about early penetration efforts with one's finger(s), which brought us, finally, directly to one of this young man's most specific and pressing questions.

"What the hell do you do when the girl you're with says that *it hurts*?"

"That's an excellent and important question, because you absolutely must try to avoid hurting her, or anyone. There is a totally simple way to patiently, and sensually work through that kind of vaginal pain. So knowing exactly what to do, and how to talk to her about it in a calm and confident way, will totally help."

As for the hymen: I first explained to him what it isn't, and then I explained what it is. Spending time to build the information logically, he eventually understood that the tightest point of penetration in a vagina is found several inches inward, and that, except in very rare cases, the hymen is actually a tissue-ring of tightness around the outer vaginal-wall, rather than a fully or even predominantly blocking film-of-skin, which is how it is still pictured by so many young men. I also carefully explained how the very first part of the pussy "tunnel" is much more easily spread wide and made open; but the mid-point of initial and early penetrations of the tunnel (especially for younger and sometimes smaller girls) is different in terms of its inherent elasticity, and that this point is where you have to be patient and literally massage open any reserving tightness, whether that be with your fingers or the head of your cock, or whatever else may be helpful (see details at beginning of this chapter, in sub-chapter "Abbey").

I continued by explaining that if all else has failed, the strategy should be to continue playing with your cock in the opening part of the vagina tunnel, pulling it slowly back and then pushing it in only as far as the girl indicates—which will make her hornier and hornier with every little slide—until she, herself, starts screaming at you to "Put it all-the-way-in!"

That has been my honest and actual experience multiple times, even when the girl could tell that the final push-through was going to cause a fair amount of pain—so I had to share that information too. And I continued my instructions by telling the young man that if this specific still-painful penetration option ever happened to him with a girl he should instantly hold totally-still inside her after the initial push-through—which allows the pain to subside—until the girl gave him the go ahead to move again.

After the momentous shock of that kind of push-through, the girls' that I have been with all had a temporary reaction of painful tightening throughout their entire bodies—followed fairly quickly by a bodily reaction of a profound relaxing within the girls vagina at that exact ring-of-tightness, which the girls all seemed to feel with a wide-eyed wonder, which then led them to beg to be fucked more deeply, and strongly, and with all the wild passion they had hoped would fill them.

Of course, we generously covered the subject of lubrication. And I also went into the lesser known field of understanding the emotionally-lubricating and loosening effect that patience, and the feelings of safety, and trust, have on the inner vaginal tightness of a girl, which is a subtle but nevertheless real bodily coordination that I have known about ever since I first sensed it and felt it.

Interestingly, almost all this exact same advice applies to penetrating the anal tunnel; which is also a sexual organ plain-and-simple, even if our educational systems don't understand or acknowledged the fact. Minus the above discussed rare dermal obstruction in vaginas, the sexual penetration similarities of patiently working open the tightness of the anus are both striking and instructional. And since this young man had also mentioned the subject of anal sex (heterosexual), we covered all this as well.

Then we talked about his un-asked questions on how to maximize the enjoyment for himself: with sub-sections on how to best present his swelling cock to the girl (hygiene, attitude, and timing are all important); as well as understanding the dynamics of having and maintaining a hard-on during a sexual event; controlling ejaculation; and some basic methods of extended porn-stud style fucking, which required us to discuss the advanced uses and methods of masturbation including the goal of increased awareness of, and the ability to control and/or extend, orgasm—for both the male and the female.

And I was as frank as is possible on the overwhelming importance of birth control, and unwanted pregnancies, and having unplanned children.

And I remembered to talk about overall hygiene too, and pre-fuck session preparations, and the special importance of excellently clipped and smoothed finger nails—emphasizing how important, in an often long-lasting way, first experiences could be.

And because he was uncircumcised, we covered that topic in full detail, including how to best deal with a girl who seemed taken back by it. My advice being to simply smile confidently at the girl, and while exposing the head of his cock with his own hands to tell her that uncircumcised cocks get even bigger than circumcised ones (a point that can't be proven or disproven—while the power of a positive spin is beyond doubt).

We also talked about how he could keep the verbal conversation relaxed and open with his partner, like we were doing, and how he could use that conversation to make the girl feel better about her hesitant touching of him, or herself. And we discussed how he could talk in a similarly calming way about any other sexual subject and any other things that came up.

"How do I get a girl to suck my cock?" He asked with extra focus.

"Just ask her if she wants to, and don't be pushy. And if she hesitates, ask her if you can lick her pussy, which will often lead the girl toward at least considering returning the oral favor." I replied. "And make sure to tell her she doesn't have to, and that you don't expect it, but if she does want to try it, even just a little, you're cool with that."

Then he surprised me by excitedly asking about "biting", which he said he'd seen in an old magazine buried in his father's pornography stash and was somewhat aroused by, but was unsure of. So I spoke to him about that subject in terms of personal fetishes, predominantly letting him know that biting and other such specifically angled sexual acts were somewhat rarer pleasures that needed the recipient's fully willing participation or even request. Emphasizing the point, I cautioned him to enter into any "biting" only on the most playful level, and only if his partner gave positive feedback from the beginning. I also encouraged him to wait on more expansive and experimental sexual acts until he felt comfortable enough to simply ask the girl if she would like to try them—and then to ask away without hesitation—and without attachment.

Finally, after discussing all the detailed questions and answers that could have only been brought forth by that young man himself, we then finished with a good dose of information on how to best end a sexual meeting, and how to encourage a sexual relationship forward in a respectful and more successful way by making sure that both people involved are clear and direct in a considerate and uncomplicated way with each other about what they want out of the relationship, both sexually and otherwise.

And by the time those two hours had gone by, and we were done talking for that day, my young friend knew more about vaginas and how to please them, and how to get back into them, than perhaps ninety-nine percent of the men in our American culture. And, he understood the power of sexual respect.

In addition, this young man also had my friendly commitment to any follow-up advice he might seek, or questions he might come up with in the future, which is a very valuable and necessary resource in any kind of education.

As that young man re-packed his gym bag and prepared to leave, something told me that some young woman in his high school was about to get some very special and respectful attention.

"Jesus, Dude! Thanks for telling me all that great shit! I can't wait to get to my girlfriend's house! We were both so nervous yesterday I felt like I was going to puke. But now I'm not hardly nervous at all! Hey Rory, for real—thanks! I gotta split. I'll see you tomorrow and tell you how it goes!"

"You're welcome! Remember to stay calm, dude. Talk to her, and 'ask' her before you make your moves. Take your time and enjoy yourselves. Good luck!"

I say: If we just open our mouths and try to talk openly and honestly about it, even the most important points about sex and sexual contact can be shared, instead of treating the issues of sexual contact like an embarrassing and unspeakable mystery.

Because of the laws preventing sexual contact—of any kind—between persons of such disparate ages like me and my young friend, I had risked an illegal discussion and criminally shared pornography with that "underage" young man. And I'd do it again in a heartbeat, because sex *is not* and *should not be* unspeakable, un-sharable, or a confusing mystery.

All sexual subjects from early masturbation, to hymens, to bi-sexual bondage, to prostitution for the handicapped, to reverse gang bangs, to cum swallowing, to the desire to participate in all kinds of other sexual fetishes can become easy to talk about, and interesting, and we can learn a lot by just talking, which is so much better than knowing almost nothing at all.

Our American culture is deceptively comfortable with talking about sex as a religious judgment, as procreation, as a somehow morally staining and crushing danger, as an insult, as a swear-word, as a bawdy joke, and as all the openly tempting, often nearly pedophilic, and overdramatic and unrealistic media presentations—but *not* as a simply real, personal, important, complex, multi-layered social challenge and daily reality that begins in your early or even pre-teens.

Instead of being afraid to learn more about sex and sexuality we should be afraid of what happens when you keep one of the most important human issues legally cut off, socially under-fed, and educationally stunted.

We need to learn more about sex directly from each other, starting no later than the age of fifteen.

I never forgot what I learned from listening to and being with Abbey and her friends. And now I've shown how that kind of intimate knowledge can be passed on.

And I am privileged to share it.

Chapter Ten

Fucking Strangers

As American "adults" we graduate into a different stratosphere of possibilities of pursuing sexual contact. Supposedly those possibilities are greatly opened up, but are they really?

The way I've always seen it, having lived my life inside the issue, outside the usual dating dynamics, which include the boyfriend/girlfriend phase, then fiancé, and finally husband/wife relationships, the hindering so-called mores and the potential social and legal consequences of seeking un-traditional sexual contact in our society impede us all the way into and throughout adulthood.

To appreciate what I am trying to point out we could first stop to consider, for instance, that marital infidelity, or sexual contact by a married person with a partner outside that marriage—is illegal—for the married person. And it can cost the "guilty" party their marriage, the parental charge of their children, roughly half their income, their home, and often times many of their other important social connections including friends, jobs, etc.

"Oh, don't be ridiculous." Many people would say. "There's all kinds of sexual options for adults, of course there are! If you're a grown up you can do whatever you want. Hell, there's even legalized prostitution in the United States!"

No, there isn't. And no, you can't.

To be clear, the infinitesimal amount of legal prostitution in America—which exists in exactly two tiny counties in the Nevada desert—absolutely does not count. Not only is it geographically remote, it is also financially extreme, both limits meaning "beyond reach" for all but the exceedingly few. In fact, wealth is also one of the substantial barriers in all but the lowest of the illegal options, and even there it is forbidding (which really pisses me off). Plus—*even then*—as far as marriage contracts go, even *if* you can afford an upper-level option, or even *if* the extra marital sex is with a "legal" sex worker, the guilty party still risks losing their family and fortune just the same.

And the new millennium internet porn content, while impressive in terms of porn expansion, has nothing to do with actual sexual contact—unless perhaps in adding to the unquenchable desire for it (admittedly while often exhausting a person's immediate sexual energy).

And the internet sex hook-up websites are, and have always been, a total mess. I've observed and used them from the start. But the multi-layered shortcomings, not the least of which is the unreal cybernetic reaches they all "exist" in, plague nearly every variation of the functioning concept, including, to my dismay, even the most non-financially based local and purposely direct public "meeting" and access sites. And even when that direction does result in an actual sexual contact event, those avenues are still treacherous at best, and they still carry a person toward all the worst possible consequences—because that person is still living in this America.

This is also true: If a person isn't in a traditional relationship, and they instead (somehow manage to) have sex with a random string of partners, or a string of randomly sexed partners, or a string of randomly deviant sexual partners, or with legal or illegal prostitutes—and they are open about it—or they are discovered—they will have made themselves unacceptable to both the majority of American society in general, including their families, the people they work with, etc., as well as the majority of additional potential relationship partners.

Or, to try to avoid those kinds of judgments from their society a person can "choose" to drastically reduce the population they consider themselves to be a part of, and they can "join" one of the separated-off alternative-sexuality subcultures, which will likely award them with a single letter designation (LGBTQIAP, etc.) But once a person is labeled, and "accepted," what good does that really do for their sexual contact reality? Not only are these subcultures limited in population, and by specific sexual preferences, they are also limited in terms of presenting an actual supply of sexual contact options. For one thing, many of the people in these populations are also partisan to developing a nearly, or exactly traditional replica of having singular partners and committed relationships parameters. Ultimately, and importantly, these subcultures were never primarily meant to supply the kinds of wide-ranging sexual contact options that I believe we need—which, by definition must be freer from such constrictions, and are perhaps less focused on political goals.

Simply stated, that's pretty much the picture—both when I was younger, and still. So yes, I feel that we are very restricted in our sexual contact and non-traditional sexual relationship options. And I think that hinders our deeper personal sexual evolutions, and our greater social gratification.

In fact, I've had revealing conversations with perhaps several hundreds of adults, most of whom were otherwise fairly well established and reasonably successful persons, and heard over and over how they've had only a few, at most, truly cherished and personally gratifying sexual experiences. And many have had none. So, along with my intense disappointment at most people's first-sex stories, comes my enduring sadness at how, even after a long life, so few people have enjoyed anything close to the sex that they had always hoped to.

And I am sorry for those people, because I have had the bright universe of unfastened and passionate sex with many hundreds of partners, literally thousands upon thousands of times—much of it with strangers I'd just met. And almost all of it outside the traditional boundaries of our American societal structure and legal system.

As much as our general society might not believe or understand it, outside the acceptable limits of sexual contact, and also beyond the sexual identity subcultures, a much broader visioned sexual empathy and instinctive sexual generosity does exist, but in a more disparate, undefined, and usually disconnected number of individuals.

And this kind of hypersexual generosity *is* special—*it is a special sexual element because it is all about totally accessible and safe sexual contact availability*—and it should be shared with society and the whole human world more openly, and professionally as well as all other consensual dynamics, in newly conceived, clean, and completely safe environments.

Dirty and dangerous illegal prostitution, and other old standards like one-night stands, or meet-at-a-bar and fuck somewhere sessions, which can result in later social awkwardness and risk, guilt, and possible professional or marital consequences, and unplanned pregnancy, and worry about undiagnosed diseases—are all so far away from what I'm talking about I would call the differences galactic, or at least planetary.

Making successful and importantly gratifying sexual contact could become so simple compared to how complex and potentially negatively consequential it currently is, if only we could swing open the door to wide-open non-traditional sexual contact options.

Advanced Class – Abbey

There is an additional level to the phenomenon of fucking strangers that needs to be appreciated. I observed its full reality at the age of thirty, and it is undoubtedly one of the preeminent cornerstones of what I now understand about sexual contact.

As previously mentioned, I've been a part of this satisfying sexual phenomenon with strangers my whole life. But what I got to witness with my wife, Abbey, when she hit her full sexual stride at the very end of her twenties and began playing nasty with strangers, is the best possible example that I can reveal—because it happened to Abbey, a person *not* from the hypersexual world. And, because I had known Abbey throughout her entire sexual history—what I observed offered me (and now all of us) a nearly unmatchable breadth of context and comprehension.

Having known Abbey for fifteen years by then, and having fucked her so many, many times, I was fairly certain that I had seen the entire range of her sexual personality.

I was wrong: And I was in for a momentous lesson.

Throughout those first fifteen years of our relationship and marriage Abbey had given me my sexual freedom, and when the time came, she knew that I would give her that same freedom. (Both of which are powerfully supportive arguments that hypersexuality and long-term committed relationships do not need to be opposed to each other.)

When Abbey was ready, she asked me if she could start off her exploration with a few of my boxing and self-defense workout friends. I know that isn't exactly a "stranger," but my workout friends weren't her friends, and they had only casually met Abbey.

None of them had ever met the "naked Abbey," and that is how she saw it.

What Abbey didn't know (but might well have suspected) was that I had already shared some of my other girlfriends with several of those men, which meant that I already knew which guys I could trust the most.

Trust can be the most powerfully facilitating factor in releasing sexual contact, as I've mentioned previously, which is definitely why Abbey first leaned in the direction of that group of men. Because she felt certain that none of those men would ever do anything the least bit untoward, awkward, or pushy with her—even if she were naked—she felt exactly the kind of trust she needed.

The real reason Abbey knew that none of them would act unseemly, in any way, was the fact that, after nineteen years of training I had become a considerably experienced, seriously dangerous, skillfully malicious and even a cruel fighter that damn near nobody would want to cross—especially when it came to confrontations caused by physically disrespectful or bullying behaviors, which (due to my emotional history and make-up) made me mean in the worst of ways. And all the men who trained with me knew about that mean-streak in me. And those who had seen me actually street fight, and had seen me put someone down, relished in telling the stories to those who hadn't.

Of course, I'm not the toughest or most dangerous man a person might meet, but I might be one of them. I've studied and fought so hard and so often, all my life, against all comers, especially bullies, everywhere I've ever lived or traveled—whenever necessary—all because of a very powerful original reason: getting raped as an eleven year old, and then attacked again soon after in an even scarier attempted abduction incident as a twelve year old, which produced an amazingly dynamic fighting and survival energy in me, along with an explosive and lasting fury, and an undying determination.

And, I don't fight fair. If I really want to hurt someone, I won't just knock them out; I'll push one of their eyeballs into the middle of their skull so fast they won't even have time to blink. And, my weapon specialty is knife-fighting. And, I often carried a gun.

Among the men that I trained with at that time in my life, at the time of Abbey's sexual expansions, I was certainly the most feared.

Pardon the digression.

Suffice it to say, Abbey felt tremendously safe: And so the sexual results were equally spectacular.

To my astonishment (which I don't mind admitting), when the four buddies I had selected began to answer my questions about what had transpired during their first sexual encounters with Abbey, all of which happened during a four-day weekend run—I discovered that she was using my position of authority over them in order to become a totally unleashed dominatrix!

Fortunately, because I had already gotten them all laid before, our sexual conversation was a well-practiced and open one.

Respectfully (if somewhat hesitantly), they each told me that she absolutely blew their heads off, for four and five hours at a time! Seemingly stumped for words, not one of them was satisfied with their attempts to describe how unleashed and amazing Abbey was during her sex with them. And all of them assumed that I already knew all about this part of Abbey. And to a man, they simply could not thank me enough for the experiences.

I know they shed tears of thankfulness at Abbey's naked feet.

The completeness of her safety, plus the carefully and protected *detached-from-the-normal-world anonymity* of the secret meetings, had produced a totally released Abbey. I had even assured her, as she'd wished, that I would know nothing specific about what had happened during her encounters (which I obviously, actually, did). And everyone involved also knew that each meeting was a one-off event, with no questions. In fact, it was pre-agreed that none of them would ever talk about any of it socially, or in Abbey's presence—ever—unless she opened the conversation herself.

All of which made Abbey feel incredibly sexually empowered.

I had never met the Dominatrix Abbey. I had certainly allowed her to take the lead in our sex play any time that she had wanted throughout our entire life together, but with us that usually meant that she would simply tell me what she wanted and I would do it to her.

On a whole different level, my workout friends told me that the minute they were behind closed doors Abbey would take total control of them, grabbing them by their arms or face with absolute dominance, while verbally making a crystal clear threat of instant discontinuation of the sexual encounter if they didn't fully obey her.

Coming up on thirty years old Abbey was a gorgeously maturing woman: slightly taller than average and slender, with ivory skin, long curly brunette hair, big dark brown eyes, an extra fine European featured face, a long neck, gorgeous smaller sized breasts with big red nipples, a burning hot pink cunt, a sleek athletic bottom, and femininely muscled legs, all coordinated with the physical grace and confidence of a professional ballerina (which, had she not met me, she may well have become).

And the things that Abbey would make those men do were almost too much for me to hear—which was such a new and wild experience for me! Not because I hadn't known of and/or participated in most of the sexual acts she was doing—but because she had never once done anything close to that kind of dominant or aggressive sexual behavior with me! And the amount of time that she would spend with those men was also difficult for me to endure, which was never less than three or four hours, which was as long or longer than *we* had ever had sex! It was stupefying, and confusing to me as a hypersexual!

Of course, out of respect for Abbey's own sexual universe, as she had always tried so hard to respect mine, I never once mentioned any of my thoughts about her rather abundant enjoyment of the freedom that I had given her.

She would tell me what she wanted to, when she wanted to, if she wanted to.

As I said, it was a little hard to take at first. But the one thing that I am not, is a hypocrite. I will absolutely give what I have been given, or have even asked for.

Plus, I already knew that jealousy is the lowest snaking destroyer of trust between people that was ever bred into humans; even I have been invaded by its curling presence inside my heart, and made violent by its constrictions, and temporarily insane by its slithering threat. But I have always had to be far too free to be caught up or anchored by any of that; I was meant for all that can be known beyond the common restricting limits.

Jealousy is like a straight-jacket, which makes you go insane.

Plus, for me Abbey's integrity of love is one thing that I know I should never doubt or stain with something as discolored and ugly as small-minded doubt and jealousy.

I gave Abbey her sexual space. And before you knew it, I was in for the outrageous sexual benefit that my respect had earned me.

Soon, she came back to me to tell me what she had experienced, and found. And hearing about it all from Abbey's own trembling lips, with the meanings it all held pouring out of her heart, and the questions that she had flowing through her mind right there before me, was as amazing a sexual experience as I've ever had.

To be a witness of her unhidden truth was an honor; to be included was an enlightenment.

Each of my few chosen friends got to be with Abbey only once, twice, or three times over the course of about six months.

What she told me then, was that after being with each of them *more than* once or twice something about the encounters changed in a not-better way. And it took us some real creative investigation, and very deep and open thought, (plus all the info that I had secretly gathered about her unrestricted behavior), to figure out what had changed.

What we closed in on, was the super-thrill of the very first encounters.

"It" was the "stranger factor:" Sex with a stranger is what had set Abbey even freer than I had. And she wanted more.

Do you understand what I am willing to tell you? What I am willing to give?

At the time, it seemed that Abbey was setting foot into the wild territory of my lifelong lascivious lifestyle—but could, within a surprising but logically defined personal space, explore it only in a freedom beyond me.

In my whole life I had never been left behind sexually—I am the sexual leader! Well, my mentor left me, roaming onward, but Abbey was *my creation*—wasn't she?

Still, I am who I am. So I observed, and marveled at Abbey's sudden hyper-expansion.

Because it needs to be revealed, let me describe a few of the things that she did with the men she dominated. I know the readers must be wondering.

And there'll be no need to dress this up.

Abbey did wear black stockings on her long white legs, with no panties so that my friends could better see her pouting shaved clean pussy, and she did pull her little soft white pert breasts out over the top of the little lacy bra. But those few sexy accoutrements were so secondary to her intrinsic sexiness they played almost no part in the descriptions that my friends gave of Abbey.

Both my friends and Abbey told me that the moment they entered our house she was waiting for them, waiting to lock the door behind them, waiting in her obvious nakedness, shining in the emboldened exhibitionism.

Without words she immediately took control of them, with her index finger pointing to where their clothing should be discarded. In each case she then first bid them:

"Stand still."

And then she began by walking around their naked body, unabashedly touching wherever she wanted with her delicate and demanding hands.

Soon, she would be kneeling in front of them with their balls and cock gathered-up in both of her hands, with as much of their cock as she could fit stuffed into her mouth.

Like I said, there was no complicated teasing design and no need for it, she was only planning to get a good look and taste of the cock that she would be using, and to let herself gorge on it for a moment before she moved onto other pleasures.

Nothing needed to be saved; nothing would be left out.

After working a cock up to its dripping and straining utmost, using both her hands and her mouth as if they were one sexual organ, rubbing the cock and sliding the balls all over her lips and face, stuffing them into her mouth until she was choking, choking as if that were better than life, breathing again in gasping moans hidden from no one, almost shouting to show her effort in backing off from her orgasmic pursuit even a little bit, eventually, achingly, she would take their entire cock out of her mouth, let go of it, and stand-up ready to proceed.

Rarely looking into their eyes for more than a coy second, she would instead stare at their bodies in a way that made them shiver. The men said that the way she looked at their bodies the whole time, rather than at their faces or eyes, and how she almost never let them talk, made her seem even less like someone they knew, and vice-versa.

Rather than telling them to move she would more often move their bodies, almost impatiently, with her own hands. The effect that this has on a man is extraordinary: Not knowing where she is leading you—you go more willing than you have ever gone anywhere before.

If she needed them across the room, she would merely point.

When she wanted to order them around it was with a calm, curt, and confidently bossy attitude.

"Go over there and sit on the ground with your back against the wall."

"No, flat on your ass...with your legs out...and together. Yes. Pull your cock and balls all the way up on top of your thighs."

"Yes. Now put your hands behind your back, and don't talk or move."

I was told that this was often the last time that Abbey would speak for the better part of the first hour, at which point she might finally allow them to cum for the first time, after she had already cum uncountable multiple shivering times.

But first she would sit them on the ground with their backs against the wall. Then she would walk forward over their extended legs, with her feet to the sides of their thighs, until her lovely legs and swelling bare cunt stood like a tower of feminine perfection in front of, and above their faces.

Then Abbey would begin touching herself, playing with her breasts and tummy, pulling her pussy open and leaning it in toward their faces, not teasing—promising.

Sometimes she would also use our rather large dildo, which helped her pulsing pink hole swell open even wider. If they opened their mouths and tried to move toward her without her permission she would reach her hand down around their jawbone and shut their mouth, pushing their head back against the wall where it belonged. The men also told me that sometimes she would punish them for moving without her saying so by shutting their eyelids for a while with her fingertips (which was certainly a torture).

With their eyes open or shut, being still or being lightly punished, she would eventually give in to her pushing desire and she would step in closer, tilting their heads back with both her hands. Then, straddling their faces, nearly sitting on them, she would begin rubbing her by then swollen-fully-open cunt, dripping with girl cum, all over their faces.

Focusing on the man's closed mouth and chin area, but not exclusively, she would hold his head in her hands and abandon herself to humping his face, and falling toward orgasm.

Whenever it suited her, not even looking at them, she would order them around like a soldier.

"Open your mouth and eat my pussy, now."

Or:

"Eat me you nasty fucker."

Or:

"Suck on me…"

And:

"YES. Suck on my cunt. Suck on meeeeeeeeee!"

Often banging their heads against the wall with the wild trusts of her hips, she would push and rub her lower tummy and entire cunt crack into their face until she shook like a gorgeous dark haired tree in a beautiful hurricane, with her sweet sweat and flowing pre-cum falling onto them in the raging storm—until the center of her sexual core broke all the way open and Abbey's squirting full orgasm of cum and loosened piss sprayed down over their face, chest, naked body, and into their forced open mouths.

Above them stood Abbey, gone beyond, screaming, magnificent, wholly woman, free, floating in wild orgasm—risen!

If a human can find a portal straight into sexual heaven Abbey had found it for herself—and she dragged those men through that portal with her.

Those who witnessed it bowed their entire bodies in worship.

I am *not* her sexual God—She is.

But I am the dark angel that set her free.

And when I did, I saw the sexual-secret of "It" more clearly than I ever had before!

"It" was directly connected to the "stranger factor": Being with a human you've never even met, specifically and only for the purpose of totally complication-free and brand-newly explored sexual contact.

I had always been with strangers out of what I felt was a forced necessity, not fully realizing the special potential it held.

However, by definition, after a couple of repetitions my friends were no longer "strangers"—enough—for Abbey. They still did exactly what Abbey told them to do, and she still blew their minds—but not her own, as much. Through direct experience she came to *know* that being naked and nasty with a man for the *very first time* was *the* most releasing.

In its own way, this is an amazing and ultimate expression of sexual variety.

Having come to this understanding, I revealed to her what it could be like to have sex with *total strangers* (even beyond bedroom strangers), which she knew I was expert at. And the very moment that she had the real thought of having sex with a total stranger—she damn near came in her pants.

(Seriously, we had to stop talking about it and fuck for a while—which was my first glimpse of the Dominatrix Abbey!)

Then she also realized, desperately disappointed for a moment (the dear), that she could probably never have the trust and safety that she required with a total stranger. To which I calmly replied, while stroking her naked skin, that she certainly could if I were with her. Even if I just sat in the other room of a hotel suite, or better yet watched, her safety would be complete.

Like someone who had won a lottery, Abbey was thrilled beyond description.

(And we had to fuck again, hard, and according to Abbey's instructions.)

So, mostly by coincidence of timing, on our next wedding anniversary, Abbey had her first "total stranger." And I not only got to accompany and witness the fully emboldened Dominatrix Abbey: Even more; I, her former master—became one of her slaves.

The combination of having me meet with the men first to make sure that they understood *exactly* how everything would be led by Abbey, and then her meeting them with my protection just across the room, or even better in an adjacent but out-of-sight suite section of the room, and my first listening to and then watching her be the Dominatrix—worked perfectly.

Watching Abbey take that amazing control over another man was so arousing I felt like I was tripping hallucinogens. Her eventually taking that same control of me, in front of them, and then her controlling two male sex slaves, ruling us in her beautiful naked flesh universe until she had cum dozens of times upon us, was one of the most surprisingly extraordinary sexual things that I've ever been a part of.

And Abbey and I discovered another level of the stranger-factor, which we refined by being inside the experience together. When we both noticed that her sexual behavior with me had become as unloosened as the behavior that was originally set free by strangers, we realized that she had learned how to be "whoever she wanted to sexually be" completely disconnected from any past or future social expectations: *She was the stranger!*

Also noteworthy is the fact that during that time of our life I felt almost no need for extra sex. I still *had* extra sex, on a daily basis, but the feeling of intense need for it virtually disappeared.

For one thing, towards the end of her adventures Abbey even developed a special passion for bi-sexual men joining us, and directing me and the men to have every kind of sex with each other for her own pleasure. She had always known about that part of my sexual being, and so she sought to be inside it with me; so even my safety go-to-kink was included in the course of my open sexual life with her.

In addition, Abbey also thoroughly explored and gratified both of our curiosities related to pure lesbian sexual contact by allowing me to watch and in one case participate with her during the half-dozen or so sexual events she had with two very wonderfully released women that she chose and pursued all on her own.

And the whole thing was surprisingly fulfilling! And I remember sleeping better in those days than I ever had since becoming a young, hiding, hyperactive, too penile-hard child.

Abbey becoming a later-blooming temporary hypersexual through this revealing avenue was an astonishing thing: I believe worthy of doctorate level study, and worthy of international artistic recognition.

She is certainly a legend among those lucky twenty-three men that she got naked with during her expansion.

I want that for every person who is seeking it, whenever they are seeking it.

What I also don't think I had previously witnessed in the same way that I was able to with Abbey, because of our lifelong and lasting closeness, is how deep, and wide, and real some seriously big sexual gratification can be. Because after barely two and-a-half years, Abbey was so sexually fulfilled I could feel it before she decided to say it outloud.

After just a couple of years of (intermittent) hypersexual activity, Abbey was just plain sexually fulfilled. There is no other word or description for it. She had simply filled up the cup of her sexual needs, and to this day sixteen years later she still enjoys the wickedly contenting bliss of having had all those actual sexual experiences, even though she has no current desire to physically repeat them.

So what I also came to understand, then, is that some people can become temporary-hypersexuals. And that's cool too, of course.

If you are to respect each person's own sexual choices, then that also applies to when that person chooses not to continue engaging in certain kinds of sex, for whatever reason. Even if they do not feel the desire for sex at all—you have to respect that—which is another very important reason for needing other, acceptable, non-committed, and non-life threatening options.

Husbands and wives don't need to limit or force or change each other sexually, so much as respect each other more completely. And maybe gratifying extra-marital and or non-traditional sexual desires is a smaller matter than we think?

Furthermore, and most profound as far as our personal relationship goes: Abbey was finally able to see directly into what I had been unable to adequately explain to her about my lifelong need for sex with new partners and strangers. Sharing this understanding on a truth-experience level meant the world to us. And it healed both our hearts.

For me that was the closest I had ever come to finding myself in the full-light.

And, for me the discovery and experience of Abbey's temporary hypersexuality—and specifically the fulfillment of it—was tantamount to the personal sexual enlightenment that I had always been looking for.

I understood then that if Abbey, a magnificent temporary hypersexual could be so fulfilled—and *if even I could feel an absence of the terrible side of sexual need*—then there was certainly a very widely applicable positive principle contained in the act of people having sex with other partners, and multiple partners, and unknown-to-them partners, which was my own life's path!

Seeing someone like Abbey benefit so directly and so importantly and so completely from sex with strangers was like seeing myself in the same sexual mirror as the rest of humankind for the first time in my adult life!

And I realized that *something* about what I was doing was *right*, and I felt so much less alone!

And that was the first time that I knew for certain that hypersexuals could help save people other than themselves.

By now, my ideas are strongly defined.

I deeply believe that if general society could be allowed multiple kinds of completely legal, easily available, and totally affordable sexual contact options like well-designed and socially supported public sex arenas, and properly created houses of prostitution serviced by a staff of hypersexuals, and also temporarily hypersexual angels (like Abbey was during her sexual rushes)—we could redefine the whole sex and sexual contact paradigm in America and make great advances in reducing the number of our sex crime victims, and in reducing the number of our sex criminals, as well as better dealing with a the entire long list of our society's other sex related problems.

In general society, utter sexual loneliness and isolation would affect way fewer people. People not necessarily meant to be in a couple, or any other type of currently common or traditional relationship, could still enjoy the human right, necessity, and gratification of physical sexual contact.

And it might be surprising how powerful that sexually concentrated kind of human connection might be in the scope of that person's greater life. Maybe some people don't really need all those other relationship dressings, perhaps the only missing element for their best personal life format is a little casual fucking.

Perhaps then the deep piles of tension caused by all the unfulfilled sexual desires of so many people would lift and vanish from their bodies and faces.

Perhaps this sexual stress is also to blame for some, or a majority of, the pent-up petty and over-aggressive anger that we are finding increasingly exhibited in our society.

More than equally as important, if we really opened up the sexual services to our whole population, a group currently regarded as *untouchable* sexually, which includes all the medically termed physically handicapped, deformed, permanently mangled, mentally injured, and perhaps even the mentally disabled could be equally sexually loved and adored.

How about a new wing in the severely injured care unit of each Veterans Administration facility? Sex for vets!

Hypersexuals, and I believe many others would welcome and adore these kinds of sexual expansions! The full circle of possibilities is so inviting.

What if this could also become a way for so-called "disabilities" to become newly-explored as *abilities?*

How about sex with a hypersexualized blind person? Or sex supplied for a blind person by a well fitted hypersexual partner? I can't imagine all the tactile, spatial, mental reference, and other experiential differences that particular special sexual coupling could include. And the extended possibilities, to other disabilities are countless!

How about saving all the wasted public attention, and political, military, and public service careers lost to consensual sexual contact scandals—all gone in an instant because adult sexual issues, including infidelity, would be the private business of the individuals involved and no one else would need to give a damn—which would happen as soon as the gavel strikes on the change of sex laws and society can start looking at sexual contact in a decidedly new and much less entangled way.

And, in a world with this kind of sexual openness, variety, and available gratification, most of the people who are currently driven criminally insane because of the lack of available sex options would never even know that frustration.

I also believe that in an expertly developed system the remaining violent sex criminals could be more easily lured-out. Empowered hypersexuals could much better spot and even draw out any suspicious fellow hypers still looking to go beyond the boundaries of sexual choice and trust.

A system revolution that is this truly wide reaching is exactly what we need to change the current paradigm. If we did it across our whole country—just like we do with so many kinds of Federal decisions and programs—our remaining sexually resistant citizens, who stridently support maximum controls and laws against sexual contact, would finally have to "get over it", and religious opinions would become just that, opinions. And we could create a cultural shift and a social benefit for our entire nation the likes of which has not been seen before.

It is not my way to think small, and I have been quickly challenged on my theory by remarkably intelligent and historically informed people doubting it mainly because they couldn't help but wonder why such a thing has never worked for humanity before. And my humble answer to them is that these exact social conditions have never existed before, and sex and sexual issues aren't static in history, they are ever-flowing and especially responsive to all the specific human and social pressures of the present surroundings and moment. And though I am not educated enough or factually empowered enough to conclusively argue or prove it, I feel confident that this exact idea has never been implemented before, and certainly not on the scale I propose, and certainly not in our American society.

My vision comes from experiencing the deepest sexual roots of our society, and it extends to the highest halls of our social challenges and law, and it reaches out to the widest ranges of human respect and inclusion, and it seeks the greatest levels of sexual safety that we can create in this time of mankind for all ages and people. I want it all.

Let's learn Abbey's lesson: Let's take advantage of strangers.

The current alternative, the present sexual reality, is no longer a defensible system.

Chapter Eleven

<u>Rape</u>

I know far too much about rape: From being a victim multiple times, from nearly being a victim several other times, from being in love with so many victims that I've met, from deep study, from terrible life-long fantasies, and because it is the antithesis of my entire being.

And also—because I am guilty.

In my youth I sexually convinced, cajoled, coerced, leveraged, and insistently forced myself on others in many, many different ways, and I will not deny it.

I never physically hurt or sexually terrorized anyone. But otherwise, plainly said, everything short of that dire mark was fair game to me in my immaturity.

From my inside perspective, straining to appreciating the bigger-than-me picture: I see that the experience of rape is prevalent, rather than rare; and proliferating, rather than being more effectively reduced; and monstrous towards so many of its victims, in so many ways, including our cultural inability to better deal with the threat and issues both before and after the crime. And many current American researchers believe that sexual crimes are increasing in frequency. And our society seems helpless in the face of it.

What can *I* possibly say of any real meaning? Believe me, I hesitate.

Regardless, as incomplete and/or individually skewed as it may be, I must now write and present my long considered thoughts on rape. If even one helpful detail emerges, it is *something*.

Rape happens: Day in and day out, and every night, rape of every kind happens, from infant pedophilia to rotting necrophilia, with every single other possibility penetrated in between.

To begin with, adolescent children rape other children. Especially when they've been raped. And by "children," I mean anyone about ten years or under. And by "rape" I mean creating forced sex, and/or creating sexual-contact that is not based on consent or mutual sexual respect (which aren't possible with children).

And: Slightly older youths rape children. My oldest brother did me, and he was barely twelve years-old when he first came to me, at seven years-old.

And once he took away my choice at that young age, and took away even the awareness that I had a choice, I have to tell you that it was a damn hard kind of consciousness to regain. I cannot say it any more plainly.

And rape among children and youths happens in a multitude of ways, in millions of homes. We all know that; and we all don't talk about it. I will admit that children and youths raping each other is a tricky kind of rape to put your finger on, or take aim at, because children and youths aren't the rape-attacker our society sees in their cultural mind's-eye.

But, why not? Why aren't all kids raised and educated to know exactly what-is-what when it comes to sexual contact with other kids? And why isn't the problem of youth rape dealt with more openly and much more completely?

Parents are responsible for that, and when they turn their backs and fail to address too-early sexual contact, of any kind—they have made a grave mistake. And when parents fail to properly educate children in a protective way—they have facilitated both the weakness and the danger that threatens children.

Making important sexual matters clear, even to children, doesn't seem much different to me than describing which snakes are poisonous and potentially deadly, or which animals are aggressive, or that kids need to stay away from the tops of old wells and other big holes they might fall into. Where does the sexual conversation get so difficult that parents can't even try?

Who raises kids that don't understand the wrongness of sexual force?

Well, my parents did: They raised six kids without enough specific sexual knowledge or informed respect to help me (at all).

We grew up without a word of sexual instruction or enlightenment—even though we were taught to be socially respectful toward all people generally, with my mother above all others.

Still, I used to get down on my knees and suck off my oldest brother and as many as three or four of his friends one after the next, some of them as much as five and six years older than me. And afterwards they would treat me like an outcast, and sometimes beat and bully me, and I accepted it—because we had absolutely no other framework of knowledge to give us perspective or guidance.

And I fully realize, now, that what I remember most is the (temporary) feeling of the powerful acceptance of those older boys when I was sexually pleasing them, and that I opened my mouth with a terrible willingness that was all my own—because I thought that was what I was supposed to be trying for—and I was only seven and eight years old when it started.

There must have been some kind of more helpful, protective, or preventative knowledge that my parents (or someone) could have taught us, and me.

I did hear adults and parents tell me not to physically maul all the girls around me so much, which should have been connected to a greater understanding in my mind; but even when adults did scold me they never sat down and explained anything about it to me, or helped me understand why I might feel or act the way I did.

So, I was left to learn about sexual respect on my own, at a later time in life.

Children should know as much as they can as early as they can. But that is not the way of our American culture. In our culture you are allowed to begin actually studying sexual subjects in college, *if* you choose it, and pay for it.

So, in addition: Teenagers rape children, and pre-teens, and other teenagers, and sometimes vulnerable adults.

In most cases (perhaps as much as eighty five percent), these rapes are also not the classically depicted violent or fully forced attacks that our society holds a picture of. But they are definitely acts of taking the other, often younger, person's choice away. And this definitely includes females raping males in all the many ways they can, and do.

People distant from the crimes can often think that only the victim (assumed female) who is violently beaten and injured, or somehow more obviously terrorized, has actually been sexually raped.

The truth, especially for young victims, is that most of the forced and choice-less sexual contact can and does happen at a time well before the victim can even understand, be aware of, or exercise any kind of control over what happens to themselves—so the need for violence or real force on the part of the perpetrator is unnecessary, or at least greatly moderated.

My second-cousin Déjà did that to me, as you know, and it was the most physically delicious, emotionally encasing, and mentally overwhelming sexual experience a child and pre-teen boy might ever have. And, in our culture, it was also an extremely confusing experience with no social context or meaningful follow-up of processing the overwhelming event—at all.

And my relationship with Déjà is also a perfect example of another fact about rape and sexual abuse that is much less often discussed: Rape doesn't just happen *once* to each victim. Many rapes are a repetitive occurrence in the victim's life, either because of the same attacker, or because of living in proximity to other myriad possible factors that can leave a young (or not so young, or not young at all) person vulnerable.

But that's not to forget or lose awareness of all the victims who have suffered only one attack, or attacks that were random and terrorizing and not from within their closer worlds. The other sides of rape statistics guarantee that sexual attacks will show up nearly everywhere, and in nearly every shape, which should, again, tell us how prevalent rape is.

Then: Adults rape victims of every age, every day, in uncountable ways, everywhere around the world. And unfortunately, adult rapists are the most variant, and by far the most able.

Rape being "forced sex," I have to ask the question again: What if all these sexual abusers and rapists didn't *need* to force or leverage somebody in order to obtain their sex?

As I have stated previously: The current thesis that rape *isn't* primarily an act of sex couldn't be more off-mark, or absurd. That it is like saying that the gun (representing the power potential) is what is responsible for the murder (representing the rape). No: It is the motive (sexual contact) that loads the act and creates the individual decision that pulls the trigger.

Rape isn't primarily an act of anger, aggression, or control: The rapist doesn't angrily force people to do something else like shine shoes, or mow the lawn, or paint murals—they force their victims to have sex with them, often in moods quite far from anger. It is that plain and simple.

Anger, aggression, and physical control are just tools the rapists use, in different ways, depending on who they are. And, importantly, those are not the only tools rapists' use, which is an immensely important part of why we have to find every way to be more honest about the act.

Here is an important question that is almost never openly asked or dealt with: Why shouldn't a person deeply desire the ability to powerfully control one of lifes' most cherished, pleasurable, intense, intimate, physical, and emotional events of gratification? Of course people want that kind of control and power over sex; they want and work diligently to obtain that level of ability in every other scope of life, too.

In fact, those exact qualities of aggressively pursuing power and control are considered signatures of success in nearly every other kind of human endeavor. But, in our American culture, unless you are one of the very rare persons in a traditional relationship whose partner allows for total sexual domination, the only ways to actually have that much control over a sexual contact event is to buy it illegally (dangerous and prohibitively expensive), or find it in an underground sexual contact arena (dangerous and illegal), or force it (unfortunately the easiest way, for far too many predators).

Anger is about anger. Physical aggression has everything to do with the specific individual and their current stresses. And trying to subtract the human aspiration to powerfully control our sexual existences and experiences is an illusion.

But the straightforward human need for sexual contact is a much deeper human mechanism. In fact, science and medicine have long known that humans are born with three imprinted primary imperatives: food, sleep, and sexual contact; all of which are wired into us at the deepest level of survival. And when any one of these needs is denied, all hell can break loose in the person. Think about it: What happens when a human is denied sleep; they go crazy. What happens when a person is denied food; they'll steal it.

Rape *is* about sex.

It is as if our society so dislikes facing our sexual issues, they are even willing to turn away from it in their way of looking at rape!

People who haven't been raped should listen to people who have; and also to people who have made terrible mistakes and are willing to be honest about it.

In grim addition, in order to open our view as widely as possible, we must look more closely at how rape can occur not only in all the ways that I've already mentioned, but also in an endless array of other ways and circumstances. So far, we've only talked about the more conventionally recognized circumstances.

There are so many more.

Even a forced sexual act in the midst of perverted illegal public-sex counts as rape. Believe me, it counts. Unquestionably, the most violent situations that I have ever been in occurred in the kept-out-of-sight corners of public sex arenas. And I can quickly count past fifteen violent occurrences that have happened to me over the course of my life.

If that seems surprising, consider this: Rape and violence over sex is an extremely serious problem in the currently broken-off and hidden public sexual dimensions of our society, like porn shop alleys, and public parks, and street prostitution. And let me tell you that fighting off a sudden and strangling sexual attack, while already in the grip of sex—literally fighting for your life coming directly out of a previously agreed upon sexual engagement—is an extremely animalistic kind of experience. And, it can seriously redefine a hypersexual's understandings.

Hookers being forced to do things that they've said "no" to counts, too. Imagine how many times that happens? And if you didn't know that almost all hookers have their own limits, now you do (in point of fact, most of them have all kinds of differing boundaries).

If a person says "No," no matter the circumstances or the sexual orientations of the persons involved, it is rape.

I grew up thinking that the completely innocent must suffer so much more, like little kids, and perhaps the most proper people, and prim mothers, or whatever. But in deepest consideration I have also realized that in using the term "innocent" I might seem to (or actually) be denigrating anyone "less than innocent," which I most definitely do not mean to do.

I'm really not sure where we'd draw the line if we wanted to define that term in this context, or what difference we should expect it to make. I know what questions I would ask first: Is it less wrong when a man is raped? Is it less wrong when a grumpy old hag is raped? Is it less wrong when a slut is raped? Is it less wrong when a child is raped for the second, or third, or twentieth time?

The answer is "No."

I was violently raped by strangers in what I thought was a grayer zone, because of who I am, even though I was just a kid at the time. But there was nothing vague or unclear about the violently unleashed intentions of those who attacked me, or the terror I felt during and after.

Because, even if I put the full grown men's straining cocks all the way inside my eleven year-old mouth, begging them to throat-fuck me until their hot spiking cum drained into my swallowing body: If I then said, *"No. I've never let men fuck me in the ass, and I don't want to."* And they then grabbed hold of me with their huge arms and hands and ripped my pants off and fucked me anyway, while I cried quietly through some of the worst stabbing pain I have ever felt in my life—that was definitely rape.

And, even if I willingly, only months later, got into a different man's car and stuffed my pre-teen face down into his naked smelly lap: that did not mean he was welcome to suddenly hold me down there, helpless in his iron-grip, with my face pushed into his legs and stomach so hard I was choking—while he tried to drive away with me. Clearly, I was being raped (and abducted).

Being held face-down by the neck and made to become a feral animal scratching and clawing for its life, twisting and kicking and screaming, terrified to fight but unstoppably wailing in an effort to escape, and then having to jump blindly out of a fast moving vehicle—is definitely rape.

If that malevolent man had not had to suddenly steer his car with both his hands at that precise moment, to avoid slamming over the large curb of the city park's entrance—fighting for control of his steering wheel around the sharp curve—I probably could not have escaped him.

It is significant, at least to me, that even though that man did not complete his sexual effort, the occurrence was sure as hell a rape. And if he were caught he probably should have been treated as a raping/kidnapping/murderer. Because, from the conglomeration of his actions I have always believed that man would have happily killed me, like happens all the time in so many child abduction-for-sex cases.

I know that I *felt* death when my neck was being crushed in that man's steely grip.

Sadly, once I had escaped that man my biggest immediate fears became how I would explain my torn shirt and badly bruised neck to my parents. Telling them the truth was out of the question, since I knew that path would likely end-up with me being put in a children's mental ward for being where I was, and doing what I was doing.

I guess I was in a gray area after all.

To anyone like me, our current legal cut-and-dried definitions of rape don't do us justice.

Consequent to my range of contact experiences, for my entire life I have never been able to stop thinking about rape—from every viewpoint.

Later in life, when I was a twenty year-old workout fanatic, I was raped again by a weightlifting French masseuse. It sounds funny and almost stupid to me, too. But all you need to know is that I never sent that guy a single inviting signal, and all I went expecting was a much needed muscular massage, and that his only methods of seduction were his superior muscular force and the threat of injury. And, that I wasn't allowed to leave his house until my "appointment" was completed—and he had finished ass-raping me (even though I submissively offered to suck him off).

In total, on top of the times that I didn't get away, I have escaped thirteen attempted violently forced sexual situations in my life. And yes, most of those attempts were suffered in illegal sex arenas (except for the above mentioned masseuse incident, which occurred under the guise of health care in his home). And—importantly—my total number of confrontations is small-change compared to the numbers that many if not most street hookers and prostitutes would present.

Still, I have definitely had a few too many experiences with the forced side of sex. And, like sex workers of all kinds and many others, I've also dragged something back from that dark place. By the last of those attempted forced-sex incidents (all of which went very poorly for my attackers), I was coming away from them with an oddly un-ruffled—

and even an excited attitude—which I knew wasn't a mentally healthy outlook.

By the very last one, at the age of thirty-three, if I am even more honest I would tell you that I felt a thrilling and satisfying rush in my instantly crushing defense against that rude and aggressive man—along with an eerie calmness—even knowing that he would require hospitalization—which was disturbing.

There's a difference between stopping someone from doing something wrong to you, and punishing someone for a debt not earned by them alone. And, taking that much physical advantage of someone should have made me feel much more uncomfortable.

I'm glad that now-distant incident was the last of its kind, and I doubt I'll ever find myself in that situation again. But I am still an exposed denizen in a dangerous public sexual underworld.

Still further into the issue:

In the course of my many, many conversations with victims, I have also shared frank conversations with many who have been attackers. The overwhelming percentage of whom, I am happy to tell you, were genuinely remorseful and completely hopeful of being sexually harmless forevermore, which is a well-known but under-valued statistic.

I'll say it even more clearly: Most rapists don't want to rape. They *do* want sex. And I know that these offenders have a clear path to recovery, because I/we can give them sex.

I have also looked squarely into the eyes of some who *want to commit rape*, again and again. And who exist without any remorse about such actions. And those persons need to be permanently incarcerated, or otherwise controlled, because they *will* find a way to violently assault and rape again. Their hunger is for sex-penetrated-by-violence, and unlike the great majority of humankind, no other sexual taste interests them, or will gratify them.

One depth of rape that I do not know, is the experience of being viciously snatched out of the blue, stolen completely away from an entire life, beaten into a paralyzed state, tied and lost in helplessness, repeatedly and sadistically raped, held ignorant hostage, starved, terrified beyond sanity, and finally murdered and disposed of—unless all of that has happened to me in another lifetime.

I did once meet a thirty-five year-old woman named Sue who was abducted by a stranger at the age of seventeen and held for two weeks as a physically battered sex slave. And both Sue and I believe that she would have most likely died had she not escaped.

I make my leaping assumption mainly because the abductor committed suicide when his identity was discovered. Sue made her statements based on the most specific and unfortunately intimate information anyone should ever need to know about their attacker.

Sue and I were freshly naked when we found ourselves really meeting each other. And then, a half-hour later, she was a tear soaked wreck after telling me about her experience.

I should have seen it coming. Even though I am always very attentive and hyper-conscious when I lead a person into the jaws of my consuming questions, when Sue took several physically frozen minutes to begin, and then started her story with a burst of tears, I just didn't realize what I was unlocking.

And to my wrenching disappointment, no matter what I tried afterwards, our attempts at sex were dismal and quickly died out.

Before I had twisted our fast, fun, and spontaneous encounter by asking my burning hypersexual questions, I'd felt that the sex Sue and I were headed for was going to be some very strong, wild, and perhaps even playfully rough stuff. That was the vibe I was feeling, and I'm a sex-vibe tuning-fork.

After telling me her story, which was drowning in all the complex confusions of a still struggling victim, having hard rocking sex seemed awkward. And the soft petting pity-filled love that we slid into instead, was also uncomfortable, so she asked me to stop.

I always wished that, before I asked my questions, I had fucked her good and hard, and as wildly as she'd wanted, so she could have experienced sexual trust and release with me, instead of just talking about it.

My intuition told me that she wanted to be able to fight-back a little as we had sex—and for it to be "okay" for her to fight back, and for it to be a playful and laughing kind of thing—and something that she could control from her side. And what a wonderfully balancing and probably healing kind of sexual play that could have been for her!

When we'd first met at the sports bar and started flirting, and I had noticed what a physically rambunctious girl she was, I fully encouraged her with high-fives and shoulder butts, and eventually punches to the arm. And I bet she sensed that I might be the kind of guy who wouldn't have a problem taking a less dominant sexual position, and of course she was right.

Too bad. At least she had let me touch her heart. But it was her sexual body—her savagely raped sexual body—that I wanted to sooth.

The depth of my lifelong connection to rape, and my manic interest in it, and my emotional absorption with the crime of rape is something that I have never completely revealed to anyone, until now.

It is such an untoward subject to be so attracted to.

Clearly, my personal take on rape is too raw, and too intimate, and too self-focused. And my suggested solutions always seem disrespectful in the context of the current social dialogue. But my story is about hypersexuals, and where those persons overlap the discussion about rape is the exact crossroads where the most important possible public options come into the discussion.

For a person constantly needing to exercise and expand their sexual self, the difference between having acceptable places to go for sex—and having nearly no place to go, or none—is all the difference in the world.

Solving impossible social mazes to obtain sexual contact is not a healthy frustration for hypersexuals (or anyone else). For us it is like a kind of claustrophobia, and some of the escape routes we will create to break through those confines will be wildly destructive.

I've struggled in the lonely labyrinths of seeking random and variant sexual contact in our society, and I have exerted an incredible amount of time and energy, and exhausted every skill and resource that I could muster, and exposed myself to a whole host of serious dangers—all to what I would consider a bare minimum of success.

I shudder to think about all those hypersexuals whose lives have even more severe limits, and no outlets, or effectively applicable skills, or resources, or free time, or any sexual success.

Most hypersexuals aren't even allowed a decent masturbation life, let alone a fully furnished masturbatorium like mine, where they could at least more deeply pleasure themselves and let their sexual spirits wander farther. The internet, of course, is now supplying a significant boost in a mega-variety of visual material. Which can be helpful. But even with that potential, any unhurried and unhindered use of it, is severely limited under the privacy constraints of most social, familial, and close personal relationships situations. And all this is still a vast dry desert away from the wet flesh-to-flesh contact that is actually needed.

For me, seeing this layer of social reality is like watching my own minority being chained-up and starved in front of everyone else. And when one of them slips the chain, I so wish that I could feed them...

For all those hunting for sex: I simply wish to give it to them, which would remove them from everyone's danger—at least for a moment—and that's a better plan than anyone else can offer.

Imagine a society-wide sexual system so effective the about-to-offend could simply turn themselves in for a "treatment."

Another vitally important thing that I can share here, is that even a fully unrestrained hypersexual is limited by how many orgasms and how much physical energy they can exert toward sex in a given day. One-stop shopping at a proper house of variant sexual contact, or exhausting employment in such a place, with the availability of any number of sexual contact options, would wear-out even the very strongest and longest-lasting of us.

As for those humans still looking for a measure of confrontational physicality, or contested strength with their sex, it would be a powerful thing to consider that there are certainly hypersexuals willing to be involved in "rough" sex—*very rough*—which, if provided, may quell a meaningful number of the remaining potential sexual attackers.

Maybe the range of human nature and sexual desire are already more equally balanced in our population than we currently understand; maybe we already have what we need.

I say: Let the hypersexuals lead the way, and trust them with their own lives and creative careers—and perhaps general society could finally let go of so many of its difficult sexual concerns, and admitted inabilities, and valid fears—because someone qualified would (finally) be taking care of that social need (instead of the religiously based laws that have been in charge).

If we could facilitate and provide everything from fully willing fifteen year-old baby-acting sex-workers, or even midget hypers in diapers, all the way to cage-fighting submission fucking sex warriors, as well as old horny grannies and grandpas willing to act horrified and then suddenly turned-on by young exhibitionists (and visa-versa), and Dom's and Dominatrix's waiting to sexually smack-fuck the-piss-out-of somebody (anybody), and every other kind of sex a person could voice a desire for—we might nearly erase the behavior of rape.

Don't we have to try?

Chapter Twelve

Zoos

Scruffy

I distinctly remember that I was twelve years old when my initial sexual contact with an animal happened, because I was also beginning the sixth grade in a new school. Having moved to a suburban/rural edge of the greater city area, in order to save money on better housing, our family was reoriented to the new and different mixture of neighborhoods surrounded by small to medium sized ranches.

With everything else that was going on in my young life at the time, (as previously written), a newly discovered avenue of sexual contact was a particularly welcomed event. And it was an even easier thing to accept because it came in the form of our well-mannered family pet, our funny little dog, Scruffy.

(I realize that's a terribly common name for a dog, but when a common name fits a common appearance—it fits.)

Our Scruffy was a short-legged, long black-haired mixed-breed mutt whose most defining trait was his friendliness. Not a dog to keep aggressive watches, or sit at the door barking, he was much more the dog who preferred to follow a family member around just to see what they were doing.

So, when he found me sitting on the floor in my closet one day, with my hard little cock in my hand, he was duly curious. And I was surprised. For one thing, I hadn't seen him come into the room behind me. But Scruffy didn't seem surprised, he seemed calmly excited, like he always was. Wagging his tail energetically and putting his nose right up to the end of my penis, and then sniffing it, and actually touching it, without a trace of hesitation or shyness, he directly entered my sphere of sexual consideration.

Allowing him to smell my penis, or more specifically the very opening of my penis (where he seemed personally pre-occupied), I held still and waited to see what he would do. And when he slowly extended his big, fat, pink, warm and wet tongue, and licked right around and across the head of my dick—I knew exactly what *he wanted* to do.

Instantly aroused by the specific and immediate new sensual experience, it took me only a few quick jerking strokes to make myself orgasm—and when I did, Scruffy eagerly and skillfully licked up every squirt and drop of it, and kept licking as if hoping for more. All of which was unquestionably pleasurable to me (even if in a somehow different and difficult to explain way).

Wagging his tail even higher, Scruffy then looked up to my face to see what I was communicating with that part of my body. Smiling back at him, and I'm sure with an extra wide smile, I reached out with my left hand and patted his head.

"Scruffy!" I said out loud (but not too loud), "I had no idea you were such a nasty little doggie!"

Smiling back at me with his long tongue hanging out, and wagging his tail even faster, he'd then pushed his wet nose back up against my penis and hand as if playing with a toy.

"Alright Scruffy," I said with a giggle, "...knock it off. I have to do my chores and sweep the whole damn driveway and garage before five o'clock."

Later that day, when I thought back to what had happened, the simplicity of the moment in the closet disappeared. And I began to feel distinctly weird about what had happened, which was odd for me when related to sexual experiences. In fact, I began to feel a kind of shame and panic that I had never felt before. Because when I had come around to thinking about it from the perspective of the people in my life, my family, my friends, and the society that surrounded me, I was certain that they would all see this particular sexual behavior as perhaps even more repulsive and offensive than any other. And though this particular sexual contact subject was so vehemently despised it was never really spoken about out-loud (for more than a disgusted and hushed instant); I knew beyond any doubt what the level of revulsion would be.

What the hell had I been thinking? I found myself worrying. *What the hell was wrong with me? Had I crossed a disgusting sexual barrier of no-return?*

However, to my dismay in the following days none of those thoughts, worries, or hidden shame, was sufficient to make me *not* want to experience the directly pleasurable sexual parts of what had happened, or to repeatedly think back to the easy seeming moment of shared enjoyment and orgasm. All of which left me with yet another severe socially and personally separating schism in my sexual experience and understanding.

Little did I know, then, how incredibly common sexual contact between humans and non-human animals actually is. Or that it is academically accepted that this sexual behavior began before recorded history, and has remained throughout, right up into our current now. And that it is found all around the Earth, and extends into in almost every branch of human nationality and culture.

Unfortunately, in American society those facts are kept fiercely secret, and silenced, which leaves us with literally millions of children, young people, and adults with absolutely no honest gauge or knowledgeable perspective for considering their sexual contact with an animal(s).

Instead, we have the great American lie: which tells us that sexual contact with animals is incredibly rare, that it is a behavior borne from terrible insanity, and that it is deviantly devastating to both the individual and the society around them, as well as spiritually damning to the person.

All of which was bred down from the Old Testament, then further in-bred by the puritanical religious leaders of the New World, resulting in the colonial law that any such contact, or in reality even being suspected of it, was punishable by death.

And, though this American culturally founding religious judgment has since morphed itself into modern versions of both religious and non-religious social judgments, and new laws and punishments, as well as medically defined labels, and forced treatments, and irremovable stigma's—all woven into the contemporary fabric of "the great lie"—the outwardly expressed public disgust continues to be advanced under the original, unchanged from the Bible, denigrating banner of "Bestiality."

However, as I found out much later in life—it turns out that the word "bestiality," itself, is in many if not most cases, an inaccurate word. And similarly, all the other generalized judgments against sexual contact with animals are also erroneous. And the reason that I say all this in such a calm and even tempered voice is due to the fact that the horror stricken gasps of loathing and damnation that are currently used in our general society about sexual contact with an animal—need to be balanced in the clearest possible way.

Zoophilia

Zoophilia is the modern word and arena of study and experience that attempts to accurately acknowledge and respectfully encompass the full array of unbridled human sexual contact with non-human animals. It graciously includes the simplest one-time experiences, the briefest explorations, the often early life occurrences, the more developed or repeated experiences, through all the varieties of practice, including those who proclaim that their erotic physical and emotional relationships with animals are superior to those possible with humans. Admittedly, it's an open range.

Bestiality, in comparison, and in a confusingly incomplete way, refers *only* to the most generalized definition of an occurrence of physical sexual contact with an animal, with absolutely no additional specifics included, which is instantly problematic because not only is there an astonishingly wide variety of ways in which that contact can and does occur, but it is also true that almost no human act or behavior (certainly including sexual events) exists or takes place without numerous important personal factors in-play, which simply must be appreciated.

In which case, to me, "bestiality" becomes a nearly un-usable word, because its meaning has so little real meaning. As an entirely unspecific definition, the word only facilitates a singular, overreaching, critically limited, and an assumed all-negative judgment.

Zoophilia, though, in significant contrast, explicitly appreciates from the beginning that when people have sexual contact, of any kind, including with non-human animals, there is also, a vast percentage of the time, a more (or much more) complex, and even fully cognizant personal awareness, attention, investment, and even an important (in some or many ways) "relationship" content involved.

And a great percentage of these zoophilic sexual relationships are—to describe them without any drama—similar to or exactly like the common relationships we see between adoring pet owners and their pets all over the world, as well as the working relationships of people whose professions involve animal labor, or animal care. In plain fact, in a majority of cases, zoophilic relationships are borne from those exact circumstances.

All of which refutes another one of the most prominent general misunderstandings about sexual contact with animals, which is that it is purposely and pervasively physically abusive to the animals, as well as disrespectful in terms of animal rights. But who cares more for those points of respect than pet owners, or professional animal workers, or animals care givers?

I would have never even thought about hurting Scruffy, in any way, shape, or form. I described the occurrence exactly as it happened; I don't know what more I can offer. Scruffy was clearly the one who initiated our contact.

"They" are "Us"

So, the sexual contact that I had with Scruffy wasn't bestiality. It may have been a rather short and simple seeming contact, but it was also filled with a whole host of personally driven sexual components from my side, as well as the fact that Scruffy was such an affectionate animal (for all his own reasons)—which is important.

And while that contact may have been quite limited for me, and I am obviously but one among the multitudes, each with their own details, the lasting effects of not having any way to process the contact, except for the singularly worst way—misinformation leading to serious self-misconceptions—makes it evident to me that we need to bring the greatly expanded conversation of the modern zoophiles out into our general public conversation, and then we need to expand the conversation even more.

In doing my own research on sexual contact with animals, I found it interesting that over the last century several notable historical researchers and theorists from many different parts of the world have tried to discern whether or not rural farmers with their livestock, or professionals (like entertainers) with their work animals, or city and suburban dwellers with their pets, create the greater number of "offenders," which tuned out to be a question none of them could definitively answer, other than to focus on animal-to-human density and common daily interaction figures.

But what that information led *me* to ask is "why" or even "if" the answer to that question has any preeminent value? The formation of the question, itself, is much more important.

The fact that both historians and modern researchers fully acknowledge the widespread variety and diversity of the sexual activity—in *all* the different types of human populations—seems to me to be the far more important recognition. And the reason that specific recognition is so important is that it shatters three of the foundation pillars of the "great American lie" about sexual contact with animals: It isn't rare; the multitude of people who engage in it are not insane; and it obviously doesn't lead to any kind of mass social decay or destruction.

Further, after completing and contemplating my own research, together with my own hypersexual experiences and conversations, I would confidently go as far as to say that every single person in our

American society knows not only "someone," but likely several people who have had some kind of sexual contact with animals.

"They" are simply a part of our population.

Think about that for a minute, and accept it; or accept fully willing conscious denial.

Plainly, "they" are "us."

I am.

Or, at least I was. And I recently met a surprisingly candid and educated young woman who told me about an adolescent stretch of time where she enjoyed playing with her tom-cats furry balls (which he greatly enjoyed). And I've met at least twenty or so other people during my lifetime of explicit conversations that were also willing, and sometimes thrilled, to admit and talk about their sexual contact experiences with animals.

However, that *is* only twenty or so people out of hundreds and hundreds of partners and even more conversations, which means that a great number of my partners hid that particular sexual fact *even from me*.

Highlighting the fact that in regard to our greater society, despite the historical and modern facts (which, of course, are not commonly known in our society), staid attention must be given to the defensive intensity with which sexual contact with an animal is guarded and hidden, even by openly admitted perverts of so many other kinds, whose deceptions are in direct proportion to the astounding amount of revulsion that sexual contact with animals is treated with in our publicly-displayed society.

Even *I* hid that fact from almost all of my sexual partners. Sometimes even when they were admitting it to me.

The "great lie" about sexual contact with animals—makes liars of us all.

Donkeys, Etc., Etc.

In Jr. High School, a year or so after my experience with Scruffy, I met and came to know a sweet and modest girl named Evelyn who would ride her favorite stallion bareback so that she could slide forward until the area known as the withers, the prominent bone between the horses shoulders, would rub up against her vagina, rhythmically—until she had full-fledged orgasms. Riding beside her during our late afternoon breaks from doing homework, I greatly enjoyed watching how she would get into her proper position and pace, and then half-close her eyes and relax into it. And I would swear that her horses head would rise higher, and that it would flare its nostrils during those moments. And I definitely observed how her horse would stay perfectly positioned and perfectly paced for Evelyn until she let out that final shivering sigh and her eyes popped all the way back open, at which point the horse would whinny and neigh, and change its trot, and shake its head back and forth (perhaps smelling her "scent" in the air).

Evelyn would also slide right off her horse whenever it would pee, and stooping next to it she would unapologetically (and without any explanation to me) stare right at its giant cock until it had squirted and dripped its last drop, and then retreated all the way back up into its fold.

And though she never reached out for it, I definitely felt as if she would have liked to. All of which surprised me, but definitely didn't disgust me.

I also remember that the first time she showed her secret pleasure to me she described it as something that had happened by "accident," and other than that we never said much about it. And even when I would flirtingly mention her wet crotch mark on her jeans at the end of a ride, or told her that she made me terribly horny when we got back to her house, or begged her to let me make-out with her when we were alone in her room—*that* was a totally separate conversation, to both of us. All of which she would laugh-off anyway, or slap away if necessary, because she was a dedicated Christian girl who believed she was destined to remain a virgin until she was married. So the most sexual thing we ever did was French kiss, which I taught her how to do.

Fascinatingly, because Evelyn was always fully clothed when she was riding her horse, and it was done in such an unhidden way in broad daylight, and because several other usual "cues" were missing from my typical assessment of sexual contact, those horseback riding occurrences seemed so indirectly "sexual" back then I never even considered them to be the same kind of thing as the (seemingly more direct) contact that I'd had with Scruffy. But it was! It totally was.

And I'm happy that Evelyn thought of it as a wonderful, coincidental, and private gift from nature, because I wouldn't have wanted her to worry about it the way I did with Scruffy. But there's no denying it, Evelyn's horseback riding was sexual contact.

But the much more important point is that Evelyn was not a sexually or socially destructive *pervert*. Quite the opposite: She was one of the nicest people I ever knew, and she eventually became the class vice-president, the head editor of our high school newspaper, a straight "A" student who got a scholarship to an out-of-state university, and the runner-up to the valedictorian of our graduating class. And later in life I heard from old friends that she had become a loving mother of a large family. And, she has been a devout and active Christian her entire life (which I include for *all* the obvious reasons).

I also understand that she still owns and rides horses on a nearly daily basis.

Consequently, I now find it impossible to logically, philosophically, emotionally, or physically differentiate between sexual contact with dogs, or cats, or goats, or donkeys, or horses, or monkeys, or gorillas for that matter. And distinguished world historical records would add a list that would include snakes, ducks, camels, baboons, bulls, bears, alligators, lions, and too many other species to list. And nearly impossible to believe from an American perspective, many of these sexual contact acts are still traditionally supported in all kinds of foreign cultures, including advancing through sexual contact with several animals as a way of progressing toward adulthood, sex with animals as a fully accepted way to solve a lack of sexual options with human partners (sometimes for preteens and teens previous to marriage), sex with certain animals as a way of promoting vigorous health (and even ridding the body of disease), as well as sex with alligators as a way of attaining lifelong prosperity. And this list barely grazes the surface.

I understand, now, that Evelyn could have been bouncing her tingling pussy (or penetrating it, or doing whatever else she wanted) to the point of gushing orgasm on top of any animal in that obviously mutually enjoyable way, and it simply would not make a shred of difference to me—because there is no difference.

Consent

It should be further discussed that the most "modern" argument against sexual contact with animals is that a person who does *that* to an animal isn't being "respectful enough," and that they haven't gotten "consent" from the animal, which is impossible because an animal cannot communicate directly or effectively enough with humans. Those people (who privilege verbal consent as the only sufficient form of consent) also propose, and loudly lament, that all sexual contact with animals is physically abusive.

(Of which, I find the central moral position idiotic and hypocritical when considered in the context of our daily omnivorous/carnivorous reality. As humans we have the unquestioned right to chop an animals head off without warning, and gut it, and skin it, and slice and dice it up anyway we want; *but no one can even touch an animal in a sexually pleasurable way or it becomes amoral?* But I digress.)

Secondly, the fact that human verbal consent is a totally flawed concept and mechanism should also be discussed at this time (and it's about time). Because no matter what the age or education of an individual, their personal and particular social complexities at any one moment of decision making certainly have the power to confuse their ability and even their understanding of exactly *why* they give "consent".

And every day of human history is filled with people who wake-up second guessing *their own given consent*, or are caught helplessly wondering and worrying about the possible consequences of their partners questioning their own consent.

No one can refute this.

And equally true, no one can deny that humans give consent signals of many non-verbal kinds, many of which are just as clear as, if not more than, a verbally constructed consent. An example would be a big smile and opened arms, which infallibly invites an embrace. An even more intimate example would be when a person pushes their face closer to yours, and closes their eyes, and puckers their lips. It's unmistakable! And an even more vividly sexual example would be, (and this is my personal favorite), when a girl or woman tears her pants and panties off and jumps onto her back with her legs open.

To insist that verbally expressed consent is the "only" kind of consent is absurd.

Hoofed mammals (among others), have the ability to lift their tails and visibly swell-open both their vaginas and anuses as a way of signaling that penetration is welcomed. And it is also true that some breeds of monkeys signal sexual invitations in an even more animated, masturbatory, and exhibitionistic way (the Hamadryas baboon for example). Many female animals, just like the human female animal, will also spontaneously lubricate the sexual orifice along with the obvious swelling-open, which is a pretty difficult thing to misinterpret. Male animals show their growing sexual excitement even more easily, and more outwardly. And many will also push their noses right into a person's crotch or ass crack, or straight up mount them, to make sure that their sexual attraction is understood.

Plus, there's an important additional factor in interspecies sexual communication to take into consideration, and it's a powerful one. Because it doesn't matter whether you're sexually approaching a reptile, feline, canine, hoofed mammal, or a full grown primate for that matter: *every* animal has the ability to claw, squirm, bite, jump, kick, run, or donkey-stomp a human's bones into a broken mess—if they don't like what's being done to them. Not to mention the screeching vocal cues of every ear-splitting decibel. And any pet owner, or pet store owner, animal care giver, livestock farmer, farrier, veterinarian, or professional zoologist—along with those who have sexual contact with animals—will tell you the same. Under the vast majority of actual circumstances, (which would not normally include the ability to effectively restrain or sedate an animal), sexual contact is either allowed by the animal, or it is a seriously physically perilous event for the human.

All of which is essential information that few people, that I know, have ever considered.

Of course: As for anyone who outright physically hurt's, damages, sadistically uses, tortures, or even kills an animal as part of their sexual pleasure—which does, unfortunately, happen—I simply cannot agree with their sexual choices, because mine are based on mutual respect and pleasure.

Several Useful Understandings

Regardless of my own carnivorous transgressions, I am relieved to report that the projected percentage of person's that engage in violent sexual contact with animals totals less than .03% (calculated as no more than 1% of 3%), which is far-far-far less than the percentage of humans who hurt other humans in sexually related ways, seems loudly significant.

Another vitally informative truth about sexual contact with animals that is not discussed or made common knowledge in our society is that such contact with animals, or even multiple contacts, does not, in the majority of incidences, indicate a permanent or exclusively sought type of sexual contact or behavior—which makes this sexual choice, in that illuminating regard, *exactly* like the amazingly varied list of other avenues of sexual activities and contact that are sought by humans. It's simply a temporary choice—not an ultimately defining and unchanging detail.

On the other hand—and this is crucial on the human-respect level—sometimes this particular sexual choice does become a permanent or regularly occurring part of a person's preferred sexual experience and life: Like it did for Evelyn. And when it does, I now know that there are much more honest, considerate, and pertinent parameters within which we can view their rights and choices.

I didn't continue my sexual relationship with my dog Scruffy; perhaps because a certain other sexual option soon had my greatest attention (Déjà); or possibly because I mistakenly felt too shameful about it. And just now, I realize that I hope Scruffy wasn't too disappointed.

If a person has ever adored, or treasured, or loved an animal (meaning other-than the human animal), they should open their heart to those who love animals even more. Free of all the illogical and outdated judgment, sexual contact with animals is "adoration" and "petting" taken to a slightly more intimate, and sexual level—nothing more, or less.

Surely, as human animals, we should admit that we have many other well established sexual relationship paradigms, practices, and realities—within our own species—that are, in comparison, starkly riddled with severely obvious complications and harshly evident abuses.

From a Zoo's point of view, I might well reply to condemnation by saying:

"I have absolutely no interest in the often inter-personally aggressive implementation of human sexual obligations, like marital commitments, or other intimate relationship manipulations, or greedy physical control, or any of the other oddly accepted obvious coercions that people regularly enact on each other for the sake of gaining sexual control and or contact. Instead, I have an eagerly neighing and hoof-stomping sexual mate available whenever the mood strikes me, in my own leisure time. I take care of her, and she takes care of me."

Rationally and emotionally, I find it impossible to dismiss the Zoos validity.

Ultimately, as a hypersexual, I absolutely had to include this chapter and its convention shattering information because the recognition of personal sexual choices and sexual contact options, of all kinds, especially when so equally and mutually facilitated, *in spite of* general social limitations, or hypocritical mores, or outdated laws, is exactly what this book is all about.

Additionally, something else about this chapter calls out to me, which is the pesky thought that LGBTQ has no direct Z in it. I appreciate the Q, but in that case why isn't the initialism simply Q? I also exalt the important history of the political struggle, and I've been a small supportive part of it my entire adult life. And, I've also got nothing against S's—straight-up-straight persons—as long as they don't enact or back any aggressive or restrictive social or legal movements against other persons.

However, as far as this approach goes, the idea I'd really love to see put forth, and recognized in the most inclusive way is: ABCDEFGHIJKLMNOPQRSTUVWXYZ.

Chapter Thirteen

<u>Pimps and Prostitutes</u>

Though I sincerely wish that prostitutes, hookers, and whores could be honored and respected with positive titles like sex-workers, or even sexual-healers, alas, that has not been the case during my lifetime. In this story, from the point of view of authenticity, using the real terms, titles, and names that people actually lived with in my life experience is done as a matter of respect.

Pimps are often hypersexuals, and crudely effective whore-tamers, I'll admit. But they are also, way too often, ruthless criminals and evil bullies. And this applies to pimps of both sexes, and prostitutes of both sexes.

The most obvious truth about pimping on American city streets, with all the drugs, and thieves, and cops, and guns, and all the other gritty illegal what-not's, is that it basically requires a ruthless criminal to do the job. And I vehemently hate the fact that hookers, in our current social structure, so often need pimps.

But the less obvious truths of what hooker's suffer, and are endangered by, are to me, even worse.

Here's the one I hate the most: Hooker's also have to fear, (perhaps even more than their own pimps), the entirety of the army of our American law officers.

Further, it is a damn shitty living situation when so-called "polite society" also threatens you, and shuts you out, or locks you in a cage, and deprives you, and demeans you in every way they can—even eternally (in the religious judgment sense).

Why should hookers be abused so badly from both sides?

To me it is like a nurse being beaten and kicked for helping those especially in need.

Sure, my view is skewed; when you look at things from the inside they tend to be quite a bit more visceral.

I also know that there is a scattered mass of more sensible and more helpful pimps, working from different power sources than violence and depravation, giving the prostitute(s) the help and protection to do what they need to do in a more supportive and positive way. And I know very well that those pimps are the more well-meaning Madams, and the less ill-meaning male counterparts, and even helpful friends, adventurous siblings, genuine boyfriends or girlfriends, sincere spouses, experienced older relatives, co-working sisters or brothers, invested strangers, etc.

Plainly, there are a multitude of versions of illegal prostitution in practice all over our Country and the world, some much better than others. Some much worse than others, with every level of denigrating and life threatening slavery and horrifying cruelty represented—and this happens primarily because prostitution is forced into the unprotected criminal worlds.

As for me, I've spent most of my hooker hunting time out in the open air of the city streets. From there I can at least see the body language of a girl, and the energy, or lack of it, in her step. I like to see some kind of bounce in a body, and some kind of light in a personality.

Of course, I know that their "personalities" are often a complete disguise, and I appreciate the effort. At some point though, I usually get to see through to the real person.

And sometimes, what they reveal to me is so honest all the lies are left behind and made meaningless.

As were the truths that I saw through the shining green eyes of the lovely street hooker whose life I was allowed to enter for almost two years.

In the profession that I worked it would be bad form to give the specifics, so I cannot tell you exactly how I was in a position to meet this girl and to have so much information about her, and control over her schedule, and potential sway over her life. Suffice it to say that my involvement with her originally had to do with a job that I was entrusted with in the northwestern state that I was living in at that time.

Mi'Cher, as her questionably clever street-hooking mother had named her, came across my path when she was in the midst of beginning a new kind of probation program. And this was her second serious adult arrest. Of her thirty-five years of life, she had spent nearly ten of those behind bars.

Regardless of her gut-wrenching history, when I first saw Mi'Cher I quickly noticed how she moved her slender body, and fine-featured face, and delicate hands with an extra amount of consciousness. She was clearly physically confident, and fluid, like an actress.

And, because she was engaged in a difficult conversation with a probation administrator, I could also see that she had surprisingly practiced and attentive communication skills to go along with her natural skills. She followed every move the administrator made as he spoke, and she answered him with sentences constructed with a stroking sense of understanding and obedience.

Watching her, even in this cold setting, I could see that she knew how to be subtly-warm physically, and casually-languid conversationally, and intangibly-alluring—probably without ever having thought about any of those words, or phrases, or ideas.

She was beautiful, tall, and blonde with milk-white skin, and big light-green eyes, and a body that vibrated with a steady sexual electricity. And though she was unmistakably from the underbelly of the lower-class, and from well across the proverbial tracks, she looked like a taller, skinnier, and elegantly hammered-out Michelle Pfeiffer.

Luckily, I also got to see her temper break a little bit in that first moment, when a second officer (female) abruptly let her know that she wasn't going to get her way (with whatever point they were discussing). From Mi'Cher's quick and verbally sharp reply to that interrupting secondary officer, it was also obvious that she knew how to hiss!

Still, however abled, at the street experienced age of twenty-nine she had been caught driving some kind of drug from a major metropolis in one coastal state into a smaller city in another one, which she had done under the direction of her pimp Big William—who had promised her complete legal protection if it were ever needed.

However, the morning of the day that Mi'Cher got arrested driving his drugs, was the last time that Big William had ever spoken to her.

Four years and four months, and not one word had ever arrived from the pig.

Those same four years and four months later, having served nearly seventy percent of her sentence, with a two-year intensive probation just beginning, Mi'Cher was ready to make a try in the world again; but with a different plan this time.

Living alone for the first time in her life, in a city over a hundred and eighty miles from her previous troubles (and the only city she had ever lived in), with a solid part-time job (another first for her), safe in her own apartment (also a first), with state financial support, fresh out of prison, fresh into a world free of a pimp for the first time since the age of twelve when her eighteen year-old brother had started her up with his friends and drug clients.

She was free (or "semi-free," as she and I liked to say).

All Mi'Cher wanted now was a fair chance: A chance at something different, something less...horrible. And she was willing to work for it, and she was set to do just that.

And then she met me.

One long eye-locking look from across the room—neither of us caring in the least what those around us might be saying or doing—and we were hypersexually tied together. By midnight of that same day we were alone and I was tearing the sheer stockings from her long white legs, and then stuffing my face all the way into the musky apex of her thighs.

The first thing we did was fuck, for three days straight. Interspersed with sleeping, eating room-service food, and occasionally getting dressed to go to the liquor store, we spent seventy-two delirious hours together naked.

I am not joking or exaggerating in the least when I say that we spoke less than ten words to each other before we were pulling each other's clothes off.

In fact, I believe I simply told her my whole real name, and she told me hers—and then we reached for each other.

By the end of those three days we had told each other our entire and most secret personal histories, deepest beliefs, dearest hopes, favorite sexual deviations, personal horrors, worst loneliness, as well as our few life victories—and then we declared our astonishing love for each other.

In those years I had an extreme amount of control over the hours and days of my life. For one thing, I had my own apartment that I "slept" at, which worked so much better for my wife Abbey and our infant children during the week, with most weekends spent together.

I also kept very odd hours in order to fulfill my three different part-time jobs, which really opened up the whole clock-face of the spinning days and nights. And, because I could get by on no more than three or four hours of sleep per day, often taken one or two hours at a time, I was able to slide an astounding number of hours and even days at a time into my hypersexual dimension.

Flying in this way, I envisioned myself as the fully grown Son of Midnight, and often thought of Déjà and what she might think of me now.

During this time I was also maintaining several other serious lovers, and was still compulsively driven to seek totally random and brand new sexual partners wherever I found myself, but Mi'Cher definitely became my number one girlfriend and my new pet sexual focus.

For the first months, other than Mi'Cher's official appointments and part-time work hours, we spent every minute we could squirreled away in her hotel room naked, drinking, smoking, eating, talking, and pleasing each other like sexual Olympians.

For a hooker who had always genuinely loved many things about sex—after a more than four year forced break (her prison time)—our sex was like a rebirth for her. Free of everything negative that sex had ever become for her, she was having sex now as a woman free to choose her own partner, being sought, and respected, and lusted after as a free woman, being a true "girlfriend" for the first time in her life, and falling in love.

For her, my kind of love was something new. Not that my physical/sexual adoration of her was new, it wasn't, she had been "loved" in that way for most of her life. It was how I also accepted, and understood, and adored absolutely everything else about her personality, and her hypersexual history, and her spirit as a true social misfit, and also as the person she was trying to become right that minute.

I loved her for everything sexual *and* everything else about her.

The second thing we did together was heavier drugs, mostly cocaine, some meth, some ecstasy, some OxyContin, and some crack. And even though Mi'Cher had told me about her struggles with some of the heaviest drugs, I convinced her that getting high with me would be as safe and free of negativity as all our nakedness had been. I told her that I knew how to help her stay sane while enjoying drugs, and that I could definitely help her slip through her drug tests and her weekly probation interviews.

As a highly functioning constant intoxi-holic since the age of fourteen, including alcohol, weed, psychedelics, cocaine, meth, and a long list of other substances, my drug tolerance and confidence level was immense. And I began to show Mi'Cher a smoother way of dealing with the world while essentially staying exactly who she wanted to be. And I showed her how I could even protect her from overdoing drugs by being with her through the night, and getting up with her to make sure she didn't snort too much shit before she went to work. And I became her helpful protector in every other way that I could.

The third big thing we did, about five months after we met, was heroin.

I'd always wanted to take a long float in the heroin sky. Mi'Cher, it turned out, was almost as experienced with heroin as she was with mens bodies and wallets. Having made my decision, I told Mi'Cher that it was her turn to be the leader in our relationship, which made her feel like a Queen again.

Of all the drugs, heroin is perhaps the one most closely related to the mega brain-chemical cocktail that sex also creates. When you do the two together it can make you feel god-like; like gods fucking.

Naked flower petals of bliss fell through us, and a silence, an agreed upon shared deafness wrapped around us. The only thing we could see was each other's sparkling eyes; the only thing we could feel was each other's swimming flesh. Breathing each other's breath, everything else disappeared...

The way that Mi'Cher and I loved each other was the purest form of narcissism I ever experienced—because we became literally one nude squirming being in love only with itself.

I never adored anyone more: No one ever adored me more. And no one ever felt my love more than Mi'Cher did.

Then, after almost eight months had flown by in our blurring bliss, Mi'Cher and I made a mistake that began our heart-rending fall.

After a couple of months of using the local offerings of heroin, we had decided to travel back into Mi'Cher's old city (world) in order to score some of the very best heroin available in our area.

Unfortunately, dipping our toes back into the dark canal that Mi'Cher had come from awakened one of that world's more dangerous and hateful dwellers, and he didn't like the sound of our carefree laughter.

Having the courage to walk straight into Mi'Cher's old neighborhood was not my best decision. However, to show Mi'Cher the fearless love that I felt for her at that time, and to teach her the confidence that I felt she needed to understand in order to really control her own life, I'd decided to wade right in.

While we were in Mi'Cher's old stomping grounds that first time, cruising around in my nice new SUV with its tinted windows, she gave me the full tour. All the different neighborhoods, and houses, and dealers' locations, that had meant so much to her during her street life were pointed out and celebrated with the best or worst stories that she could remember. She even openly showed me the streets where she had done most of her "outside work," and finally the bar where she had done over five years of "inside work" standing at the heel of Big William.

When we drove down that street, and past that bar, Mi'Cher had shrunk down in her seat and asked me to go a little faster.

"Baby, drive faster. Let's get the hell out of here." She'd said.

Mi'Cher called me "Baby," or "Sweet Baby," or "Fucker," all with the same super-warm and loving tone. If she were completely beside herself with love for me, she would call me "Baby Jesus."

"Okay, my Mi'Cher. Let's go somewhere you really love around here! Let's go somewhere that you always loved to go when you were younger, maybe somewhere outside where we can drink a few beers and have a smoke. Tell me where to take you, my love. Anywhere …"

"Oh, you sweet Fucker.., take this next right turn onto the freeway entrance and head across the bridge…" She'd suddenly pointed.

After we had cruised across the big steel bridge and over the dark and awesomely powerful river, and crossed over some railroad tracks scattered with massive logging cars, we came to a red stoplight at a big highway entrance intersection.

"Which way, my love?"

"Would you take me to my grandmother's grave?" She asked with hesitation, looking over her far shoulder and out the side window.

"Of course, Mi'Cher," I replied looking over at her, reaching my hand over to caress hers.

Swinging her head to face me, tears welled up over her big gorgeous eyes, which instantly made me well-up in response, which in turn made Mi'Cher start crying harder, which made me start crying hard enough I could hardly see to drive!

"Don't cry my love," I pleaded. "I'll take you there, and you won't have to cry. I'll hold you, Mi'Cher…"

Which made her burst out bawling.

I'd never seen Mi'Cher cry like that before. I'd seen her laugh so hard she'd cried, and I'd seen her cum so hard she'd cried, and I'd seen her get sad-high several times—but nothing like the heart-aching sobs she was pushing out of her body at that moment.

"My love, stop crying like that…" I said, making myself stop.

"I'll be alright," she said in halting sobs that were losing their power. "Can we still go to my grandmother's gravesite?"

"Of course, my love. Where the hell are we?" I said looking up at the highway signs again, trying to make her laugh, and glad that we'd gotten such a long red-light.

"It's about thirty miles south. I hope that isn't too far."

"Baby, we have two whole days before we have to be back in 'Smallsville' for work and shit. I will take you anywhere we can get to, and get back from in that amount of time!" I said enthusiastically, hitting my left blinker for the south traveling entrance.

Smiling at me, and squeezing my hand, she then turned to look out her window into the shadowy expanses of the surrounding forest.

"Baby Jesus," she said, "You are the sweetest Fucker ever."

At her Grandmother's gravesite we pulled out the overgrown weeds and cleared away all the fallen leaves and needles, which made Mi'Cher cry again, which was okay because I could weed just fine with tears raining from my face. Then we set the wildflowers we had found on the sunken piece of hallowed ground, and then we sat on a bench next to her Grandmother and drank vodka and beers to her memory. Because the grandmother was the only relative that Mi'Cher felt had ever really tried to help her, she was given the highest emotional position in Mi'Cher's knotted family tree.

After perhaps an hour, as evening approached, we left our empty bottles on the Grandmothers headstone with little rocks stacked in their bottoms and around their bases to help keep them upright. And when we got back into the city we ate Chinese food in a restaurant that sat right by the same mighty river we had crossed earlier. Mi'Cher, as always, ordered her favorite Mongolian beef dish and pushed all the green onions to the side of her plate.

As soon as dinner was finished, we set-out to Mi'Cher's favorite dealer and picked-up some premium heroin. Driving lazily along and listening to our favorite soft blues album, we watched the sunset turn to blackness.

Then, we found a quiet motel room and tapped ourselves into a constantly ascending ecstasy.

Railing inward, anything farther away than our own nakedness and nerve-endings ceased to matter... Breathing each other's breath, everything else disappeared...

The mornings after days and nights like that, especially when we were bingeing for several days in a row, were not a pretty thing. But I would let Mi'Cher sleep all the way back to her new city, while I drove us homeward on a cocaine fueled auto-pilot.

After that first trip back to her home grounds Mi'Cher loved me as if I had known her since she was a child.

But happiness and a triumphant return to Mi'Cher's old world was not all that was in the cards for us. By the time we took our third or fourth trip into her old city, Mi'Cher's older sister, a rather grumpy lifetime hooker who was married to her pimp and had kids, warned us that we better stay clear of Big William.

Luckily, one of the places in that city that William's word didn't mean shit was Chubby's heroin house. Mi'Cher's and Chubby's families went back at least one generation farther than William's reign. And Chubby's well established ghetto family and underground business was too well connected to be fucked-with by someone like William.

Plus, Mi'Cher knew exactly how to scratch Chubby's itch, so he had a real soft spot for her in his otherwise harder heart. And because he liked Mi'Cher so much, and she adored me "like no other human being ever born", in Chubby's house we were as free as welcomed birds; birds with wings made of boiling opiate liquid.

With each trip into that city, which steadily grew from once a month to nearly once a week, often for an overnight or two, Mi'Cher's admiration of me increased, as did her attachment. And even though we stayed to ourselves and Chubby's, stories about us made their way to her old acquaintances and accomplices, mostly spread by her sister.

Interestingly, Mi'Cher was always amazingly respectful of my wife and children, and would sometimes actually insist that I go home to them. And she was one hundred percent positive that our relationship would never be a problem to my married and family life—it hadn't been for the last year, so why should it ever be. By then, Mi'Cher trusted that she had a permanent place in my world. And I'm sure some of that security came from my constantly telling her that I would love her forever.

In the meantime, in her new town (a thirty minute drive from where my family lived), I helped her live within the boundaries of her probation—barely. My duty to her was making sure she made it to her work, to her official appointments, and that she advanced from level one to level two, and on up the ladder, each two-month segment getting her a solid step closer to freedom from the correctional system.

Her responsibility to me was to let me eat away for hours in her outrageously delicious sexual garden. The way I pulled and sucked at Mi'Cher's naked body, begging her to let me cherish each and every part of her profligate flesh and its former whorish existence—*and the way she let me*—was like regaining my lost sexual mother. And Mi'Cher felt that binding and wrapping love pouring from my body and heart into hers.

To make sure she wouldn't forget that, I used to always finish my sexual loving by softly kissing her chest right over her heart. That was also the way I kissed her goodbye.

In truth, I had been in love with a mesmerizing image of Mi'Cher since the age of nine or ten, shortly after I overheard my father explaining to my older brothers what the girls walking up and down a few of the downtown city streets *were called* (circa 1969, and those few spots soon disappeared from our city). Since my youthful vision of what that description *should* mean, which had evolved and gained strength through my pre-teen and teen years, I had always known that someday I would be a hooker's perfect sexual lover and servant. And just as I had seen in that vision, instead of being Mi'Cher's pimp or john, the only other real male relationships she'd ever had, I became her true-hearted lover/slave/soldier/savior.

Each wrinkle in the road that threatened to trip her up, or piss her off too much, was my chance to show Mi'Cher how to smooth out societies shifty situations no matter how high or hung-over we might be. And every personal doubt she had was my chance to adore her more, and more specifically.

Moreover, unlike the life she had always known before, instead of everything Mi'Cher earned being torn from her fingers—everything was hers, hers, hers to share with me by her own choice.

In this way, Mi'Cher and I fought for each other in the world. And for a time we won. In fact, eventually we found ourselves in a place where the light at the end of the tunnel of her probation was coming into sight. With almost sixteen of her twenty-four months successfully completed, we were sailing along and sharing the liberation.

However, the lurking reality we didn't keep in our sights was the fact that greedy pimps don't share. They take. They often take everything away from the life of a whore but her transient bed, and the physical fear that they use as the ultra-powerful parasitic extensions of their own evil fingers. And Big William still considered Mi'Cher to be *his* whore.

In their hey-day, here's what Big William used to say to Mi'Cher about five times a day, usually when she asked a question, or spoke when she hadn't been spoken to:

"Bitch, I will fucking kill you ..."

It was a catch-all phrase for William, like the Hawaiian "Aloha," but with the cold flatness of a greasy, six-foot-four, wiry, black, lifetime criminal, knocking you across-the-room with a back-hand slap.

When a pimp gets really mad—everyone join in here, we all know the words—he will scar the face of the offending hooker. William liked to burn his girls with a cigarette along the hairline on the sides of their necks so the johns wouldn't have to see the mottled marks too directly. Mi'Cher, as William's queen, had received her punishments in a design of burns that he had started years before along the waistline of the small of her back. Though only partially done, with several serious burns and several smaller ones, it was obvious that the sadistic bastard had started to burn a thong panty-line into her flesh.

And as Mi'Cher let other stories fall about Big William, it became quite clear to me that all of the violence/dependence/hate/worship that they had shared would have had to create a very complexly layered and powerful bond between them. But I wasn't afraid of that, and fear is something that I habitually walk through anyway. Plus, William had broken their bond when he abandoned her in prison. Now, Mi'Cher hated William and adored me.

Love is supposed to be so much greater than fear; I felt that Mi'Cher needed to see that fact proven in front of her own eyes. And the last thing that I was going to fear was that lanky back-alley bastard.

Let me be clear, it wasn't that I was underestimating him: I knew exactly how mean Big William was. In fact, I had read the newspaper clipping that Mi'Cher had shown me of how William had killed a man in his favorite bar by shooting him in the face in front of eight people—none of whom were "able" to later testify in court to actually seeing the incident happen. So, William was at least strong enough to make eight bar creepers go blind and beat a murder conviction. Because the gun was a throw-away not registered in his name, he claimed the other guy had pulled it and in self-defense he'd struggled with the man and the gun went off. The truth was, the guy had simply made the mistake of getting in William's way at the pool table.

In contrast, I had a lifetime of training and a hard won history of street fighting under my own belt. And when I was on the move I carried a small frame nine-millimeter semi-automatic with hydro-shock loads in a front belt holster, and a .357 magnum with similar loads in my rear belt holster. And I had a license to carry those guns concealed, and to use them in the course of my profession and in the protection of my life. So I had a stout "fuck-you-attitude" of my own, and a skill set more than tough enough for my side of the equation.

Too bad those tools and that mind-set weren't enough. And too bad I forgot it is the unexpected lie, and the sideways move, that gets you.

When Mi'Cher's older sister called me—at my own home—and threatened me on William's behalf, and also told me about his intentions to re-hook-up with Mi'Cher soon; and I then told her to tell William to "fuck off," and sent him a colorful verbal invitation to come find me anytime he was up to it—Big William went straight for Mi'Cher.

For Mi'Cher, once she'd spoken to him on the phone and agreed to talk with him in person, it was already too late.

William's only target was Mi'Cher. In his head he still owned her; and she still owed him for all the drugs she lost when she got arrested. Plus, she was Mi'Cher—a hypersexual treasure—so I knew exactly what William had come back for.

And when she'd begged him on the telephone to leave her alone, and told him how much she loved her new, more legitimate life—he had instantly looked forward to taking all that away from her, as well.

Approximately forty-eight hours after he first spoke to her on the phone, after all this time, William and his right hand muscle, an idiot named "Bat," drove the one hundred and eighty miles to Mi'Cher's city and surprised her. And since she'd already agreed to talk with him *sometime*, William insisted "Why not now?"

Luring her into the back seat of his big car, where the muscle head gave her a quick needle hit of some nearly-too-good heroin, which put Mi'Cher straight into a super-nod, they then drove her quietly back to William's grimy river-side industrial city, where he hid her away and simply kept her.

Keeping her too high to even think for the next five days, William effectively forced Mi'Cher to miss all her scheduled work hours, as well as her next required probation interview. Forty-eight hours after that missed interview, with all means of contacting her officially exhausted, meant that Mi'Cher had committed a probation violation she could not possibly recover from—and a bench warrant for her arrest and return to prison was signed out.

When I returned to my contracted duties after a three-day break, plus the weekend following it, Mi'Cher's downfall was a matter of legal fact and her status of felon on-the-run was locked around her neck.

Because nearly everything in my life was getting over-stressed by my outrageously driven hypersexual pursuits, and now the hardest kinds of drugs, I had already seen the ending of my relationship with Mi'Cher coming. Mi'Cher in all her beauty along with her heroin wonder world, however deep and pulling, was, after all, just one amazing and fully immersed focal point among the many in my life.

I just hadn't seen *how* it would all come to an end.

About fifteen days later, at Williams prompting I'm sure, Mi'Cher's ugly intentioned sister called me again and told me exactly where and who Mi'Cher was with, and how high she was, which was at the zonked-out rock-bottom of her existence.

An ornery, jealous, and flat-faced woman, her sister also told me, with eerie delight, that Mi'Cher was already totally unwilling to leave William—and that she wanted me to forget about her. And when I asked her sister for the chance to talk with Mi'Cher at least once on the phone, she laughed at me, and warned me against coming into William's world looking for trouble. And then, she finished with a menacing and heartbreaking statement.

"You better forget about her, you stupid fucker! You're lucky you ever got to be with Mi'Cher! And you're lucky Big William ain't hurt her worse for hooking-up with you. If you keep fucking with shit, he *will* hurt her worse. You better stay away."

And I never heard from Mi'Cher, or her dreadful sister again.

But I could never forget about you, Mi'Cher.

I tried to love and help Mi'Cher, but failed. And most people would say that my failure came from obvious directions. But crossing those lines and going down those questionable roads was the only way to get to where Mi'Cher really lived.

I was greedy—I'd wanted all of her.

And, I had been but a tourist in a place full of fatally dangerous attractions.

Goodbye, Mi'Cher.

In proper legal houses of professionally provided sexual contact there would be no pimps. And no bully would ever be allowed anywhere near the workers, unless they were there to be sexually soothed and behaved themselves.

And far fewer women and men would be forced into sexual work by misfortune, or poverty, or force, or criminal violence.

And society could save the already existing fully-willing and hyper-generous hookers, even the older ones who so often get run out of the leaner and meaner pimp stables.

And we could put all the willing hypersexuals to work, even the temporary ones, all deviant in their own way, to sexually meaningful, personally profitable, and socially important work.

Then, we should take the out-of-work abusive pimps and cut both their arms off at the elbows, and cut their foul tongues out, and make them clean the new sex-houses with mops held between their teeth.

I'd turn William's big ugly head into a toilet scrub brush.

He kidnapped Mi'Cher's new life and strangled it to death right in front of her.

Or, did I?

When I think of her now, I imagine my beautiful Mi'Cher buried in the smoky backroom of some hooker/heroin-house, at the end of some dark alley in that river-bound and mist enshrouded city.

But her silky-floating green-eyed ghost will always haunt my dreams and my masturbation room, where she is properly enshrined, pictured in several beautiful and celebratory photos she gave me that were taken during her brief try at liberty.

Chapter Fourteen

<u>Necrophilia</u>

Even dead, or as a floating green-eyed ghost, I would want to have sex with Mi'Cher, or Cee Cee, or my most-beloved Abbey.

As a hypersexual I would want to know what that particular sexual contact would really *feel* like, what it would actually *be* like, how *different* it would be, how far it might *release* me, and in what ways it might increase or expand my sexual understanding.

I am compelled to uncover all that I can.

So, allow me to admit some of the additional, specific, and unfiltered reasons why a hypersexual, like me, might want to fuck the dead:

Firstly, I suppose it would be obvious that we would have to be hungrily searching for a decidedly alternative way of gaining sexual gratification. Not to say it would require outright starvation to drive one of us to necrophilic contact, as the hypersexual search for variety, alone, might well suffice as the driving spirit. But simply said, creating an intimate contact with a corpse is such a self-threatening and difficult to obtain goal I have to believe that the actual act would be fed by a distinctly built hunger.

In order to take those thoughts forward into action, obviously, we would also require private access to dead bodies, or have somehow created a way of gaining that access, like an attached profession, or a method of breaking into mortuaries, etc. For some of us, such proximity would not only be a piece of facilitation, it would also be an initial temptation, and therefore a reason.

Laid out in front of me, a silent and still Mi'Cher, or any similarly attracting fully vulnerable sexual body, would be a terrible enticement.

Reaching further into the idea, in order to complete our deviant desires we would have to be able to arrange sufficient time and control over the body and the surrounding situation. And with a project of this type there is no telling how much detail might go into the effort. The many pressures of approaching such a difficult goal often have the effect of super-charging each of the specifics. So each detail, and its sub-details, individually acquire, build, and add their energies together. And the achievement of even one important detail becomes a real step forward. And the momentum of making each necessary component fall into place can become a powerful and almost irresistible "reason" to continue.

For an event as significant and unique as fucking a dead body I would need at least five or more quiet hours, the right kind of lighting, a way to hang a sex-swing, a bag full of small supplies, a bevy of strong intoxicants, the physical security of a fully hidden-away space, and the proper mood of mounting freedom.

That said, having enough hypersexual need to enable us to embrace the deceased, and having gained sufficient access and command over the situation, we would then certainly revel in the unqualified control that we would have over the extraordinary sexual occasion, all the way from the birth of the idea through to the sexually fulfilling ending that we, alone, would design and manipulate.

And during the intercourse we would *know* beyond dispute that we were the singular life-force animating that body. And we would *feel* and *experience*, directly, that we had created a very rare, astounding, and perhaps an unsurpassable kind of sexual union.

And the undisturbed and unrivalled intimacy of the contact, and its timeless piece of gratification, might wrap around us like a perfectly fitted-sheet.

I don't know for sure. I wish I did.

But more importantly, in terms of the larger discussion, that's just one possible angle of approach to necrophilia.

In addition to those reasons there must be tens on top of hundreds of other individually fueled and crafted reasons that someone might lean towards an un-live sexual partner. Many of which, I concede, would be beyond my scope or vision. I am only one person.

I can only open the box enough to peek inside.

Perhaps there are as many reasons as there are necrophiles. I can easily imagine sexualized fantasies and behaviors ranging all the way from tender tear-filled caresses to cannibalistic zombie madness. At this level of control it would (could) all be a very personalized thing.

Interestingly, the actual medical and psychological research estimates on how common it is for humans, both male and female, to have at least some version of necrophilia or pseudo-necrophilia fantasies might seem shocking to most people: Unless a person has already admitted their own shocking fantasies to themselves.

The simple but unspoken truth is: Such dark sexual fantasies are not at all rare.

Perhaps the readers already know this.

For myself, I have always seen it as a kind of immaturely rooted sexual desire, perhaps because I had my first necrophilia visions and fantasies when I was quite young. But I also think this because the desire to have a body that you can sexually control so ultimately is such a simple and unadorned wish.

As an adolescent, one shade of this fantasy got attached to one of my momentary sexual thoughts (and then memories) that I had of looking at my ten year old sister while she was asleep. Because I was only eleven, when my mind took the un-workable sexual thoughts that I was suddenly having about my sleeping sister, which then somehow jumped into a "more-than-sleeping" version of the thought—which I'll never forget contained, even at that age, a clear attempt at finding a way *around* the moral wrongness of trying to sexually touch her while she was asleep—I was duly shocked at myself, and a little bit afraid.

I could also never forget how sexually arousing *something* about that mentally railing moral journey had been.

As far as I knew then, I was a budding necrophile at eleven years old. And while I know now that I am far from the only child who ever had thoughts like that; I have still never heard anyone else in my life talk openly about adolescent necrophilic fantasies about one's own siblings, or anyone else, or any subject even remotely connected.

Depending on a person's experience, it might also be surprising to hear that a common type of paid-for sex is one in which the payee wants the professional to act totally asleep, or completely zonked out, or so drugged—or dead—that they don't "wake up" or even move while they are being sexually used.

I've also known several persons, both male and female, who privately and keenly exhibited this intensely purposeful sexually inert behavior in their own sex lives.

As a wonderful example, I had sex a few times with a girl named Ronni who, while not at all chemically impaired, maintained a corpse-like immobility with so much discipline it was incredible—even while being moved around the room, and even while being kissed in her lolling open mouth, and even while being penetrated—holding back her own excitement in the bargain, and holding it, and holding it even when orgasmic tremors crawled across her slack skin and tears began to seep from her frozen-open and dead-still eyeballs! She even preferred it if I left her body twisted, or in a heap on the ground when I was finished and left. And I've never forgotten her.

On yet another far edge of the range of those who enjoy the immobile brink of sex, I've also known those whose most intimate passion involves being completely unconscious during the partner's, or multiple partners', sexual prowling and feasting. To achieve this, even for short periods, those persons would gladly drink themselves into a totally helpless stupor, and/or take sleeping pills, or use heroin, etc. Alexis, a Native American I met was a mistress of that sort, and being with her was so erotic I'll miss being with her until the day I pass away, myself.

As the reader can imagine, and can believe me in describing, being given that much authority as the "active" partner in such a sexual event is an extremely heady experience. And it bridges the gap, a little, between what we might admit is sexually understandable and what we hesitate to even consider as understandable.

However, while the historical existence and continuous attraction to necrophilia, and pseudo-necrophilia, is acknowledged in many traditional cultural stories and social sexual threads from around the world, including several references in the Bible, and notably in some of the horror genres of literature and movies, which establishes it as an irrefutable human phenomenon—still, even the slightest open proclivity toward the ideas and/or the acts remains damned and denounced and legally banned to the point that it is utterly beyond discussion.

Even married couples with the fullest possible legal license, both nationally and internationally—even with signed documentation—are lawfully forbidden to have sex when one of the partners is unconscious, let alone dead. And the reporting of any such act to legal authorities, by anyone including a fully uninformed outside party, could result in automatic sexual assault and/or rape charges with or without the so-called "victim" ever having agreed to a complaint.

Even so, for hypersexuals, sex workers, and many, many others, inert-behavior or death-imitating as a way of being a consummate sexual partner is just another recognizable sexual vein.

What about the dental and medical personnel who perform sexual acts on patients who are under anesthesia? What about other professionals and people who have similar access to fully vulnerable bodies, and who enact similar sexual behaviors? In simple fact, this particular variety of sexual behavior has become just another variant sexual statistic—and crime.

I've even seen comedy skits about it. But the reality of persons and professionals raping immobilized (and unaware and un-consenting) victims, and the even more extreme and sometimes murderous criminal edge of necrophilia, is definitely dangerously criminal and lethally serious.

To measure the actual fatal significance you'd have to consider the frightening statistic that approximately forty percent of documented (known) necrophiles felt they needed to kill someone in order to procure a proper body and the control necessary for their sexual needs. Sadly, that forty percent was comprised, almost entirely, of those offenders who did not have some kind of other access to (already) dead bodies.

Of course, it must be acknowledged that there are those necrophilia offenders who are more attracted to the act of killing than anything else. And I would call them murders first, and (I would guess) hypersexuals in a secondary way. And I'll admit I probably don't know how to help those persons much.

Still, I say: Too bad sex with willingly totally motionless bodies isn't much more widely available, for everyone's sake. I think it could save lives. Ronni and Alexis, during every magnificently powerful hour that I spent with them, were "lifeless" saviors to me.

If the sex act is agreed to, and it is something that is appreciated by those involved, then who—from outside the intimate contact—has the right to say otherwise?

To me it is absurd that we can't have consensual and professionally assisted fully anesthetized sexual associates. That would be something really compelling to offer.

And I'll go even further: I currently have a mark on my driver's license that, in the event of death, designates me as an organ donor.

Can anyone explain to me why I can't designate myself as a willing host for necrophilia?

R.I.P.

I've already written that I believed something sexual touched me even before I was born. So it should be understandable why I might see leaving this life through the final sexual curtain of the necrophile's to be an especially suitable one for me.

Unending Circle

It has been sincerely philosophized that the only thing certain in life is death. But there is also sex mixed-in, right from the beginning.

And deep in the middle of all the intricate and so often interrelated and overlapping sexual realities of human life, there are also babies on the verge of being born…, like Cee Cee's unborn baby.

Chapter Fifteen

<u>Inside Cee Cee</u>

Even though Cee Cee had said it to herself, I'd heard it as clear as a bell.

"I wish I could get pregnant from you…"

Those may be the most bizarre and interesting words I have ever heard from a street girl I'd just met: It was sweet, and strange as hell.

"Cee Cee, you're a nasty little cum-hungry-cunt aren't you?"

Turning her head to look directly into my eyes, Cee Cee growled playfully.

"Come over here and put something in my pussy you slow-ass fucker, and I'll show you exactly what I am!"

What I heard was the "something" part; the kinky little wench!

Looking quickly around, I saw my chubby four inch long glass pipe on the low coffee table not three feet away from her. Walking over, I grabbed the pipe and put the long end of it right between her knobby knees.

"Let me put the end of my pipe in your pussy, and then take a big hit out of it!"

"Put that fucking thing in my cunt, I don't care! I bet I can squeeze my snatch hard enough to pull a hit off that fucking pipe."

What the fuck?! Would this girl never stop surprising me? Laughing out loud, I could swear that she was serious. So I decided to find out.

"Finish my drink while I light it, Cee Cee. Here…"

Handing her my drink, I quickly loaded the bowl. Lighting it up with a few quick pulls, I then used my left index finger to hook and move the crotch of her white cotton panties over to the side of her bulging pussy.

As I'd suspected, she was shaved fairly close, maybe a couple of days close. Looking at her face, I slipped the end of the smoking glass pipe through her lovely and fleshy labia and half-way into her slightly moist hole, then a little farther, until the bowl was nearly touching her. Staring back at me, Cee Cee looked me right in the eyes and didn't change her expression even the slightest—I think I was surprising her, in her favorite way, too.

"Cee Cee, finish my drink already and see if you can really make your cunt suck on this pipe. I want to see that!"

In one quick gulp she drained the glass and handed it back to me. Quickly hiking her dress all the way up over her swollen belly, and looking down toward her pussy, she began to concentrate. Flexing her abdomen awkwardly at first, and using her arms to corral and hold onto her extended stomach, I watched as her internal muscles began to coordinate themselves.

I'd heard of girls in sex shows being able to pick up and hold onto all kinds of stuff with their pussies, so I watched hopefully for the glow of my pipe bowl. And I could hardly believe my eyes, but the bowl *was* just barely lit, not actually puffing, but it wasn't going out either!

It was unbelievable! Here I was about to do something sexual that I had never even imagined: Take a hit of weed from a girl's glistening pussy hole!

This scuffed up little girl was turning out to be such a beautifully strange little street hooker I felt as if I had hit some kind of deviant jackpot! Standing dead still, I waited to see what would happen next. And I realized—with a feeling of shock—that I was no longer leading this specific sexual descent.

For at least a minute she stared at her pussy and the pot pipe protruding from it. And as she flexed inwardly, even though I was holding the bowl lightly, the pipe moved up and down like a thermometer in someone's mouth. But I couldn't see any more light to it.

And I was so turned-on by this girl it was making my head sizzle!

"PUT YOUR FACE DOWN THERE!" She howled with laughter.

And as I leaned forward she grabbed the back of my head with one hand, and then yanked the pipe out of her hole with her other hand so fast it made a little popping sound. Holding my head just inches from her now pushing outward cunt, she held still and flexed her abdomen muscles in the opposite direction.

"WATCH." she ordered.

At first nothing happened, and I thought it hadn't worked after all. Then, as she continued pushing, and rhythmically flexing, with the sound of a quiet little pussy-fart the faintest wisp of smoke came out.

Opening my mouth wide, I planted my face down over the tiny curl of smoke and down further over her now pushing open cunt hole.

Then, lifting my face up and toward Cee Cee's widening eyes, I breathed outward as if letting out a big long hit so she could see what magic she had done!

And though there wasn't any smoke to really see, the imaginary show of it was a fine enough finish!

Giggling and laughing, and still holding onto her stomach with both arms, she finally let her legs fall back to the ground as she sat up. Pulling her dress down and her panties back over her pussy, as she scooted back into a sitting position, she struggled to speak through her laughing fit.

"I told you I could do it! Ha, ha, ha!"

"Have you ever done that before?" I asked, and was immediately confused by her negatively reacting facial expression.

"NO! Fuck you, you asshole! It was your idea. I just thought I could do it..."

Responding instantly, I smoothed the weird wrinkle over.

"And you did it! That was fucking AWESOME! I can't wait to tell my buddies, they'll never believe it!"

Having hit the mark with my comeback, she smiled, and then spoke quickly and with the hard teasing edge of her upbringing.

"Why don't you put that thing in my ass, and *then* tell your friends you smoked it, you stupid pothead! Ha, ha, ha!"

"I don't want to *lose* my pipe..." I joked dangerously, and perfectly.

"Fuck you! Ha, ha, ha!" She laughed even more loudly. "Then you better not put it in my pussy again, because I bet I could fit your fist and half your forearm in there!"

"Be quiet and let me take another cum-covered hit, Cee Cee!" I laughed along with her.

Flicking my lighter on, I took the pipe from her hand and took a hit, savoring the trace of the taste of her pussy juice along with the powerful smoke. Then I handed the pipe to her.

As we exhaled a few more hits together, emptying the bowl, still for a moment in the quiet, I felt my intoxication level finally go to full-tilt.

Looking down at Cee Cee, I tried to measure her mental and physical state. And when she leaned back into the couch and shut her eyes, and then let out that telltale body-wide sigh, as her knees fell unconsciously open—I knew that she had arrived at that fully intoxicated and relaxed place, as well.

Watching her, I held off, giving her relaxation some momentum. It was so nice to look at her in such a tranquil state. But I was definitely getting ready to get sexually serious, and seeing her laying helpless like that prodded the predator in me.

Removing my t-shirt, I then reached down and removed Cee Cee's dress by lifting it easily over her head. Without opening her eyes, Cee Cee sat up a little and shrugged the dress off into my hands.

Sliding down from my standing position like a massive snake, I then crawled up between her smooth and wide open legs.

As my bared arms and chest brushed upwards along the insides of Cee Cee's naked knees and thighs, and I pushed my shoulders up and lifted her legs up and out, and then pulled her forward to the edge of the couch until her ass was up against my stomach, she gave out another little laugh and let herself fall back into the soft leather cushions.

Worshiping her body by lightly and slowly kissing her bulging and tight stomach, I told her with my lips and tongue that I was acutely turned-on by her self-sexualized state of pregnancy.

Letting her arms fall to her sides, Cee Cee followed my face with her eyes and watched as I kissed her swollen body.

Kissing upwards to each of her enlarged and erect nipples for a moment, I then aimed back downwards and kissed and licked my way down along the extra-sensitive and clearly visible bright-red stretch mark that started from above her belly-button and reached all the way down to the top of her vagina. With my forehead lightly touching her rounded tummy, I scooted my knees backwards on the floor and dropped my head even further down.

Properly repositioned, I took an extra deep breath in and pressed my wide-open mouth down tightly over her thin-cotton panties covered pussy. Slowly, I then let out a long, steady, and heated breath—forcing the heat from inside my own body to sink deeply down and into her crotch.

Still pressing my face into the spreading warmth, I then stuffed my face even deeper into her delicious lap and took that big breath back in, even slower, and deeper, and with much greater relish, flexing my body outward as I pulled on my lungs until they'd reached their absolute limit—filling myself with all the musky, wetted, ripe, young, used, and freshly aroused scent of Cee Cee.

Hugging her hips and pussy into my face with my muscular arms, I took several more oh-so-deliciously slow, hot, pungent, and intensely pleasurable breaths of her.

Leaning her head up a little, and with an expression of genuine wonder, Cee Cee peeked over the horizon of her stomach to see what I was doing.

"Mmmmm…" She cooed.

And it wasn't just the way that I was suddenly holding her body as if it belonged only to me—with both my arms wrapped up under her legs and up around the back of her hips, with my hands locked around the back of her waist, and my head and face locked into the center of her body beyond question of removal—*it was the way that I was holding still, and just breathing her…*

Releasing my hold on her waist for a second, and sliding both my hands down to the waistband of her well-worn panties, I slipped them down and off her legs. Returning quickly back to my desperate grip around her body, with her legs wrapped over my shoulders and my face placed squarely into her fully bare and now swelling-open cunt, I resumed my worship.

Cee Cee, for her part, settled back into sexual submission, laying into my arms like one who is ready to be carried away—anywhere.

Though my body held her firmly, at first I licked and ate very softly at her ample and dripping wet pussy. With a wide-wide-open mouth and my tongue held out as far and as fat as it could be, and moving deliberately like an artist with his first brush strokes upon a new canvas, I took my time. I licked her up and down, and around, and in and out, and back up to suck and kiss at her still slightly hiding clitoris. I sucked on both sides of her labia lips, taking them fully into my mouth. And I teased her labia some more, sliding the tip of my fat tongue up-and-down between them. And then I pushed her clit around a little, and licked to the sides of it, and then right over it with more pressure, and then directly down on it with authority.

But it was way too soon to focus on any one part of the feast. So, I licked down her sex-crack all the way over and past her surprised anus. And coming back I paused, and slowly pushed the whole length of my tongue into both her loosening holes.

Before long, Cee Cee was squirming hard into it, and began moaning without any restraint, moving her hips into my face in a rhythmic and pleading way.

After six or so minutes, maybe ten (which passed too quickly for me), Cee Cee's panting suddenly became a note higher, and two beats faster. So, holding for the finish, I shoved my tongue down directly over her completely hardened clit as her shaking body snapped it up-and-down and back-and-forth across my pushing tongue and puckered mouth.

When she had completely released herself to the earthquaking liberation of the face-fucking orgasm, with her wide spread legs and feet, and tight hands, and face twitching and trembling in the un-tethered spasms of physical delight, and with beautiful beads of sweat breaking out across every expanse of her skin simultaneously, and her thick musky girl-cum leaking into my mouth—I slowly-slowly backed off my oral adulations.

Who knows how often Cee Cee meets a man who even considers if *she* gets off or not?

Licking her softly and in slower strokes, dropping my tongue back into the opening of her vaginal hole, I let her enjoy the adoration until I could feel her wanting something more.

And when she was ready, I moved my attention to where I had been headed all along—her pregnancy.

Many times the moments following an orgasm are even more important to me than the orgasm itself, because I am on my way to the innermost places opened up to me through that route. The first orgasm is the lock on door number-one opening. And there are often many doorways to be dealt with. The number of orgasms or overlapping layers of releasing pleasure that I can produce, and what I can manage to achieve with each of them, must equal the specific challenge.

Cee Cee was ready to have me go where I would: I was free to find whatever passageways I wanted. Obviously, the dam that I wanted to open in Cee Cee was her dearest and most deviantly indiscriminate fondness for becoming and being pregnant from random sex.

So, of course I was headed for that heart of her body. It certainly was the so-called (but in this case not affectionately enough) "white elephant" in the room—so it ought to be obvious that I'm going to go right up and start sucking on it.

I did have to admit that the presence of a fierce fetish-like energy had been creeping up on me ever since the moment I had seen that Cee Cee was pregnant. And it wasn't just because of the pregnancy itself, but because of how she carried her pregnancy so proudly out into her street and sexual contact life, and how she had evidently wrapped her pregnancies so completely into her own sexual deviance. I didn't just want her to tell me that she "wished" she could get pregnant from me—I wanted her to scream, and cry, and wail at me about why she "needed" to *be* pregnant in this overtly unusual way.

Kissing my way up past the top of her delicious pussy, I moved my mouth up to her massive and naked Stomach. To keep her on the edge of her still passing clitoral orgasm, I then brought my right hand up between her thighs and slipped the whole of my fat thumb, up to the wrist, into her pouting pink hole. Using that hand in a slow and steady way, while my mouth set down upon her truer center, I entered her being even further.

Once you have a female's body singing those special moaning notes, sometimes all you have to do is keep stroking the right flesh-strings, the right way, to keep that lusty song going for as long as you want. Many women can cum, and be held in the flushing and pendulous ranges of cumming, and then be made to cum again—again and again.

I've strummed that cumming song for so long I've made a number of females literally collapse, and in a handful of cases even pass-out from their ecstatic exhaustion.

(I realize that might sound doubtful: Those women couldn't believe it either—until they woke up and I was still fucking them, which, interestingly, consistently led to those women releasing positive torrents of what I call the "fuck-me-tears.")

Still, it is what I do with my mind—while my lovers are floating and humming and cumming—that gets me where I need to go. Between my kisses upon her tight and tender stomach, I spoke quietly up to her.

"My god Cee Cee, you taste like heaven! Your cum is so sweet! And your skin is so delicious! Is that because you're so pregnant? Why do you taste so fucking good?"

In delightful truth, her plumped white flesh did taste like milk-and-honey. And she also tasted like nicotine, and whiskey, and harder drugs a little deeper in. And she burned like a raging sexual fire on the edge of constant peril even deeper in—but her skin was milky sweet!

Kissing Cee Cee's sizable prize, I adored her pregnant body as if it proved to me that she was extra-special and perfect. At the same time, I used my right hand, thumb, and all four fingers to continuously fondle and partially enter her now gushing wet pussy—stroking both her physical and emotional feelings.

Unexpectedly, Cee Cee reached down and began to hold the sides of my kissing face with her hands, as if trying to hold me even closer to her bulbous stomach. And since the moment she'd entered my house—that was the first time that Cee Cee had put her hands on me—confirming that I'd hit the bull's-eye.

"I know," she replied with a purring giggle, looking down at me and her precious belly. "It's so amazing to be pregnant! My whole body gets *special!* Look at me! Look at my titties, and my huge nipples!"

Saying this, she'd taken her hands off my face and was pushing her swollen-out-of-proportion little-girl breasts together just above my face. On my knees in front of her, I had to actually back my head up a bit to see them clearly. And yes, as I'd already noticed, the nipples were magnificent! And I nodded in genuine appreciation as Cee Cee continued to talk about them, and touch them, with both her hands.

"See how dark and big they get! And they are so sensitive I can't believe it!"

Reaching my body up, I wrapped my hot tongue around one of her swollen nipples, which was about the size of the tip of a pinky-finger.

"Mmmmmmm," she cooed, in appreciation. "Hey, what's your name?"

"My name is Rory, you sweet thing." I replied, without even realizing what I had done. "What else do you love about being pregnant, Cee Cee?"

"Well, it seems like men love you even more. And most of them treat you nicer. Some will pay more, too. Some men think it's the nastiest thing ever to fuck a pregnant girl and cum inside her body with nothing to worry about! One man told me that if I lived in a big city I could ask for two-hundred dollars! Do you think that's true?"

My god, I didn't want her to stop talking! I was getting off by just listening to her spill-out some of her favorite personal notions to me. So I encouraged her.

"Yes Cee Cee, that is true. In some cities, with the right set-up, you could easily ask for double that."

"Oh my god, really?! I didn't believe that old guy! I wish I could live in a big city..."

"How many boys and men did you say you have let cum inside you, Cee Cee?"

"Twenty-eight different ones, I counted! I won't ever fuck a man and not have his cum in my pussy. I pretend that I'm getting pregnant from every one of them! You make twenty-nine! You did promise me.., you *are* gonna cum inside me...?" She questioned, suddenly serious.

What an unbelievably lovely girl!

"Hey, how come your pants aren't even off yet?" She asked in blunt wonder.

"Because I wanted to make you cum at least once, or twice, before I shoved my fat cock into your big wet cunt!" I answered. "Cee Cee, my sperm load has been building up for two whole days and it is going to swamp your yummy pussy! I really like you, and I wouldn't disappoint you for anything in the world! But I want to play nasty with you for a little while longer before I cum in you. I want to make you cum really hard again, before I do. Please? I promise to drain my cock into your body Cee Cee, but you have to tell me what nasty thing I can do to you that you really, really, *really love? Anything...*"

Now that I had kissed and petted her sexualized pregnant stomach, and she had exposed her unguarded mind to me about it, I hoped that my unconditional invitation would lead me even deeper into her swollen core.

Changing her expression to a slightly more sober one, she replied slowly.

"*Anything...?*"

"*Anything*, my dear Cee Cee. The nastier the better. I just need to play with you for a little longer before I cum into your beautiful pussy. Okay? *Anything....*"

Looking down at me as if she didn't believe me, with her mouth drawn tight and the skin around her eyes squinting, she built herself up to say it out loud.

"Okay..., fuck me with something really big. Fuck me with your fist and arm or something else really big because when something reaches that far up inside me when I'm pregnant it makes me cum so hard I'll scream! Would you fuck me like that and then cum inside me too? Do you have a big glass bottle? Or a big...?"

My lord she was so eager! I couldn't help myself; I was all the way in-love with this girl!

"Cee Cee, I will fuck you with something so big you *will* cry! I know that you want to be sexually filled-up past being filled-up—I know exactly what you mean—and I would absolutely love to do that to you!

Let me think of what to use...?"

Nodding her head in excitement, she abruptly switched her seated-back position on the couch to a fully lying down on her back one.

And as she did that, she shook and relaxed her body (kind of like an athlete does), and showed me that she was totally ready by brushing her hair back and opening her legs up and out to the sides as if on a gynecologist's table.

Coming to a decision, I knew exactly what I was going to put up Cee Cee's gaping, object-hungry, and lovely-beyond-lovely cunt—and I'd shove my hard fat cock into her asshole at the same time! And there was no way in hell that I would disappoint her!

Fucking a girl in both her holes at once is one of my favorite skills—because it grants me a rather mythical level of penetration and performance! And I am exceptionally good at it!

As a hypersexual adept, I have been performing my double-fucking move for a long time, usually with a big dildo in tandem. And I can coordinate it extremely well, in many different positions, humping away as wildly as if I were born a real double-cocked centaur! In fact, more than a few women have sworn, while kicking and screaming, that I was doing something to them that they had never felt the likes of before!

And if I grab them by the hair or throat right then, or bite them, or fuck them so raucously they feel like they're being bucked by a horse—it always brings the very best kinds of results.

However, for Cee Cee my largest available dildo in the house (a rather medium sized one that my wife kept in her drawer) just wouldn't do. Unfortunately, I couldn't leave to retrieve my tools from my masturbatorium (even though it was so near). And, using my fist and forearm would have put my cock-in-ass action out of play, or I would have happily used her idea.

So, it would have to be the only other object in the house that matched the needed description: My beautifully sculpted hard-oak Japanese fighting club, which was nearly three feet long, and hand-carved with a threateningly bulbous business end, and a gorgeously rounded knob-handle at the other.

Without a word I left Cee Cee lying on the couch, waiting, while I went to get the short, stout, and heavy club. Looking back at her lying so calmly on the couch, with her legs sprawled out to the sides, I knew that she knew, as we hypersexuals do, that her life had finally, again, led her to that perfect sexual place she was always seeking.

On the way back into the living room, I dropped my pants and slipped my favorite cock-ring over my shaved, fat, and quickly swelling cock and balls.

When I returned to the couch and held the hefty, thirty-four inch long dark wooden club out above her body, showing it to her, she responded by smiling so widely it was garish—which made my cock swell even harder, lifting its turgid head as high as it could reach.

Looking up at me, Cee Cee spoke with a trembling relish. "Rory, fuck me really, really hard, okay?"

Then, laying her head all the way back, she closed her eyes. And as I placed the fat end of the club against her magnificent vaginal opening, purposely thumping the weight of it down on her swollen open and wet pussy hole, she flinched—just once—and then opened her legs even farther.

Already panting in anticipation, Cee Cee spoke loudly and with a tone of voice that was somehow both begging and demanding.

"When you put that big thing in me, drive it all the way up until you feel the hard end of my baby. Then pound me like you're beating on a big balloon or something! Hit it all the way to the end so I can feel it like a fucking shock-wave! Just do it! I do it to myself with bottles and things and it feels so goddamn good it makes me want to push it out!"

Yes, I heard it too. And no, I wasn't going to smash anything hard up against anyone's unborn fetus. And I was pretty sure, at that point in time, that this was not exactly what Cee Cee meant.

What I did know, is that when someone tells me what they want sexually—I am created to say "yes."

But I was a bit stuck, wasn't I? Wondering just how hard Cee Cee actually needed me to push that wooden club up into her, I proceeded without fear. I've been inside and satisfied some seriously and even frighteningly needy-fuck-bodies before, and I knew how wild it could get.

And I had seen women sit down on the fat half of a baseball bat, shoving into their wide open holes—and then keep pushing down, hard.

But none of them had been such a petite and obviously late-term pregnant teenager.

Holding the club against the glistening opening of Cee Cee's cunt, adrenaline began to run into my guts again, this time feeling twice as strong as when I had first decided that I must have her.

Looking slowly up from Cee Cee at the room around me, I took a few long and relaxed breaths. Looking at all the normal things around me I remembered what day it was, and how people outside this room were going about all their usual daily tasks. I looked into the kitchen and dining area of my homes open great room, and I remembered how the day had begun with my wife and two college age children, eating eggs and toast and listening to the morning news. I looked out the window at the wind blowing through the bare tree limbs, and I took a moment to remember the very first sight that I'd had of Cee Cee walking up the road, just an hour and some odd minutes ago.

And I did all these things because I was pausing to enjoy the knowledge that I would never forget any part of this.

Looking down at Cee Cee again, all spread open and with her eyes closed, I bowed my head in deep gratitude to the powers-that-be.

Intuitively I believed that this sexual union was going to be epic, and different, and new somehow…

I could sense it with every hypersexual fiber of my being: Cee Cee was pregnant with more than just a seriously health-threatened fetus.

There was something else inside Cee Cee fighting to get out, and I was going to release it.

Chapter Sixteen

Too Far

Flexing naked above Cee Cee, I reveled in the amazing visual build-up.

With my tightly fitted cock-ring now maximizing the blood-veined swelling, creating an over-fattened and extended cock shaft, with an extra sensitive and impressively enlarged head, and an enormously engorged ball-sack; I watched as Cee Cee squirmed below me with her legs spread as wide as they could go, with the big end of the war club opening and entering her gleaming pussy hole, and with her rotund stomach looming.

Having looked around the main room of my home, gathering solid points of reference for memory, I had locked myself in time-and-place—I wanted to remember every single second of what was coming.

This kind of variant and never-before-experienced sexual event is what I live for, what I persist for. Now I was so close I could see her pink insides blossoming open toward me.

I could have stood there looking down at Cee Cee for an hour…

With my right fist clinched around the handle of the fighting club, I looked up at Cee Cee's face and noticed that her eyes were opening.

Thinking that she was getting ready to say something to me, my inner thought was, "Close your eyes Cee Cee, let me look at you…"

But Cee Cee didn't want to be *just* looked at. And because I had paused with the big end of the club just a teasing inch into her hungry pussy—for one second too long—Cee Cee's eyes came all the way open and the eerie light that shot out from them was my first clue that something was wrong.

Her facial expression came next, abruptly adjusting over her hard features like a picture refocusing itself; and her new face said—in a dreadfully clear way—*"What the fuck are you waiting for?!"*

Still adjusting my cock-ring around my ball-sack and into a perfect position, I looked down at Cee Cee and had only the slightest measurement of time to wonder what was making her so impatient?

Staring hard up into my eyes from her position on her back, Cee Cee suddenly lurched her upper body forward and grabbed the club at her end with both her hands and yanked it roughly into her body to the depth of at least six or seven inches! And if I'd completely lost hold of the handle she would have driven it even further in!

Surprised and taken aback, at first I just held the club still, and looked down at her sneering face. For some reason, the crazy little twerp was irritated to the point of being ornery with me! Maybe the other drugs she was on were starting to fade? And, not only was she taking my pleasure away by hurrying the whole thing, and trying to slam the club home herself, but I also felt the restricting need for a little bit of caution. I wanted to start slowly.

Pulling back on the handle of the club, I met an unyielding resistance. And I saw in that moment that Cee Cee had realized that her two hands might be stronger than my one.

With a vicious smirk she raced me for it, leaning forward again and then yanking on her end as hard as she could! But, by clasping my second hand over my first at the last micro-second, I won the foolish tug-of-war—barely.

But Cee Cee's cutting laughter and verbal abuse said otherwise.

"If you won't fuck me with this thing, you gay fucking chicken-shit, I will!"

Tugging strongly at the club again, and finding it still unmoving, she stared up at me as if she hated me.

Her wild mood swing had happened so fast I was confused. I understood her being sexually impatient, and high and drunk as hell, and from the rough side of the tracks and all that, but her flip from fully submissive to hellcat-fury was, at the moment, unexplainable.

I could see and hear her spitting her angry words at me, but my only natural reaction was, *"What the...?"*

And the fact that I was standing there with an annoyed expression on my face, looking down at her like she was some kind of Koo-Koo bird, did not help.

"What happened you weak-ass old man?! Did you think I was kidding about wanting that fucking thing all the way inside my cunt? Is that too fucking much for you, you pansy-ass old fucker?!"

Damn this girl had an attitude and a mouth! And the more she railed the meaner she got. And I could hardly keep up with her rushing temper.

"ALRIGHT THEN, YOU GAY FUCKING ASSHOLE FUCKER, GET THE HELL OFF ME!!!" She screamed unexpectedly, as she let go of the club and moved to get up!

Snapping out of my hesitation, my slightly delayed but fully intuitive reaction swang into play like a slamming-door. When Cee Cee took her hands off the club and threw her arms over to one side of her body in an effort to roll off the couch; I took my right hand off the club and leaning quickly forward I wrapped those fingers around her thin throat and pinned her now awkwardly struggling body back down onto the couch.

Breaking out the strength of my own body and voice, I leaned even farther forward as my left hand pushed the fighting club a couple of firm inches deeper into Cee Cee's impatient pussy, and then I shouted down into her face.

"ARE YOU TALKING TO ME, YOU BATSHIT-CRAZY FUCKING BITCH?! SHUT THE FUCK UP AND LAY THE FUCK DOWN! AND HOLD FUCKING STILL FOR THREE GODDAMN SECONDS AND WE'LL SEE JUST HOW FUCKING DEEP YOU CAN TAKE THIS CLUB!!!"

Seeing that I had her attention, I leaned still closer and staring right into her eyes I growled in an even lower tone at her.

"CALL ME A WEAK-ASS OLD MAN AGAIN..."

And nothing else I could have done or said would have pleased Cee Cee more. Watching her face was like being in the front row of a movie, her expressions were so dramatic and obvious. But the poor thing sure had one hell of a communication impediment! At least now, she understood me perfectly.

And feeling her relax beneath my grip was good, and I rewarded her by providing exactly what she craved. Slowly sliding the club a little father into Cee Cee's now sopping wet hole, I watched her face turn back toward bliss.

Whispering, Cee Cee breathed out, *"Jesus.., it's about time..."*

It should be a more common knowledge that, on the right occasions, many women adore being choked while they're being fucked. And this is so common, I have to wonder if it is a genetic memory or something similar.

Because Cee Cee and I were now locked in that powerful embrace, I enjoyed an uncommonly deep taste of that pleasure while slowly sliding the club deeper into her submissively supine body, marveling at the deepening color of blue that her white throat and face were turning as she squirmed in breathless delight under the weight of my now fully engaged physical passion.

But much more than choking, Cee Cee wanted to feel the oddly related threat of being over-stuffed, of being bodily-filled past normal boundaries, of willingly pushing oneself farther open.

How can it be wrong to test the limits of how much ecstasy one can contain?

"Push it in deeper, Rory ..." She begged in a straining whisper.

Releasing my grip from the front of her neck, I moved that hand down and under her right shoulder, and then used it to pull her firmly toward me.

"Push it in DEEPER, RORY ..." She commanded.

So I did.

And for ten minutes or so I slowly and firmly deepened, and lengthened, and strengthened the insistence of my penetrating stroke; sometimes twisting the club a little, and moving it up-and-down and side-to-side, working and building her sensual and tactile sensations like a maestro of physical ecstasy. And when I could see that as much as nine or ten inches of the club were being swallowed up by her amazing vagina—I purposely went for one inch more.

"OH RORY, YES! YES! YES! YES! OHHHHHHHHHHHH!!!" She cried!

Sensing Cee Cee's imminent and ultimate descent into her final orgasmic release, I decided that it was time for me to make my own last demands. Slowing my thrusts of the club, I bent forward over her and spoke with a crystal clarity.

"Cee Cee, I'm going to turn you over so that I can shove this club all the way into you, just like you want, from behind—while I fuck you in the ass with my cock at the same time. Then, when I'm ready, I'm going to yank this club out of your body and cum all over the inside of your wide-open pussy! Now get up, and go bend your body over that big desk."

Understanding me, Cee Cee opened her eyes wide and directly into mine. Moaning back at me almost unintelligibly as I pulled the club fully out of her clinging hole, she obeyed me with enthusiasm.

"Ohhh fuck yes, you mother-fucker, that's what I'm talking about!" She murmured as she moved.

Rolling slowly off the couch, Cee Cee stood up with as much coordination as she could manage on her spindly-looking little legs and feet. Once up, she looked directly over at the sturdy desk/table that I had pointing at.

The table I had directed her to was a big heavy steel-framed desk/table/work-area that was set up in our utility-corner of the main living room of the house. Sometimes we used it for folding laundry, sometimes we used it for paperwork, or to wrap presents, or to complete any number of other family projects on.

Today I was going to lay a very deviant little street urchin across it, and fuck her past the point of reasonable.

When Cee Cee bent herself forward and pushed her bulging body up onto the table, laying herself out on her ball-like stomach, with her spreading-open ass and sodden cunt positioned right at the perfect height for me, and with her feet and legs set wide apart and braced against the desks side for traction—I stood behind her, literally salivating for the sexual feast before me.

Wiping a big handful of that saliva from my mouth into my hand, I slathered it all over Cee Cee's twitching pink asshole.

And right then, like a flash-bulb idea, I thought of how perfect it would be to get a quick picture of Cee Cee to hang in my masturbation room: Because at that moment she was all that Cee Cee could be, laid-out wide-and-willing. A picture like that—irrefutable proof of my far reaching hypersexual powers—was exactly what I filled my secret room with.

And I realized that the brand-new digital camera that I had recently received as a gift would work perfectly—and it was sitting on the corner of the kitchen countertop not more than four steps behind me. And the fact that Cee Cee was facing the other direction at that particular moment, and wasn't watching what I was doing, made the chance impossible to pass up.

Distracting Cee Cee for a moment with my playfully aggressive and loudly stated sexual promises, I set the darkly polished club down on the nearest chair without a sound and simultaneously made my move for the camera. Sneaking backward, I spoke to her.

"Cee Cee, I am going to shove this club up into your body so hard you're gonna think you just got fucked to death!"

"GIVE IT TO ME!" She shouted back in reply, shaking her head from side-to-side in an almost animalistic gesture of readiness.

Tip-toeing quickly backward during the small span of banter, I'd grabbed the camera and hurriedly took off the lens cap and hit the three buttons I hoped would properly set it for an auto-snapshot without a flash.

Even a single shadowy picture of Cee Cee would fully resurrect her for me in the future.

Setting the camera hastily back onto the countertop and aiming it, I stepped directly back to Cee Cee's body and grabbed the club up.

Keeping myself slightly to the side for the seven-second countdown, I hoped that the camera would capture my deliciously depraved manipulations of Cee Cee in a permanently perverse and frozen-in-time frame.

And at that exact moment, with my universe rotating into its own special constellation, Cee Cee turned and looked over her naked shoulder at me with a big wicked smile, and curling her index finger back in a cutesy come-fuck-me gesture, she purred her deepest desires out loud.

"RORY, COME PUT THAT BIG FUCKING CLUB IN MY PUSSY!"

"YES, MY BEAUTIFUL CEE CEE."

It was time.

Coming up behind her all at once, trapping her bent-over vulnerability between the sturdy desk/table and my strong naked body, I grabbed a handful of her dirty-blond hair at the back of her head with my left hand. With my right hand I firmly guided the clubs bulging head back into her shivering wide-open and rear-facing cunt.

Without hesitation, one wondrous inch at a time, I slipped the rigid giant phallus firmly inward until it was all-the-way up against Cee Cee's physical hilt for the first time.

Cee Cee, now finally filled, responded with a powerful quivering all over her body, and a deep groaning, as she swaying on her bent knees.

And then, slowly, she began to pump herself forward and back. Holding the edges of the table top with her outstretched arms and hands, she was both pulling herself forward and pushing herself back toward me—and onto the monster-cock sized club.

"Keep doing that Cee Cee, I ordered. "I'm going to put my fat cock into your asshole."

"FUUUUUUCK MEEEEE …" She begged.

It might seem a little bit gymnastic, but the position I put myself in was actually fairly simple: from the usual rear-mounting position for ass fucking I lifted up my left leg and placed my foot onto a low stool, which locked my whole leg beside Cee Cee's left hip and ass-cheek.

Every stud knows this one-leg-high rear fucking position. The trickier part, in this case, was swinging my left arm around behind my hip and ass to grab the clubs handle, which was now sticking out of Cee Cee's bent over body and extended out right below my nutsack.

Once I had sunk my fully swollen and now nerve-end raging cock into Cee Cee's clenching and saliva slickened asshole, I quickly adjusted my grip on the club. And then, by simply pumping my body forward just like I usually would—both my cock and the club rammed forward into Cee Cee's two fuck holes at the same time.

And with the club filling her vaginal cavity so completely, I could also feel my engorged cock sliding all the way in-and-out of her extra tightly compressed anal passage in a way that felt so good I believed in that moment that it must be the most wonderful hole I had ever fucked!

However, one thing that was a bit distracting, was gauging the club's real depth or pressure at its deepest point. So I focused on pumping my rock-hard cock into her delicious ass, and stayed back a bit from pounding the club too deeply into her pussy—which Cee Cee allowed me to do for all of three or four lovely minutes.

"YOU GOTTA GO DEEEPER, RORY…" She soon groaned.

"YOU GOTTA GO HAAARDER…" She then begged.

And as she said it out loud, she'd also started to pull herself back-and-forth across the table's top harder, pumping her little body and bulging stomach against it with a building intensity, as if to make up for what I wasn't achieving.

And God damn it, her erratic movements were starting to mess with my ass-fucking!

"CEE CEE, HOLD STILL AND LET ME FUCK YOU!"

"FUCK ME HARDER!" She yelled back.

So, I assumed that if I wasn't getting deep enough yet—I could go a little deeper. And it would be the only thing that would shut Cee Cee up and make her do what I said.

Adjusting my grip just an inch or so farther back on the handle, I pumped myself and the war club into her again—with some extra authority.

"MORE!" Cee Cee huffed, closer now.

"Okay, Baby…"

Gripping one more inch or so back on the handle, I slapped my body forward in another firm pump—and with the hand that was holding the club, I felt the first definite bit of mushy but firm resistance.

"OHHHHhhhhhhhh, FUCK ME LIKE THAAAAAT!" Cee Cee cried out, in an expression of rapture and aching desire so pure and welling-up I couldn't question it.

"OHHH.., OHHH.., OHHH.., OHHH..," She began to chant as she shoved herself back against the club and my body.

"OHHH.., OHHHHHH.., OHHHHHHHHH..," She continued in throaty ecstasy, as I pounded my body against hers.

And when she seemed to be reaching for an apex, with her anus rhythmically clinching down on my pulsing cock, making the first drops of my pre-cum begin to flow, I set myself for a few extra firm and fast pumps to finish myself off, knowing that I would have to quickly jerk the club out of her pussy and get my cock into it at just the right moment to fill her with my promised load of sperm.

And just as I readied myself to buck harder into her—*sensing it*—Cee Cee used all her arm and leg strength to simultaneously shove herself backwards into my body and the club with a blast of power that I could not have anticipated.

And as her body slammed backwards into my thrusting hips, the perfectly timed force was so great I was almost knocked back off both my feet! And when my reactively flexing left arm and grip felt the cracking shock-wave of the fighting club smacking directly into something inside Cee Cee's body—that was seemingly as hard as the oak-wood club itself—I cringed, and came to a totally freezing stop…

"AAAAAHHHHHHHHHH!!!" Cee Cee screamed!

And in response to the shock-wave that had run straight up through her body, Cee Cee's knees buckled beneath her, and her body sagged fully onto the desktop!

Quickly using my freed right hand and my whole body to hold and help keep Cee Cee up on the desk, I basically trapped her body there for the faltering moment. And within the span of only one or two quick breaths, she started raising herself back up onto her white-knuckled hands and shaking legs.

Still stuck in the micro-moment of feeling the clubs cracking impact, and Cee Cee's collapse, I stood frozen, with my cock still in her ass (as I had followed her body forward as it slumped), and my left hands grip still locked (unconsciously) around the handle of the club. I was still *inside* Cee Cee—but with my heart stopped.

And before I could think of what to do or say next, before she was even up on her feet again, unbelievably, she began to rock herself back into my body! And alarmingly, within the span of just three or four pushes, as her breaths got deeper, and her arms and legs regained their strength, she was already building her momentum again! And then she mumbled something—and then she screamed it!

"PUSH THAT FUCKING THING UP INTO ME LIKE THAT AGAIN!"

She repeated at the top of her lungs, like someone yelling into the darkness for help, which scared me. All the while pushing back into me and the club harder, and harder, violently lost in her own sexual delirium.

Oddly unable to return directly back to the too-far sexual edge that Cee Cee evidently needed to smash herself against, as she continued to pump herself back into me and the club I found myself holding my own position more weakly.

But the more I tried to hold back, the more Cee Cee tried to make up for my lack of enthusiasm. Quickly, and very emotionally building herself up to the point where she was too-vigorously bouncing and pulling her grotesquely flattening stomach against the heavy steel-framed table, her tantrum began.

And watching her do this, turned me off. And whatever may have been left of my own sexual resolve lost its strength. Even my tightly strapped cock was starting to shrink away. And I knew that I had to change-up the situation, *somehow*...

Putting my hand softly on her heaving freckled back, I tried to stop her.

"Don't do that, Cee Cee." I said softly, meaning no judgment, while pulling back on my own body to communicate the message to her physically.

"YOU BETTER JACK THAT THING ALL THE WAY UP INSIDE ME AGAIN, YOU FUCKER!" She shouted back at me, still not looking at me, and still flailing herself against the desk.

"DON'T DO THAT, CEE CEE! YOU'RE GONNA HURT YOURSELF!" I said with nothing but brotherly love, removing the club from her body.

"OH NO YOU DON'T...!" She pled! **"COME ON, FUCKER!!! JUST FUCK ME EVEN HARDER FOR A FEW MORE**

MINUTES!!!" She screamed, begged, commanded, and threatened, ferociously hurling herself down against the desktop like a child in a dangerous fit!

"NOW STOP THAT CEE CEE! I'M NOT GOING TO LET YOU HURT YOURSELF!" I yelled with growing intensity, which only made her fight harder.

And by now she was just plain out-of-control, yanking herself so wildly around with her arms she was about to start head-butting the desktop, which was too much for me.

"STOP IT RIGHT NOW!" I scolded with powerful finality, pushing my weight and hand down onto the back of her shoulders hard enough to pin her for a second, and to remind her who was in control—which I shouldn't have done.

When Cee Cee sensed the fully chilling commitment of my restraining pressure on her back, and she stopped her raging fit for a moment—I hoped it was a good sign.

Waiting, I then lightened the pressure of my hand on her back.

"Let me fuck you on the couch again, Cee Cee." I tried, softly.

"Let me cum inside your pussy now." I continued, in a voice accidentally too quiet, too distant, and too condescending, which was an unintended mistake.

Which I realized when all the warmth in the room vanished.

Just as I can sense the slightest traces of sexual connection, impulse, and release, I can also sense the absolute absence of it, and the breaking of the connection. And when those energies take a turn in the worst kinds of directions, I can feel it like punch in the head.

Cee Cee's entire body and being had been offended.

As I mentioned earlier, the desk/table that Cee Cee was laid across was a multi-purpose utility type workspace. At the far end of the table, out in front of Cee Cee, there were a few desktop type items, and among the group of items was an over-sized pen-and-pencil holder full of various writing instruments and a few other household tools.

When Cee Cee unexpectedly kicked me backward from my position behind her, and then lunged forward across the table top, somehow rolling on her rounded stomach like a big beach ball—and then snatched the large pair of steel scissors from the pen holder—I instantly *knew* that serious violence had come into my home.

Regaining my footing while stumbling backward, I came to a stop several steps back from Cee Cee, with the fighting club still hanging loosely in my left hand.

Simultaneously watching Cee Cee moving sideways off the table with the scissors, while trying to grasp exactly what was happening, I'd barely had time to regain my mental balance before she was whipping around to face me. Switching the club to my right hand, I focused my vision on the scissors.

Gripping tightly on the glinting steel weapon in her frail right hand, Cee Cee began wailing at me like a banshee.

"FUCK YOU, YOU ASSHOLE!!! YOU DON'T FUCKING KNOW MEEEEEE!!!"

Leading with the pointed edge of the scissors, Cee Cee moved toward me slashing sideways, back-and-forth, and wildly at the air space between us.

Stepping defensively backwards, and knowing that the kitchen island-counter was no more than a few more steps behind me, I began processing my thoughts and immediate priorities at the highest possible speed.

I wanted to calm her, but Cee Cee was screaming as loud as she could and literally dancing on her tip-toes to bring out every last frantic decibel of her enraged voice. And she was slashing so wildly back and forth I seriously worried that she might stab herself.

"YOU DON'T KNOW A FUCKING THING ABOUT ME YOU FUCKING ASSHOLE MOTHERFUCKER! YOU DON'T TELL ME WHAT TO FUCKING DO! YOU DON'T TELL ME WHAT TO DO WITH MY OWN FUCKING BODY! YOU FUCKING FREAK-ASS OLD MOTHERFUCKER!!!"

Thinking at the speed of light, with my focus flashing between her furious eyes and the scissors, I watched in horror as Cee Cee suddenly stopped her forward advancing and slashing movements, and then slowly lifted the scissors above her head—and then held still.

And the horror was this: I could not tell if Cee Cee was thinking of plunging the scissor-blades down at me—or into her own belly...?

The fighting club in my hand was ready, and I definitely could have struck her with it in one unstoppable movement (right across her thin wrist, breaking it) to make her drop the scissors—*if I struck instantly.*

But I just didn't want to hit her.

Dropping the club to the floor, I held my opened hands out.

Taking up my very best weapon, I decided to pit my empathic abilities against Cee Cee's tragically confused and clearly impending violence.

I was also absolutely ready to jump in and put my own hands in the way of the scissor-blades, if she tried to stab herself.

Inching forward, and looking directly into her raging eyes, I spoke softly.

"Please put down the scissors, Cee Cee. I'm so sorry. Really, Cee Cee, I adore you. We were having fun. I just thought you were going to hurt your tummy..."

Curling-back lips are frightening on the face of any animal—but on the face of the naked and pregnant little drug-smeared girl in front of me, holding a six-inch two-pronged metal spike above her head, it was the worst thing I had ever seen.

I can't remember if I started to cry first, or if she did. Hers were shaking tears of insane rage. Mine fell because Cee Cee had to live with that kind of demon burning alive inside her.

"Please Cee Cee..., I adore you..., I just didn't want you to get hurt..., and I don't want to get hurt..., please Cee Cee..., I don't want anyone to get hurt..."

Now I was begging, holding my empty hands out to her as tears rolled down my face. I was still ready to protect myself, or her, and fight for the scissors. I wasn't really afraid for myself, I was just afraid.

And I realized then, with a sense of great sadness, that I had reached that most revealing dimension with Cee Cee; and that I was witnessing her whole unraveling self.

With the scissors still above her head, snarling and shaking with fury, and with eyes so fiercely alight her face seemed to be on fire, Cee Cee actually managed to begin voicing her truest individual self:

"DON'T YOU CALL ME CEE CEE!!! MY NAME IS ALICE!!!"

And with her own truth having risen so close to the surface, she broke.

Her right foot came forward first, warning me. When the scissors came slicing down at my face, I was already moving. And as the blade and the hand that held it slipped viciously through the air space that my head had just occupied, I followed the striking path of her swipe and prepared to grab her one dangerous hand with both of mine.

I would have one chance, and one millisecond to do it in, before she became unpredictable again.

As her arm came to a stop at the bottom of its striking arc, before her mind even realized that she had missed her target, both of my arms and hands shot out and clamped down like a vice on both sides of her weapon carrying hand and wrist. Instantly pulling her arm across the front of her own body, unbalancing her, followed by quickly twisting my hips in that same direction, I took control of her physical body and her lashing-out being—including, most importantly, the scissors.

Fighting like a half-caught wildcat, Cee Cee nevertheless succumbed to my practiced skill, and to gravity, as she stumbled awkwardly in the direction of my pulling force.

With my own body's weight dropping into my powerful turning motion, my intention was to bring Cee Cee around my hips in an arc, and then set her safely down onto the floor on her back, allowing me to then simply remove the scissors from her hand.

Instead—I watched as Cee Cee unexpectedly lurched farther around me than expected, and then caught the toes of her leading foot on the corner leg of the big desk/table that we had circled back towards, which completely collapsed her front leg, tripping her precipitously sideways and down, dropping the side of her enlarged stomach right toward the steel desk's edge.

Reacting to what was unfolding as if I were electrocuted, I took a super-fast half-step in the opposite direction and yanked hard on Cee Cee's arm, now trying desperately to pull her upper body clear of the desk—and I came as close as any man could have—which was three crashing and scraping inches too short.

Violently rippling away on impact, I saw the naked side of Cee Cee's roundly-extended stomach smash into and then past the unforgiving top edge. Bashing all Cee Cee's breath out in a single blow, she wasn't even able to cry out.

Now falling straight towards the floor in an uncontrollable heap, the side of Cee Cee's head also met the edge of the table's top, brutally, sending her shimmering thin hair across her face like a floating red-blond veil, and knocking her unconscious.

With no time to even blink, I held onto her suddenly limp hand and wrist as she landed in a pile at my feet.

Before her body had come to rest on the ground, time was racing through my mind again, and I was already bent down over her, with now terrified-tears welling up, and my throat locking closed on itself.

"Oh fuck, Cee Cee...get up," I whispered to her closed eyes.

But she was completely knocked-out.

Touching her face with my shaking fingers, I realized that I had to turn her head over to see what had happened, and my tears began to run fast and freely, falling onto Cee Cee's face and cheeks.

"AWWW CEE CEE...WAKE UP PLEEEASE!" I begged the Universe, and turned her face all the way to the other side.

When I saw her fair hair bunched-up in a pink clump against her temple, I nearly fainted.

Then I pleaded to her, "OHHHHHHHH, CEE CEE...YOU GOTTA WAKE UP NOW!"

And suddenly I couldn't stop myself from bawling and shaking and I didn't care. "OHHH... OHHH... OHHHhhhhhhh... "

Moving her crumpled-up body, and laying Cee Cee flat on her back, I then looked around for something to put under her head and knees.

Sobbing, I looked up and down her limp and naked body, and noticed the fire-engine colored red scrape mark and swelling lump on the side of her asymmetrically swollen stomach.

"AHHHHHH...FUCK, NOOOOOOOOOOOOOO..." I wailed, collapsing to my elbows next to Cee Cee's limp body.

"NOOOOOOOOOOOOOOOOO..."

I was aware that I needed to get control of myself, but at that moment all I could do was cry and fight the outright denial of the situation. Senselessly, I patted Cee Cee's forehead and kept begging her to wake up. And maybe three minutes passed.

However long it was, I was still sitting there useless when I thought I heard someone else's voice...

Stopping my crying, my head shot up. And for several missing heartbeats I became even more filled with panic, suddenly gripped by the icy vision of one of my family members, or some random friend of ours, coming into my house unexpectedly. *Maybe someone was outside?*

I stopped breathing, and tried to listen to the world outside my house. And the vision of Cee Cee in a dirt grave jumped into my head: It wasn't on purpose, and not like a thought you build on. It just came into my mind all at once.

Then, out of sheer need something in my head broke loose and I stopped shaking.

Dropping Cee Cee's head softly out of my lap as I jumped up, I ran across the room and dove for the window curtain. Moving it aside just slightly, I looked out and down to my driveway..., and saw that no one was there. I then looked out the nearest front window, and then the kitchen window out to the back, and saw that no one was there, either.

And I didn't like that I couldn't quite tell what I had heard, or even *if* I had heard something. I felt like I was on the brink of losing my senses, so I started to focus as hard as I could.

Running back to Cee Cee, I noticed that most of my panic was gone. I would like to say that it was replaced by an all-consuming concern for her, or by a cold professionalism, but the truth is that I was thinking primarily of my own survival. If I could get Cee Cee back on her feet and out of my house—that would be in my very best interest. Whatever the case, I put my next focus on helping her however I could.

Using my basic first responder training, I kneeled down onto the ground at her side and reached for Cee Cee's wrist, and then lay my head down to her chest at the same time. By the time my head touched her body I knew that she had a strong pulse. And when my face touched her naked chest I felt her sternum rise, and I felt her vital body heat. She sure as hell wasn't dead, or in shock (yet).

Scooting back a little, my hands and eyes then moved to the injury on Cee Cee's side. Leaning close, I looked at it very carefully and saw that there was definitely no open part of the wound. What I did see was a bright-red fist-sized scrape that looked as if it had occurred while she was sliding down along the edge of the table. Touching softly around it and pressing a little with the fingertips of both my hands, I searched the area for anything that would tell me there was definitely a deeper injury. I felt her ribs, and around her back a little on each side, and that all seemed normal. But I knew that there was no way for me to quickly assess her internal injuries.

Next, I knew that I needed to look at her head and neck. Her head had hit the desk pretty hard, but probably not hard enough to break her young skull. Of course, a part of me was praying constantly that everything would be alright. But everything already wasn't "alright," so I just kept moving to the next thing that I thought of. Shuffling on my knees I moved to her upper most body, and turned my attention toward her right temple.

Looking up to her head my eyes stopped on her silent young face, which, when slack and totally relaxed like this, looked so trouble-free.

And for a moment I felt so sorry for how things had taken this turn for the worst, and I almost let myself go back to tears.

Reaching out to stroke her pale face for a second before I inspected her temple, in my mind, for that moment, I pretended that she was just sleeping…

And as I sat there looking down at her, blinking slowly at first, Cee Cee suddenly opened her eyes and looked up at me, like a child trying to re-focus after waking from a nap.

Shocked, I sat stock-still, staring at her. And after a just a few seconds, I could see that she was going to speak.

"Get off me fucker…," she said sleepily, and it seemed— jokingly?

I wanted to laugh: I wanted to cry; but Cee Cee's immediacy gave me time for neither.

Coming up to a sudden sitting position, by herself, right there next to me, without any trouble or apparent pain, and seemingly unaware of her head or stomach injuries, she then scooted over and nestled herself into my shoulder. Turning her face up towards mine, Cee Cee looked calmly into my eyes. And, similar to when I had first met her, she didn't seem in any hurry to speak.

Sitting on the floor with her, I lifted her chin toward my face and looked back into her eyes (to see if the pupils were oddly or differently dilated), and I was damned glad to see that they weren't. Smiling quietly, I reaching my right hand up to the back of her neck, and in the guise of a loving caress, I felt the line-up of her upper vertebrae, and watched for any sensitive spots—and found none. And as the (relative) clarity returned to Cee Cee's eyes, I felt more and more hopeful that she wouldn't have to be hospitalized, which was the point where I knew that my *other* life would have become seriously compromised.

I also knew that even the slightest scalp injuries could be temporary bleeders, and that serious head and/or neck injuries, or bad concussions, rarely had the victim sitting up with a joke on their lips this quickly.

"Holy shit," I allowed myself to think, *"maybe my hypersexual karmic-shield will hold up for me just this one more time!"*

For another second, I let myself imagine that Cee Cee might even have some permanent short-term memory loss, due to the knock-out blow. It happens all the time.

"How come we're on the floor?" She asked quietly, and calmly.

"What do you remember, Baby?" I replied softly.

"Did I pass out?" She asked, in a tone not full of surprise.

"Yeah, you did, kinda…"

"Oh man…" She sighed.

"Do you know what day it is?" I asked gently.

"No…, but I never do." She answered, without concern.

"Do you remember your name, Baby?"

Hesitating, she looked up at me and replied slowly. "You mean…, the sweet one you gave me—Cee Cee?"

"Yes, Cee Cee, my sweetheart!" I said with a rush of relief.

"Can I have some more of that whiskey?"

"Yes, Baby." I almost laughed. "But let's sit here for another minute first." I finished.

"Why?"

Wrapping my left arm around her to meet my right one, I hugged her softly to me.

"Just sit here with me for a minute, and then we'll get a drink."

Sitting with her in my arms was so quiet then, and my sense of relief was so great, and I felt nearly back-to-safety. And whether it was an effect of her regaining consciousness, or perhaps a reactive mix of brain chemicals from the physical impact, Cee Cee seemed more sober and settled than at any time before. Or, maybe she was just groggy.

Of course, inside my head I could still hear the raging fear-thoughts and mad dashing worries from just moments ago—*and the echoes of Cee Cee's screeching murderous voice as she attacked me*—but the room and our bodies were so quiet and so still for that moment, it felt almost transcendent.

Returning to rational thought, I realized that if Cee Cee didn't remember what had happened, I could just tell her that she had hit herself on the desk when she passed out.

Holding her lovingly, I said a sinister prayer inside my own mind, and I felt like a demon crawling into a cave: *"Darkness, cover me now..."*

"How did I pass out?"

"What do you remember, sweetie?"

"I...I...," she stammered.

"I remember you were fucking me over there on the couch with that big wood thing!" She chirped in sudden gleeful memory.

"Yes. You're such a nasty girl, Cee Cee."

"Yes..., I am..., thank you for doing that! I'm sorry I passed-out." She spoke genuinely, looking up to my face again.

And as she looked up at me, I saw her right hand slip unconsciously down over the bruised area on the side of her stomach. Then her hand slid gently back up over it, and stopped at the central welt and rawest patch of flesh. Feeling it, her eyebrows furrowed together, followed quickly by her head swiveling down to see what her fingers were touching.

"Oh crap," She started. "I slammed my side up pretty shitty!" She finished with a snort, and a no-big-deal kind of tough-girl from the streets attitude.

I couldn't believe it! She was actually making a funny-face to show how silly she thought it all was! So I just went with it.

"You smacked your head a little too, Baby. But I don't think it's too bad. You might have a goose-egg and a little scrape…"

"What the fuck?! No shit?" She laughed.

Then, lifting her other hand up and around to touch the exact place of the head injury, she looked at her fingers to see if there was any blood.

When she saw only a tiny smear of pink, I'd swear she was disappointed.

Then, excited, she swung the injured side of her head around toward me.

"What does it look like? Let me see it! Where's a mirror?" She sang out, trying to get up.

Holding onto her, I distracted her with promises.

"Just relax a minute more, Cee Cee. I'll get you a mirror in a second. It's always good to relax when you've just passed out. It's not much to look at anyway. I'll wash it off for you."

And man, was I glad to be able to say all that! Having finally gotten another good look at it, I was extremely relieved to see that the injury was smaller than I'd thought. And there was barely a noticeable bump on her head, which amazed me, and the small scrape/cut must have stopped bleeding almost instantly.

Still, I reminded myself that I had no way of knowing what the actual extent of her injuries were. What if her pain-tolerance, or remaining intoxication, was so high she couldn't even tell that she was hurt? Cee Cee's head could be worse than it looked, and I would definitely expect her to feel some wicked whiplash in her neck before long. Maybe the deeper pain of the injuries hadn't even kicked in yet...and what about *inside* her actual womb?

My mind skipped off that line of thinking with the slickness of a teflon-conscience. If Cee Cee thought she was "alright"; she was alright.

That was all there was to it. The faster I could move her back out into her own life, and her own responsibility, the better.

"That's fucking hilarious!" She piped in, again. "Shit fucker, that's the funniest thing that's happened to me in a long time!" Chuckling, and wagging her head back and forth, she seemed to relish the injurious incident in an openly excited way.

Then, for whatever reason, she became quiet and seemed introspective, staring blankly at the floor beneath her legs, perhaps looking for more of the memory to laugh at. And then, from her searching expressions, I could tell that she was definitely trying to remember *something*...

What could I do but just sit there?

Actually, I could hardly believe my ability to be so outwardly calm and emotionally fluid with Cee Cee. While internally, I was feeling as weirdly disconnected as I ever had in my life. I felt like I was floating, or maybe falling, and I couldn't tell the difference.

And even though things had quieted down, and Cee Cee was taking her injuries so well, I still felt like something was rushing toward me. But whatever it was, it was too shadowy, or so well-hidden even I couldn't see it coming.

While I sat there holding her in both my arms, staring at the side of her face, Cee Cee's eyes wandered around and eventually came open a little wider, and then her head came up a little higher, and her expression was more awake.

"How'd we get over on this side of the room?" She asked, sharply curious.

Then, turning herself a little to one side and then the other, her eyes panned around our immediate part of the room with intent. And when she turned and looked far enough over her left shoulder, she saw the one thing that I wished she hadn't, and I felt it in her body.

How had I not thought to hide it..? I realized helplessly.

Behind me by a few feet, the stainless steel scissors lay brightly on the blue carpeted floor, right next to the dark wooden club.

Staring at them, she didn't say anything for perhaps a whole minute. And then it started to come.

"You..., I..., you..., I...," She stammered.

Unable to stop her, I felt utterly cornered. And I felt a deep sorrow rising inside my heart. And then, I felt the mental heat of self-protection, as I prepared myself for another battle.

Waiting to feel her body tense all the way up, I turned my fighting-mind on early this time, and instantly had my plan in place: If I had to, I would simply pin Cee Cee to the ground and make her understand that it was all an accident. And I would hold her there until she relaxed—even if it took the next two hours to do it!

In my mind I strategized: If I could get her to calm down and be more-or-less alright with what had happened, perhaps I could also convince her to accept a reasonable sum of money to let it all slide by.

She was from a very low-down part of town, so kicking even this kind of shit down-the-road (as they say) should be possible for her—at some reasonably do-able dollar amount.

I felt emotionally as cold as ice, and one hundred percent absent from my nakedness.

And then Cee Cee remembered another piece of the puzzle, or put something important together, and her mind took it like a hard slap.

Pulling her lightly toward me, I prepared for the grim job in front of me.

Feeling my tears building-up again, and absolutely past the point of any artifice—I made an additional decision, and just told her straight.

"Cee Cee, I'm so sorry. I adore you. It was totally an accident. I'm so sorry. Please let me help you…"

Feeling her body relax in my arms confused me, and then alerted me, and stopped me mid-sentence. Waiting for the worst, I braced myself in every way.

"I tried to stab you…," she began, calmly.

Staying silent, I wondered at the absence of anger?

"Why did I try to stab you?" She said, almost apologetically.

Where was she coming from?

Leaning her head away from our embrace a little, she turned and looked up at me with an expression of pure, open, and honest questioning. And I said nothing.

And because she wasn't fighting me in any way, when she decided to move away from me by scooting her sitting position on the floor around to face me, I just opened my arms and let her.

Changing her question, she continued, "What did you do?"

What parts wasn't she remembering?

"Why did I get mad?" She asked more pointedly.

I didn't know the answer to that!

"Why don't you answer me?" She pressed, with her expression beginning to harden.

"Calm down, sweetie. I'll answer you, the best I can. Please don't get mad. I told you, I adore you. I didn't try to do anything..."

"You don't know me." She interrupted, in a tone that still wasn't angry, but instead seemed to contain a mixture of cold wonder and dismissiveness mixed together.

"I might know you a little more than you think." I countered, with an intention of inclusiveness.

"You don't know shit about shit, and I don't know you." She continued evenly, "Just tell me why I got so mad I tried to stab you? Did you say something? Just tell me."

Maybe her insane behavior was just as confusing to her as it was for me?

"I don't know what made you so mad, Cee Cee. I swear, I don't know..."

"What was happening when I lost my temper?"

"You got mad so fast I didn't know why, or what..."

"Just tell me what was happening."

She wasn't going to let it go. So I pictured myself guiltless, and went from there.

"Okay, Cee Cee," I said, filled with returning fear. "I'll tell you. We were fucking on the desk and...,"

And that was all it took.

Powerless, I watched as her eyes popped-open as another scene returned to her memory.

"*You said...*," She started, letting it come to her. "That..., you were going to stop fucking me because you thought I was going to hurt myself..."

Speaking mostly to herself, and thinking it through as she said it out-loud, she looked across the room.

"And then I grabbed the scissors *because...*"

And then she had her epiphany: I could tell because her face went through half a dozen different expressions, each one indicating a different hard-edged emotion, one after the next, with each one somehow adding a progressively heavier layer of psychological weight to her being.

I could also measure the personal significance of the series of thoughts because her parade of emotions ended in a private, nearly silent, and fully unrestricted flow of tears.

Whatever it was that Cee Cee had just thought her way through, it held some of the gravest meaning in her life.

For a few short minutes she let herself go. Sitting so close to her, but now separate, I wished that I was still holding her.

Her head now hanging, with her tears falling, and her anger nowhere in sight, Cee Cee sat still, reflective, and oddly calm—and I had no idea why, or where her mind had finally settled.

And I realized then that I would never understand this girl: She was right—I didn't know shit about shit.

"Are you okay...?" I eventually whispered.

Snorting in reply, which also sounded like a helpless laugh, Cee Cee struggled for the words. And when she looked up at me, it was with eyes that were so profoundly weary they looked almost incapable of any more tears.

"Am I okay? Am I? *Look at me...,*" she said softly, and self derisively, and with a voice so tired and hollow-out it seemed finally exhausted.

"I don't think you're too hurt..."

"I'm not even talking about that!" She spat softly.

"What *are* you talking about, Cee Cee?" I replied even softer. "Please tell me."

Taking her own time, and staring at my face in a way so contemplative it shocked me, as if she were trying to correctly place me in the greater scheme of her thorny universe and lonely existence, she then decided to explain herself.

"You are one of the nicest, and weirdest, and craziest old perverts I have ever met. But you act like you know everything. I'll tell you something you don't know. You don't know the first fucking thing about me, and you live in a stupid dream-world."

"I'm sorry, I certainly didn't mean to...,"

"Just like that, you asshole! Why the fuck do you apologize to me? You didn't even listen to me for two-goddamn-seconds! I was going to tell you something..."

"Okay!" I said quickly, and then clamped my mouth tightly-shut for her to see.

"You still think you're a smart fucker..." She sneered, seriously.

In stern response, I wagged my head from side to side to tell her that I didn't.

"I'm too fucking tired to argue anymore." She sighed. "Help me get my ass off the floor, and go get me that fucking whiskey drink."

"I'm not talking anymore—I promise!" I entreated. "You were going to tell me something..."

"Fuck! I just want to go home. Get me up and get me that whiskey drink, and maybe I'll finish what I was saying."

"Okay, Cee Cee." I said, as I stood up to help her.

"I already told you, *my name* is Alice." She said plainly, reaching her hands up towards mine.

Chapter Seventeen

<u>Her Babies</u>

Without even looking toward her clothes, Alice walked across the room and plopped her naked and battered body heavily onto the couch.

Watching her as I walked into the kitchen, I again noticed that we were naked. And it aroused me, again. But the blood stain in her hair was hard to look at.

Wetting a couple of paper-towels, I walked back over to her.

"Let me clean off your hair, Alice."

"Fuck, alright." She replied peevishly, leaning her head over to give me a better angle to work with.

It was weird how physically "okay" she seemed. And when she had indicated that she wanted to go home, those words were like magic to me. And I felt almost "safe" again. So, after washing the small splotch of blood out of her hair, I was glad to get her one more glass of whiskey.

And, I was still willing to hear whatever last bit of personal expression this wildly unpredictable girl had decided to share with me. I couldn't help but wonder.

What I got, instead of an anecdote of some kind, was the most unadulterated release of private truth I may have ever witnessed.

Walking back into the living room, I held out her drink.

Alice, as if lost in thought, stopped messing with the lumpy bruise on the side of her gargantuan stomach and accepted the glass with an oddly polite smile.

"Thank you." She said, just like a normal girl.

"You're welcome." I replied, in kind.

As always, it was hard for me to hold my tongue. But, biting back my own thoughts and words and questions, I sipped at my drink and sat down, looking around at nothing. If I had to, I was going to smoke a couple of hits of weed to keep myself quiet.

Alice looked at her drink, and her feet, and around at the same "nothing" that I was looking at, and drained her glass in the meantime. I had barely taken two sips, and her drink was already gone. And I was reminded that there had been many things that I'd liked about this girl.

I took a last big swallow to catch up, and found myself staring at Cee Cee's swollen little titties with their giant dark nipples. And as the whiskey started a warm buzz in my stomach and head, I also caught myself wondering if there might still be time to find a way back inside Cee Cee's feverishly hot little body. Part of me still wanted to join the musky club of men who had cum inside her.

"You said that you thought I might hurt myself." She started.

Looking up at her face I waited, but she added nothing.

"Yes?" I replied.

"That's what made me so mad."

"Uh-huh…" I continued, patiently.

"The things people say make me so furious. People talk like they know shit, when they are really just fucking stupid and blind, like you. You think you know me? You think you know what *hurts* me? You think you can tell *me* what to do with my own fucking body? That's how stupid and conceited you are. You'll do whatever *you* want with my body—but when *I* fucking decide, you say I can't."

It was eerie how coolly she was saying all this. I'd say that she was being icy, but she was really being glacial. And I didn't understand the last part she'd said, so I broke my silence briefly.

"When did I say that you couldn't decide something?" I said, as soothingly and un-interrupting as I could.

"Shut up, I'm going to fucking tell you!" She said louder, warning me.

"Do you know how many times I've been pregnant?" She asked (rhetorically), squinting at me. "At least four, and I probably had some early miscarriages too." She answered, and then continued. "But do you know what happens to my babies when they're born?" She asked again, this time more ominously. "My foster parents make the State take them away from me."

Oh no, I realized, *the poor girl was going to tell me too much.*

Taking a short and deliberate breath, she continued, "When I'm not pregnant they get me arrested for stealing shit and swear in court to all kinds of things to make me an 'unfit mother,' even though they know damn well that I usually get in trouble after getting drugs from my foster uncle and his friends, or when I'm getting food for everybody…"

Maybe I didn't want to know this.

Taking a deeper breath she began to rail, "When I am pregnant they all laugh at me, and say I'm so stupid they don't know how I even figured out how to get pregnant! They call me stupid! But they're the ones who made me stop going to school! And they say it's wrong to be 'against life', but they call my babies 'hell-bound bastards', and they could care less what happens to them after they're born! They treat me like a slave and laugh at me, and they promise me that I'll never lay eyes on any of my babies—ever—because the State knows I'm a godforsaken deviant whore!" She shouted, beginning to break, and with tears filling her eyes.

No…

"But the first two times I did go full-term and gave birth–I DID SEE THOSE BABIES!!! I SAW THEIR FACES AND THEIR LITTLE HANDS AND WIGGLY FEET AND EVERYTHING!!! AND I HATE EVERYONE IN THIS GODDAMN WORLD FOR TAKING THOSE BABIES AWAY FROM ME!!! AND I MISS THOSE BABIES LIKE I'M BURNIN' IN HELL!!!" She bawled and shook!

And then she paused for a second to catch her heaving breath, and her already disturbing facial expression changed to an even worse one. When she began again, she was screaming and crying out her confession so loudly she was literally howling—as if speared through the heart.

"AND THAT NEXT BABY THAT DIDN'T LIVE—IT DIED BECAUSE I AIN'T NEVER GONNA LET ANYONE TAKE MY BABIES AWAY FROM ME EVER AGAIN! THE ONLY BABY I DON'T MISS—IS THE ONE THEY NEVER TOOK AWAY FROM MEEEEEEE!!!"

Choking on her tears, Alice's hideous declarations came to a stop. *It was too much.*

When Alice saw that I was crying, her own tears ran freely.

When I moved to sit closer to her, she stood up and started wiping her face off. Stepping toward her clothes, she stopped and looked grimly down at me.

"I burn in Hell every day, now and forever. What do you know about that, smart fucker?!"

Overwhelmed by her irreconcilable question, I felt so ignorant I forgot how to talk. Instead, I just sat there mute while Alice began to throw her few clothes back on.

And then, in that terrible silence, she scathed me.

"Where's the fucking door?"

Chapter Eighteen

Help

Coming back to myself, I jumped up and replied to Alice.

"I'll show you to the door, Alice. Hang on one second while I put my pants on."

Grabbing my pants and t-shirt, and wiping my face off, I made Alice wait just a little bit. And all I could think about was how totally rotten this was ending.

I'd heard what she said. And I was pretty sure I knew what she meant.

But, instead of thinking about the specific horrors of her revelations right then and there, I found myself frantically wanting to find some way to turn this whole damn thing back toward some positive side of human experience—*even if I could take us just one step in that direction!*

Son-of-a-bitch! It was all so fucking wrong...

Beginning to process it all, I became so angry at the way the goddamned world was treating Alice I could hardly breathe. And at that moment I felt like I, too, was leaving her stomped-on.

Mother-fucker—that is not me!

No way was I going to let this end in this hopelessly indecent way! Racing my own thoughts—I begged myself internally:

There has to be at least one useful-enough piece of knowledge or power from my range of experience; something that I could give to Alice that she could use to help herself!

Pretending to fumble with my clothes, I turned away from Alice for a moment and closed my eyes.

Show me, Mother Universe…

Lifting my head and looking out my window, stalling for one last second—I suddenly saw something that had always been right in front of me.

Yes. That's it!

"Hurry." Alice pushed.

By the time I had buckled my belt and threw my t-shirt on, and slipped my shoes on, I had the rough beginnings of a good plan! And it was a plan that held so much positive potential, in this exact context, it seemed beyond too-good to-be-true. And like all my best sensed plans, this one had come from a source so close-at-hand it seemed ridiculous.

Who knows why someone receives a piece of power or important influence when they do? I have never been one to question it, nor do I shy away from it. It was my turn. I would never know or comprehend the depth of Alice's problems, but I could sure as hell try to move her one-step in a better direction. At the very least, I was going to send Alice back out into that bleak world with some significantly increased means of change.

Turning toward her, I spoke without wasting any more time.

"Alice, I will give you one hundred dollars more if you will stay and listen to me for just five minutes."

"Give it to me." She replied without hesitation.

"You have to listen to me first—one hundred dollars cash."

"Fuck you! You're one stupid old-man! All I asked for was a half-carton of cigarettes and you're going to give me one hundred and forty dollars cash? And you didn't even finish fucking me…because…"

"Alice, if you'll listen to me for just five minutes…"

"Christ Dude, I tried to fucking stab you!"

"Five minutes."

Picking up her empty glass, while taking an extra-long breath, Alice communicated her agreement by reaching for the whiskey bottle on the counter-top.

"Don't piss me off, fucker…"

"If you get mad, you don't get the hundred bucks."

"What a fucking asshole you turned out to be! Fuck! Go ahead."

"Okay. Come to the window so I can show you something."

Moving the sheer curtains aside I pointing at the house that sat just across the road, and one lot west from me. Nestled on its own corner of the mixed industrial/residential neighborhood, it was a nice sized two-story stone-built house.

I continued:

"See that house, Alice? People call it the 'GP House.' GP stands for 'Girl Power,' but that's just a nickname for the program. What they really do is help young women, just like you, to get their life together and get their children back. I ain't shitting you, Alice. Every girl over there has been in trouble with drugs or some other legal problem like stealing, or had a messy divorce from some shit-bag abusive husband and all the legal problems that came up, or her family was just too poor to feed her children while she was in jail, or she had no family, or she ran away from everything for a while, or for some other reason she had her children taken away from her—and the people in that house *right there* help those girls get back on their own feet, get a job, and then get their rightful kids back."

Pausing, I gave her time to keep up.

"I ain't making this shit up, Alice. It's *your right* to raise your own kids, and that house right over there might be some of the best spent money in the whole goddamn government welfare system of America—

because it's their job to make sure that girls in really tough situations, like you, are still granted their rights of raising their own babies."

At her young age and limited educational level I knew that Alice probably wouldn't have heard much about these kinds of places and social programs, but she must have heard *something* about such things before. Either way, I had to try to get this one important message through to her.

"Alice, exactly how did your foster parents get your two kids taken away? Just tell me in the simplest way."

"All I know is that I was too young, and they told the people they could prove I did drugs while I was pregnant, and they told them about me being a terrible slut, and that I won't go to school, and that I've been arrested for stealing, and that I hurt myself sometimes. They also said they are too poor to have any babies in their house."

"Did your babies get adopted, or what? And how long ago was it?"

"The first one was more than three years ago, and the second one was about ten months after that. But I don't know anything else about my babies because those fucking people wouldn't tell me what happened even if I begged them!"

"They're evil monsters. You have to get away from them, Alice."

"I've got nowhere to go…"

"You have that program house right over there, Alice!" I said, pointing repeatedly in the direction of the house across the street, trying to give my statement a level of reality that even Alice couldn't argue with.

"Look at those girls right there," I said, pointing to the group of four women just coming out of the side door. "Look at them, Alice. Almost every one of them is working through that program to get their kids and families back—and there is a way to do that, Alice!"

"How'd they get to go to that house?"

"Mostly they're coming out of jail, or prison, or maybe an intensive drug rehab program, and a probation counselor or some other kind of social worker has arranged it for them. But some of them are in there because they've been victims of different things, and have no family or financial means, and the state has stepped in to provide for their recovery and care. But I think that *you* could get into a place like that by telling them how you've been abused by your foster parents and their family, and by telling them that you want to get off drugs and keep your baby, and hopefully get your other kids back someday—whatever is possible. I truly believe that some, or many parts of your reality would qualify you for that program, or something like it!"

I tried to encourage her mind to open.

"Places like that even make sure that all the girls get solid jobs, go to school, and get money from the government like welfare, food stamps, and state coverage for medical bills. They'll even have all your child delivery and newborn expenses taken care of. And, a lot of the time they eventually help each girl to get into her own apartment!"

"My own apartment...?" She marveled out-loud.

"Hell, yes! You know how everyone else lives, Alice. You're young now, but after getting help for a while you will be old enough to get your own job, and then your own place—just like everybody else. You will probably have to live in a group home for a while, but they will help you with all that. Nobody has to live at home forever, especially with fucked-up foster parents like yours."

"My uncle still lives at his folks' home..."

"Fuck that dumbass! Alice—look at those girls! Look at them, they're just relaxing and having a cigarette for the next half-hour, and then they will go to work, or to a class about child rearing, or to an

AA/NA meeting, or to school for something else. And then, after that they will come back to that house and have a good dinner together, and then they'll probably take a nice shower and go to sleep in a soft, quiet, safe bed. And after they complete the program, which might take as much as a year or so, they will be ready to move on and get their own lives going. Hell, you might even make some good friends over there, Alice. Friends that can help you in your life.

Pausing again, I gave her time.

"Alice, if you think I'm stupid for trying to be nice to you, and help you, wait until you see how idiotically generous those people can be! Seriously girl, those people are some crazy-ass goodie-two-shoes Christian-types with State and Federal money to throw around! And that very GP House over there is dedicated specifically to local females, from lower income backgrounds, who are trying to work out their legal troubles and/or unhealthy and bad living situations in order to bear and raise their children better—meaning you're their perfect girl!"

"I couldn't get in there."

"Yes, you could! Why do you think you couldn't?!"

"Because I can't tell those people *how* I am, or they won't help me. No way. And I've already been declared an 'unfit' mother."

I knew what she meant by "*how*" she is.

"No Alice, you don't ever have to tell anyone how you *really* are—not like you told me today. What you like to do, and what you actually do, especially sexually, is your own business and you don't *ever* have to tell anyone about that. You don't ever have to tell anyone anything *that private* about yourself, or about your past, or about anything else that you don't want to reveal—especially when they will hold that against you. You just have to tell them the parts they want to hear. You know how to do that. Plus, Alice, the legal reasons that your babies were taken away from you are totally different. The law said you couldn't have your babies then because of your young age and foster status, which gave temporary control to your foster family, who refused to help you keep them, and maybe some of it was because of drug allegations, or whatever.

And I'm sure that your foster family tells you that you will never get on your own feet enough to do anything with your own life; in fact, from what you said they already do anything they can to keep you down—but fuck that! You're going to be old enough to take control of your own life soon! All you have to do now is tell the right people how all those problems are in the past, and that you'll be good now, and they will help you in every way they can! And when you get past all the programs, you can decide to live however you want. But you have to tell these people what they want to hear to get them to help you. You know what I mean. Just tell them that your very worst problem is how your foster family and uncle have abused you so terribly all these years, and they will take you into that house in an instant. I'm also pretty sure there is something called 'emancipation from foster care' that you could work on. Maybe you are old enough for that? How old are you?"

"I'm fifteen. But no, I can't do any of that! If I tell the law stuff about my foster family, they'd all tell stuff about me. I ain't gonna do that. That shit would get bad fast. We'd all go to prison." She finished, with resign. "I told you I couldn't get in there…"

"Okay, okay, Alice. Listen, let me think for a minute. There's always other ways… You wouldn't necessarily have to rat on your foster parents… Let me think…"

I was tempted to find out just what kind of crazy illegal shit her foster family was into, because it might have been useful, but that seemed too complicated a route to take at the moment, and my real focus was on getting Alice away from them.

There has got to be a way, another angle… I thought to myself.

In the meantime, Alice was looking between me and the big natural-stone built house across the street, and at the girls milling around outside on the sunlit patio smoking area.

Talking to me while looking out the window, Alice pushed.

"You're a smart fucker, think of what I could tell them that has nothing to do with my foster family. I can't start a war with them."

"You're smart too, Alice."

"I'm smart enough."

"I know, that's what I mean. Okay, let me think…"

I was never more determined to answer a challenge, or prove my cleverness.

"You have to use a story that they are used to hearing," I began, "but one that is also ugly and terrible enough to get their attention…"

The test was in creating something custom-built for Alice—that only showed a shadow of her real life—but was real. And ideally I would also make it a total side-swipe away from her foster family and all their problems…, something that would take Alice outside their control.

Then an idea came to me. So I ran it through my head again, and liked it! It was superbly simple: a hideously common crime that would garner Alice all the instant sympathy and personal care the social system could offer her—and Alice was carrying all the proof she needed right out-in-front. I was convinced the plan was flawless.

"ALICE, I HAVE IT!" I said with a shout. "Would you be willing to tell a social worker or shelter counselor that you got pregnant with this baby because you were raped by a stranger eight months ago, which you never reported to your family or the police out of shame and fear? And that your family is not supportive of your keeping the child because they are too poor. And that you now realize you desperately need help dealing with all this, especially the upcoming birth and newborn baby—which you want to keep and care for with all your heart and soul regardless of the way in which the child was conceived? Could you say that much Alice?" I encouraged loudly. "Just leave everything else about your family out of your story, and blame the rape on an unknown stranger you never saw again. It's perfect!" I nearly yelled. "Your foster family won't receive any legal hassle, and they will simply have to accept that you're going to be cared for by the State until your legal adulthood. That would also mean that your foster parents would lose all control over what happens to your baby. As a rape victim who is pregnant as a result of the crime, with serious age related difficulties, and family, financial, and educational challenges, you will absolutely be accepted into some kind of social program! That's all you have to say, Alice! You can do that!" I cried out, looking at Alice for her reply.

Pausing, while looking out the window and across the street, Alice let the idea come into focus. And the fact that she was actually thinking it through, intently, was all I could have hoped for. So I waited, silently. After perhaps a full minute and-a-half, or maybe two, which seems so long in such significant and important moments, Alice looked over at me and replied.

"Yes, I could definitely say that." she spoke slowly, with an expression of both inner revelation and deepening comprehension.

"You wouldn't have to say anything else." I continued supportively. "And when they check into your history and find out about any of your other troubles, you can repeat that those are problems you want to leave in the past. Tell them that your rape and pregnancy have made you realize all the changes you needed to make in your life—they'll eat it up! They won't know any of the real details of your problems, anyway. The files for these kinds of things are so incomplete. If they drug test you, you can say that you had a recent slip and are absolutely ready to quit—*and that you know that you need help.* If they ask for more details of your home situation, you could say that the drugs aren't your family's fault, but living at their home is not a safe environment because drugs come around your part of town and the people you know. You could do that and stay clear of all your foster family's complicated crap. Alice, it would work!"

From her concentrated expression and occasionally nodding head, I could see that she was listening very closely to me. And she couldn't keep her eyes from staring at the GP House through the window.

"Alice, you could plan your time to leave your fucked-up foster home over the next week or so. Use this hundred and forty bucks I'm giving you to help make it happen, and start your life in a new direction! I wish I had more cash here, but you'll be fine once you tell your story. Just plan it for a couple of days, and then walk out of your foster home with your best clothing and anything else you want in a backpack, and buy yourself a few new clothes, and keep some money for later. Then you could just walk right into a shelter and tell them your story. And then you would never have to go back to that foster home again, Alice! Because once you get those social workers on your side you can control the whole legal conversation, and your foster parents will have to back off. If you wanted to, you could even leave those foster fuckheads a note telling them that you will never talk to anyone about anything that would get them in trouble, or whatever it takes to settle whatever they are worried about. They'll let you go, Alice. They won't screw around with the legal system and bring any more attention to themselves than they have to. As far as they are concerned, you'll be suddenly gone in the wind."

Nodding her head steadily, while still staring out the window, Alice stayed quiet for another minute, and sipped the last of her drink down.

Standing next to her I kept quiet, and looked out the window with her, surprised with the receptiveness that Alice was now showing. How could she not be captivated by it—the idea was brilliant and the opportunity too great!

Turning around abruptly, and walking over to set her empty glass down on the counter-top, Alice then walked straight over to her coat and, bending her big belly gradually over, she picked it up off the floor.

Turning toward me, her face was firm and finally set.

"Give me the hundred bucks."

"Are you going to think about it, Alice? That house across the street is just one place, and there are several of them in every city. But I swear, places like that house right over there, and all the shelter houses like it, are built for girls just like you. You have to get your own life, Alice! Then you can live however you want to."

Yes, I knew that I was probably promising too much. Shooting for the stars is my specialty. The legally boggling victim-care/treatment/social-support system that I was attempting to send Alice into was, within itself, endlessly complicated and a severe test for anyone impatient or unwilling to play-along fairly well. But absolutely *any* help or movement in the right direction would be a vast improvement over the offensive life that Alice currently suffered. At the very least, I had given Alice some very serious and potent information. I could only hope that she would find a way to use it.

Sneering again, which got my instant attention, Alice looked down her nose at me and spoke with a steely directness.

"Don't try to tell me what to do, fucker. You know some shit, but fuck you anyway. What, then you would look over there and say, 'Oh, look at how I helped that stupid girl Alice.' Fuck you! I ain't having you looking down on me. You ain't no better than me. Give me the fucking money."

"Alice," I said evenly, "I've never once called you stupid or said that I was one bit better than you. But if you can't help yourself when you know that a solution is sitting right in front of you..."

"Are you going to give me that fucking money, or not?!" Alice interrupted, making what I was trying to say seem its worst. I'd meant to finish by telling her something important.

I tried again.

"I'm going to give you the money. But listen to me Alice, you are more than smart enough to..."

"FUCK YOU OLD MAN! GIVE ME THE MONEY YOU PROMISED! I AM SO FUCKING DONE LISTENING TO YOU!"

Forced to accept this end-point, I held my hands up and replied steadily, "Okay, Alice. I'll get your money."

The last thing I wanted to do with Alice, at this point, was to confuse the simplest picture. When I came back with the money, I held it back from her grasp for one more second, and said one more thing.

"Do it, Alice. I dare you."

Snapping the money from my hand, and leaning belligerently toward my face, Alice spoke her last words to me.

"Whatever! Where's the fucking door?!"

Chapter Epilogue

As Alice left my property, walking out from the end of the driveway, I watched her from the same upstairs big picture-window that we had been looking out a few moments ago. Waddling out into the quiet and windy street, and pulling her open coat closed around her, with her thin dress whipping around her knees and her red-blond hair pulling in a swirl to the North, Alice turned left and headed toward the nearest convenience store—and walked right past the GP House without even glancing at it.

The girl knew what she wanted: a carton of cigarettes.

Though it was cold, the bright afternoon sun was shining across the smooth street surface beneath Alice's feet so intensely it looked as if she were floating away through a mirage, and that the shimmering waves were lifting her up and moving her down the road away from me.

Staring at Alice's diminishing little back, and blinking against the glaring light, I tried to hold onto the hope that I had gotten through to her.

And I cherished that we had connected so well in the beginning of our time together, and in the middle. But the madness that had become our climax was inscrutable to me, and it left me unsettled.

Chapter Nineteen

My Own Family – Part Two

By the time my family came home that evening, I had made my way back from the disastrous edge of Alice's world.

After straightening-up the kitchen and living room I'd let the dogs out of the basement, which sent them on a frantic sniffing mission throughout the entire house. I'd then put my now tainted fighting club back by the side of my private desk, and then removed the memory card from the camera (not knowing what might be on it, and pre-planning to tuck it away in my masturbatorium the next day). After that I replaced the camera card with a spare empty one, and set the camera back where it had been. Then, I'd lit some incense and climbed into the shower.

In the warm shower I rinsed and rinsed my body, while quietly talking myself down.

After that I'd tried to take a short nap to help clear my mind. But, try as I may, I'd just lain there with my eyes stretched open by the too-fresh memories of the day.

With only forty-five minutes remaining to find my usual home-face and façade, I decided to take our three dogs out into the field and creek-bed that lay behind the property that I managed and lived on.

Maybe watching the dogs goof around, and a quiet dose of nature, would help me realign my emotional and familial placement?

And right on schedule, my lovely wife Abbey arrived home from her work at around five-thirty. Followed soon after by our twenty-two year old son Kye and our twenty-one year-old daughter Lula, who were returning from their long days at the College. And thankfully, the dinner that we shared was chock-full of delightfully ordinary conversations about the soothingly common and predominantly positive occurrences in their daily lives.

Unlike the poverty stricken and multiply mutilated horror-show that was Alice's tragic life; the lives of my own children had been surrounded by warm familial love, relative middle-class affluence, artistic education, progressive spirituality, an appreciation for travel and nature, and sexual safety.

And this has been especially true of the last seventeen year period of our lives: In all those years my wife and children have never suffered a single moment from my sexual infidelities, which have been successfully removed to a different dimension.

It is an achievement that I am proud of: Not one single incident where the worlds have crossed. That is an important part of how it works, even in a situation that implodes into a black-hole like the one I'd just survived with Alice; pieces of truth from one world just don't go well with the other.

Sitting at the table with my family that night, with everyone safe, and reasonably happy—was all the proof I needed of my trans-dimensional abilities.

Admittedly, learning how to be a hypersexual—who also has fully-committed life-long familial relationships—was a rough journey at first, for both Abbey and me. In fact, until our children were approaching the ages of four and five, I was a wild hypersexual set on a chaotic mission with only the loosest of directions. It is also true to say that the difficult lessons that I learned during those earlier years were more than worth the protection they earned for our family. Which is why I'll describe them here, and I'll start, once again, at the beginning.

The Earlier Years

In an impossible to explain twist of my life's karma, my then fourteen year-old girlfriend and wife-to-be, Abbey, not only adored having sex with me but also quietly accepted my need for secret and extra sexual activities beyond our relationship.

I do not know how or why she was able to do this, and neither does she: there is simply nothing in her background that would have prepared her for that life—other than her unusually genuine kindness.

In return, I adored her with a never ending river of loving attention to her every spoken thought, and every detail of her ideas, and her difficulties, and the joys in her daily life. From the day we met, even though her parents did not like me, and my parents had recently moved our family all the way across the city, not one day went by when Abbey and I didn't find a way to be together for as long as possible, or at least spend an hour or two on the phone.

Just two years later, at barely sixteen years old, Abbey had even been able to absorb some of the beginning details of my young homosexual activities with my oldest brother and his friends, and my deviant time with Déjà.

By the time we were married, on Abbey's eighteenth birthday, we had an amazingly workable groove going.

In fact, as a perfect example of Abbey's always impressive way, just three days before our wedding she "gave" me to a wonderful and painfully physically shy virgin, who was a girlfriend that had recently graduated from high school. (The timing of all this was coincidental, brought together mainly by the fact that we were all going in different directions in the coming months of our lives).

In careless form for me, I got caught with that girl by someone in my family, who told my mother, who told Abbey; who then told them both that she knew exactly who I was with, and precisely why, and that they should mind their own business!

That's how Abbey loved me.

During the summer immediately following our marriage, determined to get out of our hometown and geographic area, and away from our conservative and religiously bent families, we decided to become part of a private college/organic farming community in the Northwest that was comprised of several thousand people who had created an impressive compound as a multi-layered hub for the cultivation oriented and educationally progressive activities they were focused on.

Because this small private college, which had been slowly and smartly growing for almost ten years, also offered student-work programs and on-campus student-staff positions, it seemed like the perfect place for us to get away, and redefine our lives.

Nestled alongside a powerful river and surrounded by towering redwoods, and cedar trees, and giant firs, and deep forests full of a plethora of other flora, just sixty-some miles from the rocky coast and the Pacific Ocean, it was verdant and lush and teaming.

Most of the people who joined the community became both students and also went to work on the farm or at the college, and lived on-campus. And then, as the community's numbers increased, especially pushed by the families that came, an expansion occurred during the time that Abbey and I entered the community, with many of the members finding or creating all kinds of independent jobs for themselves either connected to the organic community or relying on the population of the surrounding small city. During this expansion an almost equal part of the community began living in apartments and houses located off the compound, even though they were devoted supporters of the organic farm and were daily participants in the educational and progressively spiritual programs offered on the campus. At that time the community also created its own private elementary, middle, and high schools, all sharing a common thread of higher education complimented by organic life education and progressive spiritual exploration. And, of course, many of the teachers and professors were the parents of the children, and some of the older students and workers were the youngest of the parents, and all were involved in their own ways in the evolution of the community.

On the whole, it was an extremely lively and "earthy" college population that was steadily knitting itself into the small city that it was built on the outskirts of. And through the ever widening number of interconnected people and their varied professions, and their children's lives, their daily shopping, and all types of other commerce, the intermixing of the two communities was increasingly open and flowing (though there had been early local grumblings and a little trouble from some of the belligerent locals who eventually settled on calling our community members by the term "Organics" or "Org's" for short—as in, "those goddamn Org's"—which in 1980 was meant as a "dirty hippie" type of insult).

All-in-all, Abbey and I found it to be an exceptionally exhilarating and inviting new place. And among that energetic and interesting mixture of people, adding myself in as just another nice young man with a nice smile, and immediately utilizing my own specific skill set, I was unobtrusively able to begin my growth into a prevailing sexual figure.

As Abbey went forward into her young adulthood, obtaining and holding one valuable job position after the next within the organic community; I set forth on every sexually seducible body I could find.

However, for Abbey, even with her incredibly loving intentions, for whatever personal, or cultural, or species driven reasons, her post-marital consent for my extra sexual activities was extremely difficult for her, and it was given at a great cost, which we eventually came to call the "Dark Promise."

Because having specific knowledge of (even some of) what I was doing sexually on a daily basis eventually became too emotionally difficult for her, in the sixth month of our marriage, (in reaction to my latest lover, a gorgeous older female yoga instructor), Abbey had commanded me to keep my extra sexual activities so well hidden she would never even know of their existence—until the day that she would ask me for the whole truth.

The Dark Promise was a valiant effort in what seemed like the right direction, of more fully respecting individual sexual rights, and I more than admire Abbey for her startlingly creative and consummately loving attempt. And I more than gladly accepted the conditions of her request.

But I will also admit that Abbey's side of the promise was made without her having full knowledge of the floodgate she was opening.

Still, my returned promise to Abbey—especially with all that she was willing to give to me—was that I would never leave her as her husband, and best friend, and protector, and partner. I could not give her exclusive control of my sexual life, but I could give her the knowledge that we would always be together: And my promise was for life, and beyond if there is such a thing.

However, in reality the Dark Promise was warped and twisted by the opposing forces of my dutiful development of deception in my own home, and being honor bound to eventually tell Abbey what she could never understand.

And the plain truth is, because it was faultily constructed, the dam of the Dark Promise began leaking barely three years into its life span.

Part of it came from my still developing skills with guile. And part of it came from the challenges presented by the relatively smallish and closely interwoven community. And another part of it came from Abbey occasionally deciding that it was time for me to spill some of the dark truth.

Even then, though, Abbey saw only the smallest drip of details, with my admitting only the very least amounts of guilt possible, and her quickly asking me to stop.

All the rest of the swollen errant river of my sexual activities was kept behind levees of lies and ridiculously defended stories and excuses that I built from the sands of loose information that I surrounded my daily activities with.

To be blunt, within just a handful of years, if Abbey hadn't been willing to turn squarely away—she would have had to face a churning ocean.

In the mixed population of the college community, and soon after in the nearby city, everything sexually ingrained that I had been born with, and all the earliest skills that I had developed with my brother and other boys, and everything that Déjà had taught me, and all the brilliantly open and generous love that Abbey had shown me, and my expanding freedom of time, and my more adequate financial resources, all became a very powerfully seductive hypersexual mixture.

Still, in a hypersexual sense, it started out slowly. And it took me approximately eight weeks to find my first new sexual partner in the community. She was beautiful and special and became very dear to me, and her physical flexibility and developed strength was a great match for my desires—but she was also just one woman, with a limited amount of time and a limited amount of sexual hunger. So my eyes and ears and sexual-aural-feelers were always searching, everywhere.

In the first year I also spent a lot of time working in the storage barns of the farm where heavy lifting was part of the job, which kept my daily exposure to females a bit limited. In that first year I believe I made only a paltry total of four sexual contacts.

Though the intellectual and liberal community definitely had a vaguely stated expansive acceptance for all things humanistic, progressive, positive, and loving, they were also surprisingly conservative in other ways. In fact, the farm and college had been founded by leaders who felt very strongly about not being seen by the surrounding city and greater American society as "too progressive." For instance, they would have never used words like "commune" to describe the community, and they strictly avoided any direct religious or spiritual associations. In fact, the word "spiritual" wasn't even used (officially) for the "self-improvement" studies and activities that they taught on campus and practiced.

Still, for me, even the understated and ambiguous-openness was *enough* of an openness.

At the end of the first year of work I had earned enough credits to sign up for two semesters as a part-time student. Abbey had moved on to working for the compound administration for cash paychecks instead of school credit, and she was more interested in excelling at that office work and building our bank account than she was in going back to school.

Most part-time students kept working for the farm, but with Abbey's first year's work credits added on top of mine (a generous deal on the part of the college) I decided to quit the farm work and see what I could make happen as a full-time student. Because of Abbey's continued work we also had on-campus housing and food privileges, which made our dollars (Abbey's paychecks) stretch that much farther. And, the ever expanding curriculum at the college had become surprisingly diverse.

Signing up for two sword fighting courses, two philosophy classes, and a creative writing class, all of them lasting two semesters, I quickly spent my credits. With enough spare time I also joined the soccer team and became the dominating terror (hyperactive physical achiever) of the favored (only) team-sport on our tiny campus. As a nod from nature, it was a piece of pure luck that soccer was the only team sport I had ever enjoyed as a kid (and that was briefly). And before I knew it, I was a starting forward in the first inter-college sporting match that was ever played by our little college. And I led our team to a slim victory over the opposing private college team!

And my intimate proximity to the college students and the instructors was like hooking into a life giving vein.

At the end of that college year, when my school credits ran out, I purchased a small used truck and secured myself a self-created part-time job as a delivery driver for some of the farm and greenhouse produce, as well as their bread bakery, and I also continued on (voluntarily) as an assistant coach (practice mate) of the soccer team. All of which supplied me with a widely varied schedule that often got me out early in the morning and kept me out into the late evening (when, because I had turned twenty-one, I could purchase and deliver liquor to my college friends in the dorms, or their town apartments). And through those kinds of growing arteries of connection, I began to find even more freedom, and more sexual partners.

In that year I also started physically training again, three evenings a week, at the biggest and best gym in the nearby city, which offered boxing along with a surprising variety of other fighting arts.

With my delivery job relationships also expanding, in all of my several circuits, and my knowledge of the closest surrounding cities increasing by the day, (which among other things allowed me to start obtaining and sharing a steady stash of weed), I was soon presented with a level of access and opportunity that far surpassed any I had ever had before.

Unsurprisingly, by the third year I had also gotten my own small apartment off-campus, where a string of loosely managed roommates and I held parties and "slept." Soon, I was staying there at least half of the time, which worked so much better for Abbey than my constantly coming back to the campus apartment in the wee-hours with wild explanations that she didn't believe.

With my own apartment, I could also catch one and two hour naps to make up for lost nights. And before long, I was spending only one or two weeknights and some of the weekends with Abbey.

Time itself, I realized then, is an incredibly value sexual currency, a magnificent resource, and so potent it is almost an actual skill.

It takes time to traverse so widely.

So, over the next set of years, as I entered my mid- and then later twenties, I fucked my way across every college girl and any woman I could seduce in the ever changing and expanding organic community and college population, and all their willing friends, and several wild college girls from the nearby city college, and their friends, and some young wives and young mothers from both the community and the city, as well as random working women I met on my delivery routes.

And it was glorious, glorious, and glorious! And I bow in gratitude.

I was also, instantly, as in my life before, skating on as thin of ice as I dared.

I had no other way to get where I was going.

In one early surprising case, a progressive middle-aged single mother, whom I'd met at the organic market one morning, set me up with her seventeen year-old daughter the next afternoon—because the mother had never experienced such open and compassionate sexual love as the way she had with me—and she could not hold back from sending me into her sexually expanding daughter's life (who was just a few years younger than me). It made sense to the mother, and the daughter, and the daughter's friend from out of town, who I also fucked that week. But I wouldn't have told anyone else in the community about it.

In another situation during those first years, a male college student acquaintance sent me to his girlfriend in one of the dorms to get her past her painful virginity, and that turned into a small line of connected virgin missions with her dorm friends, almost exactly as I had done with Abbey and her friends a few years before in high school.

In another layer of that time, I became steady lovers with three young mothers in the community who were all good friends. And, of course, none of their husbands knew, and none of the five children of those families knew, or needed the family-unit threat and danger that I represented in their lives.

In yet another instance, I became a dear friend of a family of five: a father and mother, with two college aged kids, and a teenager. And by the time I had known them for two years, I was having excellent and adoring sex with three of them (separately).

In another occurrence during those years, I had the pleasure of spending time with an especially interesting brother and sister duo who, in the midst of their world-traveling lifestyle, had recently come to the community. Both of whom were in their mid-twenties, and both of whom, for some wonderful reason, actively sought and gained enjoyment from supporting each other's sexual pleasures, as well as each other's extreme intoxication and careless sexual submission. And, both of whom intrigued me in an additional way because they were the children of a very well-known philosophy scholar.

And there was the tall German girl, who was undoubtedly a hypersexual herself, and who insisted that I have sex with her in public places scattered around the campus. Which I unhesitatingly and happily did, which greatly pleased her, for a short time.

If any of this sounds like too much, that might be due to underestimating what a hypersexual really is, and does.

"*Why,*" it should be wondered, would so many people find it so easily acceptable to have me as a sexual partner?

The answer to that question has at least four parts: Certainly, a good dose of the phenomenon came from the organic community's generally more progressive attitude toward positive personal expansion, which in-part, in the already somewhat sexually-charged 1980's, translated to many of the young adults and teens of the community as a green-light to explore "more-sexual-freedom." Which seemed to influence the local city college students, and even the high school students that the young organic community youth socialized with. Plain and simple, a (relatively) solid percentage of people were having, or wanting to have sex; I just happened to be the individual who was achieving a hypersexual amount of it. An important second part of why I was able to obtain so much sexual contact came directly from the fact that I am such a confident, sensitive, skilled, and empathic sexual partner. During this time one of my soccer friends told me that listening to me fuck girls and women was (sometimes) like listening to someone being tortured or killed—while begging for more of it. Though not all females are sexual "screamers" a lot of them are when you get them to a place they haven't been before, like the middle of an ocean of wave after wave of orgasms. And taken even farther, many of them are also "orgasmic criers", which confused my friend(s) even more. Suffice it to say, I tended to leave a big impression on my sexual partners. And my reputation often proceeded me. Thirdly, due to my carefully considerate personality, and because I had the party-house where everything had always gone smoothly, I was "the guy" that everybody had an extra amount of trust for. And I'd built that trust every day, in every way that had ever come up. And again, that reputation became well known. And lastly, I would add the dual powers of my hyper-availability—both in my wide-ranging willingness as a sexual partner—as well as the power of time. Put all together, this mixture functioned as something truly powerful and steady. Because, when someone is suddenly ready to be sexually released, and there is someone they can go to that is trustworthy, and they know that person will be willing and available, and they know that they can openly and safely share their sexual readiness with that person—there is a decidedly better chance that they will.

Even shy girls knew they could come to me, and they did. Just like Abbey had as a young virgin.

Interestingly, because the women in the community also knew that I was married to a beautiful and successful young woman, who by all appearances adored me to no end, and tolerated my extra-marital sexual activities, my worthiness was even more unquestionable to them.

And, because my life was so completely saturated in this sexual trust and confidence, even the girls I met for the first time, and from the farther away cities, who had never heard about any part of my reputation, felt my obvious sexual ability the moment they met me.

"*Why,*" it might be wondered, would people feel so specifically sure about sexually trusting me?

The answer to that question is singularly important: They could feel it, because *I knew it*.

That is one of the most important differences between me and a sexual lover who isn't as sure about what they are doing—in my hypersexually developed state I am absolutely ready and willing for whatever comes up. And without even the need for words, I am already sensing and creating and seeing the sexual event through to a wonderful ending for my partner—whomever they may be, and however they may want their sexual contact to proceed. And *I will make it happen*, if there is any possible way that I can. And before, during, and after the sexual contact, I will supply total sexual respect, trust, and social discretion to my partner(s)—and somehow, *they know it*.

For honest perspective, I did of course have sexual failures, both physical and in communicating the necessary trust. For instance, I was always dissatisfied at having my final orgasm too quickly, and/or before I'd meant to. Or not being able to get a hard-on under an odd pressure, as was the disappointing case when a young college girl threw me off by coming to me for sex just a few days after being in a car accident—*and* she was severely injured—*and* she was wearing a very complex neck and head brace that had a "halo" of actual skull-screws locked into place—*and* I think she was dangerously confused by medications—and I still think that sexual coupling, handled carefully, could have been amazing. Or the couple of times when a smell struck me wrong, (not usually bodily, but anything chemical or something old from the house or room we were in). And plenty of experiences of the more common malady of not quite "clicking" enough with someone to actually go through with the sex that we had begun. And, I should also mention my least favorite failure, which was when I knew that a girl or woman was feeling "pushed" by me, and there was no way to get back into her trust.

Otherwise, if I did get naked with a person—and we did get sexually started—I usually succeeded, and often enough, notably.

Outside the small organic community I had also learned to roam the wider ranging pervert community of the area: patrolling whatever places existed in the nearby cities for the possibility of street prostitutes, and also feeding myself with an uncountable number of anonymous male sex partners, spending thousands of hours in the porno shops/theaters, remote public park bathrooms, truck-stops, and a fairly reliable City College library restroom and gymnasium shower-room.

And almost every one of those sexual contacts was made under completely un-protected and nearly always illegal public circumstances, and there is simply no way to exaggerate the importance of this information. As soon as you are on the other side of the law you know it, and all pretenses may as well be dropped.

However, during those first half-dozen or so years, because I had managed to evade any scandalous or legally negative consequences, in my social circles in the community and nearby small city I was seen as a fully upstanding citizen.

For one thing, I eventually began volunteer-coaching the seasonal soccer for the little kids, which I thoroughly adored doing and was a natural at. And the families that I met during those seasons were a constant potential source for me, with the occasional secret sexual liaisons occurring with the seducible mothers, and on a few occasions the fathers.

Around that time, in order to add to the earnings of my delivery job, I took a part-time early evening position at the gym as a personal trainer who specialized in one-on-one instruction in boxing and self-defense. Throughout the years of my training, which by then equaled over a decade, among that population of obviously homophobic athletes I had been more-or-less a loner who often enjoyed practicing alone and only competed when a really good opportunity came along—but whose real passion was the art of street-fighting, knife-fighting, and situational awareness. And now it seemed the time had come for me to pass on some of that knowledge and skill. And so, over the next decade I had a fairly steady and successful stream of students, of both sexes, ranging from the upper teen years to sixty-something years-old. And that job was definitely the most interpersonal, interactive, empowering, trusting, fulfilling, and all-around positive working position I have ever held. And the sexual connections to some of those students, and parents, and other family members, and their friends, began to ignite immediately, and the flame of those relationships was non-stop.

And in the later part of that time, as I entered my thirties, through a contact at the gym I also obtained a job with a privatized branch of the state probation and parole system, (as crazy as that sounds for someone like me), which increased my hours of trolling, and substantially stretched my territory, and gave me some seriously enhanced hunting powers.

And throughout those years it was awe inspiring how much sexual contact I could actually fit into a day, and a week, and a month, and each year of my life.

And throughout those years, when Abbey and I were together, which had settled into an average of three or four evenings and/or days a week, our feelings toward each other were always as deep, and immediate, and as wonderful as they had been for us from the beginning. And our view of the future seemed unwavering.

Was there an element of twisted denial on Abbey's part? Yes. But it was even truer that we didn't want to waste our time together on anything but love.
We both knew that it hurt Abbey's feelings to be left alone so often, and that the reason *why* I left hurt her even more. But we also knew that the

idea of restraining the sexual animal in me was akin to my being suffocated to death, and that the animal in me would fight, horrendously.

So, it was better to let the animal run.

Abbey also knew that no matter where I was she could *always* call me if she needed to, and that if she called I would be there as fast as I humanly could. And, she equally knew *never* to call me unless she absolutely had to, which risked the worst of my tempers.

During that time of our marriage, the straining Dark Promise had all but disappeared—or at least that is what Abbey came to believe. As the evidence of all my sexual activity in our community had mounted up, Abbey just couldn't turn far enough away from it. So, having her believe that she knew what was going on, because she was allowed a measure of open awareness of some of my main affairs within the community, became just another mirror in the maze I kept her in.

Doing that undeniably cruel thing, especially to Abbey, became perhaps the most disgusting part of who I was; lacing half-truths and full lies together, and acting as if her suspicions were some kind of insanity, was gut wrenching to me. And to stay as free as I possibly could, I did it to her nearly every day.

So, with a newly developing flavor of self-loathing, I began to call what I did to Abbey the "Dark Distortion".

Clearly, the need for secrecy wasn't because Abbey couldn't accept that I, and other people, want to have sex with multiple partners, and/or with both sexes. She was fairly cool with all that, in the general philosophical sense. The problem was that the range of variant sex that I pursued (especially when I was outside the organic community), and the sheer amount of it, would have assaulted her mind and made her ill.

For instance, I doubted that Abbey could have absorbed or gotten past my specific penchant for sex with the oldest, most physically unattractive, sometimes decrepit, and even gross sexual partners—whose sexual directions could sometimes be wildly uncultured. And who knows why I first leaned in that direction; but I still enjoy their extra level of surprise and satisfaction, and often openly expressed gratitude, at having a shiny and healthy person like me as such a willing sexual partner.

And there were other kinds of grotesqueries, like the inordinately wealthy white southern pervert I knew who had divorced their spouse out of nothing other than petty spite over their children's preference for that parent, and then stole the children away and completely ignored them, and who saw themselves as infinitely "better" than others, and who also called me their "little brown nigger" during sex. Of course, what connected us together was the specific, nearly lunatic loss of sexual restraint between us, which had everything to do with the actual bondage restraints that person needed themselves to be bound by. Having built a dungeon-like chair and wall mounts into an open concrete basement shower, once that ill-tempered and conceited pervert was naked and strapped-in, with me free to do as I pleased, nearly anything went. And that included everything easily imaginable, plus, as part of the climax that person would begin insulting me and calling me a dirty little brown monkey and every other foul thing they could think of to verbally spit at me; and from my side, among other things, I went to the bathroom on that person. It could get so disgusting, sometimes I vomited. That person also paid me more cash than any other customer I ever serviced in my history, to the tune of many G's. However, for the half-dozen times that I agreed to be a partner to that person it had certainly been the variant hypersexual electricity of the contact that had supplied the currency I required.

Sometimes, after only a few hours of sleep I would wake up and spend the first half of the day getting together with several female partners one after the other, for an hour or so each, then spend eight hours having sex with random men in porno theatres, or wherever else, then return to the community to see who was partying that night, or who was still up, or who I could wake up to have sex with, equaling a lost-count-of number of partners in a single day.

In the end, my need to make my daily sexual contacts number so many, and be so variant, no matter what that required me to do, was a hard thing to explain even to myself.

As would be imagined, along the way I'd eventually gotten other mens wives pregnant. And I had been at least partially responsible for the divorces of several couples, and the breaking up of their families. And I had been rumored to have been with so many of the college aged girls it was enough to start making some of the members of the community uncomfortable.

I believed then that many of the people that I had known, for years by that time, were becoming aware (on differing levels) that they only knew a small part of me, and that something about me was too well-hidden behind too many carefully constructed and guarded layers of privacy. There were too many stories, both good and bad. And yet, my sexual, personal, and professional reputations continued to grow.

In juxtaposition to my need to keep so much of my sexual activity secret from Abbey, in the tenth and eleventh years of our marriage, in a massively genuine effort at joining-in on my hypersexual lifestyle, she had set herself on several serious sexual adventures (as discussed in Chapter Nine).

Coming out from behind the heavy curtains of the dramatic sexual play of my life, Abbey had jumped into the center-stage with her own deepest sexual breakthroughs, and had given herself to her own sexual growth in the fullest way possible.

And our sexual understandings of each other took a giant leap forward, together, and it was amazing!

And though her mighty expansion had brought us dynamically and sincerely closer, and had been important in a way that I wouldn't fully appreciated for many years—her hypersexuality was temporary—so it came-and-went as a dazzling wave across the horizon of all my other oceanic sexual activity.

Regardless of my immediately sailing on, because of what we had shared during that time Abbey continued to be devoted to me and determined to outlast the difficulties of my manic sexual searching. And I, too, was more devoted than ever to my love for her, and just as hopeful that I would one day be able to fulfill myself with some kind of sexual enlightenment, thus relieving Abbey.

It was hard for the few people who knew us to understand, but when Abbey and I were together, alone and away from everything outside our-own-loving-space, those details were as clear to us as if it were a reasonable goal.

However odd or lopsided, or unfair or untruthful it was, our life together and our love for each other continued and moved forward.

In the beginning of the twelfth year of our marriage our son Kye was born. And, though it was incredible to be a father, and I spent more nights at home, because he was but an infant, during the hours that I was free I didn't sexually slowdown in the least.

In the beginning of the thirteenth year of our marriage our daughter Lula was born. And, though it was amazingly beautiful to have a baby daughter, and I spent even more nights at home, because she was but an infant, during the hours that I was free I didn't sexually slowdown in the least.

In that same group of years I had the amazing honor of being with a beautiful, young, natural-born intersex person named Talia, who shared herself with me deeply enough to allow me past her surgically malformed limitations and into her delightfully personalized pleasures—and even showed me her wonderfully different ways of achieving orgasm. And, though I can say that she definitely wasn't a hypersexually activated person, I keenly felt her special interest in sexual contact, and always wished that our relationship could have grown. We spent only twenty some days together, mostly in the evenings, when she was in the nearby city on a college summertime study program.

During the winter of one of those years, I also had the exhilarating experience of being with Elaine, a super-sized female athlete whose best events were the shot-put and discus-throw, and who stood a foot taller than me and was so strong she literally picked my entire body up from the bed and repositioned it, several times, during each sexual session. She also had the strongest inner vaginal muscles I've ever felt: like some kind of Kegel world champion she could relax them as I penetrated into her, and then grip the muscles down like a hard fist around my cock as I pulled back outward, creating the wildest and most irresistible feeling of being slowly milked. She was also a lovely hearted newbie to sex who could not get enough of the wonderful experience, and quickly made the mistake of falling in love with me at a time where I could barely find the spare hours to see her once every week or so, which made her feel jealous, and eventually sent her on her way.

In another affair I became involved with a recently divorced woman who, after we had been together a couple of times, would start our sexual encounters by answering her door and then pushing me away as hard as she could, and then by trying to slap or punch me square in the face! And though it might be surprising to some, she was a university educated and polite and elegant woman who simply craved a raw and physically dominating man so badly she would fight like a hellcat in an attempt to make sure her sexual desires were fulfilled. Which, sadly, had not been, until she met me. Indeed, she would kick and slap me, and squirm against my grip with all her might, and fight me all the way from the front door to her bedroom, slamming us into the walls of the hallway, and grabbing onto doorframes, using absolutely every ounce of her strength against me, and absolutely forcing me to force her into naked physical submission. And she never stopped fighting, even when I was penetrating her. And if I didn't keep at least one hand around her throat she would bite me anywhere her teeth landed! And no matter how hard I held her down, or threw her back onto the bed, or choked her—she would always dare me to go harder, and farther—until I physically exhausted her with orgasms. And, at the same time, she was just one otherwise more-or-less "normal" organic community mother, who had always secretly fantasized about sex with some real muscle and undeniable authority behind it.

And I will always remember the twenty year-old hypersexual college cheerleader, Savannah, who hovered magnificently over my body for a moment on her whirring way through life, collecting me for her own growing list of mounted conquests. I still dream and daydream about how she achieved whole-body orgasm almost the instant she let herself start sitting and sliding down onto my hard cock, and how she didn't stop that sexual shivering and moaning, getting wetter and wetter, until she reluctantly heaved herself off my body because she couldn't stand any more of the ecstasy! Lying below her was so amazing! And how I would have loved to capture that gorgeous sexual humming-bird, if only for long enough to enjoy just one more of her trembling sexual flights.

During those years I had also developed and become quite attached to my newest barely-legal girlfriend. Simply put, I met her at the gym during her seventeenth year of age and immediately took over her greater physical training. Simply described, she was a beaming fresh rural girl named Sandie, who was born a bewildered hypersexual in a Christian American family, and who was one of the calmest, sweetest, and most deliciously natural submissive lovers that I have ever enjoyed.

Sandie was also perhaps the best kisser I have ever known, which is a higher compliment and honor in my world than most people would realize. At times Sandie and I would kiss, and kiss, for as many as five hours and more without taking our mouths away from each other. And I will never forget that pure-bliss.

Fortunately, I had never made any promises to Sandie. But I told her how much I loved her all the time. And she had loved me from an age almost as young as Abbey; and we adored each other like twins bred from the same kinky and always wanting to be naked DNA; and she would have married me in a heartbeat and endured absolutely any circumstances that I put before her, including being a second or third wife.

I always wished that I could have kept her. Leaving her, felt like failing true love.

And there was Schick, a nickname I gave to my one long term male sexual partner, who was many years my junior, and who was always freshly shaved smooth-and-clean from the neck down, and whose apartment I could walk into and get naked no matter what time of day it was. Wonderful were the many hours we spent laying flesh-to-warm-flesh, completely oblivious to the world outside our secret.

Also during these years, there was the amazing street prostitute Mi'Cher (Chapter thirteen), and her whole molten heroin world, which I poured myself into for a couple of years.

And yet, I was *always* still sexually hungry.

For one thing, it was right around this time (early 1990's) that I first became aware of the new possibilities for fully, surgically altered, transsexual persons. Of course, I had been with a few random cross-dressers (though even they were quite rare). But actual transexualism was a whole new level of sexual self-creation—and sexual experience—which I became obsessed with—and hunted for feverishly—and never satisfied.

Which sent me on even more intensely hyperactively energized loops of pursuit, often pushing myself to enact an even more feminine part of my sexual persona, often wearing panties and lip-gloss inside the porn theaters and public sexual arena's that I crept and prowled through.

If any of this description of endless sexual searching and variant contact seeking sounds like too much—I think we finally have a picture of just how true that is.

Plainly, the strain that my hypersexual lifestyle was putting on me and everyone around me became ludicrous. And to obtain such a steady supply of sex I had to expend a ridiculous and unhealthy amount of energy in every direction. And in that effort I was so unpredictable, mercurial, un-stoppable, and incessantly on-the-move, it was infuriating to anyone who knew me that I was *not with* at that particular moment.

I was a loving and/or sexual hero to all who knew me. And I was also a cold and vanishing villain.

And the ultra-real health dangers that I put myself through, and the diseases that I could have exposed all my other partners and lovers to, and perhaps my own children, were inexcusably heinous on a whole different and unbelievable level. Like far too many sexually active people in those years (1960's—2000's), I lived in total blind denial, compounded by my hypersexually driven need for fully bare-skin to bare-skin contact. For me "safe-sex" meant not getting caught by the police.

I remember that it was during these years that I first envisioned my ideas for a full-scale society-wide sexual revolution that would include easily available legal sex options (prostitution) and a multitude of free, nice, and secure public sexual meeting places.

My main thinking had been in how much safer such places would be for me, and the massive amount of time and effort such options could have saved me, (not to mention the other millions of American citizens searching for regular and even daily sexual contact).

I also remember that I dreamt of what life could be like if *I* could have honest and legal work in such a place...

With regard to Abbey and our toddlers, because I was gone all day and almost every night too, the intensifying experience of myself as a selfish and abandoning phantom-like father increasingly shamed me.

I also saw, with an angry clarity, that if I had been one of those men who sought financially bigger fortunes, or other kinds of larger fame, or different kinds of greater social power, like being a big corp. CEO or a full-time actor or a successful politician, I would have spent just as much *or even more* time away from my family—but my field of pursuit held only the opposite potential in our general society, of social disgust and legal condemnation!

And I thought, even if society could create such professional options on a truly society-wide level, those sex workers would still probably be broken off as a sexual sub-culture, which isn't what I wanted! I didn't want to be broken off!

And I was finally admitting to myself that the stress of that opposite-potential of my current lifestyle was wearing me out. Though I had successfully avoided any law-involved sexual scandals, both in-town and out-of-town, it had been by the skin of my teeth too many times to count. And I was spending way too much money.

Even Abbey was starting to look at me with deeply worrying doubt. And her over-used excuses for me, mostly to herself, were all worn so thin they were see-through.

Then, among all the other peaking pressures and whirl-pooling complications, and mounting heartache, and emotional exhaustion, I suddenly saw something coming at me that I absolutely could not absorb, or avoid, or hide from: My growing children would soon become too old and too aware to hide from all my grown-up realities, and they would begin their conscious lives caught up in the emotionally tumultuous and obviously physically out-of-control vortices of my own sexual storms.

I wasn't afraid of them being physically touched or sexually hurt by anyone I knew (though I am always cautious). But I knew that all the immediate, deep, mental, emotional, and dangerously wide-open sexual wells that lay everywhere around my life would become unavoidable pitfalls for them.

Through the deepening loneliness of their mother, that emotional reality was already a manifesting threat.

Just the verbal sexual content that would enter my children's ears when their waking minds opened up to the constant back and forth discussions, accusations, questioning, defending, and more often arguing that Abbey and I did about my other relationships and daily sexual escapades (that Abbey knew about) would be too much.

I had already seen my four year old son recognize the fact that the woman he was watching his father give fully loving "hugs and kisses" to—was *not his mother*. And I had seen that it had confused him in an emotionally negative way, which was a sobering-blow to my freewheeling mental stance.

Considering that specific moment, of my son looking at me with a sexually based confusion that I was causing, and my seeing that his primary emotions on this matter were tied to his mother's, and my not knowing how to sufficiently bridge the gap of understanding—reminded me of times that I had felt sexual confusions in my earliest remembered life. I recognized both the confusion, and the lack of ways in which to solve that confusion. For one thing, Abbey's emotions on this matter were never going to be something I could "solve." And they would always be a big part of Kye's personal reality. And Lula was right behind him.

So, it became obvious to me that there was no way my children could grow-up in that environment, in that place, and not come to see me for what I was—everyone else knew (even if they didn't have all the details).

What I looked most like, to myself, was Déjà—in the midst of the kind of sexual rampage that I had once witnessed—which is not what I wanted my children to see me as.

Though I certainly had the intention of communicating as much of the truth about sex as I could to them, someday, at that time in those surroundings, in this society, all I knew for sure was that I did not have the ability to even begin to explain my own actions and behaviors.

I knew, of course, that Abbey had already been hurt by my hypersexual life, in so many ways and for so many years. But I had always justified that by (over) acknowledging that Abbey had entered my life on her own accord, and with pre-knowledge of who I was.

However, with their little eyes looking up at me, I suddenly had to believe that my own children must be spared my sexual madness and its extended consequences—*no matter what it took.*

So, on an otherwise unremarkable November day, while thinking about my children in this way, it felt to me like I had come all the way around to looking at where I had begun my own conscious life, with all its unanswered and un-assuaged sexual confusions. And I became extraordinarily determined to better help my own children avoid those kinds of consequences and confusions in every way that I could.

By this time in life I had come to accept myself for what I was, within my own hypersexual context, and I understood that my life had its own story.

But, on that day, for my children I decided exactly what I didn't want planted at the root of their own lives narratives.

My curses and karma belong to me.

Standing still in the rustling leaves of that late autumn afternoon, watching my toddler children running carefree across the drying leaves and the green grass and the flecked tan sand of their favorite playground, I had the initial part of my great epiphany: I saw that I could completely protect my children from my sexual mayhem, and give Abbey everything that she had always wanted—*if* I was willing to finally give up my overt sexual crusade in this community and area, by moving my family and life far, far away from this place.

It was time.

I had been studying sex and sexual contact and everything that it meant to me, or connected to, or disturbed, or enhanced, or could be bent towards, or could be mixed up with, or could be evolved into, ever since I came to individual awareness. But I had never before asked myself to really calculate or tally the total of my experience, or to define the state of illumination of any of the answers that I had set out to find.

Now in my mid-thirties, I still didn't know if I was ready to do that. Until that moment, I honestly hadn't considered if I was actually worthy to answer such big questions.

But, I also had to ask myself how many hundreds and hundreds of sexual partners, and how many thousands of sexual experiences, and decades of time, should my study require?

I had already used up all the too-early years of my deviant youth, and my insane pre-teen and teen years, and now the nearly sixteen years of uncontrolled adult growth in the petri-dish of my current surroundings—how much time and life space could I expect to take?

And, if my studying perspective had ever had a *deeper reason*, wouldn't doing something great with that knowledge have been at the heart of it? Hadn't that very inner claim been one of my most empowering beliefs and releasing justifications ever since I was a pre-teen? Hadn't I tearfully screamed a childish version of that very prophecy at my laughing mother at the already determined age of twelve?

What was it that I had thought I could achieve?

Unable to stop thinking about this, whether awake or trying to sleep, I stared out over the rolling expanses of my gluttonous sexual memories for days, and then weeks passing into months, looking not for the individual specific delights and each limit tasted (as I usually did) but for what they all added up to, and for what those greater sums of experience might mean in the bigger picture of the future of myself and the lives of my family.

After weeks of rigorous consideration, and the coalescing organization of my most deeply connecting sexual understandings—because I would not give-up until I saw an answer to this new question—I realized that *I did* hold at least a few pieces of personal knowledge that should be sufficiently strong enough to push a giant change in my life, like moving my family far away, and also how that knowledge could provide some lasting protection for myself and my family.

I looked especially hard at six main personal truths: Firstly, I am and always will be hypersexual.

Secondly, I have an equally strong attachment to fulfilling my loving relationships with Abbey as her life-long friend and husband, and as a loving father to Kye and Lula—so I am equally as romantic as I am hypersexual.

Thirdly, my overt sexual lifestyle and the uncontrolled pace of that lifestyle, as well as the dangerous nature of that lifestyle, was threatening to ruin my family life. And the continued overlapping of my sexual "world" with my family's lives had the potential to seriously damage my children's upbringing and future lives—in a sexually caused way—with me as the *abuser*—which I could not live with.

Fourth, I saw that, though it only happens every so often, I had an unexpected and incredibly serious problem with keeping my emotional love separate from my sexual love with certain females that I was with repeatedly. And that once I am "in-love" with such a person, it is insanely hard for me to back away from that combination of physical and emotional adoration. Which led to the realization that it was my freedom to attach myself, in any substantial way to other people, sexually and or otherwise, that also defined my familial aimed limitations. Committed emotional love outside my four person family, I had to accept, was as dangerous to our futures as any sexual act.

Fifth, those four realities are, obviously, at war with each other. Which left me with only one conceivable direction of solution, which would require a total re-creation of my life in a completely different living location.

Lastly, the sixth truth, which I held in great confidence, was that I *did* have many highly-developed hypersexual skills and abilities that I could trust, and better apply—but only if I completely changed my currently too complex mode of utilizing those skills.

What I had to give up, in order to gain what I needed most in my life, became clear to me.

So, what I gave up first was my heart and mind mangling confusions over these issues.

I also gave up the illusion of the Dark Promise. Half-truths and half-measures are too weak.

I also, with an incredible amount of will and an equal amount of sorrow and resign, readied myself to give up the vast web of sexual contact that I had built-up over the years in that place, along with all the hypersexual power that I had attained.

Grudgingly (to the nth degree), I prepared to turn and walk away from all the wonderful and rank porn theaters that I knew inside-and-out; and the always changing faces of the street hookers; and the public homosexual sex spots; and the ever-present potential of my socially accessing jobs; and my one male lover; and the many wonderful and varied female sexual lovers that I had on-going relationships with at that time.

And though I couldn't emotionally afford to acknowledge it during those days—it was certainly a death of a part of myself, which included my personal intimacy to all the people I was sexually connected to. Like a vine once thriving, now severed at the trunk.

When it all came together: One day I was living and sexually flourishing in that amazing and verdant place; and the next day I was in a moving van, heading for the dry Southwest.

I gave Abbey her choice of moving our family to anywhere in the southwestern part of the United States, and where her finger landed on the map, we went.

Looking forward, I knew that my plan for a different kind of sexual future would take an epic amount of work, and discipline, and time. And that, with what would most likely be very few hours to give to my secret life, it would require patient years of slow progress to re-create even a portion of my previous hypersexual reality. But I stayed confident.

Equally important and empowering, was my determination to use this move as an opportunity to minimize my health risks.

I also began to build a new hypersexual vision that better treasured the affluence of my past sexual experiences, giving me a veritable vault of sexual ownership to sit and appreciate in well-earned fulfillment. Eventually, this idea of greater appreciation also re-defined my hypersexual focus by creating a new direction for decision-making about potential new sexual contacts—which would aim only for the highest quality and *distinctly new* sexual experiences—which by my evolving definitions must include those sexual contacts and activities being able to remain **completely invisible** to, and absolutely out of the way of my family life.

This was not a Dark Promise: This was a Golden Promise—made only to myself. No one else would ever know about it. That was part of the promise.

I never came up with a term to describe what it is when living a lie is the only way to live the truth; but I know that it is an understanding perfectly balanced by having multiple realities to take care of.

The "me" that Abbey loves is bound to her forever; but the hypersexual me could never be bound anyway.

During that time of my life it seemed that I was feeling the stars and planets moving around me, rearranging my universe. Perhaps this whole undertaking seems like more-of-the-same, or a mere sideways step. I am a human with his own limited compass. But to me this felt like a full-sailed and right-angled turn, heading myself and my family in a whole new direction.

Moving Forward

Within six months of my epiphany I had moved our family more than a thousand miles across the country to a small southwestern city where nobody knew us, where no one knew what Abbey had been through, where not a single soul outside my family knew me, and where we felt our children could be raised safely. And indeed, since that time the years had passed in amazingly successful familial bliss.

Life hasn't been perfect, of course, but to get through so many years with so few financial struggles, major medical emergencies, or any other kinds of severe personal or family struggles—and without a single hint of my former relentless sexual storms—has seemed like super smooth seas to Abbey and me.

In our new home, with Abbey continuing with her now well established career as an office controller/manager, and me bargaining my different skills into a lucrative enough property management career, both Kye and Lula had grown up in a relatively trouble free household. And they were both good students, loving people, and had enjoyed a life free of exactly the kind of sexual drama I had hoped to escape.

And Abbey was so happy to finally have me to herself it filled us both with delight. And even our sexual relationship blossomed again, though it was rather simplified and conventional.

And I successfully slowed my hypersexual-pace to an imperceptible pulse, and I began "riding my bike" for as much as a couple hours a day, and I focused on looking for safer versions of the types of sexual partners that I had known before, which was painstaking.

And I was encouraged from the beginning by how Abbey and our kids were thriving in our new home, and our new geographically gorgeous surroundings, and our much warmer climate.

I'm not trying to be all dreamy and make everything in our family's lives sound only excellent, all the time. But, when Abbey and I had successfully removed so many major difficulties from our relationship (my overt hypersexuality and all the trouble and anxieties that had come with it), we had also been able to move that freed-up attention and emotional energy onto our highest hopes for our own lives together, and for raising our children—and we'd done a pretty good job at both.

For instance: Kye and Lula's sexual education and upbringing was definitely one field of communication, knowledge, and family endeavor that we are proud of.

Children's Education

In the chaos of my life before our move I had not been the primary, or even anywhere near an "equal" parent, by any measure. When I was with Abbey and the children, of course I was loving and attentive. But, because I was more often gone, Abbey was the one who truly raised them from infants into the pre-school aged kids they had become.

Fortunately for Kye and Lula, Abbey had begun the development of their earliest communication patterns by making sure from their initial bathtub experiences, and throughout their potty training, and the first explorations of their bodies and genitals, that she always kept a totally open and completely relaxed "conversation" going with them.

In fact, (in her words) "Just to practice," she'd started talking openly to our infants about their bodies long before they had any idea of what she was babbling about. And when they fondled themselves, she'd felt it was a natural topic of conversation.

"Does that feel good little baby? Of course it does. That's a pretty important piece of equipment, so treat it gently!" I'd heard her say to Kye when he wasn't even a year-old. And I was touched by her warm and comfortable tone of voice. It was so different than the tone of voice I'd grown up with. And I was totally inspired by it! And I followed right along with it!

And I am so grateful to Abbey for that amazingly intuitive focus I doubt I'll ever be able to express how much. Because starting that kind of open communication from the earliest ages is the most important thing a parent(s) can do.

Which, I guess I *kind of* knew. But to make it real, I had to be shown—by Abbey!

And Abbey was so fluid with it she applied it to everything from poop on their hands to the common brother and sister genital curiosities (which are commonly shied away from), to openly talking about why kids like to run around naked after they get out of the bathtub.

After a three and-a-half year-old Lula had broken free from the bath towel and ran for it one day, I heard her tiny voice yell back at Abbey, "I just want to run free, Mommy!"

"Of course you do, Sweetheart! It feels so good!" Abbey had spontaneously yelled back with a laugh at the fleeing little figure.

Which my mind juxtaposed against the option of yelling angrily, *"God damn it, get back here!"* And, *"You can't run around naked for God's sake! What will people think?!"* Which were two phrases I remembered from my childhood.

I also remember being spanked with a folded belt, when I ran naked from the bath all the way out the back door into the falling snow, at around four or five years old.

They said that I was spanked because I had ignored my mother's commands, but my little mind was listening to my skin. I doubt I even heard her.

So, even if Abbey's response to naked kids running around is rather simple, it is exactly this kind of straightforwardness and honest acknowledgment that is needed. All day, every day, in every possible way.

Consequently, because of Abbey's foresight, and my appreciation of it, our own family's communication about body issues started out positive, straightforward, and loving. And we weren't tongue-tied, or anxious, or embarrassed.

One day, while my four year old son was in the bath, I remember calmly asking him, "Are you trying to put your finger up your bottom hole?"

"Yes, I think so."

"Why?" I continued, with only curiosity.

"I don't know, Dad. I just did."

"Well, your bottom hole is a great place to wash while you are in the bath. And if you do it softly it will usually, probably, feel good. But you do need to be careful not to push your finger too hard or too much inside because you might scratch your bottom hole with your finger nail, which hurts. You can also let bath water into your body, which you don't need to do. And, to be good and clean you don't have to wash quite that deeply."

"Okay, Dad."

As beautiful and beaming little caramel skinned kids, with big brown eyes and constantly widening minds, we knew that every little chance and occurrence, and daily experience, were opportunities.

At just past four years old, we noticed that are daughter was regularly rubbing her vagina in a seemingly semi-conscious way. Taking the lead, Abbey had walked over and sat down next to her. And she had spoken softly to her.

"Sweetie, do you notice what you are doing with your hand?"

Looking down into her lap, Lula had replied, "Oh yes, I see now Momma."

"Good, Honey. I know it feels good to do that, but it is more polite to do that when you have more privacy."

"Why, Momma?"

"It's kind of like what we do when we take all our clothes off, or take a bath and wash ourselves, but even a little more private. It's not that there is anything wrong with it, at all Lula. In fact, almost all people, all over the world, touch themselves and know that it is a very nice and good thing. But being private about it is what we call a cultural custom, meaning it is the way everyone expects it to be. Because of that, if you touch yourself when you're not in privacy other people will think it is odd, or not right. I don't agree with all cultural customs Lula, which we will talk more about some other time. But I think that learning to touch ourselves in privacy might actually be a good thing. I think it helps that activity to become our own private decision. We decide for our self."

"Okay, Mommy."

"Good girl, Lula. If you forget, I'll help you remember. Okay?"

"I'll remember, Momma."

Because of Abbey's way, shyness and silly embarrassment over bodily things had no place in our home from the beginning. And, of course, her example of loving communication extended to every part of her conversations with the kids, about all subjects.

And—the part about "privacy helping to teach us that sexual decisions are rightfully our own," and how that information works into a child's understanding of sexuality—*even before they know the word*—was brilliant!

When we moved our family to the Southwest, Kye and Lula were in the fifth and fourth years of their lives, respectively. And within the first few months of living in our new home, Abbey and I had spoken with each other several times, in the deepest possible detail about our biggest ideas and our highest goals for raising Kye and Lula. All of which was a new conversation, in terms of the super conscious level of it. And we talked perhaps even more intensely about how, having lived through the opposite kinds of upbringings—Catholic parochial school and Atheist-disciplinarian—plus our consideration of all my sexually related challenges—we agreed that we unequivocally owed it to our children to try to find a better way.

In moving our family I had acted out of a broader scope of protection and hopeful improvement for our children's lives; while Abbey had already known of, and laid the foundation for, what I believe was the most important part of how we would proceed—which was with open and honest communication.

One day, as the four of us sat down for a picnic lunch on a ponderosa pine covered hillside that was part of a National Forest just a few miles outside our new town, Lula suddenly made an urgent announcement.

"Mommy, my pee-pee place hurts!"

And though Kye had started to laugh, and I'd begun to hush him, Abbey was, of course, immediately engaged.

"Okay sweetie, let's take a look at it." Abbey had replied, hoisting her up onto the big stone picnic table.

"No. I don't want to." Lula had said, surprisingly stubborn.

"Okay, Lula." Abbey had said calmly, taking a half step back. "*Why* don't you want to show us?"

"Because…, a rock scratched it." Lula replied, obviously evasively.

Seeing Abbey's momentary baffled expression, I entered the conversation.

"When did that happen, Lula?" I asked softly.

"When you were doing the garden in the morning." She answered, as if we should have known.

"Alright, Lula." Abbey returned. "It's okay that a rock scratched you. It was just an accident. Let Mommy take a look now." She directed, but unhurriedly.

And then, after closely inspecting the scratch, Abbey continued.

"It's not such a bad scratch, Honey. We'll put some nice salve on it when we get home and it will be fine." She consoled. And then, without a trace of awkwardness or drama, she asked, "What gave you the idea of touching your vagina with a rock, Honey?"

"My *what?*" Lula giggled.

"Your pee-pee place is called a vagina, Lula. I've told you that before." Abbey continued, in a good natured tone.

"It's such a funny word, Mommy."

"Yeah, it is a funny word." Kye interjected.

"Yes, I suppose it *is* a funny word." Abbey continued patiently.

"But my question, Lula, was what gave you the idea of touching your vagina with a rock? It's okay, of course. But Mommy would like to know."

Having been dressed in a skirt without pockets that morning, Lula pulled her skirt to both sides and said, "I didn't have any pockets, Momma. So I put the rock in my panties."

Taking a few moments to consider Lula's answer, Abbey had looked over at me.

"Sweetie," I started. "Did you put the rock in your panties so it would fall down and touch your vagina? Is that what happened?" I smiled. "Or was it something else? You can say it."

And then, after a short moment, Lula replied.

"Yes, Daddy. I did. I thought it might feel good. But I got scratched."

"Ouch!" I responded quickly, and a little bit comically. Which made Lula smile.

"Well, Lula, there's a simple saying," I continued, "It goes, 'Live and Learn', which is true. And I'm so happy that you aren't scratched badly. And I'm very happy that you knew you could tell us what happened. You can always tell us everything that happens—even if you think you might have done something wrong. You know that, right Lula?"

"Yes. You told me you won't get mad no matter what I tell you. I remember, Dad." She said, repeating a sentiment we'd stated to our children many, many times.

"That's right, Lula. We will only help you, no matter what. We love you."

"Good girl, Lula." Abbey had added, with a warm and lighter note. And then smoothly changing the subject. "Who wants a sandwich?!"

And in the following mix, as Abbey set lunch out, I heard Kye making sure to ask Lula.

"Are ya alright, kid?"

And Lula was correct about our never getting mad—no matter what. For Abbey and me, anger and punishment were no part of how we raised Kye and Lula. Anger produces reactions of fear, and shame, and often returned anger; and the idea of punishment comes from the illusion that you can change a person through judgment, and disrespect, and imposed personal discomforts, including extended torture and imprisonments of many kinds—none of which we would ever do to Kye or Lula.

Soon after that day, we'd followed up with an intimate conversation with Lula about the several different physical constructions of her vagina, using the visual aids of a mirror and a picture book we purchased (after an extremely long search through what little usable material was actually available for this purpose). Abbey also reminded Lula that if she ever wanted to see her (Abbey's) vagina in a more specific way, for any reason, she would be happy to show Lula and answer any questions (which, of course, eventually happened). We also made sure to include a creative back and forth discussion about many of the things that a curious female child might try to do with their vagina, including too early penetration, which we described frankly and with enough detail for her to understand.

In Abbey and my observations and memories most parents slighted-off these kinds of awkward situations as quickly as possible, or are too surprised and embarrassed to deal with what comes up, or instead laugh and make jokes about it, or worse—tease about it, or only give the kinds of condensed answers that allow them to immediately change the subject. And the older the child gets, and the more clearly sexually related the arising questions and issues are, the more evasive and elusive those parents become.

That is a mistake.

The smallest things are the biggest things when a child's education begins. In fact, *everything* is the "biggest thing yet" at that point of awareness and learning. And the conversations and answers they get (or don't get) to even the smallest questions, can hold great importance.

About four months after settling into our new home, as we were beginning to look at preschools and elementary schools, Kye and Lula began learning in a more specific way that the "cuddly love" that our family and our closest friends shared with each other is both a caring way to enjoy the experience of positive human connection, as well as the physical sensations of touch and being embraced. Acknowledging exactly what physical and sensual touching is, and how it is shared, clarifies things so importantly, and protectively.

As a way to encourage the conversation, I suggested that we each share a description of one of our favorite ways of cuddling, or an experience related to that kind of physical closeness, like holding hands, or holding each other while falling asleep, or being held while watching television, or a long hug before leaving home, or a big kiss when returning home. And then we talked about it, all around, in an easy and positive atmosphere. In that way, Kye and Lula continued to learn about how open conversation, in both directions, is a wonderful and beneficial way to both share and continue to learn about our individual and personal sensations, and feelings, and thoughts.

In the next stage of this conversation, they learned that this kind of physical contact, especially at their age, is meant explicitly—and only—for our closest family and friends. So, if anyone else tried to be that physically or emotionally close with them it was something they should avoid, and then come straight to us to tell us about.

Additionally, throughout their toddler and adolescent years, Abbey and I made sure to find opportunities for the whole family to casually get naked together, so that it wouldn't become an awkward or in any way an uncommon occurrence. Since one of our favorite family activities was swimming in remote lakes and river swimming holes, which we sought out on many of our weekends and holidays, we were able to use the moments of changing into and out of our swimming suits as excellent and relaxed opportunities to be naked with them. Of course, we also took advantage of those opportunities to continue our conversations about our bodies, and genitals, and about physical and sexual maturity, and to show them the clear differences between our grown-up bodies and theirs, and to explain what roll those differences made in when and how sexual contact takes place.

Obviously, the best illumination of these interconnected subjects must include both the sexes, and both the older and the younger generations. How else can it be fully explained?

On days and nights before Abbey and I knew that we would be going out on a swimming excursion, as part of the many preparations we would get excited and plan the physical body and sensually illuminating conversation with Kye and Lula that would best follow the conversations before!

Early on, as would be expected, we also explained to them that this kind of conversation and casual nakedness was only appropriate among our own family (recognizing the context of our current general American society). And that, (again because of the cultural customs), no one else should be talking to them about these subjects. And we explained that their genitals were the most-private parts of their bodies. And that no one else should be trying to see or touch them. All of which would change, in stages, as they became young adults and adults.

And they learned that the reasons for these boundaries were NOT because of something gross, or wrong, or terrible about nakedness, or sensuality, or sex, or sexual contact itself. But instead, because such contact is a special thing that is shared when people are old enough and close enough to understand that contact.

All of which may seem difficult to communicate to early adolescents, but Abbey and I would say that idea is an underestimation of our children, that we should let go of.

Then, as they got a little older, we made sure that Kye and Lula knew exactly what we meant by inappropriate physical contact and/or the attempt of it, by calmly practicing several mock scenarios that exemplified exactly what was not alright. Which was a little bit awkward at first—but Abbey and I weren't worried about that. We'd already developed the necessary trust with Kye and Lula. Plus, what we cared more about, was much more important than any awkwardness.

When talking with Kye and Lula about some of the reasons that inappropriate and unwanted physical contact happens, we didn't try to scare them. I just told them straight-out that some people, of both younger and older ages, want to have close physical and even sexual contact with other people so badly they might try to do it with someone they don't know well enough, or someone that is too young, or someone who doesn't want to do it. And I told them about how some people don't grow up with any, or hardly any positive physical affection, which is a sad and lonely thing. And that some persons, again of almost any age, can be very aggressive about their desire to have physical and or sexual contact—even when they know it isn't right. And that people who are lonely and confused like this can be helped.

Importantly, they learned to be aware that inappropriate and unwanted physical and sexual contact can come from nearly any age group.

It was all positively explained, with none of the creepiness, negativity, judgment, shame, paranoia, or any other unnecessary dramatic flavor. And we successfully developed an open conversation with them about sexual behaviors and misbehaviors that has never closed down—to this very day—which may be one of the most effective and protective things we ever did.

When our family was out in public, Abbey and I also helped Kye and Lula form a habit of spotting adults that they should be able to go to for help. Like clear authority figures including the obvious choices of policemen and fireman and teachers, and other parents with kids (ideally with both parents, for added protective effectiveness), as well as mature females because of their greater availability in children's environments, like schools, libraries, retail shops, and parks, etc.

Plain and simple, children need to be taught how to spot the potential problems and hazards around them, and how to act and react, and speak out, and get adult help, and to get as out-in-public as they can about any potentially threatening problems, as immediately and as out-loudly as they can, to as many people as it takes to achieve a return to safety. To be **out-loud**, instead of *silent*, engages perhaps the greatest safety net we have!

But children aren't taught this by our society or culture! Through observing the actual hesitating and awkwardness of most adults when it comes to sexual issues, and even the turning-away and hushing reactions that too many people have toward sexually related situations, children too often learn to stay quiet about the subject, and to hesitate, and even to doubt their own observations or thoughts, and what actions they may need to initiate.

So, of course our children also learned that screaming—the very second they became seriously afraid of anything—is a fabulous survival tactic. And we practiced it, and reminded ourselves of it on regular occasion. At first (within the sound-proofing confines of our basement), we even let them have a contest to see who could create the most "attention drawing" scream, which was an excellent exercise! And they understood the exercise so completely it astonished us. And their extra-alarming and pleading screams were astounding!

Early adolescent training definitely has to include screaming, and learning to move immediately away from a threat, and to run to safety as fast as they can. When a child really understands these things as survival skills, and practices them with these understandings in mind, it greatly helps them to leave behind the inability to act, and the thoughtless response of "freezing in-place." Lessons like these plant the seeds of long-lasting empowerment.

I can't say it loud enough: Teach your children to scream, it is, at the very least, a powerful step away from inaction, or being stuck in uncertainty, or being muted by self-doubt, or being unprepared because of debilitating ignorance.

Around the same time, as they became old enough to play in the neighborhood and the closest parks without us, I taught them to make sure to stay in small groups with the other kids so that at least three kids or more were together, and to never go out alone, for the sake of all kinds of safety concerns pertinent to being children—including dealing with inappropriate physical contact situations.

Then, at around nine and ten years old, I returned to some of our previous lessons and extended that knowledge by talking with them—without hesitation—about the even more dangerous derangements of sexual abusers and even kidnappers. And I tried to show them *exactly* what some of the attackers might look like, some of whose faces I had seen in my own childhood, by letting forth the flush of the actual sexual vibrations of such persons and such sexual desires from my own body. And when I moved towards them to touch and grab them in that kind of moment—*they felt it coming!*

Just as I had felt it coming, all those times in my own childhood!

I also showed Kye and Lula what some of the other things about predators looked like, and how they acted like hunters, stalking from a farther distance but no-less-focused. Which they were rather fascinated by, in the best kind of awareness expanding way! I emphasized, with my own imitating expressions, that it is often the unusual visual attention that gives dangerous people (of many kinds) away. And I insisted that they should trust their feelings about anyone they think is concentrating directly on them. Ultimately, I focused on teaching them that there is never any harm in being cautious. And that taking the initiative toward safety was exactly that, and not necessarily a negative assumption or accusation. Sometimes people are just spacing-out when they seem to be staring. Still, it's both smarter and safer to be cautious.

Soon after that day, we went to the biggest park in town and I expanded their training even further by pretending to "lurk" them, first in my vehicle, and then on foot, starting from all the way across the park.

And I tested them on how soon they noticed me. And then I finished by closing in on them in a much quicker-than-they-expected way, which gave them a good scare and an impression of what I was talking about, and what to look out for!

Then they'd practiced running-away from me as fast as they could, and using objects or even other groups of people in the park to help keep from being grabbed. And they practiced racing to our car, or pretending to race to another family for protection. And they learned that kids their size and ages *can* outrun and outmaneuver even an adult.

And they noticed that this was a very grim version of their childhood game of tag, which is when I sat them down and explained to them that nearly all our cultural games and sports represent, and often come from, some version of human survival and/or combat skills.

Because they were absorbing the lessons so well, and seemed actually exhilarated by the empowering knowledge, I also taught them about why, as parents, we had never let them go into a public bathroom alone. And this time I did scare them.

Taking them right up to the doorway of the most distant bathroom in that park, I revealed a glimpse of my own worst experiences to them, explaining that I, myself, was physically taken control of, and physically hurt in a place like this when I was their age. Which was one of the big reasons their mother and I had always been so careful about these kinds of safety considerations. And again, they understood.

And Kye asked me, "Dad, why don't any of my friends know about this? I've never heard anyone else talk about this. I heard a kid once say, 'Watch out for the pervs.' But I had no idea what he really meant."

I could only answer, "I don't know exactly why so few people talk about these things, Kye. I've always thought they should. But now you and Lula know. And public park bathrooms aren't the only place you'll have to watch out for yourselves, which we'll talk more about later. And by the way kids, the word 'perv' isn't a nice one. It's a prejudiced and hateful word."

After that day, Kye and Lula still played in parks like carefree kids, but their awareness was expanded in an extremely important way. In part, because I followed-up in the next half-a-dozen months with surprise versions of my "stalking game", which I would enact until they noticed. And which, due to the repetition, did not make them paranoid—but rather, made them more used to simply considering their own surroundings and safety.

    I explained it to a friend of mine by saying that this education was not so different from how I taught my kids to know that if a dog looked at them a certain way—*they absolutely had to be afraid, and move immediately toward safety!* If the dogs ears were laid back low, and there was extra intensity in its body position, and its stare was too steady, and it was creeping toward them—*they had to instantly move away from the threat*, in the smartest possible way, or they might get bitten, and even mauled, possibly to death! Its straightforward reality, and something all humans should understand.

    We don't have to create a mood of totally surrounding doom or paranoia, it is better kept candid, real, and plain.

    Of course, I also explained to them that only a very few persons, out of the huge number of persons around us, would ever even think about actually physically or sexually attacking a child, or someone else—but those few persons absolutely do exist.

    Our kids were also instructed to avoid being in a closed room by themselves with an adult, or an older kid, or even a kid their own ages that they didn't trust, even when they were at school. And to unhesitatingly inform anyone they could that they had been told by their parents to avoid certain situations, and that they would like to call their parents immediately (the clear statement of which, by any child, would warn off most potential adult sexual abusers). And their teachers and school officials were informed of our family instruction, directly by Abbey and me, each and every school year. (And they almost always acted as if we were being dramatic and unreasonable—and we never gave a fuck when they did.)

During their eleventh and twelfth years, as they grew up and out of their little kid bodies, getting taller and thinner and beginning to show their more definite facial features, and their genders, they also began studying hand-to-hand self-defense, with me as their instructor.

Interestingly, this was also around the time that we stopped being naked with Kye and Lula, after Lula asked to change into her swimming suit in private, at some lake or another that we were visiting. Because she asked, the answer was "yes."

In the beginning of their self-defense training we focused on how they could protect themselves from strikes and grabs, and how to effectively escape from an attacker, including how to be aware enough to utilize everything possible in their surroundings to their advantage, like the effectiveness of maneuvering an attacker backwards or sideways into and over a chair, or anything else that the attacker doesn't see, thus causing them to trip and fall. Or, throwing an ashtray, not only as a weapon but also as a distraction giving them to time run. And they learned from the beginning that survival is about escaping and gaining safety—not the commonly glorified and prideful image of "winning a fight" and standing victorious over the conquered foe kind-of-thing that so many people think of. That kind of thinking, I taught them in every specific way I could think of, is idiotically dangerous.

After learning blocking and grip releases, and escaping techniques, and spatial and situational awareness, we added the study of effective striking and kicking with their hands and feet. A year or so later we expanded that striking study with the basics of stick and sword fighting, which are great ways to expand the knowledge of how to use nearly any object in your environment, whether fixed in-place or loosely available, as a weapon of both offense and defense against your attacker(s).

After a year of stick and sword fighting, they were then introduced to one of my fighting specialties, knife-fighting. So, from their earliest teen years on they carried razor sharp snap-out knives in their pockets wherever they went. And we practiced and practiced using those razor sharp knives as a final escape option, and a final striking option, which was kept hidden until the last possible moment (as the strategy of tricking and surprising an opponent is the most powerful of all). And by the time they were in their mid-teens, they knew by rote the eight most effective and deadliest places to strike with a knife, as well as the location of the one most vulnerable nerve cluster in the entire human body, which if struck hard enough or penetrated by even an inch, would instantly drop any attacker to the ground and/or kill them. And I share this detail to make sure that I am defining precisely how serious I was, and am about this subject.

On another side of personal and sexual issues, the older a child gets, obviously, the more there is to know about their own positive sensuality and sexuality. And when a young person reaches their early and mid-teens you have to be ready to openly discuss *anything and everything* about *all* the sides of sensuality and sexuality, and sexual contact. Which, to repeat an all-important point, is best prepared for by having an already well-established conversation.

So, during the same years that they were studying the many aspects of keeping themselves physically safe, Kye and Lula also progressed in their knowledge about the sense of touch, and the inner sensuality that can be enlivened by it, and the sexual desires that these sensations and emotions can give rise to. And we showed them how sensuality and sexuality are wide-ranging and wonderful worlds of possibilities that include sensual pleasures ranging from the simplicity of a cool breeze, to a warm bath, to the enjoyment of massages, to the more private pleasures of masturbation, to kissing, to eventual inter-personal sexual contact like sexual touching, and exploring the body further, in due course evolving into whatever sexual relationships and activities they wanted to experience, with an agreeing partner.

They also learned that sensuality and sexuality sometimes can and does have surprisingly and even overpowering emotions and mental forces driving it, and that this applies to persons of all ages, which can and will cause personal challenges, and even mistakes in decisions related to when and how to explore sensuality and sexuality. Which was a follow-up layer to discussions we'd had with them since their adolescent years.

Kye and Lula learned through multiple perspectives, about the multiple important points involved in interpersonal interactions, that the most intimate touching that occurs between people requires the highest levels of mutual respect, and the reasons why. All of which added up to how and why sexual contact should always be a non-pressured choice of "yes" or "no," that each person gets to make for themselves—every time, all the time, including second-by-second changes of mind. It really is that simple.

From that foundation of understanding, Kye and Lula built their respect for alternative sexual choices, and different personal orientations, and the full range of gender expressions, and relationships of all kinds. Including the newly more openly discussed and medically possible option of becoming a fully transgendered person. All of which Kye and Lula viewed from the same root of sexual respect, which engenders acceptance.

To maintain this wonderful and powerful level of communication we made sure to talk to them regularly about things that happened at school, or things they saw, or heard about from other kids. And everything from schoolyard kissing to stories about events at other kids homes that bordered on incest got brought up. And an even greater number of their questions seemed to come from what they saw on television, in the movies, and online—so much of which was confusing and differently angled than our own family viewpoints.

Some of the specific questions and surprising subjects of discussion that Kye and Lula brought up over the years were incredible, usually preceded by one of them announcing to everyone at the dinner table, "Okay, here's a good question about something sexual…" And no matter what was said or asked, it was listened to without shock. And even if it was hilarious, it was taken seriously.

And more often than not, both Kye and Lula expressed relatively insightful perspectives of consideration and respect, which made me and Abbey so proud.

Kye, for instance, as he got older, had seemed to take our sexual openness invitation as a challenge. And I had to wonder if his energetic search for sexual conundrums, which might eventually cause complications for his own life, was a flip-side effect of our family tradition. If it was, Abbey and I could accept that. We believed it was better to be actively informed, rather than ignorant.

On one occasion, when Kye and Lula were in their first years of high school, Kye brought up something that really astounded his mom and me.

"Okay, here's a good question about something sexual. One of the seniors was telling me and some of the other skaters that he has sex with his BMX bicycle. But he says that he doesn't use his penis or his anus or anything like that, but that he does feel physically, mentally, and emotionally ecstatic and 'orgasmic' when he's riding his bike, and even when he is just thinking about riding his bike. He said he's had intercourse and oral sex with several girls, and jacked off a million times, and used dildos. But he definitely feels *even more* fully orgasmic when he rides his bike. What do you guys think about that?"

Looking at each other for a long moment, Abbey silently handed the question over to me.

"Does he ejaculate while he's riding?" I asked.

"Daaaaad…" Our daughter interjected.

"Lulaaaaaa…" I replied with a smile, as I looked back toward Kye.

"No. He doesn't." Kye answered.

Thinking about it for a few moments, I carefully constructed my response.

"I've got to admit that is one of the more interesting things I've ever heard, Kye. Whatever my own opinions might be, I definitely can't discount his own personal experience. And I actually find the idea pretty fascinating. But I'm going to have to say that this question is beyond my ability to answer. I grew up thinking of 'sex' as actual sexual contact between people, and I always considered masturbation somewhere just a smidge below that. But I realize that this is only my own limited opinion, and that all kinds of new ideas and groundbreaking individual experiences are out there. What do you two think?" I finished, inviting both Kye and Lula's opinions.

"Sometimes when I'm practicing and playing my flute, I like to think that I'm kissing it and touching it in a *special* way…" Lula piped in. "And I won't tell you what else, because that's my private business!" She finished, with a firm expression of personal empowerment.

"Don't tell anyone at school about that, Lula." Kye responded to her, mostly jokingly. But also because he was being protective.

"But otherwise, I don't know Dad." He said with obvious depth of thought. "That dude is super good at riding his bike, he's probably going to be a pro, and he's on it like fifteen hours a day. So maybe he knows something we don't."

Getting up to clear the dishes, Abbey chimed in. "I like that answer, Kye."

"I do, too." I remember saying (while beginning my own captivated considerations of this incredible idea of what sexual contact might possibly include, and actually *be*).

One of Lula's memorable questions was:

"My friend Masha says that dead things sexually arouse her, and that she is going to be a vampire when she cuts her boyfriend and sucks his blood. But I don't get it, because vampires are supposed to be the 'Undead'. But *real* dead stuff is totally gross! Plus, you can get gnarly infections from both dead shit and cut sucking."

"Did you say, *cut sucking*?" I stammered.

"Yes...?" Lula replied slowly.

"Oh! I get it." I recovered. "Right. Um..., that's true. You can get bad infections from mouth to open wound contact. And dead things are nothing to play with."

"I know that, Dad. But why do you think she says that stuff about dead things..., like dead animals even? It kind of freaks me out."

"Do you think she has actually looked at many dead animals?" I followed.

"Yes. We were dissecting a rodent in natural sciences class when she told me! And she was all poking it around and giggling, and saying that she was going to steal it to give to her boyfriend."

"Did she steal it?" I asked.

"No."

"But still, she seems pretty specific and genuine about her statements. Do you know if she cut her boyfriend and sucked his blood?"

"I don't think so. She was waiting for him to tell her when. I think she would tell me about it. Maybe."

"Well, the cutting part is dangerous. I know it's been a niche trend for a while now, especially among teenagers. And I know the cuts are usually tiny. But it's dangerous. As you well know Lu, one slip of a sharp blade can be serious. But as far as the sexual arousal from dead things goes, which I'm sure you know is generally referred to as 'necrophilia,' that's been a 'thing' since the dawn of man. Theories about it include a range of explanations that reaches all the way from a simple feeling of physical dominance and power over the body, which may be connected to, or transferred into a host of different control related sexual arousal points, progressing all the way to a god-complex manifestation which may actually require the killing of the body and person. Other ideas go toward the almost opposite end of the spectrum, which is the unconscious or conscious desire for one's own total submission, which is a very common sexual thread. Or one's own death or suicide, which is far less common but is definitely understandable as an extremely powerful expression of personal control, and in that self-controlled death or suicide there is likely an imagined total physical and personal release that only orgasm can hope to describe. And I'm just simplifying some of the ideas on the subject."

Noticing Lula's unsatisfied expression, I attempted to better connect to the possibilities that might make the most sense in relationship to her friend.

"In your friend's case it is possible that her boyfriend introduced the idea to her as being especially exciting because it is seen by conservative people, like the school teachers, and their parents, and church leaders, and probably most people, as being unequivocally wrong, and perhaps even evil. Which, if your friend and her boyfriend took part in, would set them apart from all those people, and beyond their control, representing a state of 'freedom'. Some Satanists would view an initial event of this kind as a baptism into Evil, which frees the participants from Christian and modern social controls. It's always been interesting to me that no matter what specific sexual behavior you look at, there is always a context to it that is equally as important as the arousal point itself." I finished, attempting to tie-up that thought.

But, with Lula still staring at me with her eyebrows crossed, I continued.

"Or, your friend or her boyfriend's reality may be much, much more serious. A person who would kill an animal, any animal, or perhaps take part in serious and more dangerous cutting as a part of their sexual arousal, probably has some problems, which could present a an even greater threat. I don't want to pre-judge, Lula. Whatever the case, I think your friend said what she said because it is 'true' to her in some way. Specifically 'how' it is true, is the real question. Maybe you can ask her? I'd love to hear her answers." I concluded, finally making a relevant point.

"Yeah, that's totally direct. I should ask her." Lula replied.

"Remember not to call her arousal point 'gross', which might shut down her willingness to communicate about it. We can't only accept the 'attractive' personal options we come across. You know what I mean, Lu."

"I know, Dad." Lula replied. "We call that kind of social slight 'fading,' or sometimes 'sleeping' the opinion or conversation of someone we don't want to listen to. It's the same thing, basically a negative shut down. I wouldn't do that, Pops. You and Mom taught us better than that."

On another occasion, at the dinner table, Lula asked, "What about cum swallowing? Is there anything health threatening about it if you know the other person isn't sick or infected with anything?"

Fortunately prepared by my own lifetime, I was comfortable enough and ready to answer her question. But Abbey beat me to it.

"No, Lula. There isn't." Abbey responded, with a tone of elegant openness. "If the person is healthy, there is no risk or problem with it at all. The taste and texture isn't everyone's cup of tea. But otherwise, it is totally fine."

"That's what I thought. But I couldn't help asking you guys. It's so awesome. Thanks, Mom." Lula responded, in graceful kind.

I also remember asking Kye and Lula if they, or any of the other kids talked with any of their teachers about sexual questions and topics like this.

"Oh, hell no!" Kye had exclaimed. "I only know of one teacher on the entire staff who is cool enough to ask something like that. And even he would tell a student, straight-out, that a sexually focused conversation like that could get a teacher fired, and even destroy their career under the worst of circumstances. But, at least he wouldn't report you to the counselor."

"What about the counselor? Is there only one?" I asked.

"Oh, Dad! She's a total witch!" Lula had smirked loudly. "Plus, she's a judgmental Christian who would make *way* too big a deal out of any little sexual thing! She might even try to have charges pressed against a sexually active kid, which could be big-points career-wise for a counselor like her. For real, Dad. But no student would make the mistake of telling her anything. The kids don't talk to the adults. It's so lame Dad, you wouldn't believe it."

"But the teachers must hear *some* sexual talk among the students, even accidentally." I conjectured. "What happens then?"

"You're right, Dad." Kye replied. "The kids talk about sex shit all day, and every teacher acts like they never hear a single word. They literally act like their deaf to it! And if a teacher does stop and ask a question about something they heard, the kids just laugh at them and say they were joking around. Which makes the teacher walk away. Basically, there's a total wall of silence between the students and the teachers when it comes to anything sexually related."

"What a shame." I concluded.

"Maybe." Lula rejoined, connecting to my tone of regret. "But I don't think the teachers know how to talk about it, anyway. Not like we do, Dad."

During the last part of those high school years I also remember introducing the idea to them that they could go beyond focusing on, and getting hung-up on, the explicitly defined sexual orientations or 'identities' of their classmates, which had become such a popular thing to "claim" (often, due to incomplete information, with layers of misunderstandings present in the teenager involved in the claiming). And I mentioned that perhaps they (Kye and Lula) might consider the fact that, while they obviously respected other people's openly stated choices, sexual-privacy about those kinds of personal choices is also a completely sincere and perhaps even an advanced level of respect, which included acknowledging one's own, as well as others rights to privacy. Which had become an almost disrespected perspective among their peers, where the kids often acted like you "had to" openly sexually define yourself.

"But we already knew that, Dad." Lula had replied with surprise. "You and Mom taught us sexual respect from the beginning, for all personal choices, and you taught us about privacy too. So the option of respecting a person's choice of privacy goes without saying. Plus, nobody at school tries to push or convince me or Kye to *be* any certain way. They know better. In fact, the other kids often ask us what *we* think about stuff."

"Pops, come on…?" Kye added, with a friendly hint of sarcasm.

"I guess *I* should have known better, with you two." I'd replied, with a chuckle and a smile full of deep approval.

After that conversation I wondered if, or when I might have the chance to talk with them about the tricky and complex issue of the actual limits of sexual privacy in our society, and also within the dynamics of most relationships. It would be good, I thought, to explore their understanding of how our assumed right-to-privacy is more an ideal, than a solid reality.

Proudly, and without any reservations, I can say that by the time Lula and Kye were juniors and seniors in high school they had a more detailed and honestly inclusive sexual education than most current university graduates, including many if not most of the upper degrees.

Regardless, even with all that shared conversation and open education, during their initial individual sexual experiences both Kye and Lula ran into situations that challenged them, and made them feel some sexual doubts and hesitations, and they were extra sensitive to the doubts and hesitations of their partners, too. But they also had so much more information to work with, as well as their developed abilities of consideration to help them deal with those specific and temporary ordeals. And they also had Abbey and me for parents, who were always available to talk to.

Some awkwardness, doubt, and confusion is bound to be present with a fairly high percentage of first experiences, they are "first-experiences." But without any meaningful education, or any context of understanding, or any opportunity for meaningful follow-up communication about the questions that may (will) arise, those early confusions can become fixed barriers, or unnecessary and unreasonable emotional and mental pressures, or even lasting prejudices or traumas.

When teenagers can come to adults and unhesitatingly share even their most embarrassing, uncomfortable, unsettling, and self-doubt causing sexual experiences, and talk them through, an important and rare (in our culture) achievement has been made.

At the end of their high school years, when Kye and Lula reached the point in their maturing where their sexual knowledge needed to include an even fuller measure of honesty, Abbey and I knew that it was time for them to hear a more inclusive story of my own main sexual confusions and difficulties, including pedophilia and incest, and hypersexuality, (some of which was still generalized in terms of exact details), as well as their mother Abbey's more expansive sexual adventures (discussed in a similar way). And an importantly broader perspective, and an even greater sexual comprehension, and another substantial layer of trust was shared between us.

Then, quicker than any parent expects, our children were suddenly young adults attending college and guiding their own inner lives forward through the world. And they were such good people, helpful, and honest. With adult size bodies, Kye now stood taller and broader than me, and looked much more Mediterranean/European than I had ever imagined he would, and much more handsome than Abbey and I could have ever expected. While Lula was about my and Abbey's same height, with features that had stayed softer and had resulted in a freckled Asian girl kind of look, and she was so beautiful she shocked us.

And thankfully, neither Kye nor Lula were burdened with the unnecessary confusions of being sexually ignorant.

I certainly don't mean to make sexually educating our children and youth sound easy, because there are plenty of tricky subjects to traverse through and deal with. But, as parents it is our responsibility to do our best. And I would love to leave it at that, but we all know that would be an incomplete picture.

The sadly obvious and intervening truth is that way too few parents have the knowledge, or the ability, or even the inclination to give or guide a proper sexual conversation and education. Which is not a popular view to take, because parents are also often prideful about personally controlling their kids' educations—right along with being sexually ignorant.

Plus, before we can even try to achieve a better sexual education for our children and society, we will have to deal with all the restrictive laws and conservative trends that keep us from doing it.

Still, it must be made clear that such an education is doable. Of course it is. But like any other outstanding educational experience, it will take fully adept instructors and a broadly reaching curriculum.

I know exactly who to hire. We could have hypersexual educators and programs available that are designed specifically for this kind of early adolescent, pre-teen, teen, and follow-up sexual education, which would also allow for valuable flexibility in dealing with kids with differing levels of experience, and visa-versa. And those educators could work hand-in-hand with hypersexual counselors, and a whole new kind of coordinated effort could benefit our children and teens. And though I believe it should be required, such an education should at the very least be an available choice within both our public and our private educational systems. I love specialized education.

Golden Safety

Now excelling in college, Kye had become a seriously intentioned writer and a budding poet, who had begun organizing his own collection of poems for a book. While Lula had become a wild young musician who couldn't decide which of her instruments she loved the most, so she continued to study all four, playing and performing in a range that included the wind instrument section of the college orchestra, to playing jazz flute in a band that also regularly accompanied a local live theatre group. And she loved to dance, to all kinds of music. And with both of them having grown up to this point in their lives relatively safe-and-sound physically, mentally, emotionally, sexually, and as financially supported and stable as we could manage, Abbey and I felt as if we had achieved a real milestone.

Proof of a "good life" is a fairly rare thing to gain, but at the present time, in all our lives, we had undeniably attained a meaningful measure of just that.

Familial and personal trust is such a beautiful gift to be able to give. And it is definitely an integral part of true love. And the feeling of having Abbey and my grown children trust me with such a loving golden glow is indescribable, and invaluable to me.

In order to protect the secret portion of sexual freedom that I've kept hidden right behind our wonderful life, I actually am, otherwise, as "golden" as I can possibly be in every other way: As a successful professional, a positively giving person in society, a sincerely attentive and loving father, and as an honestly interested, vitally connected, and genuinely adoring husband.

I love, and respect, and support everyone in my visible life with an enthusiasm that is tripled by my need to have and hide my invisible life. In fact, I wake-up most mornings wondering what good deeds I might achieve to help balance my odd debt of deception.

It would be nice if the significant people in my life could simply allow me some personal time that I didn't have to explain or defend with some carefully constructed story and cover, like long distance bicycle riding, or whatever.

I wish that real sexual privacy and our expectation of honesty weren't such enemies in our culture. But, it does no good to wish. Some people are forced to go beyond wishing.

Working with the reality I have around me, and dealing with the conditions I find myself in, I feel that I have fairly mastered my "secret sexual way." And the skillful ability with which I have been able to fly between my two worlds defines the breadth of my soaring wingspan.

Returned to the Present
The Evening after Being with Cee Cee (Alice)

Sitting at the dinner table with my family, safely returned to my present life—after having been so dangerously far-away with Cee Cee (Alice) earlier that day—reminded me of just how closely my two worlds could still find themselves, and of the massive effort it took to hold them apart.

As I often did in the evening, I also enjoyed thinking that night about the years to come, especially after Kye and Lula had moved-out, in which I could only imagine Abbey and I continuing to grow even closer, in every way, until the end of our lives.

Abbey, now in her fifties, had become an even more beautiful woman in her fuller maturity, with her deep-pooling hazel-brown eyes, and her gorgeous greying brunette hair, and her even softer ivory skin, and her lightly more freckled face, which was always complimented by her genuine and attentive expressions. She had also, if anything, become even more romantic.

Currently she liked to say, while snuggling up to me on the couch, or talking about us to the kids, or perhaps while holding my hand and sharing the sentiment with our friends at a dinner party:

"No one, and nothing in the Universe could ever separate us."

To which I always reply:

"My Love."

In lieu of the sexual freedoms that we should all have, and the greater safety that could be achieved with that kind of reality—I have at least found a safe place for one like myself, and for those whom I love, and whom depend on me.

Chapter Twenty

Gravity

The day after meeting and being with Alice, I'd woken-up and known exactly what I had to write down, which was the honest entirety of our experience together that day, and our related and expansive hypersexual histories, and our horrible struggle against each other, and my hopefully (at least partially) successful effort at helping her forward in her life—as well as the multitude of connected and interconnected sexual experiences and issues that I saw could be included in the open framework of that kind of story—right up to where I exemplified how all that information shines the sunlight directly on how and why substantial legal changes, including wide-spread publicly available and affordable prostitution, along with a variety of other sexual contact options, as well as a vastly improved sexual education system for our culture, and a completely re-detailed insight on dealing with problematic sexual issues and behaviors, are all so importantly required in our current society.

Still sitting on the edge of my bed, the idea kept pouring itself into my mind and my fore-brain, demanding my full attention. It was almost like a glimpse of a big dream that leaves you with an epic memory—except that it wasn't a dream, at all. It was a full-fledged story idea with mountains of specific points and a horizon of larger scale visions that were all laid-out across my consciousness. And I could already *see* how all-of-that would fit into one great story!

As the logical wheels of consideration continued to spin, I realized that I would eventually have to write the story out as fiction, as my secrets from my family would have to stand. Still, I reasoned, I could begin by using information from my own experiences and the many sexual events that had happened to me in my life, like my incident with Alice—as a foundation for the perspective of the story—and go from there.

    I'd been wanting to write a book that would include this level of personal, sexual, and social scope ever since my college days. And for some newly emerged reason, I'd awakened on this day with a crystal-clear vision of it. And I was emotionally super-charged in my desire to achieve the encompassing goal.

    And I believed that I could.

    Having gone straight to my desk that morning with my breakfast, I began to write and I did not stop until the end of that day. Starting again the next morning, I dove right back in and another day disappeared.

    Arranging to use my remaining five days of work vacation and my four unused sick days for the current year, I turned my work office over to my weekend manager for the next week and a half.

    Using my wild involvement and the freshly raw emotions of my episode with Alice as the hub of the wheel, I began to roll out a lifetime of interlaced sexual revelations. Gaining momentum, I let my boldest truths and my most private psychological shadows fly out of my fingertips, which raced across the keyboard with a rampant openness and an unfettered intimacy that bordered on exhibitionism.

    Freed and obsessed, I wrote fervently for as many as ten and eleven hours a day. And by the early evening of the twelfth day, I had managed to compile a substantial amount of core material. In fact, when I stepped back I was surprised to see that I had created a solid draft of the first five chapters, and a draft of a chapter from my early teen years that would definitely become a centrally important one, plus the conceptual outlines and the root ideas for many of the remaining ten or so chapters that I believed would take me all the way to my intended conclusion.

I even saw an early possibility of having a somewhat heroic and victorious ending.

Again, I accepted that I would have to re-work all the non-fiction information in order to slip myself back behind my usual veils. But I also anticipated that the effort might be an excellent opportunity to meaningfully broaden the range and view, and the number of points-of-view, and to achieve as much divergent sexual inclusion as was possible.

And I felt as excited as I had ever been, about anything I had ever tried to do. I was literally aroused, and nothing less. And I couldn't wait to get back to it the next day.

However, things changed abruptly during the latter part of the evening of that twelfth day. Which, as a distant concern, revealed that the formation of my story wasn't over.

What the Universe had left to add, was what happens when worlds collide; and the consequence of human gravity at its meanest.

Worlds Collide

Just as Abbey and I were sitting down to watch some television with Lula after dinner, an overwhelmingly oppressive surge of screeching sirens and loud vehicle engines filled the air surrounding our home.

Turning towards it, and automatically getting up from the couch to look out the upstairs windows that we were each closest to, we immediately saw the wheeling multi-colored lights of the police cars and the hulking crime-lab vans that had crammed themselves into our driveway and the neighborhood street in front.

The first coherent thought that I had, was that they had come for the pot stash that I kept and "shared" with my smoking friends.

But looking down at the growing mob of officers, amassing themselves below my window, I had the most awful intuition.

Looking quickly over at Abbey and Lula, who were fixated on the surreal scene outside, I observed a last moment of quietness, and witnessed their innocent confusion.

Then they hit in a wave: Unstoppable law enforcement officers pounding on all three doors to my home and business office at the same time, with warrants shoved into our stunned faces, followed by a pile of enraged cops violently pinning me to the living room floor and handcuffing me, with the disgusting criminal and sexual allegations against me being shouted at Abbey and Lula as if they were also guilty, and our four dogs barking like crazy, and guns drawn, and vicious language being thrown all around, with Abbey screaming the loudest, and Lula pleading the hardest!

And me, unable to find any voice at all in the less than three or four insanely wrenching minutes it took for the raiding officers to arrest and drag me out of my home.

Had they said that I was being charged with violent rape and some kind of kidnapping? I'd heard the "soliciting of prostitution" charge, and the words "underage" and "minor", and "alcohol and marijuana", which were all words that made sense to me. But the rest of what they were yelling, including something about *"homicide,"* didn't make any sense to me at all!

Caught-up in the madness and clamor of my arrest, I wanted so badly to tell Abbey and Lula that "Everything would be alright." But they couldn't have heard the weak lie over their own crying voices, and all the police officers shouting anyway.

The horror and helplessness of it made me want to crawl into a ball and die.

With the cops pushing and pulling me out the front door, Abbey, Lula, and I looked hopelessly into each other's eyes—and all we could see was the flood of tears pouring down each other's faces.

Sheets-of-tears—that was my last vision of them, as I was yanked out of my house and into the cruelest and most utter separation I have ever known.

As the lone patrol car raced away with me into the blackening night, I left my beloved wife and daughter, my soon to return home son, our dogs, my home, my professional career, and every other part of my life to the merciless machinations of an army of police—and to the even greater devastation of my revealed sexual deviance.

Inside the oddly muted sounds of the police car, I closed my eyes and tried to both deny, and grasp, what I had done.

Chapter Twenty One

Defenseless

During the first twenty-four hours that I was in jail, I was permitted to make one phone call to Abbey, which was not answered. So I'd left a message that was so long it was cut off by the time limit of the recording.

And I had received no return message since.

On the afternoon of the third day that I was in jail, I was removed from my holding cell, handcuffed, and taken into an interrogation/meeting room. After being chained to the bolted down chair, a pleasant looking, fiftyish, and clearly Asian blooded man entered the room with a briefcase in one hand and an arm full of files in the other.

"Hello, Mr. Aiken. My name is Steven Yama. I'll be representing you."

"I'm sorry, could you say your name again, just a little bit louder?"

"Yes, of course. I'm Steven Yama." He repeated, audibly louder.

"Thank you, Mr. Yama. I can't seem to hear clearly in here. The noise is getting to me…"

"Please call me Steven. We'll be speaking with each other quite a lot in the coming months, and it's just easier to use first names. May I call you Rory? Or do you prefer Mr. Aiken?"

"Rory is fine."

"Good. Rory, I may as well begin by informing you of the charges as they exist now."

Not wanting to know, I nodded my head in agreement.

"I'll start with the lesser charges and proceed from there. You've been charged with contributing to the delinquency of a minor. Delivery of a controlled substance to a minor. Delivery of alcohol to a person under age. Possession of marijuana. Solicitation of prostitution of a minor. Sexual abuse of a minor. Assault. Assault with a dangerous weapon. Statutory rape. False imprisonment. Kidnapping. Manslaughter. And feticide.

"What?!!! Oh, fuck..." I reeled inside my own mind.

I'd expected most of that list, based on the arrest and the interrogation that I had been through. But hearing it spoken out loud now, so plainly, and so concretely, and as if it were true, made me feel like I was floating out into the cold darkness of space.

Feticide...

And I thought to myself, *"Alice, how could you?"*

As Steven continued, with the details of the potential sentences for each of the separate crimes, which I'd had no way of anticipating, it was so overwhelming that, again, it seemed as if my hearing was fading away.

But I did hear him say "Twenty-five to-life." Or maybe he said it twice. Or maybe it just echoed in my head.

However, I did become alert and intrigued when Steven began saying something about statements that had been taken from several counselors from a women's shelter which said that, two days after she was allegedly at my home, Alice had tried to enter their shelter with a story of needing help keeping her unborn child, which she told them would be given to foster care because of her own destitute and fully unsupportive foster family circumstances. And when Steven said that Alice had then told them that she especially needed their help because she had been hurt in a bad fall down some stairs, I was duly shocked. And, when I was further told that she had been questioned aggressively by several of the counselors from the Christian faith-based shelter, and even accused of lying to them about the cause of her injuries, which sent Alice into a rage before running out of the shelter—only to show up in an emergency room a day later, where she miscarried violently, and then offered her newly created account of what had happened to her at my house as an explanation—I felt as if I finally understood at least some part of what had happened, and of how.

But my "understanding" of what had really happened, made no difference at all.

And when I asked Steven if he had any ideas on how I could better try to reach my wife, his answer broke my only remaining connection to sanity.

"Mr. Aiken, as your defense attorney I have spoken to your wife Abbey. She told me that your family has been forced out of your former home and that they are seeking a new residence. And that she is not able to speak with you at this time. She is cooperating with the investigations of both the prosecutor and myself, but she will not be called as a witness, and she does not intend to have anything more to do with this trial. I'm sorry, that's all she said."

He also added, respectfully, that I could certainly insist on continuing to call her according to the jail's own policy. Which I did exhaustively, each time with no answer. And each time leaving a full-length message, each of which was increasingly desperate, all without a return call. And so I drifted into inexorable depression.

And each of my subsequent meetings with Mr. Yama sank me even deeper, though he was sincere and seemed to comprehend my story.

Three months later, during the six day trial I did, of course, see Alice. However, because Alice was a "victim" in the States case against me, she was only required to be in court on the day that she gave her testimony.

Due to the fact that Steven had instructed me not to look over at her, I had restrained myself from doing so. But, when she was in the witness box, up in front of me, I did allow myself to look directly at Alice's face for a moment. I couldn't help but wonder, and perhaps hope, that something in her expressions would communicate something to me—anything. And she did return my glance, and I'm sorry to say that the look on her face was one of unqualified and burning hatred, seemingly colored by the thrill she was getting from beating me down so mercilessly—all of which was stuffed into a twisted and flushing grin.

And I could not comprehend why she hated me so much.

She did appear generally healthier, much cleaner, quite a bit smaller, and all shined up for her court appearance. According to the information Steven had garnered, Alice had been in the care of the State and living in a group recovery home ever since her release from the hospital. So it was no wonder she looked better.

At the trial, on both the first and last days, I also saw one other very important person—Jimmie—whose heretofore hidden thread in this whole story had finally reached its moment. How Jimmie discovered what had happened to me is something I may never know, but his/her presence meant the world to me. A hypersexual Canadian national born and bred, we had met at a city park and known each other for nearly the entire seventeen year period that my family had lived in this southwestern state.

An always stylishly outfitted nearly eighty year-old now, Jimmie had lost his/her religious wife, children, and extended family some twenty years ago when they'd found out that he/she was a sexually active crossdresser. Which was when he/she had moved to America, eventually settling in the same little city that I had. But Jimmie's real perversion, if I may point it out, was his/her unleashed and unrelenting desire for un-judgmental and loyal sexual friendship—of the most openly deviant kind.

Jimmie is also a person who was a transsexual before the social or surgical option existed. And by the time it did, he/she simply felt too old for the full transition. Regardless, I *experienced* Jimmie as a female presence from the beginning, sexually and as a human being. And I was but one of her many spoiled and similarly loving and appreciative friends.

In returning that spirit of friendship to Jimmie, she became one of the very few people I ever took to my masturbatorium—and the *only* one who knew how to enter it. An educated and sharply observant woman, Jimmie had quickly understood the room's hidden threat—should it ever be discovered by the wrong person—and had volunteered to be my (anonymous) safety back-up for the room, as best she could. Which was an exceptionally generous way of expressing how much she adored our sexual friendship, and what we did together. I'd always kept the room pre-paid six months in advance, but beyond that time limit lay the very serious danger of discovery.

Seeing Jimmie in court, and locking eyes with her as she shared a sad smile with me, let me know that she would pay for the room's relatively modest rent until my release from prison.

Jimmie was a sweet and truest friend indeed.

As for the rest of the trial, after an endless seeming series of predominantly monotone proceedings, and evidentiary actions, and objections, and motions, with copies of paperwork to accompany each of them—other than the exceptions of some of the more colorful and interesting witness testimony, Alice's the most vile among them—the trial droned its way to a final completion.

In the end, Steven was able to prove that there was insufficient evidence for the charges related to the death of the fetus, and those were dismissed. Importantly, several of the injuries that Alice had when she arrived at the hospital—on the third day past our being together—and which she had accused had happened at my house, had been brought into question due to the medically estimated time-stamp of their occurrences, which closer matched to my own testimony from the time of my arrest. Further, and also due to the consistency of pattern with my assertions and Steven's defense case, Steven was also able to reveal Alice's juvenile record of run-ins with her local law enforcement, which were indisputable evidence of her several years of drug use and prostitution activities. Which, most importantly, tipped the scales on the kidnapping and false imprisonment charges. But the charges of rape (statutory), the sexual abuse of a minor, assault, assault with a dangerous weapon, solicitation of prostitution of a minor, and the controlled substances charges all stuck.

Abbey, Kye, and Lula, who had been crushed by the weight of the original criminal charges against me, and by the intrusive and unrelenting law enforcement investigation that had immediately followed, and by also being thrown out of the home we'd lived in, and by being suddenly reduced financially by half, had been unable to trust me enough to contact me or be involved in the legal processes or trial. And had, instead, decided to await the court's decision.

Now that those decisions had been handed down, both guilty and not-guilty, which Abbey and my children would be notified of by Steven, along with his own summary of the case, I hoped that they would all be able to at least see the actual original event more for what it really was.

And I dearly hoped that I would talk to them all again, sometime.

I missed them so much, and felt so bad about what I'd done to them. We'd been so happy. To avoid thinking about it I looked at the ground in front of my feet, and I focused on the ten feet in front of that.

I was convicted and sentenced to a term of no more than eight years and no less than six. And I would be a registered sex offender for the rest of my life.

Chapter Twenty Two

Imprisonment

The truth is, I could never have imagined the actual personal impact of being forced into a small locked-down room, with other miserable people, knowing that there is nowhere to go for as long as your mind can stretch out in front of you. All while being gutted by inner shame, and emotional desolation, made even more infuriating by absolute twenty-four hour sobriety, leaving only the inward spiraling mental-scape of being wound-down into the tightest kinds of destructive psychological descents.

From the day of my arrest, the experience(s) of incarceration had made me detest life, and feel hateful toward our society and greater humanity in a way that I didn't expect to ever escape.

In the first month, I was sure that I would go insane.

Considering myself stripped down to my current existence, finally stopped and held in total physical non-freedom, I was led to some awfully sharp-angled places of perspective. And each unadorned view of my reality was a flaying point of clarity as inescapable as a guillotine.

What a terribly greedy deviant I've always been! Why can't I be convinced that sex outside the smallest social confines is wrong? How obvious can it be made to me?

Am I sexually insane?

At least I'd never infected Abbey, or our children, or anyone else with any kind of STD, HIV, or any other awful or potentially fatal sexual disease. I'd been running with the real razor-edged claws of those ghostly killers on the back of my neck for so long I'd almost forgotten our deadly game and gamble.

It is the way I was born: Naked. And I could never break away from my belief in, or need to touch sexual flesh directly to sexual flesh.

And most of the hypersexuals I've known, and most of the other deviants I've known, are exactly like this!

Ninety-nine percent of the time we don't even ask each other!

Perhaps we're all insane. Some of us even believe that our hypersexually expanded bodily systems, strengthened by our constantly indiscriminate sexual exposure and penetration, are what give us our immunity!

Beating Gods of Death should feel like a champion's accomplishment: But, imprisoned in this way, my last illusion, of having ever been a "winged creature of sexual beauty," was burnt away.

I had crawled across so many moral and legal lines, so far past acceptable limits, so many times; I was nothing more than a maniacal, perilously stupid, and unjustly lucky hypersexual who probably should have been stomped out of society's misery long ago—at least in this world.

Lying face-down on my prison cot, I wished that I could find a way to turn off my blistering thoughts and emotions.

And then, sometime in the end of the second month, they kind of did turn off. Which is a surprising admission to make. The main thoughts and the worst emotions didn't go completely away, but the unbearably burning edges of them did eventually become somehow dulled. And for the greater parts of each day I began to find other things to focus on.

As far as the actual external reality of this medium-sized private prison complex goes, the longer I am here the more it reminds me of some kind of lock-down medical facility. With all kinds of population segregation, and modern safety measures, and more guards, and with a better standard of cleanliness than I'd expected, and even a surprising degree of air-conditioning, all designed to keep things as calm as possible—it was remarkably more stable than I'd expected. In fact, this particular incarceration is far enough removed from the old-school kinds of prisons, and many of the threats of those more open populations, it ultimately presents its very own distinct set of dynamics to deal with.

By the end of the third month, for the most part, I was developing an attitude more fit for my surroundings. Surely, if all these other men could deal with it, I would find my own way through it.

Still, the specific dynamics of this place did include the fact that in American prison populations the rate of rape (for males) is increased by as much as seven times the rate in regular society. And even more worrisome for me, the rate of STD's, Aids, HIV, and Hepatitis C are in some cases as much as *ten times* that of the general American population. And, of course, condoms are illegal (and punishable as contraband).

In fact, and perhaps surprising to many people, sexual contact of *any kind* between inmates is illegal in all U.S. detention centers, jails, and prisons. Which sets our system oddly apart from most of the other Countries on Earth. In American prisons even masturbation is a crime.

Obviously, regardless of any that, for me a big part of surviving this sentence would include finding an inmate who would ignore all those limits. And just like on the outside, when two such people meet, and lock eyes, it takes little more than a nod and a certain smile to make that connection happen. And so, the soft papery hands and the unhurried sucking affections of the elderly inmate in my cell have begun to supply me, as well as himself, with that veritable measure of humanity. His name is Carl.

I also have my eye on one other inmate, a stout middle-aged man named Howard, who I have recently sensed harbors sexual desires that are, shall we say, less soft and submissive than Carl's.

Chapter Twenty Three

The Illumined Visitor & Writing Wings

On the occasion of Abbey's first visit to the prison, at the beginning of the fourth month, the tension and sadness between us was overwhelming.

Unbelievably, one of the first things Abbey said was, "Please forgive me." Which made me cry for at least five minutes, while I tried to choke out the exact same words to her.

After that, fumbling for the right ways to say the right things, we each from our own sides came to a close-enough and quickly accepted agreement of what I had—and had not done—in whatever event had actually occurred. And even more importantly, we somehow managed to communicate our agreement that the horrible experiences and punishments that we had already been through, that we had *all* been through, as well as the imprisonment that I faced, that we all faced, was *enough* pain and punishment. Going forward, we would focus on the light at the end of the tunnel.

Barely fitting just that much into the far-too-quick thirty minutes, which is the time-limit of every visitation period in this institution, Abbey and I had then re-pledged our eternal love for each other.

And yes, I did feel like I had been forgiven by Abbey too easily.

What I had done to her, and Kye, and Lula, and our lives should not be forgiven that quickly. And I sure as hell wasn't going to forgive myself, or the rotten system that was wronging me, and that was wronging all of us. But I could only decide those things for myself. I could not decide those things for Abbey. And of course, I hoped with all my being that her beyond-generous forgiveness would hold fast.

On the occasion of Abbey's next trip into the prison, in the end of the fifth month, I watched as she entered the white cement-block and steel-mesh-glass enclosed visiting area for the second time. This time, for some reason, she had a more settled and focused look on her face. She was also carrying a large folder and some obvious paperwork in one of her hands.

Setting the folder down on our assigned table, as I approached she turned to face me. Awkwardly, and quietly, we greeted each other in the only physical way that was allowed in this prison—a brief one-handed handshake—with NO hug, NO whisper of affection, and NO kiss.

"Hello, Abbey. Thank you for coming again. I'm so sorry about you having to come to a place like this..."

"No. Don't think about all that. It's no big deal. And we have so little time. Let's sit down, Rory."

Sitting down I again noticed the over-stuffed folder. Observing my glance, Abbey took the opportunity to explain.

"I have something important to tell you, Rory. And I don't want you to worry about any of it. Okay? When I'm finished, you'll see that it's all very good."

Sensing her seriousness, I answered her with an expression of steadiness. I was happy to help her with whatever she felt was important.

"Of course Abbey, what is it?" I replied.

With a carefully composed smile, she started.

"Last week I plugged your computer in to find some financial records from your old job and I accidentally found the drafts of the first six chapters and the outline of the book you were working on..., and I read it all Rory. All two-hundred and fifty pages, and the notes."

Holy shit..., she'd read it all...

Racing her emotions, and my response, she hurried to continue.

"But listen to me, Rory! After your arrest and the trial I pretty much figured that you had been having sex secretly, like you were having with that girl. So I wasn't surprised to read about that. But I *was* surprised to read about how terribly careful, and how much safer you've tried to be all these years, and about how much you've always adored me, and our children and our life together above everything else. I knew all those things, but it was different to read your words. And I was also surprised to read about how hard you struggled to give up your previous life…, and your relationships with all those people… But back then you never said a word! I remember you just said to me, 'It's time to move, Babe. Where do you want to go?' And Rory, *the way* that you wrote about all that.., it was like I could hear your whispering voice in it. It was all so beautiful!" She gushed, which took me completely off guard, and made me listen, rather than trying to think ahead.

"And all the parts you wrote about yourself…," She continued. "I can't tell you…, I'm so proud of you…"

And while she spoke, Abbey held my eyes with hers in that quiet and warm kind of way that tells a person that all is truly well. Which, I couldn't quite wrap my head around. So I continued listening.

"I understand so much more now." She reflected. "I guess I wanted to know more of the truth than I thought I did." She then said, seemingly to herself, and as if settling the matter, with me there to hear it.

All of which was extraordinarily difficult for me to absorb. Still hanging on her every word, a parallel part of my mind begin processing what I was hearing. She'd said that she read it *all*, but what parts was she okay with? What parts wasn't she? Where was she going with all this?

What had I done now?

"I think it's the best writing you've ever done, Rory." She continued. "I think it's the book you've always talked about writing. I *know* it is. I'm trying to be as serious as I can be. As I was reading it, I saw that you had finally found a way to tell the hidden truth of your early life, with your whole heart, and with nothing held back! You have to promise me that you will finish the book, Rory." She concluded firmly.

Still unsure as to exactly where this unexpected direction was going to leave us, I finally asked.

"Abbey, I didn't mean for you to read all that stuff…"

Leaning toward me as much as she could from across the white steel table, with a face full of smiling grace, and I'd swear a hallo of glistening lights around her face, she openly and lovingly plead with me.

"I don't care about any of the other stuff, Rory! Especially what's in the past. I want the life we had together back, whatever that takes! I love you, Rory! I always have! And you have always loved me! And we will make it through this next six years. You'll see. Then we'll put all this behind us."

Finally comprehending her, (though I could not fully grasp it yet), I responded swiftly—and with the hope of keeping us afloat in this incredible moment.

"Abbey, I do love you like I wrote! I always have! I want our life together back, too! More than anything! And we *will* make it through this damned sentence! And I'll I love you forever!"

I both plead and pledged to her, emotionally beside myself in the realization of the astounding level of acceptance she had just shown me.

"And you'll write the book." Abbey insisted.

"And I'll write the book." I promised, almost laughing, surprised that she was even talking about that.

After signaling to one of the guards by raising her hand, Abbey then pushed the folder full of papers across the table to me.

"Here it is." She said, with a widening smile.

Having forgotten about the folder, I was quickly curious. Opening it, I saw a stack of double-spaced printed pages of everything that I had written and outlined for the book so far. Plus, a hefty lined notebook with five hundred empty pages (two-sided), and a box of three pens (the limit for any one inmate).

"I just put seventy-five dollars in your commissary bank, which is the monthly maximum." Abbey started. "The guard captain told me that you can get pens and more paper when you need it. And that you can also, eventually, get hours in the library where you can use the computers. If you exceed the limit of pages that you can keep in your cell, you can give them to me or mail them. And I can keep everything organized for you!" She exclaimed. "I'm so glad that Mr. Yama helped me get all these details straightened out. He really is a nice man. He and I totally agreed that this book would at least give you something to do, with some of your time." She continued happily. "Anything else you need, I can bring with me when I visit. And oh yeah, Mr. Yama said if you do write a book—he wants to read it. How about that?!"

"Oh, Abbey..." I tried, but failed to find the words.

How can a person account for what is owed to a being like Abbey?

Then, at the shocking sound of a too-loud bell our visit was over.

That evening I opened the folder and began reading.

Remembering that Abbey had already read all of what I'd written, and that Kye and Lula were surely being told something about it by Abbey, suddenly opened up the possibility of not having to write the manuscript in a way that kept me hidden. However, I wasn't sure that I was actually willing to write and publish a non-fiction story that was this directly truthful. Not wanting to close off any possibilities, I decided to make that decision later. First, I would finish writing down everything that I needed to say. Then, I would resolve exactly how to say it.

In the days that followed I read and wrote, and thought about what I wrote, nearly every minute and hour, upon hour. And before I knew it, I was disappearing into my work on the book for as much as the entire fourteen hours of lights-on time that we had each day.

And much more than just "giving me something to do, with some of my time," the self-contained project turned my prison cell into my writing desk—and it saved me.

Submerged in my flowing memories, I soon found myself thinking and writing about Déjà.

I also found myself thinking about the theories I'd had about the potential social benefits of public sexual contact availability, as well as some of my other ideas for saving society from its own sexual ignorance.

And I remembered how I had once told someone that I believed I could even save a significant number of the young sexual victims in our society.

Of course, I also thought a great deal about Alice, who I just couldn't hate because her own life had been *so* bad. And when she got cornered, she instinctively used the weapons she knew best to fight back with, which were the sex hating judgments that society had used against her. And I hoped that she had somehow found her way into one of the better kinds of women's shelters, where she would receive some truly helpful counseling, education, and other kinds of empowerment.

And while I wrote, I also thought about the many, many other people I'd known sexually in my life, whose stories—or more precisely, the meanings of whose stories—I would do my best to include.

And I thought about Abbey, who was still by my side. And I fell asleep each night eager to wake, and to write freely.

Chapter Twenty Four

Magnitude

So my time inside has progressed, and the number of my days-served has increased.

Now approaching a year in, the most important thing that has happened is the beginning stages of the necessary healing process with Kye and Lula. Led patiently by Abbey, Kye and Lula had eventually been able to come to some important understandings, and were now willing to move forward in our relationships in whatever ways we could.

When Abbey was able to bring them both on her fourth visit, near the end of the seventh month, (which meant that I hadn't seen them in over ten months), and I heard my former names of "Dad" and even "Pops" again, spoken with such tender voices, it was all a re-humanizing experience more astonishing than any I could have imagined.

And the thirty minutes that I spent with them was at first a little awkward, and then wonderful, and then crushing, and then cathartic.

I remember that right then-and-there I'd made my children promise that they wouldn't come to this terrible place more than once every several months or so. Honestly joking with them that their mother and I desperately needed some "alone time."

Regardless of that, since their first visit, either Kye or Lula, or both of them, have accompanied their mother every-other-time she comes. Which is a great balance of spending time with them all. And by now our visits have become much more fluid and natural, and we have begun to regain many of our old conversations.

And Abbey always asks about the book, to which I reply, "It's coming along, Babe."

Which is all I can really tell her, because the more I write and the more I edit, the more I know that I'll have to re-write and re-write this manuscript in order to make it say all the things that I intend it to. Plus, I've already seen that my ongoing work will demand a considerable amount of research, which means earning time in the library, which I will get in dribbles of only a few of hours a day, a couple of days a week. So I am currently making lists of all my most ardent questions.

Now nearly one and a half year in, time continues to burn, and burn slowly by.

Even with the freeing distractions of my writing, and my family visits, and my sexual contacts, a thinly buried part of myself languishes in the daily tortures of this encasing hell.

Foremost, many days, is my furious desire for sexual partners from the feminine persuasion. The few female guards, and the female counselors, literally make my salivary glands burst open when they come anywhere near me. Of course, they also make my groin ache, as if I had been squarely smacked there.

And the memory of freeing intoxication, in all its many splendors, has become an incessant delicious terror that has invaded even my dreams.

I've also contemplated, again and again, how painfully I miss being around children, and adolescents, and teenagers. Being so absent from their youthful freshness, and laughter, is a blunt cruelty.

And sometimes I can't stop thinking about my inescapable need to walk out into the wide-open spaces of nature, like I spent so much of my previous life doing. And when I think about it, my entire being aches.

During the especially difficult times I lie down and close my eyes, and I think about Abbey, and Kye, and Lula, and all the wonderful family travels across the Country we've had, as well as the countless nature adventures we've shared. Which, when I can get all-the-way back into the memories, rescues me both emotionally and mentally in a way that makes me wonder if there *is* some kind of greater human soul, which makes my agnostic mind quake.

Now past two years in, though this may sound "off" to many, Abbey and I still haven't talked about everything directly. Of course, we have plenty of time for that. And I'll follow her lead.

But I've come to suspect that Abbey meant exactly what she said when she'd stated, "I don't care about any of the other stuff, Rory. Especially what's in the past."

And that, when she said, "I guess I wanted more of the truth than I thought I did." She was also saying that she had understood enough of that truth.

And the more time that goes by without her looking any further in that direction, the more I believe that she is also giving me some personal space that I don't have to answer for, or defend. Which I appreciate.

Matters concerning privacy have become, if anything, even more important and intriguing to me.

My masturbatorium for instance, which awaited me. And which was not mentioned in any of the initial material that Abbey had read. How, or even why, would I try to explain that place to Abbey? And if I did, how could I adequately describe to her how I miss my shrouded masturbatorium the same way I would miss a surgically removed section of my own brain or body? Or that, when I think of the treasured relics and other unfastening objects tucked away there, I instantly feel the pervading pulse of the old sexual pursuits that obtained them. And that I still honor that history. And also that, if I were free, I would do nearly anything to regain the depths of that rightful terrain.

In fact, when the days of my sentence finally do come to an end, I will return to that abundant carnal refuge. And as I approach it, I will first visit the nearby driveway of my previous home, where I met Alice, who I called Cee Cee.

I can still smell her...

In the end, no part of this punitive system will ever completely control me, or fully cage me, or extinguish my personal understandings, or deaden my individual determination, or alter my distinct desires for my own life. Even this level of punishment does not hold that magnitude.

And now, I doubt that any does.

I will survive this awful confinement and all its challenges, as I've lived my whole conscious life, with the careful cunning of my own deviant designs.

Epilogue

Embrace

Our greater population could, and I think should, feed its seriously malnourished sexual contact needs by allowing the fully-willing flesh of our hypersexuals—of every variation and aberration—to be legally and abundantly available.

Embrace us, and give us a culturally acknowledged, safe, accessible, and an honorable place to *be* hypersexual.

The End

Acknowledgments

I could not have written this book without the thorough conceptual editing of my great friend Pat. His steady compass helped keep my story on the path that joins personal experience and honesty with inclusionism. My appreciation is boundless.

My gratitude and brotherhood goes to R.S., who challenged me to broaden my scope and vision. And who also made multiple significant editing contributions to this novel.

My sincere thanks and friendship to Naomi, who saw three crucially important veins of the story that needed to be strengthened. Naomi was surgical in regards to the final body of this story.

To my longtime dear friend Steve, who swam with me through the many, many editorial waves of this manuscript—I bow. And I bow, again.

I also want to thank all those friends and acquaintances who read and commented on the early drafts of this book. Your encouragement and insightful commentaries and critiques were invaluable to me. You know who you are. B.Z., J.S., T.P., and L.N., thank you, thank you, thank you.

My unending gratefulness goes to N.C. and M.D., who encouraged me at every step, and then pushed me to publish this book—until it happened.

Finally, my eternal love to my wife and best friend; who was the first person to support my writing this novel, and the first person to read it.

Made in the USA
Lexington, KY
08 March 2018